# CONTENTS

# HEART OF DARKNESS
## AND OTHER TALES

JOSEPH CONRAD was born Józef Teodor Konrad Korzeniowski in the Russian part of Poland in 1857. His parents were punished by the Russians for their Polish nationalist activities and both died while Conrad was still a child. In 1874 he left Poland for France and in 1878 began a career with the British merchant navy. He spent nearly twenty years as a sailor before becoming a full-time novelist. He became a British subject in 1886 and settled permanently in England after his marriage to Jessie George in 1896.

Conrad is a writer of extreme subtlety and sophistication; works such as 'Heart of Darkness', *Lord Jim*, and *Nostromo* display technical complexities which have established him as one of the first English 'Modernists'. He is also noted for the unprecedented vividness with which he communicates a pessimist's view of man's personal and social destiny in such works as *The Secret Agent*, *Under Western Eyes*, and *Victory*. Despite the immediate critical recognition that they received in his lifetime, Conrad's major novels did not sell, and he lived in relative poverty until the commercial success of *Chance* (1914) secured for him a wider public and an assured income. In 1923 he visited the United States, to great acclaim, and he was offered a knighthood (which he declined) shortly before his death in 1924. Since then his reputation has steadily grown, and he is now seen as a writer who revolutionized the English novel and was arguably the most important literary innovator of the twentieth century.

CEDRIC WATTS is Professor of English at the University of Sussex. His books on Conrad include *Conrad's 'Heart of Darkness': A Critical and Contextual Discussion* (1977), *A Preface to Conrad* (1982, 2nd edn. 1993), *The Deceptive Text* (1984), *Joseph Conrad: A Literary Life* (1989), and *Joseph Conrad* (1994). His other works include *A Preface to Greene* and (with John Sutherland) *Henry V, War Criminal? and Other Shakespeare Puzzles*. He has edited numerous texts by Shakespeare, Hardy, Cunninghame Graham, and Conrad.

MARA KALNINS is the General Editor of the Works of Joseph Conrad in the Oxford World's Classics series. She is a Fellow of Corpus Christi College, Cambridge, and Staff Tutor in Literature, Board of Continuing Education.

# OXFORD WORLD'S CLASSICS

*For over 100 years Oxford World's Classics have brought
readers closer to the world's great literature. Now with over 700
titles—from the 4,000-year-old myths of Mesopotamia to the
twentieth century's greatest novels—the series makes available
lesser-known as well as celebrated writing.*

*The pocket-sized hardbacks of the early years contained
introductions by Virginia Woolf, T. S. Eliot, Graham Greene,
and other literary figures which enriched the experience of reading.
Today the series is recognized for its fine scholarship and
reliability in texts that span world literature, drama and poetry,
religion, philosophy and politics. Each edition includes perceptive
commentary and essential background information to meet the
changing needs of readers.*

OXFORD WORLD'S CLASSICS

JOSEPH CONRAD

# *Heart of Darkness*
## and Other Tales

*Edited with an Introduction and Notes by*
CEDRIC WATTS

OXFORD
UNIVERSITY PRESS

# OXFORD

UNIVERSITY PRESS

Great Clarendon Street, Oxford OX2 6DP

Oxford University Press is a department of the University of Oxford.
It furthers the University's objective of excellence in research, scholarship,
and education by publishing worldwide in

Oxford New York

Auckland Bangkok Buenos Aires Cape Town Chennai
Dar es Salaam Delhi Hong Kong Istanbul Karachi Kolkata
Kuala Lumpur Madrid Melbourne Mexico City Mumbai Nairobi
São Paulo Shanghai Singapore Taipei Tokyo Toronto

with an associated company in Berlin

Oxford is a registered trade mark of Oxford University Press
in the UK and in certain other countries

Published in the United States
by Oxford University Press Inc., New York

Introduction, Note on the Text, Explanatory Notes,
and Glossary © Cedric Watts, 1990, 2002
General Editor's Preface, Select Bibliography,
Chronology © Mara Kalnins, 2002

First published as an Oxford World's Classics paperback 1990
This revised edition first published 2002

British Library Cataloguing in Publication Data

Data available

Library of Congress Cataloging in Publication Data

Data available

ISBN 0–19–280172–4

5

Typeset in Ehrhardt
by RefineCatch Limited, Bungay, Suffolk
Printed in Great Britain by
Clays Ltd., St Ives plc

# GENERAL EDITOR'S PREFACE

Conrad is acknowledged as one of the great writers of the twentieth century, but neither in his lifetime nor after have his works been available in authoritative texts. This was partly because Conrad himself revised his writings at several stages (in manuscript, typescript, and proofs), partly because many of his works appeared in different versions (slightly so in the English and American editions, significantly so in serial and book form), and partly because he himself continued to revise them for subsequent publication. Moreover he was involved in still further revision of the texts when his works were issued in the collected editions of Doubleday and Heinemann in 1921, though the extent of his involvement varied considerably from work to work. Like many authors, he also suffered from the well-meant, but often misguided, editorial efforts of his publishers who not only imposed their own house styling but sometimes changed his grammar, spelling, and punctuation, and even altered whole phrases. The textual history of Conrad's works—the revisions they underwent and their transmission and publication—is therefore an intricate and complicated one. A scholarly edition of the *Letters and Works* is currently being prepared by Cambridge University Press and six volumes of the *Letters* as well as two novels have been published to date.

In the absence of authoritative texts which accurately incorporate Conrad's corrections and revisions and which remove the editorial interference, house styling, and printing errors of his publishers, the base-texts for this new Oxford World's Classics edition must be the English first editions. These editions are important because they are what Conrad originally expected to be published, because they were the texts which first shaped his reputation as a writer, and because they are free of later layers of editorial interference. As late as 1919, when Conrad was correcting copy for a limited Collected Edition, he still affirmed their importance: 'I devote particular care to the text of the English Edition always and it is to be considered the standard one' (letter to Fisher Unwin, 27 May 1919). At the same time, however, they are themselves flawed by numerous misprints and some idiosyncratic house styling. The present edition therefore aims to correct such errors in order to restore Conrad's idiom and distinctive prose style.

In this edition the following emendations have been made silently throughout: (*a*) obvious spelling errors and typesetter's mistakes have been corrected; (*b*) inadvertent omissions have been supplied in the case of incomplete quotation marks, final stops, apostrophes in colloquial contractions (e.g. 'o'clock') and the stop following a title (e.g. 'Mr.'); (*c*) the convention of hyphenating words such as 'to-day', 'to-night', 'good-bye' has been dropped in accordance with modern usage; (*d*) inconsistencies in punctuation inside or outside quotation marks have been standardized and other inconsistencies—such as hyphenated words—have been regularized in accordance with Conrad's most frequent practice in each work; (*e*) paragraphs have been indented throughout in accordance with modern conventions and a few typographical details—such as display capitals, chapter numbers and headings, and running titles—have been regularized. However, where the sense of a phrase has been occluded or where there is a controversial reading or some specific textual difficulty, the editor of each volume will record the editorial emendation and explain the adopted reading briefly in the Note on the Text or in an explanatory note where the reader may also be directed to further reading on the issue.

Each volume has an Introduction which seeks to relate the work to Conrad's life and other writings, to place it in its literary and cultural context, and to offer a cogent argument for its relevance both to his time and ours. Although Conrad is a modern writer, his specialized terminology is not always familiar to contemporary readers nor are the literary, historical, and political allusions always clear. Explanatory notes are therefore supplied but it is assumed that words or expressions found in a good dictionary will not need to be glossed. Appendixes in each volume will also provide material useful to the reader, such as a glossary of nautical or foreign terms, maps, or important additional texts. Conrad's own series of prefaces and Author's Notes (the latter written between 1917 and 1920) are reprinted as an appendix to each volume.

Finally, any work on so major a figure as Conrad must be deeply indebted to the research of many scholars and critics, but I would like to express my gratitude especially to Jacques Berthoud, Jim Boulton, Andrew Brown, Laurence Davies, George Donaldson,

Donald Rude, J. H. Stape and Cedric Watts for sharing their expertise, and to Judith Luna of Oxford University Press for her unfailing encouragement and advice.

Mara Kalnins

*Corpus Christi, Cambridge*

# ACKNOWLEDGEMENTS

Cedric Watts wishes to express his gratitude to the staff of Sussex University Library and to numerous Conradians, including Mario Curreli, Laurence Davies, Anthony Fothergill, Hans Lippe, Seiji Minamida, Gene Moore, S. W. Reid, and Norman Sherry. The late Hans van Marle made many shrewd contributions; Brian Nicholas provided astute guidance on Gallicisms; and Robert Hampson was unfailingly helpful. The endnotes to this volume have been augmented by reference to the following works: *Youth: A Narrative | Heart of Darkness | The End of the Tether*, with an introduction by C. B. Cox and notes by Norman Sherry (London: Dent; Vermont: Tuttle, 1974); Anthony Fothergill (ed.), *Tales of Unrest* (London: Everyman, Dent; Vermont: Tuttle, 2000), Robert Hampson (ed.), *Heart of Darkness* (London: Penguin, 1995), and Gene M. Moore (ed.), *'Heart of Darkness' and Other Stories* (Ware: Wordsworth Editions, 1999).

# INTRODUCTION

## I

The four tales in this volume were written between June 1896 and March 1899, a period during which Conrad matured rapidly in stylistic virtuosity and conceptual boldness. With 'Heart of Darkness' (first published in *Blackwood's Edinburgh Magazine*, February to April 1899) he reached the height of his powers as a writer of consummate eloquence, verve, subtlety, and originality. The tales chosen to accompany 'Heart of Darkness' here have various thematic and technical relationships to it. The earliest, 'An Outpost of Progress' (which appeared in *Cosmopolis*, June and July 1897), is also set in central Africa and offers a ruthlessly ironic view of European colonialism and the pretensions of civilization. 'Karain' (*Blackwood's*, November 1897), with locations in the Malay Archipelago, again depicts confrontations between European traders and the indigenous inhabitants of the exotic region. In this case, however, the ironies are relatively mild and benign. The narrative structure is that of 'the tale within the tale', a mode which was widely employed in nineteenth-century fiction and whose full potential was to be demonstrated in 'Heart of Darkness'. 'Youth' (*Blackwood's*, September 1898) is another experiment in oblique narration. It, too, appraises imperial adventure, though a stronger preoccupation is the partly nostalgic rendering of a bizarrely ill-fated voyage. All these works are concerned with illusions (variously sustaining, tantalizing, or corrupting), with the tension between romanticism and scepticism, and with a cluster of human qualities which are gnomically suggested by Stein in Conrad's *Lord Jim*:

'This magnificent butterfly finds a little heap of dirt and sits still on it; but man he will never on his heap of mud keep still. He want to be so, and again he want to be so [. . .] He wants to be a saint, and he wants to be a devil—and every time he shuts his eyes he sees himself as a very fine fellow—so fine as he can never be. . . . In a dream. . . .' [1]

---

[1] Conrad, *Lord Jim: A Tale* (Edinburgh: Blackwood, 1900), 215.

## II

During the twentieth century, the word 'imperialism' gained increasingly pejorative associations. Today, so many people (for sound reasons) regard the history of imperialism as a predominantly sordid saga of imposition and exploitation that, in order to appreciate the bold panache of 'An Outpost of Progress', we need to recall the tale's date. The year of Queen Victoria's Diamond Jubilee, 1897, was a time of imperialistic fervour in Britain. England's power extended round the world; a quarter of the human race was subject to the Queen. The June issue of *Cosmopolis* included, with the first part of 'An Outpost of Progress', an article by Sir Richard Temple entitled 'The Reign of Queen Victoria', which extolled the growth of British economic power, military strength, and territory. In 'The Globe and the Island', the regular political commentator, Henry Norman, praised British gunboat diplomacy in Africa. The July number of the magazine, in which Conrad's Kayerts shoots the unarmed Carlier and hangs himself from a cross, contained a commentary on the Jubilee celebrations in which Norman remarked:

Britain is imperialistic now. The 'Little Englander' has wisely decided to efface himself. The political party which should talk of reducing the navy or snubbing the Colonies would have a short shrift. We are Imperialists first, and Liberals or Tories afterwards. I said this, for my own part, years ago, when the sentiment was not quite so popular. Now it has happily become a commonplace. The Jubilee is its culminating expression [. . .][2]

This context emphasizes by contrast the sardonic radicalism of Conrad's tale, in which the European emissaries of 'progress' become demoralized and deranged by their isolation in Africa, and in which the 'civilizing mission' is depicted as primarily an avidity for commercial profit.

  If we ask why Conrad should have been so exceptional in his scepticism about imperial expansion, one answer lies in his Polish upbringing. Having been born into a nation which had vanished from the map of Europe after its annexation by Russia from the east, Prussia from the west, and Austria from the south-west, Conrad had good reason to question the right of great powers to impose their wills on weaker nations. His many years of travels and voyages had

[2] *Cosmopolis*, 7 (July 1897), 81.

culminated in his African venture of 1890, when, travelling through the heart of the Congo (which the Belgian King, Leopold II, had claimed as his personal property), he observed the rapacity and brutality of Europeans in the 'dark continent'. Conrad would prove capable of enthusiastic tribute to British traditions; and certainly, of the various kinds of imperialism, he regarded British imperialism as the least malign. Nevertheless, all forms of imperialism were to him deeply suspect, and his abhorrence for the Russian, German, and Belgian forms remained lifelong.

'An Outpost of Progress' provides various clues to enable the reader to identify Kayerts and Carlier as Belgian and the country of their outpost as 'The Congo Free State' (as it was hypocritically designated); but, characteristically, Conrad does not explicitly name their nationality or that location. As we infer them, the tale becomes in part an indictment of Belgian colonialism, but that degree of reticence encourages us to consider how far the tale's criticism may apply to colonialism in general. Indeed, the tale assails the presumptions of civilization by both implying and alleging that civilization is hollow at the core, being a deceptive system of conventions, institutions, and sustaining illusions. Isolate individuals from that system, and the hollowness is revealed:

Few men realise that their life, the very essence of their character, their capabilities and their audacities, are only the expression of their belief in the safety of their surroundings. The courage, the composure, the confidence; the emotions and principles; every great and every insignificant thought belongs not to the individual but to the crowd: to the crowd that believes blindly in the irresistible force of its institutions and of its morals, in the power of its police and of its opinion. But the contact with pure unmitigated savagery, with primitive nature and primitive man, brings sudden and profound trouble into the heart.

The most quotably explanatory part of a text is, however, seldom its best part. This passage is readily isolable and solicits quotation because it epitomizes some of the sceptical themes of 'An Outpost' and of numerous other Conradian works. The force of the tale lies rather in its graphic accumulation of ironies, and these culminate in the final scene when Kayerts is discovered:

He had evidently climbed the grave, which was high and narrow, and after tying the end of the strap to the arm, had swung himself off. His toes were only a couple of inches above the ground; his arms hung stiffly down; he seemed to be standing rigidly at attention, but with one purple cheek playfully posed on the shoulder. And, irreverently, he was putting out a swollen tongue at his Managing Director.

A dangling man suspended from a cross, with a 'purple cheek playfully posed' as he extends his 'swollen tongue'. It is a ferociously sardonic image. Here Conrad, writing in 1897, is—by his unflinchingly bold scepticism—generating the technical and moral shock-tactics of Modernism.

The symbolic, cinematic ironies are already distinctively Conradian; but, like virtually every author, he had begun by learning from others. 'An Outpost of Progress' is indebted in various ways to Maupassant and Flaubert. From both, Conrad had learned the art of literary connoisseurship of the base and wretched. What is described may be sordid or horrifying, yet the manner of description implies a highly civilized concern with linguistic precision and tonal control. In this tale (which he later declared his best),[3] Conrad showed that he was capable of surpassing his French mentors. Among the literary progenitors of Kayerts and Carlier are the eponymous heroes of Flaubert's *Bouvard et Pécuchet*, who, like the Conradian characters, are ingenuous incompetents in an unfamiliar region; but, whereas Flaubert's narrative is long, repetitive, and diffuse, Conrad's is a masterpiece of compression which, in its brief span, proves to be far more incisive and far wider in its implications.

## III

'Karain' is a gentler, slower-paced tale, coloured by those abundant descriptions of the exotic locality which characterize Conrad's works with Malaysian settings. Conrad called it 'magazine'ish',[4] and its handling of the patronizing relationship between the British traders and their Malay friend does bring to mind both the magazine fiction of that day (particularly that in *Blackwood's*, where the tale was first published) and an early reviewer's claim that Conrad might become 'the Kipling of the Malay Archipelago'.[5] Conrad distrusted

---

[3] 'My Best Story and Why I Think So', *Grand Magazine*, 3 (Mar. 1906), 87.

[4] C. T. Watts (ed.), *Joseph Conrad's Letters to R. B. Cunninghame Graham* (London: Cambridge University Press, 1969), p. 82.

[5] *Spectator*, 19 Oct. 1895, p. 530.

Kipling's outlook but admired his technical skill; and certainly 'Karain', though descriptively more luxuriant, resembles a Kipling tale in its reminiscential form, its sympathetic presentation of the group of British friends, its treatment of oriental superstition, the apparently knowledgeable detail in the account of local politics, and the half-ironic, half-serious tribute to the exorcistic power of Queen Victoria's image on a coin—a silver coin which (being gilded) may be doubly fraudulent.

The inner narrative, Karain's confession of his lethal treachery to his friend, derives from a Polish ballad, Adam Mickiewicz's 'Czaty' ('The Ambush').[6] In 'Czaty', a Polish governor finds that his wife has taken a lover. The governor and his henchman (a Cossack) prepare an ambush for the couple; but the Cossack, pitying the wife, then shoots his master. Thus both 'Karain' and 'Czaty' feature a double betrayal: the woman is wayward, and her charms subvert the bond of loyalty between two men, so that a determined avenger perishes at the hand of his trusted companion. Knowledge of the source extends the resonance of 'Karain', for such recognition emphasizes a familiar Conradian theme, that human nature varies little from region to region: different races are united in their capacity for infatuation, treachery, and subjection to illusions. Indeed, the conditions of tropical life may reveal more nakedly the vices and follies which the trappings of northerly civilization contrive to conceal. The ending of the tale effects an appropriately ironic connection between the outer narrative and the inner. Hollis's sense that Karain's haunting may hold more reality than the familiar world of urban London is challenged by the narrator, but the description of the city's crowded streets with their confused turmoil sustains the possibility that Karain's intense experience may be more significant than the hubbub of life in a European metropolis.

## IV

'Youth' introduces Captain Charles Marlow as narrator: he will reappear in 'Heart of Darkness', *Lord Jim*, and *Chance*. Being a civilized, philosophically-minded, and much-travelled Englishman who recounts his past experiences, he proved to be an ideal 'surrogate author'. 'Of all my people', said Conrad, 'he's the one that has

[6] The derivation was first noted by Andrzej Busza in *Antemurale*, 10 (1966), 209–11.

never been a vexation to my spirit. A most discreet, understanding man. . . .'[7] Conrad could now enjoy an exceptional freedom in commentary, since cynical or sceptical ideas could thus be ascribed (however nominally) to the narrating character rather than to the author; so Marlow served, in part, as a mask through which Conrad could speak more fluently and diversely. Cumulatively, Marlow was to become the fullest, most sophisticated, and most convincing character in the whole of Conrad's literary work, and one implying a generous tribute from the Polish-born author to the value of British civilization at its best—as he then saw it.

This generosity of response to his adoptive country can be seen in Conrad's transformation of the facts which provided the basis for 'Youth'. To a large extent, the story of the ill-fated voyage of the *Judea* is based on the *Palestine*'s attempted voyage, between 1881 and 1883, from England to Bangkok. The storms which threatened to sink the ship, the months of repairs at Falmouth, the burning coal in the hold, the explosion and conflagration which destroyed the vessel, the landfall in open boats: all these incidents really occurred. Naturally, various changes have been made for literary and political purposes. When the *Palestine* sank, the boats took fewer than fourteen hours to reach land;[8] in the tale, they take 'many days', a change which accentuates the thematic emphasis on the crew's courageous persistence in the face of all setbacks. Again, the description of the landfall stresses the aromatically exotic glamour of the orient ('strange odours of blossoms, of aromatic wood,' . . . 'impalpable and enslaving, like a charm, like a whispered promise of mysterious delight'); whereas in reality, as Conrad told Richard Curle, the landfall had been made at Muntok—'a damned hole without any beach and without any glamour'.[9] A particularly significant modification concerns the crew's origins. In the *Palestine*, the hard-working crew consisted of a black seaman from St Kitts, a Belgian, an Irishman, two men and a boy from Devon, three men from Cornwall, and a Norwegian; the officers were an Englishman, an Irishman, and (of

---

[7] 'Author's Note' [1917] to *Youth | A Narrative | and Two Other Stories* (London: J. M. Dent and Sons, 1917), p. viii.

[8] Report of the Court of Inquiry, repr. in Norman Sherry, *Conrad's Eastern World* (London: Cambridge University Press, 1966), 298.

[9] Letter of 24 Apr. 1922, quoted in Zdzisław Najder, *Joseph Conrad: A Chronicle* (Cambridge: Cambridge University Press, 1983), 77.

course) a Pole.[10] In the fictional *Judea*, the men are depicted as distinctively and courageously English: 'That crew of Liverpool hard cases had in them the right stuff. It's my experience they always have.'

'Youth' illustrates, thereby, the process of patriotic myth-making. It is also a tale concerned to memorialize, with vividness, lyrical romanticism, wry humour, and an eye for local absurdities, the trials and dour heroism of life under sail in the merchant navy. The nostalgia is frank and unashamed: a middle-aged Marlow looks back indulgently on the ardent optimism of his younger self, and, licensed by the claret bottle, veers finally towards a sentimentality which the anonymous narrator endorses in a concluding paragraph of rhythmic vigour and logical vapidity.

## V

In 1876, Leopold II, King of the Belgians, had declared:

To open to civilisation the sole part of the globe which it has not yet penetrated, to pierce the darkness which envelops the entire population: this, I venture to say, is a crusade worthy of this century of progress.[11]

Fourteen years later, Conrad travelled through that 'part of the globe': the hypocritically named Congo Free State. There he witnessed the brutality with which, in the quest for ivory, the Belgians were exploiting the indigenous population and the imported African labourers. Among the entries in his 'Congo Diary' are these:

Met an off[ice]r of the State inspecting. A few minutes afterwards saw at a camp[ing] place the dead body of a Backongo. Shot? Horrid smell [. . .] Saw another dead body lying by the path in an attitude of meditative repose [. . .] On the road to day passed a skeleton tied-up to a post. Also white man's grave—No name [. . .] Row between the carriers and a man stating himself in gov[ernment] employ, about a mat.—Blows with sticks raining hard—Stopped it. Chief came with a youth about 13 suffering from gunshot wound in the head [. . .] Gave him a little glycerine to put on the wound [. . .][12]

---

[10] Jerry Allen, *The Sea Years of Joseph Conrad* (London: Methuen, 1987), 319.

[11] Quoted in Maurice H. Hennessy's *Congo: A Brief History and Appraisal* (London: Pall Mall Press, 1961), 13.

[12] Robert Hampson (ed.), Joseph Conrad: *'Heart of Darkness' with 'The Congo Diary'* (London: Penguin, 1995), 152, 153, 158, 160–1.

Conrad's travels in the Congo lasted approximately six months. Eventually, having been afflicted with dysentery and fever, he returned to London via Brussels. He never forgot the horrors of the African journey. In 1903, when writing to a socialist friend, he compared the Belgian colonialists to the Spanish *conquistadores*:

Their achievement is monstrous enough in all conscience—but not as a great human force let loose, but rather like that of a gigantic and obscene beast. Leopold is their Pizarro, Thys their Cortez and their 'lances' are recruited amongst the souteneurs, sous-offs, maquereaux, fruit-secs [ponces, N.C.O.s, pimps, and losers] of all sorts on the pavements of Brussels and Antwerp.[13]

From Conrad's embittering African experience emerged 'Heart of Darkness': a work supreme among his *novelle* or longer tales. It is exciting and profound, lucid and bewildering; highly compressed, immensely rich in texture and implication; and it has a recessive adroitness, for its paradoxes repeatedly ambush the conceptualizing reader or critic. Thematically, it holds a remarkably wide range of reference to problems of politics and psychology, morality and religion, social order and evolution. In a critical interplay, the narra- tive dextrously embodies literary theories and techniques which were yet to be formulated and labelled. 'Heart of Darkness' can be related to a diversity of traditions, generic and technical, including political satire, protest literature, traveller's tale, psychological odys- sey, symbolic novel, and mediated autobiography; while, to those readers who seek prophecies, it speaks eloquently of the brutalities and follies of subsequent history. The tale's influence extends to works as diverse as John Powell's *Rhapsodie nègre*, Malinowski's *Diary*,[14] T. S. Eliot's 'The Hollow Men', Chinua Achebe's *Things Fall Apart*, Graham Greene's 'The Third Man' and *A Burnt-out*

[13] Frederick R. Karl and Laurence Davies (ed.), *The Collected Letters of Joseph Conrad*, iii (Cambridge: Cambridge University Press, 1988), 101. (This series will subsequently be cited as *Letters*.)

[14] Bronisław Malinowski, the eminent Polish anthropologist, declared when he was young: '[W. H. R.] Rivers is the Rider Haggard of anthropology; I shall be the Conrad.' See Raymond Firth (ed.), *Man and Culture: An Evaluation of the Work of Bronisław Malinowski* (London: Routledge & Kegan Paul, 1957), 6. While working in New Guinea, Malinowski read the *Youth* volume, which contained 'Heart of Darkness'. On 21 Jan. 1915, he confided to his journal: 'On the whole my feelings toward the natives are decidedly tending to "*Exterminate the brutes*."' (The italicized words were in Eng- lish, while the other words were originally in Polish.) See his *A Diary in the Strict Sense of the Term* (London: Routledge & Kegan Paul, 1967), 69.

*Case*, William Golding's *The Inheritors*, Ngugi wa Thiong'o's *A Grain of Wheat*, Robert Stone's *Dog Soldiers*, George Steiner's *The Portage to San Cristóbal of A. H.*, and Robert Edric's *The Book of the Heathen*. Films, videos, and adaptations for radio and the theatre have further extended its range. The second of Orson Welles's two radio versions (1938 and 1945) depicted Kurtz explicitly as a fore-runner of Adolf Hitler, while Coppola's film *Apocalypse Now* (1979) demonstrated that this tale about Africa in 1890 entailed, among many other possibilities, a sardonic commentary on the Vietnam War of the 1970s. A documentary about Coppola's work, *Hearts of Darkness: A Film-Maker's Apocalypse* (1991) suggested that the film-makers embodied and extended the corruption described in the tale. Other films included Nicolas Roeg's version for television and video (1994) and Jonathan Lawton's spoof entitled *Cannibal Women in the Avocado Jungle of Death*. One test of literary merit is fecundity, the ability to generate offspring; and this test has been amply passed by the story that appeared in the closing years of the Victorian Age.

As in 'Youth', 'Heart of Darkness' employs doubly oblique narra-tion: an anonymous character reports the story told by Marlow. This time, however, the oblique narrative technique is used much more searchingly, so that one of the main co-ordinators of the story is a linguistic theme, which emphasizes not only the difficulty of com-municating what is obscure or profound but also the attractions and perils of charismatic eloquence. Indeed, one of the many paradoxes of 'Heart of Darkness' is that this narrative offers eloquent warnings about eloquence, while effectively communicating the difficulty of effective communication. An important political aspect of this theme is displayed by the tale's demonstration that there is an imperialism of discourse which both licenses and conceals the excesses of eco-nomic exploitation. The generative and transformative relationship of language to the world is made problematically evident.

The sophistication, compression, and obliquities of the tale are such that, in order to be adequately comprehended, it needs to be read at least twice. At a first reading, many ironies are likely to pass unnoticed. We may not see, for instance, that Marlow's initial descriptions of the Roman trireme-commander and the 'decent young citizen in a toga' offer ironic counterparts to Marlow himself and Kurtz in Africa; nor may we see that the tale has a covert murder-plot, in which the manager schemes to destroy the ailing

Kurtz by delaying the steamer which is supposed to relieve Kurtz's outpost. Certainly, the satiric indictment of colonialism in Africa is graphically clear at a first reading, as is the mockery of the myopic arrogance of Europeans in daring to impose themselves on alien territory. Many of the 'pilgrims' function as mere avaricious automata; and as for Kurtz himself, who has brought idealistic ambitions to the wilderness, he proves to be depraved and deranged. In its accumulation of images of absurdity, of savage farce, of wanton destruction and demented energy, 'Heart of Darkness' can be seen as a fiercely pessimistic narrative. Its positive values lie partly in the quality of civilization represented by Marlow, who, though flawed, usually preserves a vigilant humanity; they lie largely in the authorial indignation at man's inhumanity to man and, indeed, at the despoliation of the earth in the name of 'progress'; and they are richly implicit in the articulate intelligence, sensitivity, and exuberance of the text.

The general critical consensus, which met some fierce challenges in the late twentieth century, is that the strengths of the tale greatly outweigh its flaws. One apparent flaw, postulated long ago by F. R. Leavis, Jocelyn Baines, and other commentators, is a tendency to vapidly portentous phrasing, 'an adjectival and worse than super-erogatory insistence on "unspeakable rites", "unspeakable secrets", "monstrous passions", "inconceivable mystery", and so on'.[15] This criticism has some force, but the force is reduced by the following considerations. The speaker who offers such 'adjectival insistence' is ostensibly not Conrad but Marlow, a narrator who, by his dry comments on Kurtz's inflated prose style, himself invites us to beware of waffle. In any case, Marlow emphasizes that during the journey (on which he was stricken with fever), he frequently encountered experiences which, in their baffling, bewildering, or disorientating nature, were hard to capture in words. The marked use of polysyllabic privative adjectives ('inconceivable', 'unspeakable', etc.) may have thematic justification, if not vindication, in a liminal text which explores, and looks beyond, limits: limits of experience, of morality, and of language. The 'darkness' of the work's title has numerous referents: moral corruption, night, death, ignorance, and that

---

[15] F. R. Leavis, *The Great Tradition* [1948] (Harmondsworth: Penguin, 1962), 198–200; quoted, p. 198; Jocelyn Baines, *Joseph Conrad: A Critical Biography* (London: Weidenfeld & Nicolson, 1960), 225.

encompassing obscurity of the pre-rational and pre-verbal which words seek to illuminate. An important co-ordinator of the tale is a sequence of literal and symbolic images of light shining briefly amid obscurity; and one of the searchingly experimental features is the incorporation of conspicuous opacities—opacities in characterization, plot, and situation which are made conspicuous by the frustrated questioning that surrounds them. Indeed, commentators may too readily fall into the trap of postulating specific and partial answers, when the text is often determined to maintain ambiguity, doubt, uncertainty, and symbolic multiplicity. Its images shimmer and shift on the borders between realism, symbolism, and expressionism.

A second, and far graver, objection to 'Heart of Darkness' was that offered most forcefully by the Nigerian novelist, Chinua Achebe, who asserted that the tale reveals Conrad as 'a bloody racist'.[16] He argued that Conrad dramatizes Africa as 'a place of negations [. . .] in comparison with which Europe's own state of spiritual grace will be manifest'. The blacks, Achebe alleged, are dehumanized and degraded, seen as grotesques or as a howling mob; they are denied speech, or are granted speech only to condemn themselves out of their own mouths. In short, 'Heart of Darkness' is 'an offensive and totally deplorable book' in which Conrad has adopted 'the role of purveyor of comforting myths'. The tale, Achebe insists, promotes racial intolerance and is therefore to be condemned. (It may, however, have helped to prompt Achebe's fine novel, *Things Fall Apart*, which depicts imperialism from the indigenes' point of view.)

Achebe's criticism became widely influential and drew attention to ways in which 'Heart of Darkness', though so proleptic, bears signs of its Victorian origins. Within Marlow's credibly mixed range of responses to the Africans, there are certainly some attitudes which can seem patronizing or misguided. His use of the term 'niggers' has given offence, though it was historically realistic: the obnoxious term was widely and casually used by whites in the 1890s and long afterwards; indeed, it could be heard in American films more than a

---

[16] 'An Image of Africa' (originally a lecture given in 1975) in *Massachusetts Review*, 18 (Winter 1977), 782–94. The phrase 'a bloody racist' is on p. 788. In the subsequent, revised version of this article, the phrase became 'a thoroughgoing racist', and a passage linking Conrad with Nazism was cut.

century later. In one respect, Achebe's criticisms could have gone further. Marlow notes that Kurtz is drawn to a nocturnal ritual in the jungle which is attended by a sinister figure:

a black figure stood up, strode on long black legs, waving long black arms, across the glow. It had horns—antelope horns, I think—on its head. Some sorcerer, some witch-man, no doubt: it looked fiend-like enough.

Achebe objected to the tautological iteration of the adjective 'black'; but another objection might be that here we encounter—in a dramatically visual form—'demonization of the other'. Details of phrasing ('I think', 'no doubt') indicate the faint but distinct suspicion that the figure observed might be truly Satanic, so that for a while there is a fleeting fusion of an African and a diabolic entity. Nevertheless, the speaker there is not Joseph Conrad but Charles Marlow, the character. Achebe says that he sees no difference between Marlow and Conrad, to which one response is that Conrad has deliberately chosen to use the convention of doubly oblique narration, which tends to generate ambiguities.

Achebe's attack was fierce, sweeping, and polemically influential; later, he moderated its ferocity. Other 'postcolonial' writers, including Ngugi wa Thiong'o, Wilson Harris, Frances B. Singh, and C. P. Sarvan, argued that while Conrad was ambivalent on racial matters, 'Heart of Darkness' was progressive in its satiric accounts of the colonialists.[17] Singh noted that though the tale was vulnerable in several respects, including that association of Africans with supernatural evil, the story should remain in 'the canon of works indicting colonialism'. Sarvan concluded: 'Conrad [. . .] was not entirely immune to the infection of the beliefs and attitudes of his age, but he was ahead of most in trying to break free'. To be fair to 'Heart of Darkness', as to any literary text, we need to take account of its date: 1899. As Sarvan indicates, relative to the standards prevailing in the 1890s, the heyday of Victorian imperialism, the tale was indeed progressive in its criticism of imperialist activities in Africa, and, indeed, of imperialist activities generally. Marlow says: 'The conquest of the earth [. . .] mostly means the taking it away from those who have a different complexion or slightly flatter noses than

---

[17] Ngugi wa Thiong'o is quoted in Robert Kimbrough (ed.), *Heart of Darkness* (New York: Norton, 1988), 285, within C. P. Sarvan's essay (pp. 280–5); Wilson Harris's piece is on pp. 262–8, and Frances B. Singh's is on pp. 268–80.

ourselves'; and, though he attempts to postulate some redemptive factor, his own narrative shows that in Africa, at any rate, 'the conquest of the earth' is predominantly 'robbery with violence, aggravated murder on a great scale'. Achebe claimed that Africa was depicted by Conrad as 'a place of negations' so as to emphasize by contrast 'Europe's own state of spiritual grace'; but in a variety of ways the tale challenges such a contrast. As Africa is to present-day Europeans, so, Marlow suggests, England was to Roman colonists. When he describes depopulated regions of Africa, Marlow reflects that the Kentish countryside would also become rapidly depopulated if it were invaded by heavily armed strangers. The sound of drums in the jungle has 'perhaps [. . .] as profound a meaning as the sound of bells in a Christian country'. The whites of the Eldorado Expedition ride their donkeys into the jungle, and Marlow comments: 'Long afterwards the news came that all the donkeys were dead. I know nothing as to the fate of the less valuable animals.' (If he had referred to blacks rather than whites as 'less valuable animals', critics would have cited this as evidence of racism.) Kurtz, we are told, is not worth 'the life we lost in getting to him': the life of the black helmsman. The cannibal crew evinces remarkable restraint; it is Kurtz, the European, who 'lacked restraint in the gratification of his various lusts', and who, it is implied, may have drunk blood and consumed human flesh. A particularly bold attempt to subvert conventional prejudice is made near the end of the tale, when Marlow notes the kinship between the idealistic fiancée and the black consort: their similarity in gesture, stretching out their arms towards the Kurtz of memory, shows that both are alike in unavailing fidelity to the egotist who attracted their devotion.

In a late essay, Conrad referred to the Belgian exploitation of Africa as 'the vilest scramble for loot that ever disfigured the history of human conscience'.[18] Generally, the satiric animus which 'Heart of Darkness' directs against the European 'pilgrims' is so intense as to be, in one respect, unhistorical; for the tale's depiction of their senselessly chaotic attempts at construction can make us briefly forget the enduring technological achievements (the railways, the roads, the establishment of new townships) which, for all the depredations, changed the face of Africa. Marlow says nothing about the atrocities

[18] 'Geography and Some Explorers', in *Last Essays* (London: Dent, 1926), 25.

committed by black imperialists such as the ruling dynasty of the kingdom of Benin; nor does he mention the slave-trading conducted on a large scale by Arabs and their local accomplices. In the tale, there is only group of people which seems to be vital, happy, and in harmony with the environment, and that group is not European: it is the singing blacks who, with 'wild vitality' and 'intense energy of movement', paddle their boat through the coastal surf. 'They'—unlike the whites—'wanted no excuse for being there.' These energetic boatmen make a stark contrast to the enslaved and dying men of the chain gang and the grove of death. In many respects the tale is ambiguous, but it seems unambiguous when it stresses, by means of such graphically effective scenes, the hypocritical and callous cruelty which, in the name of progress and for the sake of profit, the European invaders have inflicted on their fellow human beings.

In practice, 'Heart of Darkness' contributed to the international campaign of protest which eventually curbed the Belgian excesses in the Congo. E. D. Morel, leader of the Congo Reform Association, stated that 'Heart of Darkness' was 'the most powerful thing ever written on the subject';[19] and Conrad sent encouraging letters to his acquaintance (and Morel's collaborator in the campaign), Roger Casement, who in 1904 published a parliamentary report documenting the atrocities committed by the Belgian administrators. On 21 December 1903, Conrad wrote to Casement:

You cannot doubt that I form the warmest wishes for your success. A King, wealthy and unscrupulous, is certainly no mean adversary [. . .]

And the fact remains that [. . .] there exists in Africa a Congo State, created by the act of European Powers[,] where ruthless, systematic cruelty towards the blacks is the basis of administration [. . .]

[M]ake any use you like of what I write to you.[20]

The material supplied by Conrad was quoted in Morel's book, *King Leopold's Rule in Africa* (1904); and the London *Morning*

---

[19] Letter of 7 Oct. 1909, quoted in W. R. Louis and Jean Stengers, *E. D. Morel's History of the Congo Reform Movement* (London: Oxford University Press, 1968), 205.

[20] *Letters*, iii. 95, 97. In 1913, Morel declared that most of the campaign's goals had been achieved: 'The native of the Congo is once more a free man [. . .] The rubber-tax—the "blood tax"—has been abolished.' (*E. D. Morel's History*, 208.) The Congo gained independence in 1960. A century after Conrad's journey there, corruption, disorder, and poverty were widespread.

*Post*, in a laudatory review, gave prominence to Conrad's 'heavy indictment'.[21] Meanwhile, Conrad and F. M. Hueffer, in their novel *The Inheritors* (1901), satirized Leopold II as the grasping and unscrupulous Duc de Mersch. In 'Heart of Darkness', Conrad makes sure that the indictment is not of Belgian imperialism alone. Neither Brussels nor the Congo Free State is named, and 'all Europe contributed to the making of Kurtz': furthermore, that Europe includes England, for Kurtz was 'educated partly in England', and, while his father was half-French, '[his] mother was half-English'. Such details erode Marlow's early attempt to distinguish the British Empire as a place where 'real work' is done; and they ambush unwary commentators who underestimate Conrad's resourcefulness. As Peter Nazareth has said, 'Conrad was a mental liberator.'[22]

Predictably, Conrad was assailed as a male chauvinist. Nina Pelikan Straus, Bette London, Johanna M. Smith, and Elaine Showalter were among those feminists who argued that 'Heart of Darkness' was both imperialist and sexist.[23] Straus, for instance, declared: 'The woman reader [. . .] is in the position to insist that Marlow's cowardice consists of his inability to face the dangerous self that is the form of his own masculinist vulnerability: his own complicity in the racist, sexist, imperialistic, and finally libidinally satisfying world he has inhabited with Kurtz.' In the tale, a man (Marlow) tells a group of men a story about 'men's work' in Africa; women are subordinated. He says, notoriously: 'It's queer how out of touch with truth women are. They live in a world of their own [. . .] It is too beautiful altogether [. . .]'. Eventually he lies to the Intended, denying her (mercifully enough) access to the truth about Kurtz. Nevertheless, in the later work *Chance* (1914), Marlow says that women know the whole truth but mercifully conceal it from men, who live in 'fool's paradise'. In 'Heart of Darkness', females are depicted in diverse and contrasting ways. The African consort

---

[21] *Morning Post*, 12 Oct. 1904, p. 8.

[22] Peter Nazareth, 'Out of Darkness: Conrad and Other Third World Writers', *Conradiana*, 14 (1982), 173–87; quotation, p. 178.

[23] Straus, 'The Exclusion of the Intended from Secret Sharing in Conrad's *Heart of Darkness*', *Novel*, 20 (1987), 123–37. (The subsequent quotation is from p. 135.) London, *The Appropriated Voice* (Ann Arbor: University of Michigan Press, 1990). Smith, '"Too Beautiful Altogether": Patriarchal Ideology in *Heart of Darkness*', in Ross C. Murfin (ed.), *Joseph Conrad, 'Heart of Darkness': A Case Study in Contemporary Criticism* (New York: St. Martin's Press, 1989). Showalter, *Sexual Anarchy* (London: Bloomsbury, 1991).

knows what the Intended does not. At the company's offices in the city, the two mysterious females who meet the applicants are apparently prescient, even fateful. Marlow's aunt cannot be living entirely 'in a world of her own', for it is she whose influence with the company gains employment for her nephew. Characteristically masculine activities (waging war, or trading in—and exploiting—territories abroad) are depicted satirically. Those feminist critics did not mention that Conrad was a postulant of female suffrage, although in 1910 he signed an open letter to the Prime Minister, Herbert Asquith, advocating votes for women.[24]

Critics who allege that Conrad is imperialistic may themselves be practising ideological and temporal imperialism. They assail the text for failing to endorse their own present-day beliefs or prejudices; and thereby they seek to subordinate the literary work to their own value systems. The novelist Julian Barnes once said: '[W]hat a curious vanity it is of the present to expect the past to suck up to it.' Or, as a better-known story-teller put it, 'He that is without sin among you, let him first cast a stone.'[25] In 1907 Conrad wrote an essay ('The Censor of Plays') denouncing censorship as a contemptible weapon of tyranny. If we abolished all those past texts which, in our fallible understandings, failed to endorse today's preferred notions, few works would survive, and every library would become merely a hall of mirrors. A literary work may have a diversity of political implications and consequences, but it is not a political manifesto. It is an imaginative work which offers a voluntary and hypothetical experience. Its linguistic texture may be progressive when its paraphrasable content may not. All its implications remain within the invisible quotation-marks of the fictional. Awareness of the tentacular complexity of 'Heart of Darkness' may alert to us a current critical tendency: the reductive treatment of past texts in the attempt to vindicate the political gestures of the present. 'Heart of Darkness' reminds us that this tendency resembles an earlier one: the adoption of a demeaning attitude to colonized people in order to vindicate

---

[24] The letter was reported and quoted in *The Times*, 15 June 1910, p. 7. The list of signatories included Cunninghame Graham, Sarah Grand, Bernard Shaw, and May Sinclair. See also *Letters*, iv (1990), 327.

[25] Julian Barnes, *Flaubert's Parrot* (London: Cape, 1984), 130; John 8: 7. J. W. Burrow adds: 'To illustrate the racial prejudices of our ancestors [. . .] provides both an easy research strategy and a cheaply won moral superiority' (*Times Literary Supplement*, 13 June 1986, p. 653).

the exploitative actions of the colonizer. Naturally, readers discuss political aspects of literary texts; but to use political criteria as a 'master-discourse', as the final tribunal of judgement, is to commit an error of categorization. (An equivalent error would be to condemn *The Communist Manifesto* for lacking the lyricism of Shelley's 'Ode to a Skylark'.)

Conrad earned his living as an entertainer, not as a writer of religious or political tracts. We read fiction for pleasures of diverse kinds. The pleasures generated by 'Heart of Darkness' have many sources. They lie in part in its evocative vividness, its linguistic intelligence, its diverse modes of suspense, and its power to question and to provoke thought. Paraphrase is a necessary critical tool, but paraphrase is never an equivalent of the original, the vitality of which permeates its combinations of the particular and the general, the rational and the emotional. The tale's paradoxical complexities expose by contrast the relatively limited and predictable narratives offered by so much non-fictional critical and political writing. In 1895, Conrad wrote: 'Theory is a cold and lying tombstone of departed truth.' He thus anticipated, by about eighty-eight years, Edward Said's anti-theoretical theory. Said declared:

[I]t is the critic's job to provide resistances to theory, to open it up toward historical reality, toward society, toward human needs and interests, to point up those concrete instances drawn from everyday reality that lie outside or just beyond the interpretive area necessarily designated in advance and thereafter circumscribed by every theory.[26]

'The critic's job'? Conrad knew that this had long been the creative writer's job. In 'Heart of Darkness', various theories, clichés, and jargonic phrases are tested against the rich particularities of the work's texture. The political is challenged by the aesthetic. The tale has sombre implications, and so does the story of its reception over the years, but the imaginative intelligence with which the narrative addressed its era was exemplary. To those English-speaking critics who have deemed the work racist, sexist, and imperialist, we may reply: 'Try writing a better tale; and don't forget to write it in Polish, in order to emulate Joseph Conrad's ability to cross frontiers of

---

[26] Conrad, *Letters*, i (1983), 205. Edward Said, *The World, the Text, and the Critic* [1983] (London: Faber & Faber, 1984), 242.

language, nationality, and culture.' In the virtuosity of this Polish author's command of English, he was profoundly anti-imperialistic, for he was liberating new possibilities of experience from the benighted empire of inarticulacy.

# NOTE ON THE TEXT

The four tales in this volume are arranged in chronological order of composition. 'An Outpost of Progress' was written in July 1896, and the manuscript is held at the Beinecke Rare Book and Manuscript Library, Yale University. 'Karain' was mooted early in February 1897 and completed by 14 April of that year. The manuscript, having been sold to John Quinn, the American collector, is believed to have sunk with the *Titanic* in 1912 on its way to New York. 'Youth' was begun early in 1898 and finished by 3 June. Its manuscript is at Colgate University, while a single handwritten leaf is in the National Library of Scotland. The writing of 'Heart of Darkness' (originally 'The Heart of Darkness') extended from December 1898 to February 1899. Part of the original manuscript has survived and is in the Beinecke Rare Book and Manuscript Library, while a fragment of the typescript is in the Berg Collection, New York Public Library.

The first publication of 'An Outpost of Progress' was in the magazine *Cosmopolis* in June and July 1897, and 'Karain: A Memory' made its début in *Blackwood's Edinburgh Magazine* in November of the same year. Both tales were next published in the volume *Tales of Unrest* (London: Fisher Unwin; New York: Scribner's) in 1898. The first publication of 'Youth: A Narrative' was in *Blackwood's* in September 1898; that of 'Heart of Darkness' was in the issues of the same magazine for February, March, and April, 1899. These two works first appeared in book form in *Youth: A Narrative | and | Two Other Stories* (Edinburgh: Blackwood, 1902). The third item in that volume was the long story entitled 'The End of the Tether'. The 'Author's Note' to *Youth* was written in 1917 for the second edition of that volume (London: Dent), and subsequently appeared in the Collected Editions issued by Doubleday and Heinemann. The base-text here is the 1917 (Dent) version. A discussion of 'The End of the Tether' has been deleted from it, as that tale is not part of the present collection.

Important editions of 'Heart of Darkness' are by Robert Kimbrough (New York: Norton, 1963, 1971, 1988), D. C. R. A. Goonetilleke (Broadview: Peterborough, Ontario, 1995), and Robert Hampson (London: Penguin, 1995). I am variously and gratefully indebted to these editors. Hampson's base-text is the first British edition of *Youth*. The serial is the base-text for the Everyman paperback, *The Heart of Darkness*, ed. Cedric Watts (London: Dent; Vermont: Tuttle, 1995). Anthony Fothergill's edition of *Tales of Unrest* (London: Everyman, Dent; Vermont: Tuttle, 2000) proved helpful for the annotations of 'Karain' and 'An Outpost of Progress'. Another useful volume was Ross C. Murfin (ed.), *Heart of Darkness* (2nd edn.: Basingstoke: Macmillan; Boston: St Martin's Press, 1996). S. W. Reid kindly provided relevant documents.

In the present volume, I have followed the procedures described in the 'General Editor's Preface'. The base-texts of the fictional works are those of the first British publications in book form, which I have compared with the British serial versions (where such versions exist). Various emendations are listed below. (The textual annotations towards the end of this volume include references to problematic or divergent phrasings.) In the textual apparatus which follows, the page and line numbers refer to emendations in this edition, and each reading after the square bracket is that of the first British book edition. With the exception of four entries, which are emended from the periodical version (*Per.*), all corrections are the editor's.

### An Outpost of Progress

25: 13–14   up, the fog *Per.*] up the fog

### Karain

53: 30   should not die? *Per.*] should not die!
56: 24   forest. *Per.*] forest."
58: 1   Sulu] Sula
61: 25   that I] that "I
61: 25   think so.] think so."
63: 33   —shook] shook

### Youth

71        YOUTH: A NARRATIVE *Per.*] YOUTH

### Heart of Darkness

106: 1   say 'knights'?] say Knights?
108: 34–5   Trading Society] Trading society
116: 28   way of] way or

122: 32  You must] you must
124: 27  Kurtz!', broke] Kurtz!' broke
124: 31  I tell?] I tell,
126: 16  Anyway] Anyways
128: 6   moonlight; the] moonlight, the
138: 15  word 'ivory'] word ivory
141: 17  Towser,] Tower,
145: 19  good tuck-in] good tuck in
152: 37  shoes?] shoes.
166: 29–30   means 'short'] means short
170: 11  He suspected] 'He suspected
170: 12  that—] that—'

I have preserved some spellings which, according to the *Oxford English Dictionary*, are correct but archaic or uncommon (e.g. 'lounged' for 'lunged', 'calipers' for 'callipers', and 'dumfounded' for 'dumbfounded'). I have also retained Conradian Gallicisms, such as 'I heard all round me like a pent-up breath released' and 'I felt like a chill grip on my chest'.

# SELECT BIBLIOGRAPHY

### *Biographies and Letters*

Baines, Jocelyn, *Joseph Conrad: A Critical Biography* (London: Weidenfeld & Nicolson, 1960).

Batchelor, John, *The Life of Joseph Conrad* (Oxford: Blackwell, 1994).

Ford, Ford Madox, *Joseph Conrad: A Personal Remembrance* (Boston: Little, Brown, 1924; New York: Ecco, 1989).

Jean-Aubry, G., *Joseph Conrad: Life and Letters*, 2 vols. (London: Heinemann, 1927).

Karl, Frederick R., *Joseph Conrad: The Three Lives* (London: Faber, 1979).

—— and Davies, Laurence (eds.), *The Collected Letters of Joseph Conrad* (Cambridge: Cambridge University Press, 1983–   ).

Knowles, Owen, *A Conrad Chronology* (Basingstoke: Macmillan, 1989).

Najder, Zdzisław, *Conrad's Polish Background* (Oxford: Oxford University Press, 1964).

—— *Joseph Conrad: A Chronicle* (Cambridge: Cambridge University Press, 1983).

Ray, Martin (ed.), *Joseph Conrad: Interviews and Recollections* (Basingstoke: Macmillan, 1990).

Sherry, Norman, *Conrad's Eastern World* (London: Cambridge University Press, 1966).

—— *Conrad's Western World* (London: Cambridge University Press, 1971).

—— *Conrad and His World* (London: Thames & Hudson, 1972).

Stape, J. H., and Knowles, Owen (eds.), *A Portrait in Letters: Correspondence to and about Conrad* (Amsterdam: Rodopi, 1996).

Watts, Cedric, *Joseph Conrad: A Literary Life* (Basingstoke: Macmillan, 1989).


### *Criticism*

Berthoud, Jacques, *Joseph Conrad: The Major Phase* (Cambridge: Cambridge University Press, 1978).

Bradbrook, Muriel, *Joseph Conrad: Poland's English Genius* (Cambridge: Cambridge University Press, 1941).

Daleski, Hillel M., *Joseph Conrad: The Way of Dispossession* (London: Faber, 1977).

Erdinast-Vulcan, Daphna, *Joseph Conrad and the Modern Temper* (Oxford: Oxford University Press, 1991).

Fogel, Aaron, *Coercion to Speak: Conrad's Poetics of Dialogue* (Cambridge, Mass.: Harvard University Press, 1985).

Gordon, John Dozier, *Joseph Conrad: The Making of a Novelist* (Cambridge, Mass.: Harvard University Press, 1985).

Guerard, Albert J., *Conrad the Novelist* (Cambridge, Mass.: Harvard University Press, 1958).

Hampson, Robert, *Joseph Conrad: Betrayal and Identity* (Basingstoke: Macmillan, 1992).

Hawthorn, Jeremy, *Joseph Conrad: Language and Fictional Self-Consciousness* (London: Edward Arnold, 1979).

—— *Joseph Conrad: Narrative Technique and Ideological Commitment* (London: Edward Arnold, 1990).

Knowles, Owen, and Moore, Gene (eds.), *The Oxford Reader's Companion to Conrad* (Oxford: Oxford University Press, 2000).

Lothe, Jakob, *Conrad's Narrative Method* (Oxford: Oxford University Press, 1989).

Morf, Gustav, *The Polish Shades and Ghosts of Joseph Conrad* (New York: Astra, 1976).

Moser, Thomas, *Joseph Conrad: Achievement and Decline* (Cambridge, Mass.: Harvard University Press, 1957).

Murfin, Ross (ed.), *Conrad Revisited: Essays for the Eighties* (Tuscaloosa, Ala.: University of Alabama Press, 1985).

Said, Edward, *Joseph Conrad and the Fiction of Autobiography* (Cambridge, Mass.: Harvard University Press, 1966).

Sherry, Norman (ed.), *Conrad: The Critical Heritage* (London: Routledge & Kegan Paul, 1973).

Spittles, Brian, *Joseph Conrad* (Basingstoke: Macmillan, 1992).

Stape, J. H. (ed.), *The Cambridge Companion to Joseph Conrad* (Cambridge: Cambridge University Press, 1996).

Watt, Ian, *Conrad in the Nineteenth Century* (London: Chatto & Windus, 1980).

—— *Essays on Conrad* (Cambridge: Cambridge University Press, 2000).

Watts, Cedric, *A Preface to Conrad* (London: Longman, 1982).

—— *The Deceptive Text: An Introduction to Covert Plots* (Brighton: Harvester, 1984).

### Chapters on Conrad in Critical Texts

Armstrong, Paul B., *The Challenge of Bewilderment: Understanding and Representation in James, Conrad and Ford* (Ithaca, NY: Cornell University Press, 1987).

Graham, Kenneth, *Indirections of the Novel: James, Conrad and Ford* (Cambridge: Cambridge University Press, 1988).

Leavis, F. R., *The Great Tradition: George Eliot, Henry James, Joseph Conrad* (London: Chatto & Windus, 1948).

Levenson, Michael, *A Genealogy of Modernism* (Cambridge: Cambridge University Press, 1984).

—— *Modernism and the Fate of Individuality* (Cambridge: Cambridge University Press, 1991).

White, Allon, *The Uses of Obscurity: The Fiction of Early Modernism* (London: Routledge & Kegan Paul, 1981).

Whiteley, Patrick J., *Knowledge and Experimental Realism in Conrad, Lawrence and Woolf* (Baton Rouge: Louisiana State University Press, 1987).

### Periodicals and Bibliographies

There are two important journals devoted to Conrad—*The Conradian* and *Conradiana*—and several scholarly critical bibliographies, though to date there is no single comprehensive bibliography of Conrad's entire oeuvre. The most helpful selective guide for the student and general reader is Owen Knowles's *An Annotated Critical Bibliography of Joseph Conrad* (Hemel Hempstead: Harvester Wheatsheaf, 1992). Further details of recent scholarship can be found in the *MLA International Bibliography* which is also available on CD-Rom and on-line.

### Useful Web Sites

http://lang.nagoya-u.ac.jp/~matsuoka/Conrad.html [offers a large number of hyperlinks to many other specialized Conrad web sites or relevant parts of other web sites]

http://www.library.utoronto.ca/utel/authors/conradj.html [a sound academic complement to the above]

http://members.tripod.com/~JTKNK/ [focuses mainly on the activities of the Joseph Conrad Foundation but also provides access to a number of e-texts]

### On the Stories in This Volume

Achebe, Chinua, 'An Image of Africa', in *The Chancellor's Lecture Series: 1974–75* (Amherst: University of Massachusetts, 1975), reprinted in *Massachusetts Review*, 18 (1977), and in *Research in African Literatures*, 9 (1978). A substantially revised version appears in Achebe's *Hopes and Impediments* (London: Heinemann, 1988; New York: Doubleday, 1989) and in the 1988 volume edited by Kimbrough, cited below.

Adams, Richard, *Joseph Conrad: 'Heart of Darkness'* (London: Penguin, 1991).

Beerbohm, Max, 'The Feast', in *A Christmas Garland* (London: Heinemann, 1912).

Bender, Todd K. (ed.), *A Concordance to Conrad's 'Heart of Darkness'* (New York: Garland, 1979).

Bloom, Harold (ed.), *Joseph Conrad's 'Heart of Darkness'* (New York: Chelsea House, 1987).

Burden, Robert, *Heart of Darkness* (Basingstoke: Macmillan, 1991).

Carlier, J. C., 'Roland Barthes's Resurrection of the Author and Redemption of Biography', *Cambridge Quarterly*, 29 (Autumn 2000).

Dean, L. F. (ed.), *Heart of Darkness: Backgrounds and Criticism* (Englewood Cliffs, NJ: Prentice-Hall, 1960).

Dryden, Linda, *Joseph Conrad and the Imperial Romance* (Basingstoke: Macmillan; New York: St Martin's Press, 2000).

Fothergill, Anthony, *Heart of Darkness* (Milton Keynes: Open University Press, 1989).

—— (ed.), *Tales of Unrest* (London: Everyman, Dent; Vermont: Tuttle, 2000).

Hampson, Robert (ed.), Joseph Conrad: *Heart of Darkness* (London: Penguin, 1995).

Harkness, Bruce (ed.), *Conrad's 'Heart of Darkness' and the Critics* (Belmont: Wadsworth, 1960).

Hawkins, Hunt, 'Conrad's Critique of Imperialism in *Heart of Darkness*', *Publications of the Modern Language Association of America*, 94 (Jan. 1979).

—— 'Joseph Conrad, Roger Casement, and the Congo Reform Movement', *Journal of Modern Literature*, 9 (1981); repr. in Kimbrough, 1988.

—— 'The Issue of Racism in *Heart of Darkness*', *Conradiana*, 14 (1982).

Kimbrough, Robert (ed.), Joseph Conrad: *Heart of Darkness* (New York: Norton, 1963, 1971, 1988).

Lyon, John (ed.), Joseph Conrad: *Youth | Heart of Darkness | The End of the Tether* (London: Penguin, 1995).

Mahood, M. M. *The Colonial Encounter* (London: Collings, 1977).

Murfin, Ross C. (ed.), *Joseph Conrad, 'Heart of Darkness': A Case Study in Contemporary Criticism* (New York: St Martin's Press, 1989; 2nd edn., 1996).

Nazareth, Peter, 'Out of Darkness: Conrad and Other Third World Writers', *Conradiana*, 14 (1982).

Sarvan, C. P., 'Racism and the *Heart of Darkness*', *International Fiction Review*, 7 (1980); repr. in Kimbrough, 1988.

Singh, Frances B., 'The Colonialistic Bias of *Heart of Darkness*', *Conradiana*, 10 (1978); repr. in Kimbrough, 1988.

Straus, Nina Pelikan, 'The Exclusion of the Intended from Secret Sharing in Conrad's *Heart of Darkness*', *Novel*, 20 (1980).

Tallack, Douglas (ed.), *Literary Theory at Work: Three Texts* (London: Batsford; Totoya, NJ: Barnes and Noble, 1987).

van de Vriesenaerde, Jetty, *Conrad Criticism 1965–1985: 'Heart of Darkness'* (Groningen: Phoenix Press, 1988).

Watts, Cedric, *Conrad's 'Heart of Darkness': A Critical and Contextual Discussion* (Milan: Mursia, 1977).

—— '"A Bloody Racist": About Achebe's View of Conrad', *Yearbook of English Studies*, 13 (1983).

White, Andrea, *Joseph Conrad and the Adventure Tradition* (Cambridge: Cambridge University Press, 1993).

### Further Reading in Oxford World's Classics

Conrad, Joseph, *Chance*, ed. Martin Ray.
—— *An Outcast of the Islands*, ed. J. H. Stape.
—— *The Lagoon and Other Stories*, ed. William Atkinson.
—— *Lord Jim*, ed. Jacques Berthoud.
—— *Nostromo*, ed. Keith Carabine.
—— *The Secret Agent*, ed. Roger Tennant.
—— *The Shadow-Line*, ed. Jeremy Hawthorn.
—— *Typhoon and Other Tales*, ed. Cedric Watts.
—— *Under Western Eyes*, ed. Jeremy Hawthorn.
—— *Victory*, ed. John Batchelor.

# A CHRONOLOGY OF JOSEPH CONRAD

| *Life* | *Historical and Cultural Background* |
|---|---|
| *The Polish Years: 1857–1873* | |
| 1857 3 December: Józef Teodor Konrad Korzeniowski born to Apollo Korzeniowski and Ewa (née Bobrowska) Korzeniowska in Berdyczów (Berdichev), Polish Ukraine | Indian Mutiny; Flaubert, *Madame Bovary* 1859: Darwin, *On the Origin of Species* 1860: Turgenev, *On the Eve* |
| 1861 October: Conrad's father arrested and imprisoned in Warsaw by the Russian authorities for anti-Russian conspiracy | American Civil War begins; emancipation of the serfs in Russia; Dickens, *Great Expectations* |
| 1862 May: Conrad's parents convicted of 'political activities' and exiled to Vologda, Russia; Conrad goes with them | Rise of Bismarck in Prussia; Turgenev, *Fathers and Sons*; Victor Hugo, *Les Misérables* |
| 1863 Exile continues in Chernikhov | Polish insurrection; death of Thackeray |
| 1865 18 April: death of Ewa Korzeniowska | American Civil War ends; Tolstoy, *War and Peace* (1865–72) 1866: Dostoevsky, *Crime and Punishment* 1867: Karl Marx, *Das Kapital* |
| 1868 Korzeniowski permitted to leave Russia; settles with his son in Lwów, Austrian Poland | Dostoevsky, *The Idiot* |
| 1869 February: Conrad and his father move to Cracow; 23 May: death of Apollo Korzeniowski; Conrad's uncle Tadeusz Bobrowski becomes his unofficial guardian | Suez Canal opens; Flaubert, *L'Éducation sentimentale*; Matthew Arnold, *Culture and Anarchy*; J. S. Mill, *The Subjection of Women* |
| 1870–3 Lives in Cracow with his maternal grandmother, Teofila Bobrowska; studies with his tutor, Adam Pulman | Franco-Prussian War; Education Act; death of Dickens 1871: Darwin, *The Descent of Man* 1872: George Eliot, *Middlemarch* |
| 1873 Goes to school in Lwów; May–June: tours Switzerland and N. Italy with his tutor | Death of J. S. Mill, publication of his *Autobiography* |

| *Life* | *Historical and Cultural Background* |
|---|---|

*The Years at Sea: 1874–1893*

| | | |
|---|---|---|
| 1874 | September: leaves for Marseille and takes a position with Delestang et Fils, bankers and shippers; December: Conrad's sea-life begins; sails as passenger in the *Mont-Blanc* to Martinique | First Impressionist Exhibition in Paris; Britain extends influence in Malaya |
| 1875 | June–December: sails across the Atlantic as apprentice in the *Mont-Blanc* | Tolstoy, *Anna Karenina* (1875–6) |
| 1876–7 | July–February: steward in the *Saint-Antoine* sailing from Marseille to South America | Alexander Graham Bell demonstrates the telephone; Wagner's 'The Ring Cycle' performed in Bayreuth; death of George Sand |
| 1877 | March–December: possibly involved in Carlist arms-smuggling to Spain | Russia declares war on Turkey; Britain annexes Transvaal |
| 1878 | March: apparent suicide attempt; April: sails in British steamer *Mavis*; June: lands in England for first time; July: joins British coastal ship *Skimmer of the Sea* as ordinary seaman; October: departs from London in the *Duke of Sutherland* bound for Australia | The Congress of Berlin; James, *The Europeans* |
| 1879–80 | October: arrives back in London; December–January: sails in the *Europa* bound for Australia | British Zulu War; Ibsen, *A Doll's House*; James, *Daisy Miller*; Meredith, *The Egoist* |
| 1880 | Takes lodgings in London; May: passes second-mate's examination; August: joins the *Loch Etive* bound for Australia as third mate | Edison develops electric lighting; deaths of George Eliot and Flaubert; Dostoevsky, *The Brothers Karamazov* |
| 1881 | September: signs on as second mate in the *Palestine* bound for Bangkok | Tsar Alexander II assassinated; deaths of Dostoevsky and Carlyle |

| *Life* | *Historical and Cultural Background* |
|---|---|
| 1882–3 The *Palestine* repaired in Falmouth but sinks off Sumatra | Married Women's Property Act in Britain; deaths of Darwin and Garibaldi |
| 1883 July: reunited with his uncle Tadeusz Bobrowski at Marienbad; September: signs on as second mate in the *Riversdale* bound for South Africa and Madras, India | Nietzsche, *Also Sprach Zarathustra*; deaths of Turgenev, Wagner, and Marx |
| 1884 June: sails in the *Narcissus* from Bombay, India, to Dunkirk as second mate; December: passes examination as first mate | Berlin Conference (14 nations), 'The Scramble for Africa'; the Fabian Society founded; Mark Twain, *Huckleberry Finn* |
| 1885 April: sails for Calcutta and Singapore aboard the *Tilkhurst* as second mate | Death of General Gordon at Khartoum; Zola, *Germinal* |
| 1886 August: becomes a naturalized British subject; November: gains his Master's Certificate; briefly signs on as second mate in the *Falconhurst* | Stevenson, *Dr. Jekyll and Mr. Hyde*; Nietzsche, *Beyond Good and Evil* |
| 1887–8 Makes four voyages to the Malay Archipelago as first mate; February (1887): sails for Java in the *Highland Forest* but is injured and hospitalized in Singapore; August: joins the *Vidar* in Singapore bound for Borneo; January (1888): appointed Master of the *Otago* at Bangkok and sails for Australia | Queen Victoria's Golden Jubilee; Verdi, *Otello* 1888: Wilhelm II becomes Kaiser; British 'protectorate' over Matabeleland, Sarawak, North Borneo, and Brunei; death of Matthew Arnold |
| 1889 Resigns from the *Otago*; March: released from his status as a Russian subject; June: settles briefly in London and in the autumn begins writing *Almayer's Folly* | London Dock Strike; Cecil Rhodes founds the British South Africa Co.; death of Robert Browning |

| *Life* | *Historical and Cultural Background* |
|---|---|
| 1890 February: returns to Polish Ukraine for the first time in 16 years and visits his uncle Tadeusz Bobrowski; April: in Brussels; appointed by the Société Anonyme Belge pour le Commerce du Haut-Congo; Mid-May: sails for the Congo; August–September: commands the *Roi des Belges* from Stanley Falls to Kinshasa but falls ill with dysentery and malaria; sails for Europe in November | The Partition of Africa; Ibsen, *Hedda Gabler*; William Morris, *News from Nowhere*; J. G. Frazer, *The Golden Bough* (1890–1914) |
| 1891–3 January (1891): back in England; February–March: hospitalized in London; April–May: travels to Champel-les-Bains near Geneva for a cure and returns to London in June, to be temporarily employed by Barr, Moering & Co.; November: joins the *Torrens*, his last sailing ship, and makes four voyages as first mate; meets John Galsworthy and Edward (Ted) Sanderson on one return passage; July (1893): resigns from the *Torrens* but remains on the payroll till mid-October; August–September: visits his uncle in Ukraine; November: briefly joins the *Adowa* at Rouen, France | 1891: Hardy, *Tess of the D'Urbervilles*; Wilde, *The Picture of Dorian Gray* 1892: Death of Tennyson 1893: Dvořák, 'New World' Symphony, Verdi, *Falstaff* |

| *Life* | *Historical and Cultural Background* |
|---|---|

*Conrad the Writer: 1894–1924*

| | | |
|---|---|---|
| 1894 | January: leaves the *Adowa* and returns to London; 10 February: Tadeusz Bobrowski dies; April–May: finishes and revises *Almayer's Folly*; August: again at Champel-les-Bains for hydrotherapy; October: meets Edward Garnett; November: meets Jessie George, his future wife | Greenwich bomb outrage; Nicholas II becomes Tsar; 'Dreyfus case' in France; death of Robert Louis Stevenson |
| 1895 | April: *Almayer's Folly* published | Crane, *The Red Badge of Courage*; H. G. Wells, *The Time Machine*; death of Engels; Hardy, *Jude the Obscure* |
| 1896 | March: *An Outcast of the Islands*; marries Jessie George; they live in Stanford-le-Hope, Essex | Puccini, *La Bohème*; death of William Morris |
| 1897 | Meets R. B. Cunninghame Graham, Henry James and Stephen Crane; March: moves to Ivy Walls, Essex; December: *The Nigger of the 'Narcissus'* | Queen Victoria's Diamond Jubilee; H. G. Wells, *The Invisible Man* |
| 1898 | Meets Ford Madox (Hueffer) Ford and H. G. Wells; 15 January: Alfred Borys Conrad born; April: *Tales of Unrest*; October: leases Pent Farm, Postling, Kent | Curies discover radium; Wilde, *The Ballad of Reading Gaol*; H. G. Wells, *The War of the Worlds* |
| 1899 | February: finishes 'Heart of Darkness' | Boer War begins |
| 1900 | September: J. B. Pinker becomes Conrad's literary agent; October: *Lord Jim* | Russia occupies Manchuria; Freud, *The Interpretation of Dreams*; deaths of Oscar Wilde, Ruskin, Nietzsche, Crane |
| 1901 | June: *The Inheritors* (with Ford) | Death of Queen Victoria; Marconi transmits first transatlantic Morse Code signal; Kipling, *Kim* |

| | *Life* | *Historical and Cultural Background* |
|---|---|---|
| 1902 | November: *Youth: A Narrative and Two Other Stories* ('Heart of Darkness' and 'The End of the Tether') | Balfour's Education Act; death of Zola; Gorky, *The Lower Depths* |
| 1903 | April: *Typhoon and Other Stories*<br>October: *Romance* (with Ford) | Wright brothers' first flight; Shaw, *Man and Superman*; James, *The Ambassadors*; Butler, *The Way of All Flesh* |
| 1904 | October: *Nostromo* | Russo–Japanese War; Anglo-French *Entente Cordiale*; Chekhov, *The Cherry Orchard*; James, *The Golden Bowl*; death of Chekhov |
| 1905 | January–May: resides in Capri, Italy;<br>June: *One Day More* staged in London | Abortive revolution in Russia; beginning of the Women's Suffrage Movement; Freud, *Three Essays on the Theory of Sexuality*; Debussy, *La Mer* |
| 1906 | Meets Arthur Marwood, who becomes a close friend;<br>2 August: John Conrad born;<br>October: *The Mirror of the Sea: Memories and Impressions* | Anglo–Russian Entente; death of Ibsen; Galsworthy, *The Man of Property* |
| 1907 | May–August: at Champel-les-Bains for the children's health;<br>September: *The Secret Agent*; moves to Someries, Luton Hoo, Bedfordshire | Cubist Exhibition in Paris; Shaw, *Major Barbara* |
| 1908 | August: *A Set of Six* | Bennett, *The Old Wives' Tale* |
| 1909 | February: moves to rented rooms in Aldington, near Hythe, Kent;<br>July: deteriorating relations with Ford culminate in a break | Peary reaches the North Pole; Blériot flies across the Channel; Marinetti launches the Futurist movement |
| 1910 | January: quarrels with Pinker; physical and mental breakdown for three months;<br>June: moves to new home, Capel House, Orlestone, Kent | The Union of South Africa created; death of Tolstoy; Post-Impressionist Exhibition, London; E. M. Forster, *Howards End*; Yeats, *The Green Helmet* |
| 1911 | October: *Under Western Eyes* | Amundsen reaches the South Pole; the *Blaue Reiter* group formed, Munich |
| 1912 | January: *Some Reminiscences* (later retitled *A Personal Record*);<br>October: *'Twixt Land and Sea* | *Titanic* sinks; Schoenberg, *Pierrot Lunaire*; Pound, *Ripostes*; Mann, *Death in Venice* |

| *Life* | *Historical and Cultural Background* |
|---|---|
| 1913 | March: meets F. N. Doubleday to discuss a collected edition of his work; September: first meets Bertrand Russell | D. H. Lawrence, *Sons and Lovers*; Proust, *A la recherche du temps perdu* (1913–27); Stravinsky, *The Rite of Spring* |
| 1914 | January: *Chance*; July–November: visits Poland with his family and is detained for several weeks by the outbreak of the war | Outbreak of First World War; Polish Legion fights Russians; Joyce, *Dubliners* |
| 1915 | February: *Within the Tides*; March: *Victory* (USA; September in UK) | Germans sink the *Lusitania*; Einstein, *General Theory of Relativity*; Pound, *Cathay*; D. H. Lawrence, *The Rainbow*; Ford, *The Good Soldier* |
| 1916 | March: sits for a bust by the sculptor Jo Davidson; August: visits Foreign Office and Admiralty to discuss propaganda articles | Battles of Verdun and Somme; Joyce, *A Portrait of the Artist as a Young Man*; death of Henry James |
| 1917 | March: *The Shadow-Line*; November: London for a three-month stay | The Russian Revolution; USA enters war; Jung, *The Psychology of the Unconscious*; T. S. Eliot, *Prufrock and Other Observations*; Shaw, *Heartbreak House* |
| 1918 | May: first meets G. Jean-Aubry; October: his son Borys hospitalized in Rouen, suffering from shell-shock | Spengler, *The Decline of the West*; death of Wilfred Owen; November, Armistice signed; Polish Republic restored |
| 1919 | March: stage version of *Victory* in London; April: *The Arrow of Gold*; May: sells film rights to four of his novels; October: moves to his last home—Oswalds, Bishopsbourne, near Canterbury, Kent | Treaty of Versailles; Keynes, *The Economic Consequences of the Peace*; Walter Gropius founds the *Bauhaus* |
| 1920 | May: *The Rescue* (USA; June in UK) | League of Nations founded; Poles rout Russian invaders; D. H. Lawrence, *Women in Love* |
| 1921 | February: *Notes on Life and Letters*; the Collected Edition begins publication in England (Heinemann) and the USA (Doubleday) | Irish Free State created; Rutherford and Chadwick work on splitting the atom |

| *Life* | *Historical and Cultural Background* |
|---|---|
| 1922 November: stage version of *The Secret Agent*, London | Mussolini forms fascist government in Italy; BBC founded; T. S. Eliot, *The Waste Land*; Joyce, *Ulysses*; Woolf, *Jacob's Room* |
| 1923 May–June: visits USA; December: *The Rover* | Yeats wins Nobel Prize for Literature |
| 1924 11 January: birth of first grandson, Philip James; March: sits for sculptor Jacob Epstein; May: declines knighthood; 3 August: dies of a heart attack; buried in Canterbury Cemetery; September: *The Nature of a Crime* (with Ford); October: *Laughing Anne & One Day More: Two Plays*; November: Ford, *Joseph Conrad: A Personal Remembrance* | Death of Lenin; E. M. Forster, *A Passage to India*; Mann, *The Magic Mountain*; Shaw, *St. Joan* |
| 1925 January: *Tales of Hearsay*; September: *Suspense* (unfinished) | Fall of Trotsky, rise of Stalin; Shaw wins the Nobel Prize for Literature; Hitler, *Mein Kampf*; Woolf, *Mrs. Dalloway* |
| 1926 March: *Last Essays* | General Strike; Kafka, *The Castle* |
| 1928 June: *The Sisters* | Death of Thomas Hardy; D. H. Lawrence, *Lady Chatterley's Lover* |

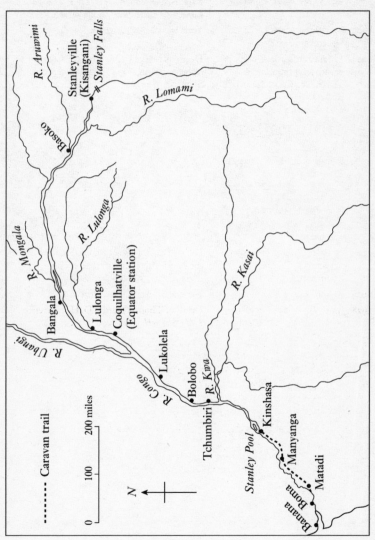

The River Congo

# AN OUTPOST OF PROGRESS

# AN OUTPOST OF PROGRESS

## I

THERE were two white men in charge of the trading station. Kayerts, the chief, was short and fat; Carlier, the assistant, was tall, with a large head and a very broad trunk perched upon a long pair of thin legs.* The third man on the staff was a Sierra Leone nigger, who maintained that his name was Henry Price.* However, for some reason or other, the natives down the river had given him the name of Makola, and it stuck to him through all his wanderings about the country. He spoke English and French with a warbling accent, wrote a beautiful hand, understood book-keeping, and cherished in his innermost heart the worship of evil spirits. His wife was a negress from Loanda, very large and very noisy. Three children rolled about in sunshine before the door of his low, shed-like dwelling. Makola, taciturn and impenetrable, despised the two white men. He had charge of a small clay storehouse with a dried-grass roof, and pretended to keep a correct account of beads, cotton cloth, red kerchiefs, brass wire, and other trade goods it contained. Besides the storehouse and Makola's hut, there was only one large building in the cleared ground of the station. It was built neatly of reeds, with a verandah on all the four sides. There were three rooms in it. The one in the middle was the living-room, and had two rough tables and a few stools in it. The other two were the bedrooms for the white men. Each had a bedstead and a mosquito net for all furniture.* The plank floor was littered with the belongings of the white men; open half-empty boxes, torn wearing apparel,* old boots; all the things dirty, and all the things broken, that accumulate mysteriously round untidy men. There was also another dwelling-place some distance away from the buildings. In it, under a tall cross much out of the perpendicular, slept the man who had seen the beginning of all this; who had planned and had watched the construction of this outpost of progress. He had been, at home, an unsuccessful painter who, weary of pursuing fame on an empty stomach, had gone out there through high protections. He had been the first chief of that station. Makola had watched the energetic artist die of fever in the just finished house with his usual kind of "I told you so" indifference. Then, for a time, he dwelt alone with his family, his account books, and the Evil Spirit that rules the lands under the equator. He got on very well with his god. Perhaps he had propitiated him by a promise of more white men to play with, by and by. At any rate the director of the Great Trading Company, coming up in a steamer that resembled an enormous sardine box with a flat-roofed shed erected on it, found the station in good order, and Makola as usual quietly diligent. The director had the cross put up over the first agent's grave, and appointed Kayerts to the post. Carlier was told off as second in charge. The director was a man ruthless and efficient, who at times, but very imperceptibly, indulged in grim humour. He made a speech to Kayerts and Carlier, pointing out to them the promising aspect of their station.\* The nearest trading-post was about three hundred miles away. It was an exceptional opportunity for them to distinguish themselves and to earn percentages on the trade. This appointment was a favour done to beginners. Kayerts was moved almost to tears by his director's kindness. He would, he said, by doing his best, try to justify the flattering confidence, &c., &c. Kayerts had been in the Administration of the Telegraphs, and knew how to express himself correctly. Carlier, an ex-non-commissioned officer of cavalry in an army guaranteed from harm by several European Powers,\* was less impressed. If there were commissions to get, so much the better; and, trailing a sulky glance over the river, the forests, the impenetrable bush that seemed to cut off the station from the rest of the world, he muttered between his teeth, "We shall see, very soon."

Next day, some bales of cotton goods and a few cases of provisions having been thrown on shore, the sardine-box steamer went off, not to return for another six months. On the deck the director touched his cap to the two agents, who stood on the bank waving their hats, and turning to an old servant of the Company on his passage to headquarters, said, "Look at those two imbeciles. They must be mad at home to send me such specimens. I told those fellows to plant a vegetable garden, build new storehouses and fences, and construct a landing-stage. I bet nothing will be done! They won't know how to begin.\* I always thought the station on this river useless, and they just fit the station!"

"They will form themselves there," said the old stager with a quiet smile.

"At any rate, I am rid of them for six months," retorted the director.

The two men watched the steamer round the bend, then, ascending arm in arm the slope of the bank, returned to the station. They had been in this vast and dark country only a very short time, and as yet always in the midst of other white men, under the eye and guidance of their superiors. And now, dull as they were to the subtle influences of surroundings, they felt themselves very much alone, when suddenly left unassisted to face the wilderness; a wilderness rendered more strange, more incomprehensible by the mysterious glimpses of the vigorous life it contained. They were two perfectly insignificant and incapable individuals, whose existence is only rendered possible through the high organisation of civilised crowds. Few men realise that their life, the very essence of their character, their capabilities and their audacities, are only the expression of their belief in the safety of their surroundings. The courage, the composure, the confidence; the emotions and principles; every great and every insignificant thought belongs not to the individual but to the crowd: to the crowd that believes blindly in the irresistible force of its institutions and of its morals, in the power of its police and of its opinion.* But the contact with pure unmitigated savagery, with primitive nature and primitive man, brings sudden and profound trouble into the heart. To the sentiment of being alone of one's kind, to the clear perception of the loneliness of one's thoughts, of one's sensations—to the negation of the habitual, which is safe, there is added the affirmation of the unusual, which is dangerous; a suggestion of things vague, uncontrollable, and repulsive, whose discomposing intrusion excites the imagination and tries the civilised nerves of the foolish and the wise alike.

Kayerts and Carlier walked arm in arm, drawing close to one another as children do in the dark; and they had the same, not altogether unpleasant, sense of danger which one half suspects to be imaginary. They chatted persistently in familiar tones. "Our station is prettily situated," said one. The other assented with enthusiasm, enlarging volubly on the beauties of the situation. Then they passed near the grave. "Poor devil!" said Kayerts. "He died of fever, didn't he?" muttered Carlier, stopping short. "Why," retorted Kayerts, with indignation, "I've been told that the fellow exposed himself recklessly to the sun. The climate here, everybody says, is not at all worse than at home, as long as you keep out of the sun. Do you hear that, Carlier? I am chief here, and my orders are that you should not expose yourself to the sun!" He assumed his superiority jocularly, but his meaning was serious. The idea that he would, perhaps, have to bury Carlier and remain alone, gave him an inward shiver. He felt suddenly that this Carlier was more precious to him here, in the centre of Africa, than a brother could be anywhere else. Carlier, entering into the spirit of the thing, made a military salute and answered in a brisk tone, "Your orders shall be attended to, chief!" Then he burst out laughing, slapped Kayerts on the back, and shouted, "We shall let life run easily here! Just sit still and gather in the ivory those savages will bring. This country has its good points, after all!" They both laughed loudly while Carlier thought: That poor Kayerts; he is so fat and unhealthy. It would be awful if I had to bury him here. He is a man I respect. . . . Before they reached the verandah of their house they called one another "my dear fellow."

The first day they were very active, pottering about with hammers and nails and red calico, to put up curtains, make their house habitable and pretty; resolved to settle down comfortably to their new life. For them an impossible task. To grapple effectually with even purely material problems requires more serenity of mind and more lofty courage than people generally imagine. No two beings could have been more unfitted for such a struggle. Society, not from any tenderness, but because of its strange needs, had taken care of those two men, forbidding them all independent thought, all initiative, all departure from routine; and forbidding it under pain of death. They could only live on condition of being machines. And now, released from the fostering care of men with pens behind the ears, or of men with gold lace on the sleeves, they were like those lifelong prisoners who, liberated after many years, do not know what use to make of their freedom. They did not know what use to make of their faculties, being both, through want of practice, incapable of independent thought.

At the end of two months Kayerts often would say, "If it was not for my Melie, you wouldn't catch me here." Melie was his daughter. He had thrown up his post in the Administration of the Telegraphs, though he had been for seventeen years perfectly happy there, to earn a dowry for his girl. His wife was dead, and the child was being brought up by his sisters. He regretted the streets, the pavements, the cafés, his friends of many years; all the things he used to see, day after day; all the thoughts suggested by familiar things—the thoughts effortless, monotonous, and soothing of a Government clerk; he regretted all the gossip, the small enmities, the mild venom, and the little jokes of Government offices. "If I had had a decent brother-in-law," Carlier would remark, "a fellow with a heart, I would not be here." He had left the army and had made himself so obnoxious to his family by his laziness and impudence, that an exasperated brother-in-law had made superhuman efforts to procure him an appointment in the Company as a second-class agent. Having not a penny in the world, he was compelled to accept this means of livelihood as soon as it became quite clear to him that there was nothing more to squeeze out of his relations. He, like Kayerts, regretted his old life. He regretted the clink of sabre and spurs on a fine afternoon, the barrack-room witticisms, the girls of garrison towns; but, besides, he had also a sense of grievance. He was evidently a much ill-used man. This made him moody, at times. But the two men got on well together in the fellowship of their stupidity and laziness. Together they did nothing, absolutely nothing, and enjoyed the sense of the idleness for which they were paid. And in time they came to feel something resembling affection for one another.

They lived like blind men in a large room, aware only of what came in contact with them (and of that only imperfectly), but unable to see the general aspect of things. The river, the forest, all the great land throbbing with life, were like a great emptiness. Even the brilliant sunshine disclosed nothing intelligible. Things appeared and disappeared before their eyes in an unconnected and aimless kind of way. The river seemed to come from nowhere and flow nowhither. It flowed through a void. Out of that void, at times, came canoes, and men with spears in their hands would suddenly crowd the yard of the station. They were naked, glossy black, ornamented with snowy shells and glistening brass wire, perfect of limb. They made an uncouth babbling noise when they spoke, moved in a stately manner, and sent quick, wild glances out of their startled, never-resting eyes. Those warriors would squat in long rows, four or more deep, before the verandah, while their chiefs bargained for hours with Makola over an elephant tusk. Kayerts sat on his chair and looked down on the proceedings, understanding nothing. He stared at them with his round blue eyes, called out to Carlier, "Here, look! look at that fellow there—and that other one, to the left. Did you ever see such a face? Oh, the funny brute!"

Carlier, smoking native tobacco in a short wooden pipe, would swagger up twirling his moustaches, and, surveying the warriors with haughty indulgence, would say—

"Fine animals. Brought any bone? Yes? It's not any too soon. Look at the muscles of that fellow—third from the end. I wouldn't care to get a punch on the nose from him. Fine arms, but legs no good below the knee. Couldn't make cavalry men of them." And after glancing down complacently at his own shanks, he always concluded: "Pah! Don't they stink! You, Makola! Take that herd over to the fetish" (the storehouse was in every station called the fetish, perhaps because of the spirit of civilisation it contained) "and give them up some of the rubbish you keep there. I'd rather see it full of bone than full of rags."

Kayerts approved.

"Yes, yes! Go and finish that palaver over there, Mr. Makola. I will come round when you are ready, to weigh the tusk. We must be careful." Then, turning to his companion: "This is the tribe that lives down the river; they are rather aromatic. I remember, they had been once before here. D'ye hear that row? What a fellow has got to put up with in this dog of a country! My head is split."

Such profitable visits were rare. For days the two pioneers of trade and progress would look on their empty courtyard in the vibrating brilliance of vertical sunshine. Below the high bank, the silent river flowed on glittering and steady. On the sands in the middle of the stream, hippos and alligators sunned themselves side by side.* And stretching away in all directions, surrounding the insignificant cleared spot of the trading post, immense forests, hiding fateful complications of fantastic life, lay in the eloquent silence of mute greatness. The two men understood nothing, cared for nothing but for the passage of days that separated them from the steamer's return. Their predecessor had left some torn books. They took up these wrecks of novels, and, as they had never read anything of the kind before, they were surprised and amused. Then during long days there were interminable and silly discussions about plots and personages. In the centre of Africa they made the acquaintance of Richelieu and of d'Artagnan, of Hawk's Eye and of Father Goriot, and of many other people.* All these imaginary personages became subjects for gossip as if they had been living friends. They discounted their virtues, suspected their motives, decried their successes; were scandalised at their duplicity or were doubtful about their courage. The accounts of crimes filled them with indignation, while tender or pathetic passages moved them deeply. Carlier cleared his throat and said in a soldierly voice, "What nonsense!" Kayerts, his round eyes suffused with tears, his fat cheeks quivering, rubbed his bald head, and declared, "This is a splendid book. I had no idea there were such clever fellows in the world." They also found some old copies of a home paper. That print discussed what it was pleased to call "Our Colonial Expansion" in high-flown language. It spoke much of the rights and duties of civilisation, of the sacredness of the civilising work, and extolled the merits of those who went about bringing light, and faith, and commerce to the dark places of the earth.* Carlier and Kayerts read, wondered, and began to think better of themselves. Carlier said one evening, waving his hand about, "In a hundred years, there will be perhaps a town here. Quays, and warehouses, and barracks, and—and—billiard-rooms. Civilisation, my boy, and virtue—and all. And then, chaps will read that two good fellows, Kayerts and Carlier, were the first civilised men to live in this very spot!" Kayerts nodded, "Yes, it is a consolation to think of that." They seemed to forget their dead predecessor; but, early one day, Carlier went out and replanted the cross firmly. "It used to make me squint whenever I walked that way," he explained to Kayerts over the morning coffee. "It made me squint, leaning over so much. So I just planted it upright. And solid, I promise you! I suspended myself with both hands to the cross-piece. Not a move. Oh, I did that properly."

At times Gobila came to see them. Gobila was the chief of the neighbouring villages. He was a grey-headed savage, thin and black, with a white cloth round his loins and a mangy panther skin hanging over his back. He came up with long strides of his skeleton legs, swinging a staff as tall as himself, and, entering the common room of the station, would squat on his heels to the left of the door. There he sat, watching Kayerts, and now and then making a speech which the other did not understand. Kayerts, without interrupting his occupation, would from time to time say in a friendly manner: "How goes it, you old image?" and they would smile at one another. The two whites had a liking for that old and incomprehensible creature, and

called him Father Gobila.* Gobila's manner was paternal, and he
seemed really to love all white men. They all appeared to him very
young, indistinguishably alike (except for stature), and he knew that
they were all brothers, and also immortal. The death of the artist,
who was the first white man whom he knew intimately, did not
disturb this belief, because he was firmly convinced that the white
stranger had pretended to die and got himself buried for some mysterious purpose of his own, into which it was useless to inquire.
Perhaps it was his way of going home to his own country? At any
rate, these were his brothers, and he transferred his absurd affection
to them. They returned it in a way. Carlier slapped him on the back,
and recklessly struck off matches for his amusement. Kayerts was
always ready to let him have a sniff at the ammonia bottle. In short,
they behaved just like that other white creature that had hidden itself
in a hole in the ground. Gobila considered them attentively. Perhaps
they were the same being with the other—or one of them was. He
couldn't decide—clear up that mystery; but he remained always very
friendly. In consequence of that friendship the women of Gobila's
village walked in single file through the reedy grass, bringing every
morning to the station, fowls, and sweet potatoes, and palm wine,
and sometimes a goat. The Company never provisions the stations
fully, and the agents required those local supplies to live. They had
them through the good-will of Gobila, and lived well. Now and then
one of them had a bout of fever, and the other nursed him with
gentle devotion. They did not think much of it. It left them weaker,
and their appearance changed for the worse. Carlier was hollow-
eyed and irritable. Kayerts showed a drawn, flabby face above the
rotundity of his stomach, which gave him a weird aspect. But
being constantly together, they did not notice the change that took
place gradually in their appearance, and also in their dispositions.

Five months passed in that way.

Then, one morning, as Kayerts and Carlier, lounging in their
chairs under the verandah, talked about the approaching visit of the
steamer, a knot of armed men came out of the forest and advanced
towards the station. They were strangers to that part of the country.
They were tall, slight, draped classically from neck to heel in blue
fringed cloths, and carried percussion muskets over their bare right
shoulders. Makola showed signs of excitement, and ran out of the
storehouse (where he spent all his days) to meet these visitors. They

*note actions*

came into the courtyard and looked about them with steady, scornful glances. Their leader, a powerful and determined-looking negro with bloodshot eyes, stood in front of the verandah and made a long speech. He gesticulated much, and ceased very suddenly.

There was something in his intonation, in the sounds of the long sentences he used, that startled the two whites. It was like a reminiscence of something not exactly familiar, and yet resembling the speech of civilised men. It sounded like one of those impossible languages which sometimes we hear in our dreams.

"What lingo is that?" said the amazed Carlier. "In the first moment I fancied the fellow was going to speak French. Anyway, it is a different kind of gibberish to what we ever heard."

"Yes," replied Kayerts. "Hey, Makola, what does he say? Where do they come from? Who are they?"

But Makola, who seemed to be standing on hot bricks, answered hurriedly, "I don't know. They come from very far. Perhaps Mrs. Price will understand. They are perhaps bad men."

The leader, after waiting for a while, said something sharply to Makola, who shook his head. Then the man, after looking round, noticed Makola's hut and walked over there. The next moment Mrs. Makola was heard speaking with great volubility. The other strangers—they were six in all—strolled about with an air of ease, put their heads through the door of the store-room, congregated round the grave, pointed understandingly at the cross, and generally made themselves at home.

"I don't like those chaps—and, I say, Kayerts, they must be from the coast; they've got firearms," observed the sagacious Carlier.

Kayerts also did not like those chaps. They both, for the first time, became aware that they lived in conditions where the unusual may be dangerous, and that there was no power on earth outside of themselves to stand between them and the unusual. They became uneasy, went in and loaded their revolvers. Kayerts said, "We must order Makola to tell them to go away before dark."

The strangers left in the afternoon, after eating a meal prepared for them by Mrs. Makola. The immense woman was excited, and talked much with the visitors. She rattled away shrilly, pointing here and pointing there at the forests and at the river. Makola sat apart and watched. At times he got up and whispered to his wife. He accompanied the strangers across the ravine at the back of the station-ground, and returned slowly looking very thoughtful. When questioned by the white men he was very strange, seemed not to understand, seemed to have forgotten French—seemed to have forgotten how to speak altogether. Kayerts and Carlier agreed that the nigger had had too much palm wine.

There was some talk about keeping a watch in turn, but in the evening everything seemed so quiet and peaceful that they retired as usual. All night they were disturbed by a lot of drumming in the villages. A deep, rapid roll near by would be followed by another far off—then all ceased. Soon short appeals would rattle out here and there, then all mingle together, increase, become vigorous and sustained, would spread out over the forest, roll through the night, unbroken and ceaseless, near and far, as if the whole land had been one immense drum booming out steadily an appeal to heaven. And through the deep and tremendous noise sudden yells that resembled snatches of songs from a madhouse darted shrill and high in discordant jets of sound which seemed to rush far above the earth and drive all peace from under the stars.

Carlier and Kayerts slept badly. They both thought they had heard shots fired during the night—but they could not agree as to the direction. In the morning Makola was gone somewhere. He returned about noon with one of yesterday's strangers, and eluded all Kayerts' attempts to close with him: had become deaf apparently. Kayerts wondered. Carlier, who had been fishing off the bank, came back and remarked while he showed his catch, "The niggers seem to be in a deuce of a stir; I wonder what's up. I saw about fifteen canoes cross the river during the two hours I was there fishing." Kayerts, worried, said, "Isn't this Makola very queer today?" Carlier advised, "Keep all our men together in case of some trouble."

*war drums, yet white men have absolutely no clue.*

# II

THERE were ten station men who had been left by the Director. Those fellows, having engaged themselves to the Company for six months (without having any idea of a month in particular and only a very faint notion of time in general), had been serving the cause of progress for upwards of two years. Belonging to a tribe from a very distant part of this land of darkness and sorrow, they did not run away, naturally supposing that as wandering strangers they would be killed by the inhabitants of the country; in which they were right. They lived in straw huts on the slope of a ravine overgrown with reedy grass, just behind the station buildings. They were not happy, regretting the festive incantations, the sorceries, the human sacrifices of their own land; where they also had parents, brothers, sisters, admired chiefs, respected magicians, loved friends, and other ties supposed generally to be human. Besides, the rice rations served out by the Company did not agree with them, being a food unknown to their land, and to which they could not get used. Consequently they were unhealthy and miserable. Had they been of any other tribe they would have made up their minds to die—for nothing is easier to certain savages than suicide—and so have escaped from the puzzling difficulties of existence. But belonging, as they did, to a warlike tribe with filed teeth, they had more grit, and went on stupidly living through disease and sorrow. They did very little work, and had lost their splendid physique. Carlier and Kayerts doctored them assiduously without being able to bring them back into condition again. They were mustered every morning and told off to different tasks—grass-cutting, fence-building, tree-felling, &c., &c., which no power on earth could induce them to execute efficiently. The two whites had practically very little control over them.

In the afternoon Makola came over to the big house and found Kayerts watching three heavy columns of smoke rising above the forests. "What is that?" asked Kayerts. "Some villages burn," answered Makola, who seemed to have regained his wits. Then he said abruptly: "We have got very little ivory; bad six months' trading. Do you like get a little more ivory?"

"Yes," said Kayerts eagerly. He thought of percentages which were low.    *focus on money, etc.*

"Those men who came yesterday are traders from Loanda who have got more ivory than they can carry home. Shall I buy? I know their camp."

"Certainly," said Kayerts, "What are those traders?"

"Bad fellows," said Makola indifferently. "They fight with people, and catch women and children. They are bad men, and got guns. There is a great disturbance in the country. Do you want ivory?"    *but...*

"Yes," said Kayerts. Makola said nothing for a while. Then: "Those workmen of ours are no good at all," he muttered, looking round. "Station in very bad order, sir. Director will growl. Better get a fine lot of ivory, then he say nothing."

"I can't help it; the men won't work," said Kayerts. "When will you get that ivory?"

"Very soon," said Makola. "Perhaps tonight. You leave it to me, and keep indoors, sir. I think you had better give some palm wine to our men to make a dance this evening. Enjoy themselves. Work better tomorrow. There's plenty palm wine—gone a little sour."

Kayerts said yes, and Makola, with his own hands, carried the big calabashes to the door of his hut. They stood there till the evening, and Mrs. Makola looked into every one. The men got them at sunset. When Kayerts and Carlier retired, a big bonfire was flaring before the men's huts. They could hear their shouts and drumming. Some men from Gobila's village had joined the station hands, and the entertainment was a great success.

In the middle of the night, Carlier waking suddenly, heard a man shout loudly; then a shot was fired. Only one. Carlier ran out and met Kayerts on the verandah. They were both startled. As they went across the yard to call Makola, they saw shadows moving in the night. One of them cried, "Don't shoot! It's me, Price." Then Makola appeared close to them. "Go back, go back, please," he urged, "you spoil all." "There are strange men about," said Carlier. "Never mind; I know," said Makola. Then he whispered, "All right. Bring ivory. Say nothing! I know my business." The two white men reluctantly went back to the house, but did not sleep. They heard footsteps, whispers, some groans. It seemed as if a lot of men came in, dumped heavy things on the ground, squabbled a long time, then went away. They lay on their hard beds and thought: "This Makola is invaluable." In the morning Carlier came out, very sleepy, and pulled at the cord of the big bell. The station hands mustered every morning to the sound of the bell. That morning nobody came. Kayerts turned out also, yawning. Across the yard they saw Makola come out of his hut, a tin basin of soapy water in his hand. Makola, a civilised nigger, was very neat in his person. He threw the soapsuds skilfully over a wretched little yellow cur he had, then turning his face to the agent's house, he shouted from the distance, "All the men gone last night!"

They heard him plainly, but in their surprise they both yelled out together: "What!" Then they stared at one another. "We are in a proper fix now," growled Carlier. "It's incredible!" muttered Kayerts. "I will go to the huts and see," said Carlier, striding off. Makola coming up found Kayerts standing alone.

"I can hardly believe it," said Kayerts tearfully. "We took care of them as if they had been our children."

"They went with the coast people," said Makola after a moment of hesitation.

"What do I care with whom they went—the ungrateful brutes!" exclaimed the other. Then with sudden suspicion, and looking hard at Makola, he added: "What do you know about it?"

Makola moved his shoulders, looking down on the ground. "What do I know? I think only. Will you come and look at the ivory I've got there? It is a fine lot. You never saw such."

He moved towards the store. Kayerts followed him mechanically, thinking about the incredible desertion of the men. On the ground before the door of the fetish lay six splendid tusks.

"What did you give for it?" asked Kayerts, after surveying the lot with satisfaction.

"No regular trade," said Makola. "They brought the ivory and gave it to me. I told them to take what they most wanted in the station. It is a beautiful lot. No station can show such tusks. Those traders wanted carriers badly, and our men were no good here. No trade, no entry in books; all correct."

Kayerts nearly burst with indignation. "Why!" he shouted, "I believe you have sold our men for these tusks!" Makola stood impassive and silent. "I—I—will—I," stuttered Kayerts. "You fiend!" he yelled out.

"I did the best for you and the Company," said Makola imperturbably. "Why you shout so much? Look at this tusk."

"I dismiss you! I will report you—I won't look at the tusk. I forbid you to touch them. I order you to throw them into the river. You— you!" *emotion blinds logic: being irrational*

"You very red, Mr. Kayerts. If you are so irritable in the sun, you will get fever and die—like the first chief!" pronounced Makola impressively.

They stood still, contemplating one another with intense eyes, as if they had been looking with effort across immense distances. Kayerts shivered. Makola had meant no more than he said, but his words seemed to Kayerts full of ominous menace! He turned sharply and went away to the house. Makola retired into the bosom of his family; and the tusks, left lying before the store, looked very large and valuable in the sunshine.

Carlier came back on the verandah. "They're all gone, hey?" asked Kayerts from the far end of the common room in a muffled voice. "You did not find anybody?"

"Oh, yes," said Carlier, "I found one of Gobila's people lying dead before the huts—shot through the body. We heard that shot last night."

Kayerts came out quickly. He found his companion staring grimly over the yard at the tusks, away by the store. They both sat in silence for a while. Then Kayerts related his conversation with Makola. Carlier said nothing. At the mid-day meal they ate very little. They hardly exchanged a word that day. A great silence seemed to lie heavily over the station and press on their lips. Makola did not open the store; he spent the day playing with his children. He lay full-length on a mat outside his door, and the youngsters sat on his chest and clambered all over him. It was a touching picture. Mrs. Makola was busy cooking all day as usual. The white men made a somewhat better meal in the evening. Afterwards, Carlier smoking his pipe strolled over to the store; he stood for a long time over the tusks, touched one or two with his foot, even tried to lift the largest one by its small end. He came back to his chief, who had not stirred from the verandah, threw himself in the chair and said—

"I can see it! They were pounced upon while they slept heavily after drinking all that palm wine you've allowed Makola to give them. A put-up job! See? The worst is, some of Gobila's people were there, and got carried off too, no doubt. The least drunk woke up, and got shot for his sobriety. This is a funny country. What will you do now?"

"We can't touch it, of course," said Kayerts.

"Of course not," assented Carlier.

"Slavery is an awful thing," stammered out Kayerts in an unsteady voice.

"Frightful—the sufferings," grunted Carlier, with conviction.

They believed their words. Everybody shows a respectful deference to certain sounds that he and his fellows can make. But about feelings people really know nothing. We talk with indignation or enthusiasm; we talk about oppression, cruelty, crime, devotion, self-sacrifice, virtue, and we know nothing real beyond the words. Nobody knows what suffering or sacrifice mean—except, perhaps, the victims of the mysterious purpose of these illusions.

Next morning they saw Makola very busy setting up in the yard the big scales used for weighing ivory. By and by Carlier said: "What's that filthy scoundrel up to?" and lounged out into the yard. Kayerts followed. They stood by watching. Makola took no notice. When the balance was swung true, he tried to lift a tusk into the scale. It was too heavy. He looked up helplessly without a word, and for a minute they stood round that balance as mute and still as three statues. Suddenly Carlier said: "Catch hold of the other end, Makola—you beast!" and together they swung the tusk up. Kayerts trembled in every limb. He muttered, "I say! O! I say!" and putting his hand in his pocket found there a dirty bit of paper and the stump of a pencil. He turned his back on the others, as if about to do something tricky, and noted stealthily the weights which Carlier shouted out to him with unnecessary loudness. When all was over Makola whispered to himself: "The sun's very strong here for the tusks." Carlier said to Kayerts in a careless tone: "I say, chief, I might just as well give him a lift with this lot into the store."

As they were going back to the house Kayerts observed with a sigh: "It had to be done." And Carlier said: "It's deplorable, but, the men being Company's men, the ivory is Company's ivory. We must look after it." "I will report to the Director, of course," said Kayerts. "Of course; let him decide," approved Carlier.

At mid-day they made a hearty meal. Kayerts sighed from time to time. Whenever they mentioned Makola's name they always added to it an opprobrious epithet. It eased their conscience. Makola gave himself a half-holiday, and bathed his children in the river. No one from Gobila's villages came near the station that day. No one came the next day, and the next, nor for a whole week. Gobila's people might have all been dead and buried for any sign of life they gave. But they were only mourning for those they had lost by the witch-craft of white men, who had brought wicked people into their coun-try. The wicked people were gone, but fear remained. Fear always remains. A man may destroy everything within himself, love and hate and belief, and even doubt; but as long as he clings to life he cannot destroy fear: the fear, subtle, indestructible, and terrible, that pervades his being; that tinges his thoughts; that lurks in his heart; that watches on his lips the struggle of his last breath. In his fear, the mild old Gobila offered extra human sacrifices to all the Evil Spirits that had taken possession of his white friends. His heart was heavy. Some warriors spoke about burning and killing, but the cautious old savage dissuaded them. Who could foresee the woe those mysterious creatures, if irritated, might bring? They should be left alone. Per-haps in time they would disappear into the earth as the first one had disappeared. His people must keep away from them, and hope for the best.

Kayerts and Carlier did not disappear, but remained above on this earth, that, somehow, they fancied had become bigger and very empty. It was not the absolute and dumb solitude of the post that impressed them so much as an inarticulate feeling that something from within them was gone, something that worked for their safety, and had kept the wilderness from interfering with their hearts. The images of home; the memory of people like them, of men that thought and felt as they used to think and feel, receded into distances made indistinct by the glare of unclouded sunshine. And out of the great silence of the surrounding wilderness, its very hopelessness and savagery seemed to approach them nearer, to draw them gently, to look upon them, to envelop them with a solicitude irresistible, familiar, and disgusting.

Days lengthened into weeks, then into months. Gobila's people drummed and yelled to every new moon, as of yore, but kept away from the station. Makola and Carlier tried once in a canoe to open communications, but were received with a shower of arrows, and had to fly back to the station for dear life. That attempt set the country

*— effect of usury transaction=*
*no more gifts from Gobila's village, thus no more food*

up and down the river into an uproar that could be very distinctly heard for days. The steamer was late. At first they spoke of delay jauntily, then anxiously, then gloomily. The matter was becoming serious. Stores were running short. Carlier cast his lines off the bank, but the river was low, and the fish kept out in the stream. They dared not stroll far away from the station to shoot. Moreover, there was no game in the impenetrable forest. Once Carlier shot a hippo in the river. They had no boat to secure it, and it sank. When it floated up it drifted away, and Gobila's people secured the carcase. It was the occasion for a national holiday, but Carlier had a fit of rage over it, and talked about the necessity of exterminating all the niggers before the country could be made habitable.* Kayerts mooned about silently; spent hours looking at the portrait of his Melie. It represented a little girl with long bleached tresses and a rather sour face. His legs were much swollen, and he could hardly walk. Carlier, undermined by fever, could not swagger any more, but kept tottering about, still with a devil-may-care air, as became a man who remembered his crack regiment. He had become hoarse, sarcastic, and inclined to say unpleasant things. He called it "being frank with you." They had long ago reckoned their percentages on trade, including in them that last deal of "this infamous Makola." They had also concluded not to say anything about it. Kayerts hesitated at first—was afraid of the Director.

"He has seen worse things done on the quiet," maintained Carlier, with a hoarse laugh. "Trust him! He won't thank you if you blab. He is no better than you or me. Who will talk if we hold our tongues? There is nobody here."

That was the root of the trouble! There was nobody there; and being left there alone with their weakness, they became daily more like a pair of accomplices than like a couple of devoted friends. They had heard nothing from home for eight months. Every evening they said, "Tomorrow we shall see the steamer." But one of the Company's steamers had been wrecked, and the Director was busy with the other, relieving very distant and important stations on the main river. He thought that the useless station, and the useless men, could wait. Meantime Kayerts and Carlier lived on rice boiled without salt, and cursed the Company, all Africa, and the day they were born. One must have lived on such diet to discover what ghastly trouble the necessity of swallowing one's food may become. There was literally nothing else in the station but rice and coffee; they drank the coffee without sugar. The last fifteen lumps Kayerts had solemnly locked away in his box, together with a half-bottle of Cognac, "in case of sickness," he explained. Carlier approved. "When one is sick," he said, "any little extra like that is cheering."

They waited. Rank grass began to sprout over the courtyard. The bell never rang now. Days passed, silent, exasperating, and slow. When the two men spoke, they snarled; and their silences were bitter, as if tinged by the bitterness of their thoughts.

One day after a lunch of boiled rice, Carlier put down his cup untasted, and said: "Hang it all! Let's have a decent cup of coffee for once. Bring out that sugar, Kayerts!"*

"For the sick," muttered Kayerts, without looking up.

"For the sick," mocked Carlier. "Bosh! . . . Well! I am sick."

"You are no more sick than I am, and I go without," said Kayerts in a peaceful tone.

"Come! out with that sugar, you stingy old slave-dealer."

Kayerts looked up quickly. Carlier was smiling with marked insolence. And suddenly it seemed to Kayerts that he had never seen that man before. Who was he? He knew nothing about him. What was he capable of? There was a surprising flash of violent emotion within him, as if in the presence of something undreamt-of, dangerous, and final. But he managed to pronounce with composure—

"That joke is in very bad taste. Don't repeat it."

"Joke!" said Carlier, hitching himself forward on his seat. "I am hungry—I am sick—I don't joke! I hate hypocrites. You are a hypocrite. You are a slave-dealer. I am a slave-dealer. There's nothing but slave-dealers in this cursed country. I mean to have sugar in my coffee today, anyhow!"

"I forbid you to speak to me in that way," said Kayerts with a fair show of resolution.

"You!—What?" shouted Carlier, jumping up.

Kayerts stood up also. "I am your chief," he began, trying to master the shakiness of his voice.

"What?" yelled the other. "Who's chief? There's no chief here. There's nothing here: there's nothing but you and I. Fetch the sugar—you pot-bellied ass."

"Hold your tongue. Go out of this room," screamed Kayerts. "I dismiss you—you scoundrel!"

Carlier swung a stool. All at once he looked dangerously in earnest. "You flabby, good-for-nothing civilian—take that!" he howled.

Kayerts dropped under the table, and the stool struck the grass inner wall of the room. Then, as Carlier was trying to upset the table, Kayerts in desperation made a blind rush, head low, like a cornered pig would do, and overturning his friend, bolted along the verandah, and into his room. He locked the door, snatched his revolver, and stood panting. In less than a minute Carlier was kicking at the door furiously, howling, "If you don't bring out that sugar, I will shoot you at sight, like a dog. Now then—one—two—three. You won't? I will show you who's the master."

Kayerts thought the door would fall in, and scrambled through the square hole that served for a window in his room. There was then the whole breadth of the house between them. But the other was apparently not strong enough to break in the door, and Kayerts heard him running round. Then he also began to run laboriously on his swollen legs. He ran as quickly as he could, grasping the revolver, and unable yet to understand what was happening to him. He saw in succession Makola's house, the store, the river, the ravine, and the low bushes; and he saw all those things again as he ran for the second time round the house. Then again they flashed past him. That morning he could not have walked a yard without a groan.

And now he ran. He ran fast enough to keep out of sight of the other man.

Then as, weak and desperate, he thought, "Before I finish the next round I shall die," he heard the other man stumble heavily, then stop. He stopped also. He had the back and Carlier the front of the house, as before. He heard him drop into a chair cursing, and suddenly his own legs gave way, and he slid down into a sitting posture with his back to the wall. His mouth was as dry as a cinder, and his face was wet with perspiration—and tears. What was it all about? He thought it must be a horrible illusion; he thought he was dreaming; he thought he was going mad! After a while he collected his senses. What did they quarrel about? That sugar! How absurd! He would give it to him—didn't want it himself. And he began scrambling to his feet with a sudden feeling of security. But before he had fairly stood upright, a common-sense reflection occurred to him and drove him back into despair. He thought: If I give way now to that brute of a soldier, he will begin this horror again tomorrow—and the day after—every day—raise other pretensions, trample on me, torture me, make me his slave—and I will be lost! Lost! The steamer may not come for days—may never come. He shook so that he had to sit down on the floor again. He shivered forlornly. He felt he could not, would not move any more. He was completely distracted by the sudden perception that the position was without issue—that death and life had in a moment become equally difficult and terrible.

All at once he heard the other push his chair back; and he leaped to his feet with extreme facility. He listened and got confused. Must run again! Right or left? He heard footsteps. He darted to the left, grasping his revolver, and at the very same instant, as it seemed to him, they came into violent collision. Both shouted with surprise. A loud explosion took place between them; a roar of red fire, thick smoke; and Kayerts, deafened and blinded, rushed back thinking: I am hit—it's all over. He expected the other to come round—to gloat over his agony. He caught hold of an upright of the roof—"All over!" Then he heard a crashing fall on the other side of the house, as if somebody had tumbled headlong over a chair—then silence. Nothing more happened. He did not die. Only his shoulder felt as if it had been badly wrenched, and he had lost his revolver. He was disarmed and helpless! He waited for his fate. The other man made no sound. It was a stratagem. He was stalking him now! Along what side? Perhaps he was taking aim this very minute!

After a few moments of an agony frightful and absurd, he decided to go and meet his doom. He was prepared for every surrender. He turned the corner, steadying himself with one hand on the wall; made a few paces, and nearly swooned. He had seen on the floor, protruding past the other corner, a pair of turned-up feet. A pair of white naked feet in red slippers. He felt deadly sick, and stood for a time in profound darkness. Then Makola appeared before him, saying quietly: "Come along, Mr. Kayerts. He is dead." He burst into tears of gratitude; a loud, sobbing fit of crying. After a time he found himself sitting in a chair and looking at Carlier, who lay stretched on his back. Makola was kneeling over the body.

"Is this your revolver?" asked Makola, getting up.

"Yes," said Kayerts; then he added very quickly, "He ran after me to shoot me—you saw!"

"Yes, I saw," said Makola. "There is only one revolver; where's his?"

"Don't know," whispered Kayerts in a voice that had become suddenly very faint.

"I will go and look for it," said the other gently. He made the round along the verandah, while Kayerts sat still and looked at the corpse. Makola came back empty-handed, stood in deep thought, then stepped quietly into the dead man's room, and came out directly with a revolver, which he held up before Kayerts. Kayerts shut his eyes. Everything was going round. He found life more terrible and difficult than death. He had shot an unarmed man.

After meditating for a while, Makola said softly, pointing at the dead man who lay there with his right eye blown out—*

"He died of fever." Kayerts looked at him with a stony stare. "Yes," repeated Makola thoughtfully, stepping over the corpse, "I think he died of fever. Bury him tomorrow."

And he went away slowly to his expectant wife, leaving the two white men alone on the verandah.

Night came, and Kayerts sat unmoving on his chair. He sat quiet as if he had taken a dose of opium. The violence of the emotions he had passed through produced a feeling of exhausted serenity. He had plumbed in one short afternoon the depths of horror and despair, and now found repose in the conviction that life had no more secrets for him: neither had death! He sat by the corpse thinking; thinking very actively, thinking very new thoughts. He seemed to have broken loose from himself altogether. His old thoughts, convictions, likes and dislikes, things he respected and things he abhorred, appeared in their true light at last! Appeared contemptible and childish, false and ridiculous. He revelled in his new wisdom while he sat by the man he had killed. He argued with himself about all things under heaven with that kind of wrong-headed lucidity which may be observed in some lunatics. Incidentally he reflected that the fellow dead there had been a noxious beast anyway; that men died every day in thousands; perhaps in hundreds of thousands—who could tell?—and that in the number, that one death could not possibly make any difference; couldn't have any importance, at least to a thinking creature. He, Kayerts, was a thinking creature. He had been all his life, till that moment, a believer in a lot of nonsense like the rest of mankind—who are fools; but now he thought! He knew! He was at

peace; he was familiar with the highest wisdom! Then he tried to
imagine himself dead, and Carlier sitting in his chair watching him;
and his attempt met with such unexpected success, that in a very few
moments he became not at all sure who was dead and who was alive.
This extraordinary achievement of his fancy startled him, however,
and by a clever and timely effort of mind he saved himself just in
time from becoming Carlier. His heart thumped, and he felt hot all
over at the thought of that danger. Carlier! What a beastly thing! To
compose his now disturbed nerves—and no wonder!—he tried to
whistle a little. Then, suddenly, he fell asleep, or thought he had
slept; but at any rate there was a fog, and somebody had whistled in
the fog.

He stood up. The day had come, and a heavy mist had descended
upon the land: the mist penetrating, enveloping, and silent; the
morning mist of tropical lands; the mist that clings and kills; the mist
white and deadly, immaculate and poisonous. He stood up, saw the
body, and threw his arms above his head with a cry like that of a man
who, waking from a trance, finds himself immured for ever in a tomb.
"*Help! . . . My God!*"

A shriek inhuman, vibrating and sudden, pierced like a sharp dart
the white shroud of that land of sorrow. Three short, impatient
screeches followed, and then, for a time, the fog-wreaths rolled on,
undisturbed, through a formidable silence. Then many more shrieks,
rapid and piercing, like the yells of some exasperated and ruthless
creature, rent the air. Progress was calling to Kayerts from the river.
Progress and civilisation and all the virtues. Society was calling to its
accomplished child to come, to be taken care of, to be instructed, to
be judged, to be condemned; it called him to return to that rubbish
heap from which he had wandered away, so that justice could be
done.

Kayerts heard and understood. He stumbled out of the verandah,
leaving the other man quite alone for the first time since they had
been thrown there together. He groped his way through the fog,
calling in his ignorance upon the invisible heaven to undo its work.
Makola flitted by in the mist, shouting as he ran—

"Steamer! Steamer! They can't see. They whistle for the station. I
go ring the bell. Go down to the landing, sir. I ring."

He disappeared. Kayerts stood still. He looked upwards; the fog
rolled low over his head. He looked round like a man who has lost his

way; and he saw a dark smudge, a cross-shaped stain, upon the shifting purity of the mist. As he began to stumble towards it, the station bell rang in a tumultuous peal its answer to the impatient clamour of the steamer.

The Managing Director of the Great Civilising Company (since we know that civilisation follows trade) landed first, and incontinently lost sight of the steamer. The fog down by the river was exceedingly dense; above, at the station, the bell rang unceasing and brazen.

The Director shouted loudly to the steamer.

"There is nobody down to meet us; there may be something wrong, though they are ringing. You had better come, too!"

And he began to toil up the steep bank. The captain and the engine-driver of the boat followed behind. As they scrambled up, the fog thinned, and they could see their Director a good way ahead. Suddenly they saw him start forward, calling to them over his shoulder:—"Run! Run to the house! I've found one of them. Run, look for the other!"

He had found one of them! And even he, the man of varied and startling experience, was somewhat discomposed by the manner of this finding. He stood and fumbled in his pockets (for a knife) while he faced Kayerts, who was hanging by a leather strap from the cross. He had evidently climbed the grave, which was high and narrow, and after tying the end of the strap to the arm, had swung himself off. His toes were only a couple of inches above the ground; his arms hung stiffly down; he seemed to be standing rigidly at attention, but with one purple cheek playfully posed on the shoulder. And, irreverently, he was putting out a swollen tongue at his Managing Director.

# KARAIN: A MEMORY

# KARAIN: A MEMORY

## I

WE knew him in those unprotected days when we were content to
hold in our hands our lives and our property. None of us, I believe,
has any property now, and I hear that many, negligently, have lost
their lives; but I am sure that the few who survive are not yet so dim-
eyed as to miss in the befogged respectability of their newspapers the
intelligence of various native risings in the Eastern Archipelago.
Sunshine gleams between the lines of those short paragraphs—
sunshine and the glitter of the sea. A strange name wakes up memories; the printed words scent the smoky atmosphere of today faintly,
with the subtle and penetrating perfume as of land breezes breathing
through the starlight of bygone nights; a signal fire gleams like a
jewel on the high brow of a sombre cliff; great trees, the advanced
sentries of immense forests, stand watchful and still over sleeping
stretches of open water; a line of white surf thunders on an empty
beach, the shallow water foams on the reefs; and green islets scattered through the calm of noonday lie upon the level of a polished
sea, like a handful of emeralds on a buckler of steel.

There are faces too—faces dark, truculent, and smiling; the frank
audacious faces of men barefooted, well armed and noiseless. They
thronged the narrow length of our schooner's decks with their
ornamented and barbarous crowd, with the variegated colours of
checkered sarongs, red turbans, white jackets, embroideries; with the
gleam of scabbards, gold rings, charms, armlets, lance blades, and
jewelled handles of their weapons. They had an independent bearing, resolute eyes, a restrained manner; and we seem yet to hear their
soft voices speaking of battles, travels, and escapes; boasting with
composure, joking quietly; sometimes in well-bred murmurs extol-
ling their own valour, our generosity; or celebrating with loyal
enthusiasm the virtues of their ruler. We remember the faces, the
eyes, the voices, we see again the gleam of silk and metal; the murmuring stir of that crowd, brilliant, festive, and martial; and we seem
to feel the touch of friendly brown hands that, after one short grasp,
return to rest on a chased hilt. They were Karain's people—a

devoted following. Their movements hung on his lips; they read their thoughts in his eyes; he murmured to them nonchalantly of life and death, and they accepted his words humbly, like gifts of fate. They were all free men, and when speaking to him said, "Your slave." On his passage voices died out as though he had walked guarded by silence; awed whispers followed him. They called him their war-chief. He was the ruler of three villages on a narrow plain; the master of an insignificant foothold on the earth—of a conquered foothold that, shaped like a young moon, lay ignored between the hills and the sea.

From the deck of our schooner, anchored in the middle of the bay, he indicated by a theatrical sweep of his arm along the jagged outline of the hills the whole of his domain; and the ample movement seemed to drive back its limits, augmenting it suddenly into something so immense and vague that for a moment it appeared to be bounded only by the sky. And really, looking at that place, landlocked from the sea and shut off from the land by the precipitous slopes of mountains, it was difficult to believe in the existence of any neighbourhood. It was still, complete, unknown, and full of a life that went on stealthily with a troubling effect of solitude; of a life that seemed unaccountably empty of anything that would stir the thought, touch the heart, give a hint of the ominous sequence of days. It appeared to us a land without memories, regrets, and hopes; a land where nothing could survive the coming of the night, and where each sunrise, like a dazzling act of special creation, was disconnected from the eve and the morrow.

Karain* swept his hand over it. "All mine!" He struck the deck with his long staff; the gold head flashed like a falling star; very close behind him a silent old fellow in a richly embroidered black jacket alone of all the Malays around did not follow the masterful gesture with a look. He did not even lift his eyelids. He bowed his head behind his master, and without stirring held hilt up over his right shoulder a long blade in a silver scabbard. He was there on duty, but without curiosity, and seemed weary, not with age, but with the possession of a burdensome secret of existence. Karain, heavy and proud, had a lofty pose and breathed calmly. It was our first visit, and we looked about curiously.

The bay was like a bottomless pit of intense light. The circular sheet of water reflected a luminous sky, and the shores enclosing it made an opaque ring of earth floating in an emptiness of transparent blue. The hills, purple and arid, stood out heavily on the sky: their summits seemed to fade into a coloured tremble as of ascending vapour; their steep sides were streaked with the green of narrow ravines; at their foot lay rice-fields, plantain-patches, yellow sands. A torrent wound about like a dropped thread. Clumps of fruit-trees marked the villages; slim palms put their nodding heads together above the low houses; dried palm-leaf roofs shone afar, like roofs of gold, behind the dark colonnades of tree-trunks; figures passed vivid and vanishing; the smoke of fires stood upright above the masses of flowering bushes; bamboo fences glittered, running away in broken lines between the fields. A sudden cry on the shore sounded plaintive in the distance, and ceased abruptly, as if stifled in the downpour of sunshine; a puff of breeze made a flash of darkness on the smooth water, touched our faces, and became forgotten. Nothing moved. The sun blazed down into a shadowless hollow of colours and stillness.

It was the stage where, dressed splendidly for his part, he strutted, incomparably dignified, made important by the power he had to awaken an absurd expectation of something heroic going to take place—a burst of action or song—upon the vibrating tone of a wonderful sunshine. He was ornate and disturbing, for one could not imagine what depth of horrible void such an elaborate front could be worthy to hide. He was not masked—there was too much life in him, and a mask is only a lifeless thing; but he presented himself essentially as an actor, as a human being aggressively disguised. His smallest acts were prepared and unexpected, his speeches grave, his sentences ominous like hints and complicated like arabesques. He was treated with a solemn respect accorded in the irreverent West only to the monarchs of the stage, and he accepted the profound homage with a sustained dignity seen nowhere else but behind the footlights and in the condensed falseness of some grossly tragic situation. It was almost impossible to remember who he was—only a petty chief of a conveniently isolated corner of Mindanao, where we could in comparative safety break the law against the traffic in fire-arms and ammunition with the natives. What would happen should one of the moribund Spanish gun-boats be suddenly galvanised into a flicker of active life did not trouble us, once we were inside the bay—so completely did it appear out of the reach of a meddling

world; and besides, in those days we were imaginative enough to look
with a kind of joyous equanimity on any chance there was of being
quietly hanged somewhere out of the way of diplomatic remon-
strance. As to Karain, nothing could happen to him unless what
happens to all—failure and death; but his quality was to appear
clothed in the illusion of unavoidable success. He seemed too effective, too necessary there, too much of an essential condition for the
existence of his land and his people, to be destroyed by anything short
of an earthquake. He summed up his race, his country, the elemental
force of ardent life, of tropical nature. He had its luxuriant strength,
its fascination; and, like it, he carried the seed of peril within.

In many successive visits we came to know his stage well—
the purple semicircle of hills, the slim trees leaning over houses, the
yellow sands, the streaming green of ravines. All that had the crude
and blended colouring, the appropriateness almost excessive, the
suspicious immobility of a painted scene;* and it enclosed so perfectly
the accomplished acting of his amazing pretences that the rest of the
world seemed shut out for ever from the gorgeous spectacle. There
could be nothing outside. It was as if the earth had gone on spinning,
and had left that crumb of its surface alone in space. He appeared
utterly cut off from everything but the sunshine, and that even
seemed to be made for him alone. Once when asked what was on the
other side of the hills, he said, with a meaning smile, "Friends and
enemies—many enemies; else why should I buy your rifles and powder?" He was always like this—word-perfect in his part, playing up
faithfully to the mysteries and certitudes of his surroundings.
"Friends and enemies"—nothing else. It was impalpable and vast.
The earth had indeed rolled away from under his land, and he, with
his handful of people, stood surrounded by a silent tumult as of
contending shades. Certainly no sound came from outside. "Friends
and enemies!" He might have added, "and memories," at least as far
as he himself was concerned; but he neglected to make that point
then. It made itself later on, though; but it was after the daily
performance—in the wings, so to speak, and with the lights out.
Meantime he filled the stage with barbarous dignity. Some ten years
ago he had led his people—a scratch lot of wandering Bugis—to the
conquest of the bay, and now in his august care they had forgotten all
the past, and had lost all concern for the future. He gave them
wisdom, advice, reward, punishment, life or death, with the same

serenity of attitude and voice. He understood irrigation and the art of war—the qualities of weapons and the craft of boat-building. He could conceal his heart; had more endurance; he could swim longer, and steer a canoe better than any of his people; he could shoot straighter, and negotiate more tortuously than any man of his race I knew. He was an adventurer of the sea, an outcast, a ruler—and my very good friend. I wish him a quick death in a stand-up fight, a death in sunshine; for he had known remorse and power, and no man can demand more from life. Day after day he appeared before us, incomparably faithful to the illusions of the stage, and at sunset the night descended upon him quickly, like a falling curtain. The seamed hills became black shadows towering high upon a clear sky; above them the glittering confusion of stars resembled a mad turmoil stilled by a gesture; sounds ceased, men slept, forms vanished—and the reality of the universe alone remained—a marvellous thing of darkness and glimmers.

BUT it was at night that he talked openly, forgetting the exactions of his stage. In the daytime there were affairs to be discussed in state. There were at first between him and me his own splendour, my shabby suspicions, and the scenic landscape that intruded upon the reality of our lives by its motionless fantasy of outline and colour. His followers thronged round him; above his head the broad blades of their spears made a spiked halo of iron points, and they hedged him from humanity by the shimmer of silks, the gleam of weapons, the excited and respectful hum of eager voices. Before sunset he would take leave with ceremony, and go off sitting under a red umbrella, and escorted by a score of boats. All the paddles flashed and struck together with a mighty splash that reverberated loudly in the monumental amphitheatre of hills. A broad stream of dazzling foam trailed behind the flotilla. The canoes appeared very black on the white hiss of water; turbaned heads swayed back and forth; a multitude of arms in crimson and yellow rose and fell with one movement; the spearmen upright in the bows of canoes had variegated sarongs and gleaming shoulders like bronze statues; the muttered strophes of the paddlers' song ended periodically in a plaintive shout. They diminished in the distance; the song ceased; they swarmed on the beach in the long shadows of the western hills. The sunlight lingered on the purple crests, and we could see him leading the way to his stockade, a burly bareheaded figure walking far in advance of a straggling *cortège*, and swinging regularly an ebony staff taller than himself. The darkness deepened fast; torches gleamed fitfully, passing behind bushes; a long hail or two trailed in the silence of the evening; and at last the night stretched its smooth veil over the shore, the lights, and the voices.

Then, just as we were thinking of repose, the watchmen of the schooner would hail a splash of paddles away in the starlit gloom of the bay; a voice would respond in cautious tones, and our serang, putting his head down the open skylight, would inform us without surprise, "That Rajah, he coming. He here now." Karain appeared noiselessly in the doorway of the little cabin. He was simplicity itself then; all in white; muffled about his head; for arms only a kriss with a plain buffalo-horn handle, which he would politely conceal within a fold of his sarong before stepping over the threshold.* The old sword-bearer's face, the worn-out and mournful face so covered with wrinkles that it seemed to look out through the meshes of a fine dark net, could be seen close above his shoulder. Karain never moved without that attendant, who stood or squatted close at his back. He had a dislike of an open space behind him. It was more than a dislike—it resembled fear, a nervous preoccupation of what went on where he could not see. This, in view of the evident and fierce loyalty that surrounded him, was inexplicable. He was there alone in the midst of devoted men; he was safe from neighbourly ambushes, from fraternal ambitions; and yet more than one of our visitors had assured us that their ruler could not bear to be alone. They said, "Even when he eats and sleeps there is always one on the watch near him who has strength and weapons." There was indeed always one near him, though our informants had no conception of that watcher's strength and weapons, which were both shadowy and terrible. We knew, but only later on, when we had heard the story. Meantime we noticed that, even during the most important interviews, Karain would often give a start, and interrupting his discourse, would sweep his arm back with a sudden movement, to feel whether the old fellow was there. The old fellow, impenetrable and weary, was always there. He shared his food, his repose, and his thoughts; he knew his plans, guarded his secrets; and, impassive behind his master's agitation, without stirring the least bit, murmured above his head in a soothing tone some words difficult to catch.

It was only on board the schooner, when surrounded by white faces, by unfamiliar sights and sounds, that Karain seemed to forget the strange obsession that wound like a black thread through the gorgeous pomp of his public life. At night we treated him in a free and easy manner, which just stopped short of slapping him on the back, for there are liberties one must not take with a Malay. He said himself that on such occasions he was only a private gentleman coming to see other gentlemen whom he supposed as well born as himself. I fancy that to the last he believed us to be emissaries of Government, darkly official persons furthering by our illegal traffic some dark scheme of high statecraft. Our denials and protestations were unavailing. He only smiled with discreet politeness and inquired about the Queen. Every visit began with that inquiry; he was insatiable of details; he was fascinated by the holder of a sceptre the shadow of which, stretching from the westward over the earth and over the seas, passed far beyond his own hand's-breadth of conquered land. He multiplied questions; he could never know enough of the Monarch of whom he spoke with wonder and chivalrous respect—with a kind of affectionate awe! Afterwards, when we had learned that he was the son of a woman who had many years ago ruled a small Bugis state, we came to suspect that the memory of his mother (of whom he spoke with enthusiasm) mingled somehow in his mind with the image he tried to form for himself of the far-off Queen whom he called Great, Invincible, Pious, and Fortunate. We had to invent details at last to satisfy his craving curiosity; and our loyalty must be pardoned, for we tried to make them fit for his august and resplendent ideal. We talked. The night slipped over us, over the still schooner, over the sleeping land, and over the sleepless sea that thundered amongst the reefs outside the bay. His paddlers, two trustworthy men, slept in the canoe at the foot of our side-ladder. The old confidant, relieved from duty, dozed on his heels, with his back against the companion-doorway; and Karain sat squarely in the ship's wooden armchair, under the slight sway of the cabin lamp, a cheroot between his dark fingers, and a glass of lemonade before him. He was amused by the fizz of the thing, but after a sip or two would let it get flat, and with a courteous wave of his hand ask for a fresh bottle. He decimated our slender stock; but we did not begrudge it to him, for, when he began, he talked well. He must have been a great Bugis dandy in his time, for even then (and when we knew him he was no longer young) his splendour was spotlessly neat, and he dyed his hair a light shade of brown. The quiet dignity of his bearing transformed the dim-lit cuddy of the schooner into an audience-hall. He talked of inter-island politics with an ironic and melancholy shrewdness. He had travelled much, suffered not a little, intrigued, fought. He knew native Courts, European Settlements, the forests, the sea, and, as he said himself, had spoken in his time to many great men. He liked to talk with me because I had known some of these men: he seemed to think that I could understand him, and, with a fine confidence, assumed that I, at least, could appreciate how much greater he was himself. But he preferred to talk of his native country—a small Bugis state on the island of Celebes. I had visited it some time before, and he asked eagerly for news. As men's names came up in conversation he would say, "We swam against one another when we were boys;" or, "We had hunted the deer together—he could use the noose and the spear as well as I." Now and then his big dreamy eyes would roll restlessly; he frowned or smiled, or he would become pensive, and, staring in silence, would nod slightly for a time at some regretted vision of the past.

His mother had been the ruler of a small semi-independent state on the sea-coast at the head of the Gulf of Boni.* He spoke of her with pride. She had been a woman resolute in affairs of state and of her own heart. After the death of her first husband, undismayed by the turbulent opposition of the chiefs, she married a rich trader, a Korinchi man of no family.* Karain was her son by that second marriage, but his unfortunate descent had apparently nothing to do with his exile. He said nothing as to its cause, though once he let slip with a sigh, "Ha! my land will not feel any more the weight of my body." But he related willingly the story of his wanderings, and told us all about the conquest of the bay. Alluding to the people beyond the hills, he would murmur gently, with a careless wave of the hand, "They came over the hills once to fight us, but those who got away never came again." He thought for a while, smiling to himself. "Very few got away," he added, with proud serenity. He cherished the recollections of his successes; he had an exulting eagerness for endeavour; when he talked, his aspect was warlike, chivalrous, and uplifting. No wonder his people admired him. We saw him once walking in daylight amongst the houses of the settlement. At the doors of huts groups of women turned to look after him, warbling softly, and with gleaming eyes; armed men stood out of the way, submissive and erect; others approached from the side, bending their backs to address him humbly; an old woman stretched out a draped lean arm—"Blessings on thy head!" she cried from a dark doorway; a fiery-eyed man showed above the low fence of a plantain-patch a streaming face, a bare breast scarred in two places, and bellowed out pantingly after him, "God give victory to our master!" Karain walked fast, and with firm long strides; he answered greetings right and left by quick piercing glances. Children ran forward between the houses, peeped fearfully round corners; young boys kept up with him, gliding between bushes: their eyes gleamed through the dark leaves. The old sword-bearer, shouldering the silver scabbard, shuffled hastily at his heels with bowed head, and his eyes on the

ground. And in the midst of a great stir they passed swift and
absorbed, like two men hurrying through a great solitude.

In his council hall he was surrounded by the gravity of armed
chiefs, while two long rows of old headmen dressed in cotton stuffs
squatted on their heels, with idle arms hanging over their knees.
Under the thatch roof supported by smooth columns, of which each
one had cost the life of a straight-stemmed young palm, the scent of
flowering hedges drifted in warm waves. The sun was sinking. In the
open courtyard suppliants walked through the gate, raising, when
yet far off, their joined hands above bowed heads, and bending low in
the bright stream of sunlight. Young girls, with flowers in their laps,
sat under the wide-spreading boughs of a big tree. The blue smoke
of wood fires spread in a thin mist above the high-pitched roofs of
houses that had glistening walls of woven reeds, and all round them
rough wooden pillars under the sloping eaves. He dispensed justice
in the shade; from a high seat he gave orders, advice, reproof. Now
and then the hum of approbation rose louder, and idle spearmen that
lounged listlessly against the posts, looking at the girls, would turn
their heads slowly. To no man had been given the shelter of so much
respect, confidence, and awe. Yet at times he would lean forward and
appear to listen as for a far-off note of discord, as if expecting to hear
some faint voice, the sound of light footsteps; or he would start half
up in his seat, as though he had been familiarly touched on the
shoulder. He glanced back with apprehension; his aged follower
whispered inaudibly at his ear; the chiefs turned their eyes away in
silence, for the old wizard, the man who could command ghosts and
send evil spirits against enemies, was speaking low to their ruler.
Around the short stillness of the open place the trees rustled faintly,
the soft laughter of girls playing with the flowers rose in clear bursts
of joyous sound. At the end of upright spear-shafts the long tufts of
dyed horse-hair waved crimson and filmy in the gust of wind; and
beyond the blaze of hedges the brook of limpid quick water ran
invisible and loud under the drooping grass of the bank, with a great
murmur, passionate and gentle.

After sunset, far across the fields and over the bay, clusters of
torches could be seen burning under the high roofs of the council
shed. Smoky red flames swayed on high poles, and the fiery blaze
flickered over faces, clung to the smooth trunks of palm-trees,
kindled bright sparks on the rims of metal dishes standing on fine

floor-mats. That obscure adventurer feasted like a king. Small groups of men crouched in tight circles round the wooden platters; brown hands hovered over snowy heaps of rice. Sitting upon a rough couch apart from the others, he leaned on his elbow with inclined head; and near him a youth improvised in a high tone a song that celebrated his valour and wisdom. The singer rocked himself to and fro, rolling frenzied eyes; old women hobbled about with dishes, and men, squatting low, lifted their heads to listen gravely without ceasing to eat. The song of triumph vibrated in the night, and the stanzas rolled out mournful and fiery like the thoughts of a hermit. He silenced it with a sign, "Enough!" An owl hooted far away, exulting in the delight of deep gloom in dense foliage; overhead lizards ran in the attap thatch, calling softly; the dry leaves of the roof rustled; the rumour of mingled voices grew louder suddenly. After a circular and startled glance, as of a man waking up abruptly to the sense of danger, he would throw himself back, and under the downward gaze of the old sorcerer take up, wide-eyed, the slender thread of his dream. They watched his moods; the swelling rumour of animated talk subsided like a wave on a sloping beach. The chief is pensive. And above the spreading whisper of lowered voices only a light rattle of weapons would be heard, a single louder word distinct and alone, or the grave ring of a big brass tray.

## III

FOR two years at short intervals we visited him. We came to like him, to trust him, almost to admire him. He was plotting and preparing a war with patience, with foresight—with a fidelity to his purpose and with a steadfastness of which I would have thought him racially incapable. He seemed fearless of the future, and in his plans displayed a sagacity that was only limited by his profound ignorance of the rest of the world. We tried to enlighten him, but our attempts to make clear the irresistible nature of the forces which he desired to arrest failed to discourage his eagerness to strike a blow for his own primitive ideas. He did not understand us, and replied by arguments that almost drove one to desperation by their childish shrewdness. He was absurd and unanswerable. Sometimes we caught glimpses of a sombre, glowing fury within him—a brooding and vague sense of wrong, and a concentrated lust of violence which is dangerous in a native. He raved like one inspired. On one occasion, after we had been talking to him late in his campong, he jumped up. A great, clear fire blazed in the grove; lights and shadows danced together between the trees; in the still night bats flitted in and out of the boughs like fluttering flakes of denser darkness. He snatched the sword from the old man, whizzed it out of the scabbard, and thrust the point into the earth. Upon the thin, upright blade the silver hilt, released, swayed before him like something alive. He stepped back a pace, and in a deadened tone spoke fiercely to the vibrating steel: "If there is virtue in the fire, in the iron, in the hand that forged thee, in the words spoken over thee, in the desire of my heart, and in the wisdom of thy makers,—then we shall be victorious together!" He drew it out, looked along the edge. "Take," he said over his shoulder to the old sword-bearer. The other, unmoved on his hams, wiped the point with a corner of his sarong, and returning the weapon to its scabbard, sat nursing it on his knees without a single look upwards. Karain, suddenly very calm, reseated himself with dignity. We gave up remonstrating after this, and let him go his way to an honourable disaster. All we could do for him was to see to it that the powder was good for the money and the rifles serviceable, if old.

But the game was becoming at last too dangerous; and if we, who had faced it pretty often, thought little of the danger, it was decided for us by some very respectable people sitting safely in counting-houses that the risks were too great, and that only one more trip could be made. After giving in the usual way many misleading hints as to our destination, we slipped away quietly, and after a very quick passage entered the bay. It was early morning, and even before the anchor went to the bottom the schooner was surrounded by boats.

The first thing we heard was that Karain's mysterious sword-bearer had died a few days ago. We did not attach much importance to the news. It was certainly difficult to imagine Karain without his inseparable follower; but the fellow was old, he had never spoken to one of us, we hardly ever had heard the sound of his voice; and we had come to look upon him as upon something inanimate, as a part of our friend's trappings of state—like that sword he had carried, or the fringed red umbrella displayed during an official progress. Karain did not visit us in the afternoon as usual. A message of greeting and a present of fruit and vegetables came off for us before sunset. Our friend paid us like a banker, but treated us like a prince. We sat up for him till midnight. Under the stern awning bearded Jackson jingled an old guitar and sang, with an execrable accent, Spanish love-songs; while young Hollis and I, sprawling on the deck, had a game of chess by the light of a cargo lantern. Karain did not appear. Next day we were busy unloading, and heard that the Rajah was unwell. The expected invitation to visit him ashore did not come. We sent friendly messages, but, fearing to intrude upon some secret council, remained on board. Early on the third day we had landed all the powder and rifles, and also a six-pounder brass gun with its carriage, which we had subscribed together for a present to our friend. The afternoon was sultry. Ragged edges of black clouds peeped over the hills, and invisible thunderstorms circled outside, growling like wild beasts. We got the schooner ready for sea, intending to leave next morning at daylight. All day a merciless sun blazed down into the bay, fierce and pale, as if at white heat. Nothing moved on the land. The beach was empty, the villages seemed deserted; the trees far off stood in unstirring clumps, as if painted; the white smoke of some invisible bush-fire spread itself low over the shores of the bay like a settling fog. Late in the day three of Karain's chief men, dressed in their best and armed to the teeth, came off in a canoe, bringing a case of dollars. They were gloomy and languid, and told us they had not seen their Rajah for five days. No one had seen him! We settled all accounts, and after shaking hands in turn and in profound silence, they descended one after another into their boat, and were paddled to the shore, sitting close together, clad in vivid colours, with hanging heads: the gold embroideries of their jackets flashed dazzlingly as they went away gliding on the smooth water, and not one of them looked back once. Before sunset the growling clouds carried with a rush the ridge of hills, and came tumbling down the inner slopes. Everything disappeared; black whirling vapours filled the bay, and in the midst of them the schooner swung here and there in the shifting gusts of wind. A single clap of thunder detonated in the hollow with a violence that seemed capable of bursting into small pieces the ring of high land, and a warm deluge descended. The wind died out. We panted in the close cabin; our faces streamed; the bay outside hissed as if boiling; the water fell in perpendicular shafts as heavy as lead; it swished about the deck, poured off the spars, gurgled, sobbed, splashed, murmured in the blind night. Our lamp burned low. Hollis, stripped to the waist, lay stretched out on the lockers, with closed eyes and motionless like a despoiled corpse; at his head Jackson twanged the guitar, and gasped out in sighs a mournful dirge about hopeless love and eyes like stars. Then we heard startled voices on deck crying in the rain, hurried footsteps overhead, and suddenly Karain appeared in the doorway of the cabin. His bare breast and his face glistened in the light; his sarong, soaked, clung about his legs; he had his sheathed kriss in his left hand; and wisps of wet hair, escaping from under his red kerchief, stuck over his eyes and down his cheeks. He stepped in with a headlong stride and looking over his shoulder like a man pursued. Hollis turned on his side quickly and opened his eyes. Jackson clapped his big hand over the strings and the jingling vibration died suddenly. I stood up.

"We did not hear your boat's hail!" I exclaimed.

"Boat! The man's swum off," drawled out Hollis from the locker. "Look at him!"

He breathed heavily, wild-eyed, while we looked at him in silence. Water dripped from him, made a dark pool, and ran crookedly across the cabin floor. We could hear Jackson, who had gone out to drive away our Malay seamen from the doorway of the companion; he swore menacingly in the patter of a heavy shower, and there was a

great commotion on deck. The watchmen, scared out of their wits
by the glimpse of a shadowy figure leaping over the rail, straight out
of the night as it were, had alarmed all hands.

Then Jackson, with glittering drops of water on his hair and
beard, came back looking angry, and Hollis, who, being the youngest
of us, assumed an indolent superiority, said without stirring, "Give
him a dry sarong—give him mine; it's hanging up in the bathroom."
Karain laid the kriss on the table, hilt inwards, and murmured a few
words in a strangled voice.

"What's that?" asked Hollis, who had not heard.

"He apologises for coming in with a weapon in his hand," I said,
dazedly.

"Ceremonious beggar. Tell him we forgive a friend . . . on such a
night," drawled out Hollis. "What's wrong?"

Karain slipped the dry sarong over his head, dropped the wet one
at his feet, and stepped out of it. I pointed to the wooden armchair—
his armchair. He sat down very straight, said "Ha!" in a strong voice;
a short shiver shook his broad frame. He looked over his shoulder
uneasily, turned as if to speak to us, but only stared in a curious blind
manner, and again looked back. Jackson bellowed out, "Watch well
on deck there!" heard a faint answer from above, and reaching out
with his foot slammed-to the cabin door.

"All right now," he said.

Karain's lips moved slightly. A vivid flash of lightning made the
two round sternports facing him glimmer like a pair of cruel and
phosphorescent eyes. The flame of the lamp seemed to wither into
brown dust for an instant, and the looking-glass over the little side-
board leaped out behind his back in a smooth sheet of livid light.
The roll of thunder came near, crashed over us; the schooner trembled, and the great voice went on, threatening terribly, into the distance. For less than a minute a furious shower rattled on the decks.
Karain looked slowly from face to face, and then the silence became
so profound that we all could hear distinctly the two chronometers in
my cabin ticking along with unflagging speed against one another.

And we three, strangely moved, could not take our eyes from him.
He had become enigmatical and touching, in virtue of that mysterious cause that had driven him through the night and through the
thunderstorm to the shelter of the schooner's cuddy. Not one of us
doubted that we were looking at a fugitive, incredible as it appeared

to us. He was haggard, as though he had not slept for weeks; he had become lean, as though he had not eaten for days. His cheeks were hollow, his eyes sunk, the muscles of his chest and arms twitched slightly as if after an exhausting contest. Of course, it had been a long swim off to the schooner; but his face showed another kind of fatigue, the tormented weariness, the anger and the fear of a struggle against a thought, an idea—against something that cannot be grappled, that never rests—a shadow, a nothing, unconquerable and immortal, that preys upon life. We knew it as though he had shouted it at us. His chest expanded time after time, as if it could not contain the beating of his heart. For a moment he had the power of the possessed—the power to awaken in the beholders wonder, pain, pity, and a fearful near sense of things invisible, of things dark and mute, that surround the loneliness of mankind. His eyes roamed about aimlessly for a moment, then became still. He said with effort—

"I came here . . . I leaped out of my stockade as after a defeat. I ran in the night. The water was black. I left him calling on the edge of black water . . . I left him standing alone on the beach. I swam . . . he called out after me . . . I swam . . ."

He trembled from head to foot, sitting very upright and gazing straight before him. Left whom? Who called? We did not know. We could not understand. I said at all hazards—

"Be firm."

The sound of my voice seemed to steady him into a sudden rigidity, but otherwise he took no notice. He seemed to listen, to expect something for a moment, then went on—

"He cannot come here—therefore I sought you. You men with white faces who despise the invisible voices. He cannot abide your unbelief and your strength."

He was silent for a while, then exclaimed softly—

"Oh! the strength of unbelievers!"

"There's no one here but you—and we three," said Hollis, quietly. He reclined with his head supported on elbow and did not budge.

"I know," said Karain. "He has never followed me here. Was not the wise man ever by my side? But since the old wise man, who knew of my trouble, has died, I have heard the voice every night. I shut myself up—for many days—in the dark. I can hear the sorrowful murmurs of women, the whisper of the wind, of the running waters; the clash of weapons in the hands of faithful men, their footsteps—

and his voice! . . . Near . . . So! In my ear! I felt him near . . . His breath passed over my neck. I leaped out without a cry. All about me men slept quietly. I ran to the sea. He ran by my side without footsteps, whispering, whispering old words—whispering into my ear in his old voice. I ran into the sea; I swam off to you, with my kriss between my teeth. I, armed, I fled before a breath—to you. Take me away to your land. The wise old man has died, and with him is gone the power of his words and charms. And I can tell no one. No one. There is no one here faithful enough and wise enough to know. It is only near you, unbelievers, that my trouble fades like a mist under the eye of day."

He turned to me.

"With you I go!" he cried in a contained voice. "With you, who know so many of us. I want to leave this land—my people . . . and him—there!"

He pointed a shaking finger at random over his shoulder. It was hard for us to bear the intensity of that undisclosed distress. Hollis stared at him hard. I asked gently—

"Where is the danger?"

"Everywhere outside this place," he answered, mournfully. "In every place where I am. He waits for me on the paths, under the trees, in the place where I sleep—everywhere but here."

He looked round the little cabin, at the painted beams, at the tarnished varnish of bulkheads; he looked round as if appealing to all its shabby strangeness, to the disorderly jumble of unfamiliar things that belong to an inconceivable life of stress, of power, of endeavour, of unbelief—to the strong life of white men, which rolls on irresistible and hard on the edge of outer darkness. He stretched out his arms as if to embrace it and us. We waited. The wind and rain had ceased, and the stillness of the night round the schooner was as dumb and complete as if a dead world had been laid to rest in a grave of clouds. We expected him to speak. The necessity within him tore at his lips. There are those who say that a native will not speak to a white man. Error. No man will speak to his master; but to a wanderer and a friend, to him who does not come to teach or to rule, to him who asks for nothing and accepts all things, words are spoken by the camp-fires, in the shared solitude of the sea, in riverside villages, in resting-places surrounded by forests—words are spoken that take no account of race or colour. One heart speaks—another one listens;

and the earth, the sea, the sky, the passing wind and the stirring leaf, hear also the futile tale of the burden of life.

He spoke at last. It is impossible to convey the effect of his story. It is undying, it is but a memory, and its vividness cannot be made clear to another mind any more than the vivid emotions of a dream. One must have seen his innate splendour, one must have known him before—looked at him then. The wavering gloom of the little cabin; the breathless stillness outside, through which only the lapping of water against the schooner's sides could be heard; Hollis's pale face, with steady dark eyes; the energetic head of Jackson held up between two big palms, and with the long yellow hair of his beard flowing over the strings of the guitar lying on the table; Karain's upright and motionless pose, his tone—all this made an impression that cannot be forgotten. He faced us across the table. His dark head and bronze torso appeared above the tarnished slab of wood, gleaming and still as if cast in metal. Only his lips moved, and his eyes glowed, went out, blazed again, or stared mournfully. His expressions came straight from his tormented heart. His words sounded low, in a sad murmur as of running water; at times they rang loud like the clash of a war-gong—or trailed slowly like weary travellers—or rushed forward with the speed of fear.

# IV

THIS is, imperfectly, what he said—

"It was after the great trouble that broke the alliance of the four states of Wajo.* We fought amongst ourselves, and the Dutch watched from afar till we were weary. Then the smoke of their fire-ships was seen at the mouth of our rivers, and their great men came in boats full of soldiers to talk to us of protection and peace. We answered with caution and wisdom, for our villages were burnt, our stockades weak, the people weary, and the weapons blunt. They came and went; there had been much talk, but after they went away everything seemed to be as before, only their ships remained in sight from our coast, and very soon their traders came amongst us under a promise of safety. My brother was a Ruler, and one of those who had given the promise. I was young then, and had fought in the war, and Pata Matara* had fought by my side. We had shared hunger, danger, fatigue, and victory. His eyes saw my danger quickly, and twice my arm had preserved his life. It was his destiny. He was my friend. And he was great amongst us—one of those who were near my brother, the Ruler. He spoke in council, his courage was great, he was the chief of many villages round the great lake that is in the middle of our country as the heart is in the middle of a man's body. When his sword was carried into a campong in advance of his coming, the maidens whispered wonderingly under the fruit-trees, the rich men consulted together in the shade, and a feast was made ready with rejoicing and songs. He had the favour of the Ruler and the affection of the poor. He loved war, deer hunts, and the charms of women. He was the possessor of jewels, of lucky weapons, and of men's devotion. He was a fierce man; and I had no other friend.

"I was the chief of a stockade at the mouth of the river, and collected tolls for my brother from the passing boats. One day I saw a Dutch trader go up the river. He went up with three boats, and no toll was demanded from him, because the smoke of Dutch warships stood out from the open sea, and we were too weak to forget treaties. He went up under the promise of safety, and my brother gave him protection. He said he came to trade. He listened to our voices, for we are men who speak openly and without fear; he counted the number of our spears, he examined the trees, the running waters, the grasses of the bank, the slopes of our hills. He went up to Matara's country and obtained permission to build a house. He traded and planted. He despised our joys, our thoughts, and our sorrows. His face was red, his hair like flame, and his eyes pale, like a river mist; he moved heavily, and spoke with a deep voice; he laughed aloud like a fool, and knew no courtesy in his speech. He was a big, scornful man, who looked into women's faces and put his hand on the shoulders of free men as though he had been a noble-born chief. We bore with him. Time passed.

"Then Pata Matara's sister fled from the campong and went to live in the Dutchman's house. She was a great and wilful lady: I had seen her once carried high on slaves' shoulders amongst the people, with uncovered face, and I had heard all men say that her beauty was extreme, silencing the reason and ravishing the heart of the beholders. The people were dismayed; Matara's face was blackened with that disgrace, for she knew she had been promised to another man. Matara went to the Dutchman's house, and said, 'Give her up to die—she is the daughter of chiefs.' The white man refused, and shut himself up, while his servants kept guard night and day with loaded guns. Matara raged. My brother called a council. But the Dutch ships were near, and watched our coast greedily. My brother said, 'If he dies now our land will pay for his blood. Leave him alone till we grow stronger and the ships are gone.' Matara was wise; he waited and watched. But the white man feared for her life and went away.

"He left his house, his plantations, and his goods! He departed, armed and menacing, and left all—for her! She had ravished his heart! From my stockade I saw him put out to sea in a big boat. Matara and I watched him from the fighting platform behind the pointed stakes. He sat cross-legged, with his gun in his hands, on the roof at the stern of his prau. The barrel of his rifle glinted aslant before his big red face. The broad river was stretched under him— level, smooth, shining, like a plain of silver; and his prau, looking very short and black from the shore, glided along the silver plain and over into the blue of the sea.

"Thrice Matara, standing by my side, called aloud her name with grief and imprecations. He stirred my heart. It leaped three times; and three times with the eye of my mind I saw in the gloom within the enclosed space of the prau a woman with streaming hair going away from her land and her people. I was angry—and sorry. Why? And then I also cried out insults and threats. Matara said, 'Now they have left our land their lives are mine. I shall follow and strike—and, alone, pay the price of blood.' A great wind was sweeping towards the setting sun over the empty river. I cried, 'By your side I will go!' He lowered his head in sign of assent. It was his destiny. The sun had set, and the trees swayed their boughs with a great noise above our heads.

"On the third night we two left our land together in a trading prau.

"The sea met us—the sea, wide, pathless, and without voice. A sailing prau leaves no track. We went south. The moon was full; and, looking up, we said to one another, 'When the next moon shines as this one, we shall return and they will be dead.' It was fifteen years ago. Many moons have grown full and withered, and I have not seen my land since. We sailed south; we overtook many praus; we examined the creeks and the bays; we saw the end of our coast, of our island—a steep cape over a disturbed strait, where drift the shadows of shipwrecked praus and drowned men clamour in the night. The wide sea was all round us now. We saw a great mountain burning in the midst of water;* we saw thousands of islets scattered like bits of iron fired from a big gun; we saw a long coast of mountain and lowlands stretching away in sunshine from west to east. It was Java. We said, 'They are there; their time is near, and we shall return or die cleansed from dishonour.'

"We landed. Is there anything good in that country? The paths run straight and hard and dusty. Stone campongs, full of white faces, are surrounded by fertile fields, but every man you meet is a slave. The rulers live under the edge of a foreign sword.* We ascended mountains, we traversed valleys; at sunset we entered villages. We asked every one, 'Have you seen such a white man?' Some stared; others laughed; women gave us food, sometimes, with fear and respect, as though we had been distracted by the visitation of God; but some did not understand our language, and some cursed us, or, yawning, asked with contempt the reason of our quest. Once, as we were going away, an old man called after us, 'Desist!'

"We went on. Concealing our weapons, we stood humbly aside before the horsemen on the road; we bowed low in the courtyards of chiefs who were no better than slaves. We lost ourselves in the fields, in the jungle; and one night, in a tangled forest, we came upon a place where crumbling old walls had fallen amongst the trees, and where strange stone idols—carved images of devils with many arms and legs, with snakes twined round their bodies, with twenty heads and holding a hundred swords—seemed to live and threaten in the light of our camp-fire. Nothing dismayed us. And on the road, by every fire, in resting-places, we always talked of her and of him. Their time was near. We spoke of nothing else. No! not of hunger, thirst, weariness, and faltering hearts. No! we spoke of him and her! Of her! And we thought of them—of her! Matara brooded by the fire. I sat and thought and thought, till suddenly I could see again the image of a woman, beautiful, and young, and great, and proud, and tender, going away from her land and her people. Matara said, 'When we find them we shall kill her first to cleanse the dishonour—then the man must die.' I would say, 'It shall be so; it is your vengeance.' He stared long at me with his big sunken eyes.

"We came back to the coast. Our feet were bleeding, our bodies thin. We slept in rags under the shadow of stone enclosures; we prowled, soiled and lean, about the gateways of white men's court-yards. Their hairy dogs barked at us, and their servants shouted from afar, 'Begone!' Low-born wretches, that keep watch over the streets of stone campongs, asked us who we were. We lied, we cringed, we smiled with hate in our hearts, and we kept looking here, looking there, for them—for the white man with hair like flame, and for her, for the woman who had broken faith, and therefore must die. We looked. At last in every woman's face I thought I could see hers. We ran swiftly. No! Sometimes Matara would whisper, 'Here is the man,' and we waited, crouching. He came near. It was not the man—those Dutchmen are all alike. We suffered the anguish of deception. In my sleep I saw her face, and was both joyful and sorry. . . . Why? . . . I seemed to hear a whisper near me. I turned swiftly. She was not there! And as we trudged wearily from stone city to stone city I seemed to hear a light footstep near me. A time came when I heard it always, and I was glad. I thought, walking dizzy and weary in sunshine on the hard paths of white men—I thought, She is there—with us! . . . Matara was sombre. We were often hungry.

"We sold the carved sheaths of our krisses—the ivory sheaths with golden ferules. We sold the jewelled hilts. But we kept the blades—

for them. The blades that never touch but kill—we kept the blades for her . . . Why? She was always by our side . . . We starved. We begged. We left Java at last.

"We went West, we went East. We saw many lands, crowds of strange faces, men that live in trees and men who eat their old people. We cut rattans in the forest for a handful of rice, and for a living swept the decks of big ships and heard curses heaped upon our heads. We toiled in villages; we wandered upon the seas with the Bajow people, who have no country.* We fought for pay; we hired ourselves to work for Goram men, and were cheated; and under the orders of rough white-faces we dived for pearls in barren bays, dotted with black rocks, upon a coast of sand and desolation. And everywhere we watched, we listened, we asked. We asked traders, robbers, white men. We heard jeers, mockery, threats—words of wonder and words of contempt. We never knew rest; we never thought of home, for our work was not done. A year passed, then another. I ceased to count the number of nights, of moons, of years. I watched over Matara. He had my last handful of rice; if there was water enough for one he drank it; I covered him up when he shivered with cold; and when the hot sickness came upon him I sat sleepless through many nights and fanned his face. He was a fierce man, and my friend. He spoke of her with fury in the daytime, with sorrow in the dark; he remembered her in health, in sickness. I said nothing; but I saw her every day—always! At first I saw only her head, as of a woman walking in the low mist on a river bank. Then she sat by our fire. I saw her! I looked at her! She had tender eyes and a ravishing face. I murmured to her in the night. Matara said sleepily some- times, 'To whom are you talking? Who is there?' I answered quickly, 'No one' . . . It was a lie! She never left me. She shared the warmth of our fire, she sat on my couch of leaves, she swam on the sea to follow me . . . I saw her! . . . I tell you I saw her long black hair spread behind her upon the moonlit water as she struck out with bare arms by the side of a swift prau. She was beautiful, she was faithful, and in the silence of foreign countries she spoke to me very low in the language of my people. No one saw her; no one heard her; she was mine only! In daylight she moved with a swaying walk before me upon the weary paths; her figure was straight and flexible like the stem of a slender tree; the heels of her feet were round and polished like shells of eggs; with her round arm she made signs. At night she

looked into my face. And she was sad! Her eyes were tender and
frightened; her voice soft and pleading. Once I murmured to her,
'You shall not die,' and she smiled . . . ever after she smiled! . . . She
gave me courage to bear weariness and hardships. Those were times
of pain, and she soothed me. We wandered patient in our search. We
knew deception, false hopes; we knew captivity, sickness, thirst,
misery, despair. . . . Enough! We found them! . . ."

He cried out the last words and paused. His face was impassive,
and he kept still like a man in a trance. Hollis sat up quickly, and
spread his elbows on the table. Jackson made a brusque movement,
and accidentally touched the guitar. A plaintive resonance filled the
cabin with confused vibrations and died out slowly. Then Karain
began to speak again. The restrained fierceness of his tone seemed to
rise like a voice from outside, like a thing unspoken but heard; it
filled the cabin and enveloped in its intense and deadened murmur
the motionless figure in the chair.

"We were on our way to Atjeh, where there was war;* but the vessel
ran on a sandbank, and we had to land in Delli. We had earned a little
money, and had bought a gun from some Selangore traders; only
one gun, which was fired by the spark of a stone: Matara carried it.
We landed. Many white men lived there, planting tobacco on conquered plains, and Matara . . . But no matter. He saw him! . . . The
Dutchman! . . . At last! . . . We crept and watched. Two nights and a
day we watched. He had a house—a big house in a clearing in the
midst of his fields; flowers and bushes grew around; there were
narrow paths of yellow earth between the cut grass, and thick hedges
to keep people out. The third night we came armed, and lay behind a
hedge.

"A heavy dew seemed to soak through our flesh and made our very
entrails cold. The grass, the twigs, the leaves, covered with drops of
water, were grey in the moonlight. Matara, curled up in the grass,
shivered in his sleep. My teeth rattled in my head so loud that I was
afraid the noise would wake up all the land. Afar, the watchmen of
white men's houses struck wooden clappers and hooted in the
darkness. And, as every night, I saw her by my side. She smiled no
more! . . . The fire of anguish burned in my breast, and she whispered to me with compassion, with pity, softly—as women will; she
soothed the pain of my mind; she bent her face over me—the face of
a woman who ravishes the hearts and silences the reason of men. She

was all mine, and no one could see her—no one of living mankind! Stars shone through her bosom, through her floating hair. I was overcome with regret, with tenderness, with sorrow. Matara slept . . . Had I slept? Matara was shaking me by the shoulder, and the fire of the sun was drying the grass, the bushes, the leaves. It was day. Shreds of white mist hung between the branches of trees.

"Was it night or day? I saw nothing again till I heard Matara breathe quickly where he lay, and then outside the house I saw her. I saw them both. They had come out. She sat on a bench under the wall, and twigs laden with flowers crept high above her head, hung over her hair. She had a box on her lap, and gazed into it, counting the increase of her pearls. The Dutchman stood by looking on; he smiled down at her; his white teeth flashed; the hair on his lip was like two twisted flames. He was big and fat, and joyous, and without fear. Matara tipped fresh priming from the hollow of his palm, scraped the flint with his thumb-nail,* and gave the gun to me. To me! I took it . . . O fate!

"He whispered into my ear, lying on his stomach, 'I shall creep close and then amok . . . let her die by my hand. You take aim at the fat swine there. Let him see me strike my shame off the face of the earth—and then . . . you are my friend—kill with a sure shot.' I said nothing; there was no air in my chest—there was no air in the world. Matara had gone suddenly from my side. The grass nodded. Then a bush rustled. She lifted her head.

"I saw her! The consoler of sleepless nights, of weary days; the companion of troubled years! I saw her! She looked straight at the place where I crouched. She was there as I had seen her for years—a faithful wanderer by my side. She looked with sad eyes and had smiling lips; she looked at me . . . Smiling lips! Had I not promised that she should not die?

"She was far off and I felt her near. Her touch caressed me, and her voice murmured, whispered above me, around me, 'Who shall be thy companion, who shall console thee if I die?' I saw a flowering thicket to the left of her stir a little . . . Matara was ready . . . I cried aloud—'Return!'

"She leaped up; the box fell; the pearls streamed at her feet. The big Dutchman by her side rolled menacing eyes through the still sunshine. The gun went up to my shoulder. I was kneeling and I was firm—firmer than the trees, the rocks, the mountains. But in front of the steady long barrel the fields, the house, the earth, the sky swayed to and fro like shadows in a forest on a windy day. Matara burst out of the thicket; before him the petals of torn flowers whirled high as if driven by a tempest. I heard her cry; I saw her spring with open arms in front of the white man. She was a woman of my country and of noble blood. They are so! I heard her shriek of anguish and fear—and all stood still! The fields, the house, the earth, the sky stood still—while Matara leaped at her with uplifted arm. I pulled the trigger, saw a spark, heard nothing; the smoke drove back into my face, and then I could see Matara roll over head first and lie with stretched arms at her feet. Ha! A sure shot! The sunshine fell on my back colder than the running water. A sure shot! I flung the gun after the shot. Those two stood over the dead man as though they had been bewitched by a charm. I shouted at her, 'Live and remember!' Then for a time I stumbled about in a cold darkness.

"Behind me there were great shouts, the running of many feet; strange men surrounded me, cried meaningless words into my face, pushed me, dragged me, supported me . . . I stood before the big Dutchman: he stared as if bereft of his reason. He wanted to know, he talked fast, he spoke of gratitude, he offered me food, shelter, gold—he asked many questions. I laughed in his face. I said, 'I am a Korinchi traveller from Perak over there, and know nothing of that dead man. I was passing along the path when I heard a shot, and your senseless people rushed out and dragged me here.' He lifted his arms, he wondered, he could not believe, he could not understand, he clamoured in his own tongue! She had her arms clasped round his neck, and over her shoulder stared back at me with wide eyes. I smiled and looked at her; I smiled and waited to hear the sound of her voice. The white man asked her suddenly, 'Do you know him?' I listened—my life was in my ears! She looked at me long, she looked at me with unflinching eyes, and said aloud, 'No! I never saw him before.' . . . What! Never before? Had she forgotten already? Was it possible? Forgotten already—after so many years—so many years of wandering, of companionship, of trouble, of tender words! Forgotten already! . . . I tore myself out from the hands that held me and went away without a word . . . They let me go.

"I was weary. Did I sleep? I do not know. I remember walking upon a broad path under a clear starlight; and that strange country seemed so big, the rice-fields so vast, that, as I looked around, my head swam with the fear of space. Then I saw a forest. The joyous starlight was heavy upon me. I turned off the path and entered the forest, which was very sombre and very sad."

# V

KARAIN'S tone had been getting lower and lower, as though he had been going away from us, till the last words sounded faint but clear, as if shouted on a calm day from a very great distance. He moved not. He stared fixedly past the motionless head of Hollis, who faced him, as still as himself. Jackson had turned sideways, and with elbow on the table shaded his eyes with the palm of his hand. And I looked on, surprised and moved; I looked at that man, loyal to a vision, betrayed by his dream, spurned by his illusion, and coming to us unbelievers for help—against a thought. The silence was profound; but it seemed full of noiseless phantoms, of things sorrowful, shadowy, and mute, in whose invisible presence the firm, pulsating beat of the two ship's chronometers ticking off steadily the seconds of Greenwich Time seemed to me a protection and a relief. Karain stared stonily; and looking at his rigid figure, I thought of his wanderings, of that obscure Odyssey of revenge, of all the men that wander amongst illusions; of the illusions as restless as men; of the illusions faithful, faithless; of the illusions that give joy, that give sorrow, that give pain, that give peace; of the invincible illusions that can make life and death appear serene, inspiring, tormented, or ignoble.

A murmur was heard; that voice from outside seemed to flow out of a dreaming world into the lamplight of the cabin. Karain was speaking.

"I lived in the forest.

"She came no more. Never! Never once! I lived alone. She had forgotten. It was well. I did not want her; I wanted no one. I found an abandoned house in an old clearing. Nobody came near. Sometimes I heard in the distance the voices of people going along a path. I slept; I rested; there was wild rice, water from a running stream—and peace! Every night I sat alone by my small fire before the hut. Many nights passed over my head.

"Then, one evening, as I sat by my fire after having eaten, I looked down on the ground and began to remember my wanderings. I lifted my head. I had heard no sound, no rustle, no footsteps— but I lifted my head. A man was coming towards me across the small clearing. I waited. He came up without a greeting and squatted down into the firelight. Then he turned his face to me. It was Matara. He stared at me fiercely with his big sunken eyes. The night was cold; the heat died suddenly out of the fire, and he stared at me. I rose and went away from there, leaving him by the fire that had no heat.

"I walked all that night, all next day, and in the evening made up a big blaze and sat down—to wait for him. He did not come into the light. I heard him in the bushes here and there, whispering, whispering. I understood at last—I had heard the words before, 'You are my friend—kill with a sure shot.'

"I bore it as long as I could—then leaped away, as on this very night I leaped from my stockade and swam to you. I ran—I ran crying like a child left alone and far from the houses. He ran by my side, without footsteps, whispering, whispering—invisible and heard. I sought people—I wanted men around me! Men who had not died! And again we two wandered. I sought danger, violence, and death. I fought in the Atjeh war, and a brave people wondered at the valiance of a stranger. But we were two; he warded off the blows . . . Why? I wanted peace, not life. And no one could see him; no one knew—I dared tell no one. At times he would leave me, but not for long; then he would return and whisper or stare. My heart was torn with a strange fear, but could not die. Then I met an old man.

"You all knew him. People here called him my sorcerer, my servant and sword-bearer; but to me he was father, mother, protection, refuge, and peace. When I met him he was returning from a pilgrimage, and I heard him intoning the prayer of sunset. He had gone to the holy place with his son, his son's wife, and a little child; and on their return, by the favour of the Most High, they all died: the strong man, the young mother, the little child—they died; and the old man reached his country alone. He was a pilgrim serene and pious, very wise and very lonely. I told him all. For a time we lived together. He said over me words of compassion, of wisdom, of prayer. He warded from me the shade of the dead. I begged him for a charm that would make me safe. For a long time he refused; but at last, with a sigh and a smile, he gave me one. Doubtless he could command a spirit stronger than the unrest of my dead friend, and again I had peace; but I had become restless, and a lover of turmoil and danger. The old man never left me. We travelled together. We were welcomed by the great; his wisdom and my courage are remembered where your

strength, O white men, is forgotten! We served the Sultan of Sulu.
We fought the Spaniards.* There were victories, hopes, defeats, sorrow, blood, women's tears . . . What for? . . . We fled. We collected
wanderers of a warlike race and came here to fight again. The rest
you know. I am the ruler of a conquered land, a lover of war and
danger, a fighter and a plotter. But the old man has died, and I am
again the slave of the dead. He is not here now to drive away the
reproachful shade—to silence the lifeless voice! The power of his
charm has died with him. And I know fear; and I hear the whisper,
'Kill! kill! kill!' . . . Have I not killed enough? . . ."

For the first time that night a sudden convulsion of madness and
rage passed over his face. His wavering glances darted here and there
like scared birds in a thunderstorm. He jumped up, shouting—

"By the spirits that drink blood: by the spirits that cry in the
night: by all the spirits of fury, misfortune, and death, I swear—some
day I will strike into every heart I meet—I . . ."

He looked so dangerous that we all three leaped to our feet, and
Hollis, with the back of his hand, sent the kriss flying off the table. I
believe we shouted together. It was a short scare, and the next
moment he was again composed in his chair, with three white men
standing over him in rather foolish attitudes. We felt a little ashamed
of ourselves. Jackson picked up the kriss, and, after an inquiring
glance at me, gave it to him. He received it with a stately inclination
of the head and stuck it in the twist of his sarong, with punctilious
care to give his weapon a pacific position. Then he looked up at us
with an austere smile. We were abashed and reproved. Hollis sat
sideways on the table and, holding his chin in his hand, scrutinised
him in pensive silence. I said—

"You must abide with your people. They need you. And there is
forgetfulness in life. Even the dead cease to speak in time."

"Am I a woman, to forget long years before an eyelid has had the
time to beat twice?" he exclaimed, with bitter resentment. He startled me. It was amazing. To him his life—that cruel mirage of love
and peace—seemed as real, as undeniable, as theirs would be to any
saint, philosopher, or fool of us all. Hollis muttered—

"You won't soothe him with your platitudes."

Karain spoke to me.

"You know us. You have lived with us. Why?—we cannot know;
but you understand our sorrows and our thoughts. You have lived

with my people, and you understand our desires and our fears. With you I will go. To your land—to your people. To your people, who live in unbelief; to whom day is day, and night is night—nothing more, because you understand all things seen, and despise all else! To your land of unbelief, where the dead do not speak, where every man is wise, and alone—and at peace!"

"Capital description," murmured Hollis, with the flicker of a smile.

Karain hung his head.

"I can toil, and fight—and be faithful," he whispered, in a weary tone, "but I cannot go back to him who waits for me on the shore. No! Take me with you . . . Or else give me some of your strength— of your unbelief . . . A charm! . . ."

He seemed utterly exhausted.

"Yes, take him home," said Hollis, very low, as if debating with himself. "That would be one way. The ghosts there are in society, and talk affably to ladies and gentlemen, but would scorn a naked human being—like our princely friend. . . . Naked . . . Flayed! I should say. I am sorry for him. Impossible—of course. The end of all this shall be," he went on, looking up at us—"the end of this shall be, that some day he will run amuck amongst his faithful subjects and send *ad patres* ever so many of them before they make up their minds to the disloyalty of knocking him on the head."

I nodded. I thought it more than probable that such would be the end of Karain. It was evident that he had been hunted by his thought along the very limit of human endurance, and very little more pressing was needed to make him swerve over into the form of madness peculiar to his race. The respite he had during the old man's life made the return of the torment unbearable. That much was clear.

He lifted his head suddenly; we had imagined for a moment that he had been dozing.

"Give me your protection—or your strength!" he cried. "A charm . . . a weapon!"*

Again his chin fell on his breast. We looked at him, then looked at one another with suspicious awe in our eyes, like men who come unexpectedly upon the scene of some mysterious disaster. He had given himself up to us; he had thrust into our hands his errors and his torment, his life and his peace; and we did not know what to do with that problem from the outer darkness. We three white men, looking at that Malay, could not find one word to the purpose amongst us—if indeed there existed a word that could solve that problem. We pondered, and our hearts sank. We felt as though we three had been called to the very gate of Infernal Regions to judge, to decide the fate of a wanderer coming suddenly from a world of sunshine and illusions.*

"By Jove, he seems to have a great idea of our power," whispered Hollis, hopelessly. And then again there was a silence, the feeble plash of water, the steady tick of chronometers. Jackson, with bare arms crossed, leaned his shoulders against the bulkhead of the cabin. He was bending his head under the deck beam; his fair beard spread out magnificently over his chest; he looked colossal, ineffectual, and mild. There was something lugubrious in the aspect of the cabin; the air in it seemed to become slowly charged with the cruel chill of helplessness, with the pitiless anger of egoism against the incomprehensible form of an intruding pain. We had no idea what to do; we began to resent bitterly the hard necessity to get rid of him.

Hollis mused, muttered suddenly with a short laugh, "Strength . . . Protection . . . Charm." He slipped off the table and left the cuddy without a look at us. It seemed a base desertion. Jackson and I exchanged indignant glances. We could hear him rummaging in his pigeon-hole of a cabin. Was the fellow actually going to bed? Karain sighed. It was intolerable!

Then Hollis reappeared, holding in both hands a small leather box. He put it down gently on the table and looked at us with a queer gasp, we thought, as though he had from some cause become speechless for a moment, or were ethically uncertain about producing that box. But in an instant the insolent and unerring wisdom of his youth gave him the needed courage. He said, as he unlocked the box with a very small key, "Look as solemn as you can, you fellows."

Probably we looked only surprised and stupid, for he glanced over his shoulder, and said angrily—

"This is no play; I am going to do something for him. Look serious. Confound it! . . . Can't you lie a little . . . for a friend!"

Karain seemed to take no notice of us, but when Hollis threw open the lid of the box his eyes flew to it—and so did ours. The quilted crimson satin of the inside put in a violent patch of colour into the sombre atmosphere; it was something positive to look at—it was fascinating.

## VI

HOLLIS looked smiling into the box. He had lately made a dash home through the Canal. He had been away six months, and only joined us again just in time for this last trip. We had never seen the box before. His hands hovered above it; and he talked to us ironically, but his face became as grave as though he were pronouncing a powerful incantation over the things inside.

"Every one of us," he said, with pauses that somehow were more offensive than his words—"every one of us, you'll admit, has been haunted by some woman . . . And . . . as to friends . . . dropped by the way . . . Well! . . . ask yourselves . . ."

He paused. Karain stared. A deep rumble was heard high up under the deck. Jackson spoke seriously—

"Don't be so beastly cynical."

"Ah! You are without guile," said Hollis, sadly. "You will learn . . . Meantime this Malay has been our friend . . ."

He repeated several times thoughtfully, "Friend . . . Malay. Friend, Malay," as though weighing the words against one another, then went on more briskly—

"A good fellow—a gentleman in his way. We can't, so to speak, turn our backs on his confidence and belief in us. Those Malays are easily impressed—all nerves, you know—therefore . . ."

He turned to me sharply.

"You know him best," he said, in a practical tone. "Do you think he is fanatical—I mean very strict in his faith?"

I stammered in profound amazement that I did not think so.

"It's on account of its being a likeness—an engraved image,"* muttered Hollis, enigmatically, turning to the box. He plunged his fingers into it. Karain's lips were parted and his eyes shone. We looked into the box.

There were there a couple of reels of cotton, a packet of needles, a bit of silk ribbon, dark blue; a cabinet photograph, at which Hollis stole a glance before laying it on the table face downwards. A girl's portrait, I could see. There were, amongst a lot of various small objects, a bunch of flowers, a narrow white glove with many buttons, a slim packet of letters carefully tied up. Amulets of white men!

Charms and talismans! Charms that keep them straight, that drive them crooked, that have the power to make a young man sigh, an old man smile. Potent things that procure dreams of joy, thoughts of regret; that soften hard hearts, and can temper a soft one to the hardness of steel. Gifts of heaven—things of earth . . .

Hollis rummaged in the box.

And it seemed to me, during that moment of waiting, that the cabin of the schooner was becoming filled with a stir invisible and living as of subtle breaths. All the ghosts driven out of the unbelieving West by men who pretend to be wise and alone and at peace—all the homeless ghosts of an unbelieving world—appeared suddenly round the figure of Hollis bending over the box; all the exiled and charming shades of loved women; all the beautiful and tender ghosts of ideals, remembered, forgotten, cherished, execrated; all the cast-out and reproachful ghosts of friends admired, trusted, traduced, betrayed, left dead by the way—they all seemed to come from the inhospitable regions of the earth to crowd into the gloomy cabin, as though it had been a refuge and, in all the unbelieving world, the only place of avenging belief. . . . It lasted a second—all disappeared. Hollis was facing us alone with something small that glittered between his fingers. It looked like a coin.

"Ah! here it is," he said.

He held it up. It was a sixpence—a Jubilee sixpence. It was gilt; it had a hole punched near the rim.* Hollis looked towards Karain.

"A charm for our friend," he said to us. "The thing itself is of great power—money, you know—and his imagination is struck. A loyal vagabond; if only his puritanism doesn't shy at a likeness . . ."

We said nothing. We did not know whether to be scandalised, amused, or relieved. Hollis advanced towards Karain, who stood up as if startled, and then, holding the coin up, spoke in Malay.

"This is the image of the Great Queen, and the most powerful thing the white men know," he said, solemnly.

Karain covered the handle of his kriss in sign of respect, and stared at the crowned head.

"The Invincible, the Pious," he muttered.

"She is more powerful than Suleiman the Wise, who commanded the genii,* as you know," said Hollis, gravely. "I shall give this to you."

He held the sixpence in the palm of his hand, and looking at it thoughtfully, spoke to us in English.

"She commands a spirit, too—the spirit of her nation; a masterful, conscientious, unscrupulous, unconquerable devil . . . that does a lot of good—incidentally . . . a lot of good . . . at times—and wouldn't stand any fuss from the best ghost out for such a little thing as our friend's shot. Don't look thunderstruck, you fellows. Help me to make him believe—everything's in that."

"His people will be shocked," I murmured.

Hollis looked fixedly at Karain, who was the incarnation of the very essence of still excitement. He stood rigid, with head thrown back; his eyes rolled wildly, flashing; the dilated nostrils quivered.

"Hang it all!" said Hollis at last, "he is a good fellow. I'll give him something that I shall really miss."

He took the ribbon out of the box, smiled at it scornfully, then with a pair of scissors cut out a piece from the palm of the glove.

"I shall make him a thing like those Italian peasants wear, you know."*

He sewed the coin in the delicate leather, sewed the leather to the ribbon, tied the ends together. He worked with haste. Karain watched his fingers all the time.

"Now then," he said—then stepped up to Karain. They looked close into one another's eyes. Those of Karain stared in a lost glance, but Hollis's seemed to grow darker and looked out masterful and compelling. They were in violent contrast together—one motionless and the colour of bronze, the other dazzling white and lifting his arms, where the powerful muscles rolled slightly under a skin that gleamed like satin. Jackson moved near with the air of a man closing up to a chum in a tight place. I said impressively, pointing to Hollis—

"He is young, but he is wise. Believe him!"

Karain bent his head: Hollis threw lightly over it the dark-blue ribbon and stepped back.

"Forget, and be at peace!" I cried.

Karain seemed to wake up from a dream. He said, "Ha!"—shook himself as if throwing off a burden. He looked round with assurance. Some one on deck dragged off the skylight cover and a flood of light fell into the cabin. It was morning already.

"Time to go on deck," said Jackson.

Hollis put on a coat, and we went up, Karain leading.

The sun had risen beyond the hills, and their long shadows

stretched far over the bay in the pearly light. The air was clear, stainless, and cool. I pointed at the curved line of yellow sands.

"He is not there," I said, emphatically, to Karain. "He waits no more. He has departed for ever."

A shaft of bright hot rays darted into the bay between the summits of two hills, and the water all round broke out as if by magic into a dazzling sparkle.

"No! He is not there waiting," said Karain, after a long look over the beach. "I do not hear him," he went on, slowly. "No!"

He turned to us.

"He has departed again—for ever!" he cried.

We assented vigorously, repeatedly, and without compunction. The great thing was to impress him powerfully; to suggest absolute safety—the end of all trouble. We did our best; and I hope we affirmed our faith in the power of Hollis's charm efficiently enough to put the matter beyond the shadow of a doubt. Our voices rang around him joyously in the still air, and above his head the sky, pellucid, pure, stainless, arched its tender blue from shore to shore and over the bay, as if to envelop the water, the earth, and the man in the caress of its light.

The anchor was up, the sails hung still, and half-a-dozen big boats were seen sweeping over the bay to give us a tow out. The paddlers in the first one that came alongside lifted their heads and saw their ruler standing amongst us. A low murmur of surprise arose—then a shout of greeting.

He left us, and seemed straightway to step into the glorious splendour of his stage, to wrap himself in the illusion of unavoidable success. For a moment he stood erect, one foot over the gangway, one hand on the hilt of his kriss, in a martial pose; and, relieved from the fear of outer darkness, he held his head high, he swept a serene look over his conquered foothold on the earth. The boats far off took up the cry of greeting; a great clamour rolled on the water; the hills echoed it, and seemed to toss back at him the words invoking long life and victories.

He descended into a canoe, and as soon as he was clear of the side we gave him three cheers. They sounded faint and orderly after the wild tumult of his loyal subjects, but it was the best we could do. He stood up in the boat, lifted up both his arms, then pointed to the infallible charm. We cheered again; and the Malays in the boats stared—very much puzzled and impressed. I wonder what they thought; what he thought; . . . what the reader thinks?

We towed out slowly. We saw him land and watch us from the beach. A figure approached him humbly but openly—not at all like a ghost with a grievance. We could see other men running towards him. Perhaps he had been missed? At any rate there was a great stir. A group formed itself rapidly near him, and he walked along the sands, followed by a growing *cortège*, and kept nearly abreast of the schooner. With our glasses we could see the blue ribbon on his neck and a patch of white on his brown chest. The bay was waking up. The smoke of morning fires stood in faint spirals higher than the heads of palms; people moved between the houses; a herd of buffa-loes galloped clumsily across a green slope; the slender figures of boys brandishing sticks appeared black and leaping in the long grass; a coloured line of women, with water bamboos on their heads, moved swaying through a thin grove of fruit-trees. Karain stopped in the midst of his men and waved his hand; then, detaching himself from the splendid group, walked alone to the water's edge and waved his hand again. The schooner passed out to sea between the steep headlands that shut in the bay, and at the same instant Karain passed out of our life for ever.

But the memory remains. Some years afterwards I met Jackson, in the Strand. He was magnificent as ever. His head was high above the crowd. His beard was gold, his face red, his eyes blue; he had a wide-brimmed grey hat and no collar or waistcoat; he was inspiring; he had just come home—had landed that very day! Our meeting caused an eddy in the current of humanity. Hurried people would run against us, then walk round us, and turn back to look at that giant. We tried to compress seven years of life into seven exclamations; then, suddenly appeased, walked sedately along, giving one another the news of yesterday. Jackson gazed about him, like a man who looks for landmarks, then stopped before Bland's window.* He always had a passion for firearms; so he stopped short and contemplated the row of weapons, perfect and severe, drawn up in a line behind the black-framed panes. I stood by his side. Suddenly he said—

"Do you remember Karain?"

I nodded.

"The sight of all this made me think of him," he went on, with his face near the glass . . . and I could see another man, powerful and bearded, peering at him intently from amongst the dark and polished tubes that can cure so many illusions. "Yes; it made me think of him," he continued, slowly. "I saw a paper this morning; they are fighting over there again. He's sure to be in it. He will make it hot for the caballeros. Well, good luck to him, poor devil! He was perfectly stunning."

We walked on.

"I wonder whether the charm worked—you remember Hollis's charm, of course. If it did . . . never was a sixpence wasted to better advantage! Poor devil! I wonder whether he got rid of that friend of his. Hope so . . . Do you know, I sometimes think that——"

I stood still and looked at him.

"Yes . . . I mean, whether the thing was so, you know . . . whether it really happened to him . . . What do you think?"

"My dear chap," I cried, "you have been too long away from home. What a question to ask! Only look at all this."

A watery gleam of sunshine flashed from the west and went out between two long lines of walls; and then the broken confusion of roofs, the chimney-stacks, the gold letters sprawling over the fronts of houses, the sombre polish of windows, stood resigned and sullen under the falling gloom. The whole length of the street, deep as a well and narrow like a corridor, was full of a sombre and ceaseless stir. Our ears were filled by a headlong shuffle and beat of rapid footsteps and an underlying rumour—a rumour vast, faint, pulsating, as of panting breaths, of beating hearts, of gasping voices.* Innumerable eyes stared straight in front, feet moved hurriedly, blank faces flowed, arms swung. Over all, a narrow ragged strip of smoky sky wound about between the high roofs, extended and motionless, like a soiled streamer flying above the rout of a mob.

"Ye-e-e-s," said Jackson, meditatively.

The big wheels of hansoms turned slowly along the edge of sidewalks; a pale-faced youth strolled, overcome by weariness, by the side of his stick and with the tails of his overcoat flapping gently near his heels; horses stepped gingerly on the greasy pavement, tossing their heads; two young girls passed by, talking vivaciously and with shining eyes; a fine old fellow strutted, red-faced, stroking a white moustache; and a line of yellow boards with blue letters on them approached us slowly, tossing on high behind one another like some queer wreckage adrift upon a river of hats.*

"Ye-e-es," repeated Jackson. His clear blue eyes looked about, contemptuous, amused and hard, like the eyes of a boy. A clumsy string of red, yellow, and green omnibuses rolled swaying, monstrous and gaudy; two shabby children ran across the road; a knot of dirty men with red neckerchiefs round their bare throats lurched along, discussing filthily; a ragged old man with a face of despair yelled horribly in the mud the name of a paper; while far off, amongst the tossing heads of horses, the dull flash of harnesses, the jumble of lustrous panels and roofs of carriages, we could see a policeman, helmeted and dark, stretching out a rigid arm at the crossing of the streets.

"Yes; I see it," said Jackson, slowly. "It is there; it pants, it runs, it rolls; it is strong and alive; it would smash you if you didn't look out; but I'll be hanged if it is yet as real to me as . . . as the other thing . . . say, Karain's story."

I think that, decidedly, he had been too long away from home.

# YOUTH: A NARRATIVE

# YOUTH: A NARRATIVE

THIS could have occurred nowhere but in England, where men and sea interpenetrate, so to speak—the sea entering into the life of most men, and the men knowing something or everything about the sea, in the way of amusement, of travel, or of bread-winning.

We were sitting round a mahogany table that reflected the bottle, the claret-glasses, and our faces as we leaned on our elbows. There was a director of companies, an accountant, a lawyer, Marlow, and myself. The director had been a *Conway* boy,* the accountant had served four years at sea, the lawyer—a fine crusted Tory, High Churchman, the best of old fellows, the soul of honour—had been chief officer in the P. & O. service in the good old days when mail-boats were square-rigged at least on two masts, and used to come down the China Sea before a fair monsoon with stun'-sails set alow and aloft. We all began life in the merchant service. Between the five of us there was the strong bond of the sea, and also the fellowship of the craft, which no amount of enthusiasm for yachting, cruising, and so on can give, since one is only the amusement of life and the other is life itself.

Marlow (at least I think that is how he spelt his name) told the story, or rather the chronicle, of a voyage:—

"Yes, I have seen a little of the Eastern seas; but what I remember best is my first voyage there. You fellows know there are those voyages that seem ordered for the illustration of life, that might stand for a symbol of existence. You fight, work, sweat, nearly kill yourself, sometimes do kill yourself, trying to accomplish something—and you can't. Not from any fault of yours. You simply can do nothing, neither great nor little—not a thing in the world—not even marry an old maid, or get a wretched 600-ton cargo of coal to its port of destination.

"It was altogether a memorable affair. It was my first voyage to the East, and my first voyage as second mate; it was also my skipper's first command.* You'll admit it was time. He was sixty if a day; a little man, with a broad, not very straight back, with bowed shoulders and one leg more bandy than the other, he had that queer twisted-about appearance you see so often in men who work in the fields. He had a nut-cracker face—chin and nose trying to come together over a sunken mouth—and it was framed in iron-grey fluffy hair, that looked like a chin-strap of cotton-wool sprinkled with coal-dust. And he had blue eyes in that old face of his, which were amazingly like a boy's, with that candid expression some quite common men preserve to the end of their days by a rare internal gift of simplicity of heart and rectitude of soul. What induced him to accept me was a wonder. I had come out of a crack Australian clipper, where I had been third officer, and he seemed to have a prejudice against crack clippers as aristocratic and high-toned. He said to me, 'You know, in this ship you will have to work.' I said I had to work in every ship I had ever been in. 'Ah, but this is different, and you gentlemen out of them big ships; . . . but there! I daresay you will do. Join tomorrow.'

"I joined tomorrow. It was twenty-two years ago; and I was just twenty.* How time passes! It was one of the happiest days of my life. Fancy! Second mate for the first time—a really responsible officer! I wouldn't have thrown up my new billet for a fortune. The mate looked me over carefully. He was also an old chap, but of another stamp. He had a Roman nose, a snow-white, long beard, and his name was Mahon, but he insisted that it should be pronounced Mann. He was well connected; yet there was something wrong with his luck, and he had never got on.

"As to the captain, he had been for years in coasters, then in the Mediterranean, and last in the West Indian trade. He had never been round the Capes. He could just write a kind of sketchy hand, and didn't care for writing at all. Both were thorough good seamen of course, and between those two old chaps I felt like a small boy between two grandfathers.

"The ship also was old. Her name was the *Judea*. Queer name, isn't it? She belonged to a man Wilmer, Wilcox—some name like that; but he has been bankrupt and dead these twenty years or more, and his name don't matter. She had been laid up in Shadwell basin for ever so long. You may imagine her state. She was all rust, dust, grime—soot aloft, dirt on deck. To me it was like coming out of a palace into a ruined cottage. She was about 400 tons, had a primitive windlass, wooden latches to the doors, not a bit of brass about her, and a big square stern. There was on it, below her name in big letters, a lot of scrollwork, with the gilt off, and some sort of a coat of arms, with the motto 'Do or Die' underneath.* I remember it took my fancy immensely. There was a touch of romance in it, something that made me love the old thing—something that appealed to my youth!

"We left London in ballast—sand ballast—to load a cargo of coal in a northern port for Bankok. Bankok! I thrilled. I had been six years at sea, but had only seen Melbourne and Sydney, very good places, charming places in their way—but Bankok!

"We worked out of the Thames under canvas, with a North Sea pilot on board. His name was Jermyn, and he dodged all day long about the galley drying his handkerchief before the stove. Apparently he never slept. He was a dismal man, with a perpetual tear sparkling at the end of his nose, who either had been in trouble, or was in trouble, or expected to be in trouble—couldn't be happy unless something went wrong. He mistrusted my youth, my common-sense, and my seamanship, and made a point of showing it in a hundred little ways. I daresay he was right. It seems to me I knew very little then, and I know not much more now; but I cherish a hate for that Jermyn to this day.

"We were a week working up as far as Yarmouth Roads, and then we got into a gale—the famous October gale of twenty-two years ago. It was wind, lightning, sleet, snow, and a terrific sea. We were flying light, and you may imagine how bad it was when I tell you we had smashed bulwarks and a flooded deck. On the second night she shifted her ballast into the lee bow, and by that time we had been blown off somewhere on the Dogger Bank. There was nothing for it but go below with shovels and try to right her, and there we were in that vast hold, gloomy like a cavern, the tallow dips stuck and flickering on the beams, the gale howling above, the ship tossing about like mad on her side; there we all were, Jermyn, the captain, every one, hardly able to keep our feet, engaged on that gravedigger's work, and trying to toss shovelfuls of wet sand up to windward. At every tumble of the ship you could see vaguely in the dim light men falling down with a great flourish of shovels. One of the ship's boys (we had two), impressed by the weirdness of the scene, wept as if his heart would break. We could hear him blubbering somewhere in the shadows.

"On the third day the gale died out, and by-and-by a north-country tug picked us up. We took sixteen days in all to get from London to the Tyne! When we got into dock we had lost our turn for loading, and they hauled us off to a tier where we remained for a month. Mrs Beard (the captain's name was Beard) came from Colchester to see the old man. She lived on board. The crew of runners had left, and there remained only the officers, one boy, and the steward, a mulatto who answered to the name of Abraham.* Mrs Beard was an old woman, with a face all wrinkled and ruddy like a winter apple, and the figure of a young girl. She caught sight of me once, sewing on a button, and insisted on having my shirts to repair. This was something different from the captains' wives I had known on board crack clippers. When I brought her the shirts, she said: 'And the socks? They want mending, I am sure, and John's— Captain Beard's—things are all in order now. I would be glad of something to do.' Bless the old woman. She overhauled my outfit for me, and meantime I read for the first time *Sartor Resartus* and Burnaby's *Ride to Khiva*.* I didn't understand much of the first then; but I remember I preferred the soldier to the philosopher at the time; a preference which life has only confirmed. One was a man, and the other was either more—or less. However, they are both dead, and Mrs Beard is dead, and youth, strength, genius, thoughts, achievements, simple hearts—all dies. . . . No matter.

"They loaded us at last. We shipped a crew. Eight able seamen and two boys. We hauled off one evening to the buoys at the dock-gates, ready to go out, and with a fair prospect of beginning the voyage next day. Mrs Beard was to start for home by a late train. When the ship was fast we went to tea. We sat rather silent through the meal— Mahon, the old couple, and I. I finished first, and slipped away for a smoke, my cabin being in a deck-house just against the poop. It was high water, blowing fresh with a drizzle; the double dock-gates were opened, and the steam-colliers were going in and out in the darkness with their lights burning bright, a great plashing of propellers, rattling of winches, and a lot of hailing on the pier-heads. I watched the procession of head-lights gliding high and of green lights gliding low in the night, when suddenly a red gleam flashed at me, vanished, came into view again, and remained.* The fore-end of a steamer loomed up close. I shouted down the cabin, 'Come up, quick!' and then heard a startled voice saying afar in the dark, 'Stop her, sir.' A bell jingled. Another voice cried warningly, 'We are going right into that barque, sir.' The answer to this was a gruff 'All right,' and the next thing was a heavy crash as the steamer struck a glancing blow with the bluff of her bow about our fore-rigging. There was a moment of confusion, yelling, and running about. Steam roared. Then somebody was heard saying, 'All clear, sir.' . . . 'Are you all right?' asked the gruff voice. I had jumped forward to see the damage, and hailed back, 'I think so.' 'Easy astern,' said the gruff voice. A bell jingled. 'What steamer is that?' screamed Mahon. By that time she was no more to us than a bulky shadow manœuvring a little way off. They shouted at us some name—a woman's name, Miranda or Melissa—or some such thing. 'This means another month in this beastly hole,' said Mahon to me, as we peered with lamps about the splintered bulwarks and broken braces. 'But where's the captain?'

"We had not heard or seen anything of him all that time. We went aft to look. A doleful voice arose hailing somewhere in the middle of the dock, '*Judea* ahoy!' . . . How the devil did he get there? . . . 'Hallo!' we shouted. 'I am adrift in our boat without oars,' he cried. A belated waterman offered his services, and Mahon struck a bargain with him for half-a-crown to tow our skipper alongside; but it was Mrs Beard that came up the ladder first. They had been floating about the dock in that mizzly cold rain for nearly an hour. I was never so surprised in my life.

"It appears that when he heard my shout 'Come up' he understood at once what was the matter, caught up his wife, ran on deck, and across, and down into our boat, which was fast to the ladder. Not bad for a sixty-year-old. Just imagine that old fellow saving heroically in his arms that old woman—the woman of his life. He set her down on a thwart, and was ready to climb back on board when the painter came adrift somehow, and away they went together. Of course in the confusion we did not hear him shouting. He looked abashed. She said cheerfully, 'I suppose it does not matter my losing the train now?' 'No, Jenny—you go below and get warm,' he growled. Then to us: 'A sailor has no business with a wife—I say.* There I was, out of the ship. Well, no harm done this time. Let's go and look at what that fool of a steamer smashed.'

"It wasn't much, but it delayed us three weeks. At the end of that time, the captain being engaged with his agents, I carried Mrs Beard's bag to the railway-station and put her all comfy into a third-class carriage. She lowered the window to say, 'You are a good young man. If you see John—Captain Beard—without his muffler at night, just remind him from me to keep his throat well wrapped up.' 'Certainly, Mrs Beard,' I said. 'You are a good young man; I noticed how attentive you are to John—to Captain——' The train pulled out suddenly; I took my cap off to the old woman: I never saw her again. . . . Pass the bottle.

"We went to sea next day. When we made that start for Bankok we had been already three months out of London. We had expected to be a fortnight or so—at the outside.

"It was January, and the weather was beautiful—the beautiful sunny winter weather that has more charm than in the summer-time, because it is unexpected, and crisp, and you know it won't, it can't, last long. It's like a windfall, like a godsend, like an unexpected piece of luck.

"It lasted all down the North Sea, all down Channel; and it lasted till we were three hundred miles or so to the westward of the Lizards: then the wind went round to the sou'west and began to pipe up. In two days it blew a gale. The *Judea*, hove to, wallowed on the Atlantic like an old candle-box. It blew day after day: it blew with spite, without interval, without mercy, without rest. The world was nothing but an immensity of great foaming waves rushing at us, under a sky low enough to touch with the hand and dirty like a smoked ceiling. In the stormy space surrounding us there was as much flying spray as air. Day after day and night after night there was nothing round the ship but the howl of the wind, the tumult of the sea, the noise of water pouring over her deck. There was no rest for her and no rest for us. She tossed, she pitched, she stood on her head, she sat on her tail, she rolled, she groaned, and we had to hold on while on deck and cling to our bunks when below, in a constant effort of body and worry of mind.

"One night Mahon spoke through the small window of my berth. It opened right into my very bed, and I was lying there sleepless, in my boots, feeling as though I had not slept for years, and could not if I tried. He said excitedly—

"'You got the sounding-rod in here, Marlow? I can't get the pumps to suck. By God! it's no child's play.'

"I gave him the sounding-rod and lay down again, trying to think of various things—but I thought only of the pumps. When I came on deck they were still at it, and my watch relieved at the pumps. By the light of the lantern brought on deck to examine the sounding-rod I caught a glimpse of their weary, serious faces. We pumped all the four hours. We pumped all night, all day, all the week—watch and watch. She was working herself loose, and leaked badly—not enough to drown us at once, but enough to kill us with the work at the pumps. And while we pumped the ship was going from us piecemeal: the bulwarks went, the stanchions were torn out, the ventilators smashed, the cabin-door burst in. There was not a dry spot in the ship. She was being gutted bit by bit. The long-boat changed, as if by magic, into matchwood where she stood in her gripes. I had lashed her myself, and was rather proud of my handi-work, which had withstood so long the malice of the sea. And we pumped. And there was no break in the weather. The sea was white like a sheet of foam, like a caldron of boiling milk; there was not a break in the clouds, no—not the size of a man's hand—no, not for so much as ten seconds. There was for us no sky, there were for us no stars, no sun, no universe—nothing but angry clouds and an infuri-ated sea. We pumped watch and watch, for dear life; and it seemed to last for months, for years, for all eternity, as though we had been dead and gone to a hell for sailors. We forgot the day of the week, the name of the month, what year it was, and whether we had ever been ashore. The sails blew away, she lay broadside on under a weather-cloth, the ocean poured over her, and we did not care. We turned those handles, and had the eyes of idiots. As soon as we had crawled on deck I used to take a round turn with a rope about the men, the pumps, and the mainmast, and we turned, we turned incessantly, with the water to our waists, to our necks, over our heads. It was all one. We had forgotten how it felt to be dry.

"And there was somewhere in me the thought: By Jove! this is the deuce of an adventure—something you read about; and it is my first voyage as second mate—and I am only twenty—and here I am last-ing it out as well as any of these men, and keeping my chaps up to the mark. I was pleased. I would not have given up the experience for worlds. I had moments of exultation. Whenever the old dismantled craft pitched heavily with her counter high in the air, she seemed to me to throw up, like an appeal, like a defiance, like a cry to the clouds without mercy, the words written on her stern: '*Judea*, London. Do or Die.'

"O youth! The strength of it, the faith of it, the imagination of it! To me she was not an old rattle-trap carting about the world a lot of coal for a freight—to me she was the endeavour, the test, the trial of life. I think of her with pleasure, with affection, with regret—as you would think of some one dead you have loved. I shall never forget her. . . . Pass the bottle.

"One night when tied to the mast, as I explained, we were pumping on, deafened with the wind, and without spirit enough in us to wish ourselves dead, a heavy sea crashed aboard and swept clean over us. As soon as I got my breath I shouted, as in duty bound, 'Keep on, boys!' when suddenly I felt something hard floating on deck strike the calf of my leg. I made a grab at it and missed. It was so dark we could not see each other's faces within a foot—you understand.

"After that thump the ship kept quiet for a while, and the thing, whatever it was, struck my leg again. This time I caught it—and it was a sauce-pan. At first, being stupid with fatigue and thinking of nothing but the pumps, I did not understand what I had in my hand. Suddenly it dawned upon me, and I shouted, 'Boys, the house on deck is gone. Leave this, and let's look for the cook.'

"There was a deck-house forward, which contained the galley, the cook's berth, and the quarters of the crew. As we had expected for days to see it swept away, the hands had been ordered to sleep in the cabin—the only safe place in the ship. The steward, Abraham, however, persisted in clinging to his berth, stupidly, like a mule—from sheer fright I believe, like an animal that won't leave a stable falling in an earthquake. So we went to look for him. It was chancing death, since once out of our lashings we were as exposed as if on a raft. But we went. The house was shattered as if a shell had exploded inside. Most of it had gone overboard—stove, men's quarters, and their property, all was gone; but two posts, holding a portion of the bulkhead to which Abraham's bunk was attached, remained as if by a miracle. We groped in the ruins and came upon this, and there he was, sitting in his bunk, surrounded by foam and wreckage, jabbering cheerfully to himself. He was out of his mind; completely and for ever mad, with this sudden shock coming upon the fag-end of his endurance. We snatched him up, lugged him aft, and pitched him head-first down the cabin companion. You understand there was no time to carry him down with infinite precautions and wait to see how he got on. Those below would pick him up at the bottom of the stairs all right. We were in a hurry to go back to the pumps. That business could not wait. A bad leak is an inhuman thing.

"One would think that the sole purpose of that fiendish gale had been to make a lunatic of that poor devil of a mulatto. It eased before morning, and next day the sky cleared, and as the sea went down the leak took up. When it came to bending a fresh set of sails the crew demanded to put back—and really there was nothing else to do. Boats gone, decks swept clean, cabin gutted, men without a stitch but what they stood in, stores spoiled, ship strained. We put her head for home, and—would you believe it? The wind came east right in our teeth. It blew fresh, it blew continuously. We had to beat up every inch of the way, but she did not leak so badly, the water keeping comparatively smooth. Two hours' pumping in every four is no joke—but it kept her afloat as far as Falmouth.

"The good people there live on casualties of the sea, and no doubt were glad to see us. A hungry crowd of shipwrights sharpened their chisels at the sight of that carcass of a ship. And, by Jove! they had pretty pickings off us before they were done. I fancy the owner was already in a tight place. There were delays. Then it was decided to take part of the cargo out and caulk her topsides. This was done, the repairs finished, cargo reshipped; a new crew came on board, and we went out—for Bankok. At the end of a week we were back again. The crew said they weren't going to Bankok—a hundred and fifty days' passage—in a something hooker that wanted pumping eight hours out of the twenty-four; and the nautical papers inserted again the little paragraph: '*Judea*. Barque. Tyne to Bankok; coals; put back to Falmouth leaky and with crew refusing duty.'

"There were more delays—more tinkering. The owner came down for a day, and said she was as right as a little fiddle. Poor old Captain Beard looked like the ghost of a Geordie skipper—through the worry and humiliation of it. Remember he was sixty, and it was his first command. Mahon said it was a foolish business, and would end badly. I loved the ship more than ever, and wanted awfully to get to Bankok. To Bankok! Magic name, blessed name. Mesopotamia* wasn't a patch on it. Remember I was twenty, and it was my first second mate's billet, and the East was waiting for me.

"We went out and anchored in the outer roads with a fresh crew— the third. She leaked worse than ever. It was as if those confounded shipwrights had actually made a hole in her. This time we did not even go outside. The crew simply refused to man the windlass.

"They towed us back to the inner harbour, and we became a fixture, a feature, an institution of the place. People pointed us out to visitors as 'That 'ere barque that's going to Bankok—has been here

six months—put back three times.' On holidays the small boys pulling about in boats would hail, '*Judea*, ahoy!' and if a head showed
above the rail shouted, 'Where you bound to?—Bankok?' and jeered.
We were only three on board. The poor old skipper mooned in the
cabin. Mahon undertook the cooking, and unexpectedly developed
all a Frenchman's genius for preparing nice little messes. I looked
languidly after the rigging. We became citizens of Falmouth. Every
shopkeeper knew us. At the barber's or tobacconist's they asked
familiarly, 'Do you think you will ever get to Bankok?' Meantime the
owner, the underwriters, and the charterers squabbled amongst
themselves in London, and our pay went on. . . . Pass the bottle.

"It was horrid. Morally it was worse than pumping for life. It
seemed as though we had been forgotten by the world, belonged to
nobody, would get nowhere; it seemed that, as if bewitched, we
would have to live for ever and ever in that inner harbour, a derision
and a byword to generations of long-shore loafers and dishonest
boatmen. I obtained three months' pay and a five days' leave, and
made a rush for London. It took me a day to get there and pretty well
another to come back—but three months' pay went all the same. I
don't know what I did with it. I went to a music-hall, I believe,
lunched, dined, and supped in a swell place in Regent Street, and
was back to time, with nothing but a complete set of Byron's works
and a new railway rug to show for three months' work. The boatman
who pulled me off to the ship said: 'Hallo! I thought you had left the
old thing. *She* will never get to Bankok.' 'That's all *you* know about
it,' I said, scornfully—but I didn't like that prophecy at all.

"Suddenly a man, some kind of agent to somebody, appeared with
full powers. He had grog-blossoms all over his face, an indomitable
energy, and was a jolly soul. We leaped into life again. A hulk came
alongside, took our cargo, and then we went into dry dock to get our
copper stripped. No wonder she leaked. The poor thing, strained
beyond endurance by the gale, had, as if in disgust, spat out all the
oakum of her lower seams. She was recaulked, new coppered, and
made as tight as a bottle. We went back to the hulk and reshipped our
cargo.

"Then, on a fine moonlight night, all the rats left the ship.

"We had been infested with them. They had destroyed our sails,
consumed more stores than the crew, affably shared our beds and our
dangers, and now, when the ship was made seaworthy, concluded to

clear out.* I called Mahon to enjoy the spectacle. Rat after rat appeared on our rail, took a last look over his shoulder, and leaped with a hollow thud into the empty hulk. We tried to count them, but soon lost the tale. Mahon said: 'Well, well! don't talk to me about the intelligence of rats. They ought to have left before, when we had that narrow squeak from foundering. There you have the proof how silly is the superstition about them.* They leave a good ship for an old rotten hulk, where there is nothing to eat, too, the fools! . . . I don't believe they know what is safe or what is good for them, any more than you or I.'

"And after some more talk we agreed that the wisdom of rats had been grossly overrated, being in fact no greater than that of men.

"The story of the ship was known, by this, all up the Channel from Land's End to the Forelands, and we could get no crew on the south coast. They sent us one all complete from Liverpool, and we left once more—for Bankok.

"We had fair breezes, smooth water right into the tropics, and the old *Judea* lumbered along in the sunshine. When she went eight knots everything cracked aloft, and we tied our caps to our heads; but mostly she strolled on at the rate of three miles an hour. What could you expect? She was tired—that old ship. Her youth was where mine is—where yours is—you fellows who listen to this yarn; and what friend would throw your years and your weariness in your face? We didn't grumble at her. To us aft, at least, it seemed as though we had been born in her, reared in her, had lived in her for ages, had never known any other ship. I would just as soon have abused the old village church at home for not being a cathedral.

"And for me there was also my youth to make me patient. There was all the East before me, and all life, and the thought that I had been tried in that ship and had come out pretty well. And I thought of men of old who, centuries ago, went that road in ships that sailed no better, to the land of palms, and spices, and yellow sands, and of brown nations ruled by kings more cruel than Nero the Roman and more splendid than Solomon the Jew. The old bark lumbered on, heavy with her age and the burden of her cargo, while I lived the life of youth in ignorance and hope. She lumbered on through an interminable procession of days; and the fresh gilding flashed back at the setting sun, seemed to cry out over the darkening sea the words painted on her stern, '*Judea*, London. Do or Die.'

"Then we entered the Indian Ocean and steered northerly for Java Head. The winds were light. Weeks slipped by. She crawled on, do or die, and people at home began to think of posting us as overdue.

"One Saturday evening, I being off duty, the men asked me to give them an extra bucket of water or so—for washing clothes. As I did not wish to screw on the fresh-water pump so late, I went forward whistling, and with a key in my hand to unlock the forepeak scuttle, intending to serve the water out of a spare tank we kept there.

"The smell down below was as unexpected as it was frightful. One would have thought hundreds of paraffin-lamps had been flaring and smoking in that hole for days. I was glad to get out. The man with me coughed and said, 'Funny smell, sir.' I answered negligently, 'It's good for the health they say,' and walked aft.

"The first thing I did was to put my head down the square of the midship ventilator. As I lifted the lid a visible breath, something like a thin fog, a puff of faint haze, rose from the opening. The ascending air was hot, and had a heavy, sooty, paraffiny smell. I gave one sniff, and put down the lid gently. It was no use choking myself. The cargo was on fire.*

"Next day she began to smoke in earnest. You see it was to be expected, for though the coal was of a safe kind, that cargo had been so handled, so broken up with handling, that it looked more like smithy coal than anything else.* Then it had been wetted—more than once. It rained all the time we were taking it back from the hulk, and now with this long passage it got heated, and there was another case of spontaneous combustion.

"The captain called us into the cabin. He had a chart spread on the table, and looked unhappy. He said, 'The coast of West Australia is near, but I mean to proceed to our destination. It is the hurricane month too; but we will just keep her head for Baṇkok, and fight the fire. No more putting back anywhere, if we all get roasted. We will try first to stifle this 'ere damned combustion by want of air.'*

"We tried. We battened down everything, and still she smoked. The smoke kept coming out through imperceptible crevices; it forced itself through bulkheads and covers; it oozed here and there and everywhere in slender threads, in an invisible film, in an incomprehensible manner. It made its way into the cabin, into the forecastle; it poisoned the sheltered places on the deck, it could be sniffed as high as the mainyard. It was clear that if the smoke came out the air came in. This was disheartening. This combustion refused to be stifled.

"We resolved to try water, and took the hatches off. Enormous volumes of smoke, whitish, yellowish, thick, greasy, misty, choking, ascended as high as the trucks. All hands cleared out aft. Then the poisonous cloud blew away, and we went back to work in a smoke that was no thicker now than that of an ordinary factory chimney.

"We rigged the force-pump, got the hose along, and by-and-by it burst. Well, it was as old as the ship—a prehistoric hose, and past repair. Then we pumped with the feeble head-pump, drew water with buckets, and in this way managed in time to pour lots of Indian Ocean into the main hatch. The bright stream flashed in sunshine, fell into a layer of white crawling smoke, and vanished on the black surface of coal. Steam ascended mingling with the smoke. We poured salt water as into a barrel without a bottom. It was our fate to pump in that ship, to pump out of her, to pump into her; and after keeping water out of her to save ourselves from being drowned, we frantically poured water into her to save ourselves from being burnt.

"And she crawled on, do or die, in the serene weather. The sky was a miracle of purity, a miracle of azure. The sea was polished, was blue, was pellucid, was sparkling like a precious stone, extending on all sides, all round to the horizon—as if the whole terrestrial globe had been one jewel, one colossal sapphire, a single gem fashioned into a planet. And on the lustre of the great calm waters the *Judea* glided imperceptibly, enveloped in languid and unclean vapours, in a lazy cloud that drifted to leeward, light and slow: a pestiferous cloud defiling the splendour of sea and sky.*

"All this time of course we saw no fire. The cargo smouldered at the bottom somewhere. Once Mahon, as we were working side by side, said to me with a queer smile: 'Now, if she only would spring a tidy leak—like that time when we first left the Channel—it would put a stopper on this fire. Wouldn't it?' I remarked irrelevantly, 'Do you remember the rats?'

"We fought the fire and sailed the ship too as carefully as though nothing had been the matter. The steward cooked and attended on us. Of the other twelve men, eight worked while four rested. Every one took his turn, captain included. There was equality, and if not exactly fraternity, then a deal of good feeling. Sometimes a man, as he dashed a bucketful of water down the hatchway, would yell out,

'Hurrah for Bankok!' and the rest laughed. But generally we were taciturn and serious—and thirsty. Oh! how thirsty! And we had to be careful with the water. Strict allowance. The ship smoked, the sun blazed. . . . Pass the bottle.

"We tried everything. We even made an attempt to dig down to the fire. No good, of course. No man could remain more than a minute below. Mahon, who went first, fainted there, and the man who went to fetch him out did likewise. We lugged them out on deck. Then I leaped down to show how easily it could be done. They had learned wisdom by that time, and contented themselves by fishing for me with a chain-hook tied to a broom-handle, I believe. I did not offer to go and fetch up my shovel, which was left down below.

"Things began to look bad. We put the long-boat into the water. The second boat was ready to swing out. We had also another, a 14-foot thing, on davits aft, where it was quite safe.

"Then, behold, the smoke suddenly decreased. We redoubled our efforts to flood the bottom of the ship. In two days there was no smoke at all. Everybody was on the broad grin. This was on a Friday. On Saturday no work, but sailing the ship of course, was done. The men washed their clothes and their faces for the first time in a fortnight, and had a special dinner given them. They spoke of spontaneous combustion with contempt, and implied *they* were the boys to put out combustions. Somehow we all felt as though we each had inherited a large fortune. But a beastly smell of burning hung about the ship. Captain Beard had hollow eyes and sunken cheeks. I had never noticed so much before how twisted and bowed he was. He and Mahon prowled soberly about hatches and ventilators, sniffing. It struck me suddenly poor Mahon was a very, very old chap. As to me, I was as pleased and proud as though I had helped to win a great naval battle. O! Youth!

"The night was fine. In the morning a homeward-bound ship passed us hull down,—the first we had seen for months; but we were nearing the land at last, Java Head being about 190 miles off, and nearly due north.

"Next day it was my watch on deck from eight to twelve. At breakfast the captain observed, 'It's wonderful how that smell hangs about the cabin.' About ten, the mate being on the poop, I stepped down on the main-deck for a moment. The carpenter's bench stood abaft the mainmast: I leaned against it sucking at my pipe, and the carpenter, a young chap, came to talk to me. He remarked, 'I think we have done very well, haven't we?' and then I perceived with annoyance the fool was trying to tilt the bench. I said curtly, 'Don't, Chips,' and immediately became aware of a queer sensation, of an absurd delusion,—I seemed somehow to be in the air. I heard all round me like* a pent-up breath released—as if a thousand giants simultaneously had said Phoo!—and felt a dull concussion which made my ribs ache suddenly. No doubt about it—I was in the air, and my body was describing a short parabola. But short as it was, I had the time to think several thoughts in, as far as I can remember, the following order: 'This can't be the carpenter—What is it?—Some accident—Submarine volcano?—Coals, gas!—By Jove! we are being blown up—Everybody's dead—I am falling into the after-hatch—I see fire in it.'

"The coal-dust suspended in the air of the hold had glowed dull-red at the moment of the explosion.* In the twinkling of an eye, in an infinitesimal fraction of a second since the first tilt of the bench, I was sprawling full length on the cargo.* I picked myself up and scrambled out. It was quick like a rebound. The deck was a wilderness of smashed timber, lying crosswise like trees in a wood after a hurricane; an immense curtain of soiled rags waved gently before me—it was the mainsail blown to strips. I thought, The masts will be toppling over directly; and to get out of the way bolted on all-fours towards the poop-ladder. The first person I saw was Mahon, with eyes like saucers, his mouth open, and the long white hair standing straight on end round his head like a silver halo. He was just about to go down when the sight of the main-deck stirring, heaving up, and changing into splinters before his eyes, petrified him on the top step. I stared at him in unbelief, and he stared at me with a queer kind of shocked curiosity. I did not know that I had no hair, no eyebrows, no eyelashes, that my young moustache was burnt off, that my face was black, one cheek laid open, my nose cut, and my chin bleeding. I had lost my cap, one of my slippers, and my shirt was torn to rags. Of all this I was not aware. I was amazed to see the ship still afloat, the poop-deck whole—and, most of all, to see anybody alive. Also the peace of the sky and the serenity of the sea were distinctly surprising. I suppose I expected to see them convulsed with horror. . . . Pass the bottle.

"There was a voice hailing the ship from somewhere—in the air, in the sky—I couldn't tell. Presently I saw the captain—and he was mad. He asked me eagerly, 'Where's the cabin-table?' and to hear such a question was a frightful shock. I had just been blown up, you understand, and vibrated with that experience,—I wasn't quite sure whether I was alive. Mahon began to stamp with both feet and yelled at him, 'Good God! don't you see the deck's blown out of her?' I found my voice, and stammered out as if conscious of some gross neglect of duty, 'I don't know where the cabin-table is.' It was like an absurd dream.

"Do you know what he wanted next? Well, he wanted to trim the yards. Very placidly, and as if lost in thought, he insisted on having the foreyard squared. 'I don't know if there's anybody alive,' said Mahon, almost tearfully. 'Surely,' he said, gently, 'there will be enough left to square the foreyard.'

"The old chap, it seems, was in his own berth, winding up the chronometers, when the shock sent him spinning. Immediately it occurred to him—as he said afterwards—that the ship had struck something, and he ran out into the cabin. There, he saw, the cabin-table had vanished somewhere. The deck being blown up, it had fallen down into the lazarette of course. Where we had our breakfast that morning he saw only a great hole in the floor. This appeared to him so awfully mysterious, and impressed him so immensely, that what he saw and heard after he got on deck were mere trifles in comparison. And, mark, he noticed directly the wheel deserted and his barque off her course—and his only thought was to get that miserable, stripped, undecked, smouldering shell of a ship back again with her head pointing at her port of destination. Bankok! That's what he was after. I tell you this quiet, bowed, bandy-legged, almost deformed little man was immense in the singleness of his idea and in his placid ignorance of our agitation. He motioned us forward with a commanding gesture, and went to take the wheel himself.

"Yes; that was the first thing we did—trim the yards of that wreck! No one was killed, or even disabled, but every one was more or less hurt. You should have seen them! Some were in rags, with black faces, like coalheavers, like sweeps, and had bullet heads that seemed closely cropped, but were in fact singed to the skin. Others, of the watch below, awakened by being shot out from their collapsing bunks, shivered incessantly, and kept on groaning even as we went about our work. But they all worked. That crew of Liverpool hard cases had in them the right stuff. It's my experience they always have. It is the sea that gives it—the vastness, the loneliness surrounding their dark stolid souls. Ah! Well! we stumbled, we crept, we fell, we barked our shins on the wreckage, we hauled. The masts stood, but we did not know how much they might be charred down below. It was nearly calm, but a long swell ran from the west and made her roll. They might go at any moment. We looked at them with apprehension. One could not foresee which way they would fall.

"Then we retreated aft and looked about us. The deck was a tangle of planks on edge, of planks on end, of splinters, of ruined woodwork. The masts rose from that chaos like big trees above a matted undergrowth. The interstices of that mass of wreckage were full of something whitish, sluggish, stirring—of something that was like a greasy fog. The smoke of the invisible fire was coming up again, was trailing, like a poisonous thick mist in some valley choked with dead wood. Already lazy wisps were beginning to curl upwards amongst the mass of splinters. Here and there a piece of timber, stuck upright, resembled a post. Half of a fife-rail had been shot through the foresail, and the sky made a patch of glorious blue in the ignobly soiled canvas. A portion of several boards holding together had fallen across the rail, and one end protruded overboard, like a gangway leading upon nothing, like a gangway leading over the deep sea, leading to death—as if inviting us to walk the plank at once and be done with our ridiculous troubles.* And still the air, the sky—a ghost, something invisible was hailing the ship.

"Some one had the sense to look over, and there was the helmsman, who had impulsively jumped overboard, anxious to come back. He yelled and swam lustily like a merman, keeping up with the ship. We threw him a rope, and presently he stood amongst us streaming with water and very crestfallen. The captain had surrendered the wheel, and apart, elbow on rail and chin in hand, gazed at the sea wistfully. We asked ourselves, What next? I thought, Now, this is something like. This is great. I wonder what will happen. O youth!*

"Suddenly Mahon sighted a steamer far astern. Captain Beard said, 'We may do something with her yet.' We hoisted two flags, which said in the international language of the sea, 'On fire. Want immediate assistance.' The steamer grew bigger rapidly, and by-and-by spoke with two flags on her foremast, 'I am coming to your assistance.'

"In half an hour she was abreast, to windward, within hail, and rolling slightly, with her engines stopped. We lost our composure, and yelled all together with excitement, 'We've been blown up.' A man in a white helmet, on the bridge, cried, 'Yes! All right! all right!' and he nodded his head, and smiled, and made soothing motions with his hand as thought at a lot of frightened children. One of the boats dropped in the water, and walked towards us upon the sea with her long oars. Four Calashes pulled a swinging stroke. This was my first sight of Malay seamen. I've known them since, but what struck me then was their unconcern: they came alongside, and even the bowman standing up and holding to our main-chains with the boat-hook did not deign to lift his head for a glance. I thought people who had been blown up deserved more attention.

"A little man, dry like a chip and agile like a monkey, clambered up. It was the mate of the steamer. He gave one look, and cried, 'O boys—you had better quit.'

"We were silent. He talked apart with the captain for a time,—seemed to argue with him. Then they went away together to the steamer.

"When our skipper came back we learned that the steamer was the *Sommerville*, Captain Nash, from West Australia to Singapore *viâ* Batavia with mails, and that the agreement was she should tow us to Anjer or Batavia, if possible, where we could extinguish the fire by scuttling, and then proceed on our voyage—to Bankok! The old man seemed excited. 'We will do it yet,' he said to Mahon, fiercely. He shook his fist at the sky. Nobody else said a word.

"At noon the steamer began to tow. She went ahead slim and high, and what was left of the *Judea* followed at the end of seventy fathom of tow-rope,—followed her swiftly like a cloud of smoke with mast-heads protruding above. We went aloft to furl the sails. We coughed on the yards, and were careful about the bunts. Do you see the lot of us there, putting a neat furl on the sails of that ship doomed to arrive nowhere? There was not a man who didn't think that at any moment the masts would topple over. From aloft we could not see the ship for smoke, and they worked carefully, passing the gaskets with even turns. 'Harbour furl—aloft there!' cried Mahon from below.

"You understand this? I don't think one of those chaps expected to get down in the usual way. When we did I heard them saying to each other, 'Well, I thought we would come down overboard, in a lump—sticks and all—blame me if I didn't.' 'That's what I was thinking to myself,' would answer wearily another battered and bandaged scarecrow. And, mind, these were men without the drilled-in habit of obedience. To an onlooker they would be a lot of profane scallywags without a redeeming point. What made them do it—what made them obey me when I, thinking consciously how fine it was, made them drop the bunt of the foresail twice to try and do it better? What? They had no professional reputation—no examples, no praise. It wasn't a sense of duty; they all knew well enough how to shirk, and laze, and dodge—when they had a mind to it—and mostly they had. Was it the two pounds ten a month that sent them there? They didn't think their pay half good enough. No; it was something in them, something inborn and subtle and everlasting. I don't say positively that the crew of a French or German merchantman wouldn't have done it, but I doubt whether it would have been done in the same way.* There was a completeness in it, something solid like a principle, and masterful like an instinct—a disclosure of something secret—of that hidden something, that gift of good or evil that makes racial difference, that shapes the fate of nations.

"It was that night at ten that, for the first time since we had been fighting it, we saw the fire. The speed of the towing had fanned the smouldering destruction. A blue gleam appeared forward, shining below the wreck of the deck. It wavered in patches, it seemed to stir and creep like the light of a glowworm. I saw it first, and told Mahon. 'Then the game's up,' he said. 'We had better stop this towing, or she will burst out suddenly fore and aft before we can clear out.' We set up a yell; rang bells to attract their attention; they towed on. At last Mahon and I had to crawl forward and cut the rope with an axe. There was no time to cast off the lashings. Red tongues could be seen licking the wilderness of splinters under our feet as we made our way back to the poop.

"Of course they very soon found out in the steamer that the rope was gone. She gave a loud blast of her whistle, her lights were seen sweeping in a wide circle, she came up ranging close alongside, and stopped. We were all in a tight group on the poop looking at her. Every man had saved a little bundle or a bag. Suddenly a conical flame with a twisted top shot up forward and threw upon the black sea a circle of light, with the two vessels side by side and heaving gently in its centre. Captain Beard had been sitting on the gratings still and mute for hours, but now he rose slowly and advanced in front of us, to the mizzen-shrouds. Captain Nash hailed: 'Come along! Look sharp. I have mail-bags on board. I will take you and your boats to Singapore.'

"'Thank you! No!' said our skipper. 'We must see the last of the ship.'

"'I can't stand by any longer,' shouted the other. 'Mails—you know.'

"'Ay! ay! We are all right.'

"'Very well! I'll report you in Singapore. . . . Goodbye!'

"He waved his hand. Our men dropped their bundles quietly. The steamer moved ahead, and passing out of the circle of light, vanished at once from our sight, dazzled by the fire which burned fiercely. And then I knew that I would see the East first as commander of a small boat. I thought it fine; and the fidelity to the old ship was fine. We should see the last of her. Oh the glamour of youth! Oh the fire of it, more dazzling than the flames of the burning ship, throwing a magic light on the wide earth, leaping audaciously to the sky, presently to be quenched by time, more cruel, more pitiless, more bitter than the sea—and like the flames of the burning ship surrounded by an impenetrable night.

"The old man warned us in his gentle and inflexible way that it was part of our duty to save for the underwriters as much as we could of the ship's gear.* Accordingly we went to work aft, while she blazed forward to give us plenty of light. We lugged out a lot of rubbish. What didn't we save? An old barometer fixed with an absurd quantity of screws nearly cost me my life: a sudden rush of smoke came upon me, and I just got away in time. There were various stores, bolts of canvas, coils of rope; the poop looked like a marine bazaar, and the boats were lumbered to the gunwales. One would have thought the old man wanted to take as much as he could of his first command with him. He was very, very quiet, but off his balance evidently. Would you believe it? He wanted to take a length of old stream-cable and a kedge-anchor with him in the long-boat. We said, 'Ay, ay, sir,' deferentially, and on the quiet let the things slip overboard. The heavy medicine-chest went that way, two bags of green coffee, tins of paint—fancy, paint!—a whole lot of things. Then I was ordered with two hands into the boats to make a stowage and get them ready against the time it would be proper for us to leave the ship.

"We put everything straight, stepped the long-boat's mast for our skipper, who was to take charge of her, and I was not sorry to sit down for a moment. My face felt raw, every limb ached as if broken, I was aware of all my ribs, and would have sworn to a twist in the backbone. The boats, fast astern, lay in a deep shadow, and all around I could see the circle of the sea lighted by the fire. A gigantic flame rose forward straight and clear. It flared fierce, with noises like the whirr of wings, with rumbles as of thunder. There were cracks, detonations, and from the cone of flame the sparks flew upwards, as man is born to trouble,* to leaky ships, and to ships that burn.

"What bothered me was that the ship, lying broadside to the swell and to such wind as there was—a mere breath—the boats would not keep astern where they were safe, but persisted, in a pig-headed way boats have, in getting under the counter and then swinging along-side. They were knocking about dangerously and coming near the flame, while the ship rolled on them, and, of course, there was always the danger of the masts going over the side at any moment. I and my two boat-keepers kept them off as best we could, with oars and boat-hooks; but to be constantly at it became exasperating, since there was no reason why we should not leave at once. We could not see those on board, nor could we imagine what caused the delay. The boat-keepers were swearing feebly, and I had not only my share of the work but also had to keep at it two men who showed a constant inclination to lay themselves down and let things slide.

"At last I hailed, 'On deck there,' and some one looked over. 'We're ready here,' I said. The head disappeared, and very soon popped up again. 'The captain says, All right, sir, and to keep the boats well clear of the ship.'

"Half an hour passed. Suddenly there was a frightful racket, rattle, clanking of chain, hiss of water, and millions of sparks flew up into the shivering column of smoke that stood leaning slightly above the ship. The cat-heads had burned away, and the two red-hot anchors had gone to the bottom, tearing out after them two hundred fathom of red-hot chain. The ship trembled, the mass of flame swayed as if ready to collapse, and the fore top-gallant-mast fell. It darted down like an arrow of fire, shot under, and instantly leaping up within an oar's-length of the boats, floated quietly, very black on the luminous sea. I hailed the deck again. After some time a man in an unexpectedly cheerful but also muffled tone, as though he had been trying to speak with his mouth shut, informed me, 'Coming directly, sir,' and vanished. For a long time I heard nothing but the whirr and roar of the fire. There were also whistling sounds. The boats jumped, tugged at the painters, ran at each other playfully, knocked their sides together, or, do what we would, swung in a bunch against the ship's side. I couldn't stand it any longer, and swarming up a rope, clambered aboard over the stern.

"It was as bright as day. Coming up like this, the sheet of fire facing me, was a terrifying sight, and the heat seemed hardly bearable at first. On a settee cushion dragged out of the cabin, Captain Beard, his legs drawn up and one arm under his head, slept with the light playing on him. Do you know what the rest were busy about? They were sitting on deck right aft, round an open case, eating bread and cheese and drinking bottled stout.

"On the background of flames twisting in fierce tongues above their heads they seemed at home like salamanders, and looked like a band of desperate pirates. The fire sparkled in the whites of their eyes, gleamed on patches of white skin seen through the torn shirts. Each had the marks as of a battle about him—bandaged heads, tied-up arms, a strip of dirty rag round a knee—and each man had a bottle between his legs and a chunk of cheese in his hand. Mahon got up. With his handsome and disreputable head, his hooked profile, his long white beard, and with an uncorked bottle in his hand, he resembled one of those reckless sea-robbers of old making merry amidst violence and disaster. 'The last meal on board,' he explained solemnly. 'We had nothing to eat all day, and it was no use leaving all this.' He flourished the bottle and indicated the sleeping skipper. 'He said he couldn't swallow anything, so I got him to lie down,' he went on; and as I stared, 'I don't know whether you are aware, young fellow, the man had no sleep to speak of for days—and there will be dam' little sleep in the boats.' 'There will be no boats by-and-by if you fool about much longer,' I said, indignantly. I walked up to the skipper and shook him by the shoulder. At last he opened his eyes, but did not move. 'Time to leave her, sir,' I said, quietly.

"He got up painfully, looked at the flames, at the sea sparkling round the ship, and black, black as ink farther away; he looked at the stars shining dim through a thin veil of smoke in a sky black, black as Erebus.

"'Youngest first,' he said.

"And the ordinary seaman, wiping his mouth with the back of his hand, got up, clambered over the taffrail, and vanished. Others followed. One, on the point of going over, stopped short to drain his bottle, and with a great swing of his arm flung it at the fire. 'Take this!' he cried.

"The skipper lingered disconsolately, and we left him to commune alone for a while with his first command. Then I went up again and brought him away at last. It was time. The ironwork on the poop was hot to the touch.

"Then the painter of the long-boat was cut, and the three boats, tied together, drifted clear of the ship. It was just sixteen hours after the explosion when we abandoned her. Mahon had charge of the second boat, and I had the smallest—the 14-foot thing. The long-boat would have taken the lot of us; but the skipper said we must save as much property as we could—for the underwriters—and so I got my first command. I had two men with me, a bag of biscuits, a few tins of meat, and a breaker of water. I was ordered to keep close to the long-boat, that in case of bad weather we might be taken into her.

"And do you know what I thought? I thought I would part company as soon as I could. I wanted to have my first command all to myself. I wasn't going to sail in a squadron if there were a chance for independent cruising. I would make land by myself. I would beat the other boats. Youth! All youth! The silly, charming, beautiful youth.*

"But we did not make a start at once. We must see the last of the ship. And so the boats drifted about that night, heaving and setting on the swell. The men dozed, waked, sighed, groaned. I looked at the burning ship.

"Between the darkness of earth and heaven she was burning fiercely upon a disc of purple sea shot by the blood-red play of gleams; upon a disc of water glittering and sinister. A high, clear flame, an immense and lonely flame, ascended from the ocean, and from its summit the black smoke poured continuously at the sky. She burned furiously, mournful and imposing like a funeral pile kindled in the night, surrounded by the sea, watched over by the stars. A magnificent death had come like a grace, like a gift, like a reward to that old ship at the end of her laborious days. The surrender of her weary ghost to the keeping of stars and sea was stirring like the sight of a glorious triumph. The masts fell just before daybreak, and for a moment there was a burst and turmoil of sparks that seemed to fill with flying fire the night patient and watchful, the vast night lying silent upon the sea. At daylight she was only a charred shell, floating still under a cloud of smoke and bearing a glowing mass of coal within.

"Then the oars were got out, and the boats forming in a line moved round her remains as if in procession—the long-boat leading. As we pulled across her stern a slim dart of fire shot out viciously at us, and suddenly she went down, head first, in a great hiss of steam. The unconsumed stern was the last to sink; but the paint had gone, had cracked, had peeled off, and there were no letters, there was no word, no stubborn device that was like her soul, to flash at the rising sun her creed and her name.

"We made our way north. A breeze sprang up, and about noon all the boats came together for the last time. I had no mast or sail in mine, but I made a mast out of a spare oar and hoisted a boat-awning for a sail, with a boat-hook for a yard. She was certainly over-masted, but I had the satisfaction of knowing that with the wind aft I could beat the other two. I had to wait for them. Then we all had a look at the captain's chart, and, after a sociable meal of hard bread and water, got our last instructions. These were simple: steer north, and keep together as much as possible. 'Be careful with that jury-rig, Marlow,' said the captain; and Mahon, as I sailed proudly past his boat, wrinkled his curved nose and hailed, 'You will sail that ship of yours under water, if you don't look out, young fellow.' He was a malicious old man—and may the deep sea where he sleeps now rock him gently, rock him tenderly to the end of time!

"Before sunset a thick rain-squall passed over the two boats, which were far astern, and that was the last I saw of them for a time. Next day I sat steering my cockle-shell—my first command—with nothing but water and sky around me. I did sight in the afternoon the upper sails of a ship far away, but said nothing, and my men did not notice her. You see I was afraid she might be homeward bound, and I had no mind to turn back from the portals of the East. I was steering for Java—another blessed name—like Bankok, you know. I steered many days.

"I need not tell you what it is to be knocking about in an open boat. I remember nights and days of calm when we pulled, we pulled, and the boat seemed to stand still, as if bewitched within the circle of the sea horizon. I remember the heat, the deluge of rain-squalls that kept us baling for dear life (but filled our water-cask), and I remember sixteen hours on end with a mouth dry as a cinder and a steering-oar over the stern to keep my first command head on to a breaking sea. I did not know how good a man I was till then. I remember the drawn faces, the dejected figures of my two men, and I remember my youth and the feeling that will never come back any more—the feeling that I could last for ever, outlast the sea, the earth, and all men; the deceitful feeling that lures us on to joys, to perils, to love, to vain effort—to death; the triumphant conviction of strength, the heat of life in the handful of dust,* the glow in the heart that with every year grows dim, grows cold, grows small, and expires—and expires, too soon, too soon—before life itself.

"And this is how I see the East. I have seen its secret places and have looked into its very soul; but now I see it always from a small boat, a high outline of mountains, blue and afar in the morning; like faint mist at noon; a jagged wall of purple at sunset. I have the feel of the oar in my hand, the vision of a scorching blue sea in my eyes. And I see a bay, a wide bay, smooth as glass and polished like ice, shimmering in the dark. A red light burns far off upon the gloom of the land, and the night is soft and warm. We drag at the oars with aching arms, and suddenly a puff of wind, a puff faint and tepid and laden with strange odours of blossoms, of aromatic wood, comes out of the still night—the first sigh of the East on my face. That I can never forget. It was impalpable and enslaving, like a charm, like a whispered promise of mysterious delight.

"We had been pulling this finishing spell for eleven hours. Two pulled, and he whose turn it was to rest sat at the tiller. We had made out the red light in that bay and steered for it, guessing it must mark some small coasting port. We passed two vessels, outlandish and high-sterned, sleeping at anchor, and, approaching the light, now very dim, ran the boat's nose against the end of a jutting wharf. We were blind with fatigue. My men dropped the oars and fell off the thwarts as if dead. I made fast to a pile. A current rippled softly. The scented obscurity of the shore was grouped into vast masses, a dens-ity of colossal clumps of vegetation, probably—mute and fantastic shapes. And at their foot the semicircle of a beach gleamed faintly, like an illusion. There was not a light, not a stir, not a sound. The mysterious East faced me, perfumed like a flower, silent like death, dark like a grave.

"And I sat weary beyond expression, exulting like a conqueror, sleepless and entranced as if before a profound, a fateful enigma.

"A splashing of oars, a measured dip reverberating on the level of water, intensified by the silence of the shore into loud claps, made me jump up. A boat, a European boat, was coming in. I invoked the name of the dead; I hailed: *Judea* ahoy! A thin shout answered.

"It was the captain. I had beaten the flagship by three hours, and I was glad to hear the old man's voice again, tremulous and tired. 'Is it you, Marlow?' 'Mind the end of that jetty, sir,' I cried.

"He approached cautiously, and brought up with the deep-sea lead-line which we had saved—for the underwriters. I eased my painter and fell alongside. He sat, a broken figure at the stern, wet with dew, his hands clasped in his lap. His men were asleep already. 'I had a terrible time of it,' he murmured. 'Mahon is behind—not very far.' We conversed in whispers, in low whispers, as if afraid to wake up the land. Guns, thunder, earthquakes would not have awakened the men just then.

"Looking round as we talked, I saw away at sea a bright light travelling in the night. 'There's a steamer passing the bay,' I said. She was not passing, she was entering, and she even came close and anchored. 'I wish,' said the old man, 'you would find out whether she is English. Perhaps they could give us a passage somewhere.' He seemed nervously anxious. So by dint of punching and kicking I started one of my men into a state of somnambulism, and giving him an oar, took another and pulled towards the lights of the steamer.

"There was a murmur of voices in her, metallic hollow clangs of the engine-room, footsteps on the deck. Her ports shone, round like dilated eyes. Shapes moved about, and there was a shadowy man high up on the bridge. He heard my oars.

"And then, before I could open my lips, the East spoke to me, but it was in a Western voice. A torrent of words was poured into the enigmatical, the fateful silence; outlandish, angry words, mixed with words and even whole sentences of good English, less strange but even more surprising. The voice swore and cursed violently; it riddled the solemn peace of the bay by a volley of abuse. It began by calling me Pig, and from that went crescendo into unmentionable adjectives—in English. The man up there raged aloud in two languages, and with a sincerity in his fury that almost convinced me I had, in some way, sinned against the harmony of the universe. I could hardly see him, but began to think he would work himself into a fit.

"Suddenly he ceased, and I could hear him snorting and blowing like a porpoise. I said—

"'What steamer is this, pray?'

"'Eh? What's this? And who are you?'

"'Castaway crew of an English barque burnt at sea. We came here tonight. I am the second mate. The captain is in the long-boat, and wishes to know if you would give us a passage somewhere.'

"'Oh, my goodness! I say. . . . This is the *Celestial* from Singapore on her return trip. I'll arrange with your captain in the morning, . . . and, . . . I say, . . . did you hear me just now?'

"'I should think the whole bay heard you.'

"'I thought you were a shore-boat. Now, look here—this infernal lazy scoundrel of a caretaker has gone to sleep again—curse him. The light is out, and I nearly ran foul of the end of this damned jetty. This is the third time he plays me this trick. Now, I ask you, can anybody stand this kind of thing? It's enough to drive a man out of his mind. I'll report him. . . . I'll get the Assistant Resident to give him the sack, by . . . ! See—there's no light. It's out, isn't it? I take you to witness the light's out. There should be a light, you know. A red light on the——'

"'There was a light,' I said, mildly.

"'But it's out, man! What's the use of talking like this? You can see for yourself it's out—don't you? If you had to take a valuable steamer along this God-forsaken coast you would want a light too. I'll kick him from end to end of his miserable wharf. You'll see if I don't. I will——'

"'So I may tell my captain you'll take us?' I broke in.

"'Yes, I'll take you. Good night,' he said, brusquely.

"I pulled back, made fast again to the jetty, and then went to sleep at last. I had faced the silence of the East. I had heard some of its language. But when I opened my eyes again the silence was as complete as though it had never been broken. I was lying in a flood of light, and the sky had never looked so far, so high, before. I opened my eyes and lay without moving.

"And then I saw the men of the East—they were looking at me. The whole length of the jetty was full of people. I saw brown, bronze, yellow faces, the black eyes, the glitter, the colour of an Eastern crowd. And all these beings stared without a murmur, without a sigh, without a movement. They stared down at the boats, at the sleeping men who at night had come to them from the sea. Nothing moved. The fronds of palms stood still against the sky. Not a branch stirred along the shore, and the brown roofs of hidden houses peeped through the green foliage, through the big leaves that hung shining and still like leaves forged of heavy metal. This was the East of the ancient navigators, so old, so mysterious, resplendent and sombre, living and unchanged, full of danger and promise. And these were the men. I sat up suddenly. A wave of movement passed through the crowd from end to end, passed along the heads, swayed the bodies, ran along the jetty like a ripple on the water, like a breath of wind on a field—and all was still again. I see it now—the wide sweep of the bay, the glittering sands, the wealth of green infinite and varied, the sea blue like the sea of a dream, the crowd of attentive faces, the blaze of vivid colour—the water reflecting it all, the curve of the shore, the jetty, the high-sterned outlandish craft floating still, and the three boats with the tired men from the West sleeping, unconscious of the land and the people and of the violence of sunshine. They slept thrown across the thwarts, curled on bottom-boards, in the careless attitudes of death. The head of the old skipper, leaning back in the stern of the long-boat, had fallen on his breast, and he looked as though he would never wake. Farther out old Mahon's face was upturned to the sky, with the long white beard spread out on his breast, as though he had been shot where he sat at the tiller; and a man, all in a heap in the bows of the boat, slept with both arms embracing the stem-head and with his cheek laid on the gunwale. The East looked at them without a sound.

"I have known its fascination since: I have seen the mysterious shores, the still water, the lands of brown nations, where a stealthy Nemesis lies in wait, pursues, overtakes so many of the conquering race, who are proud of their wisdom, of their knowledge, of their strength. But for me all the East is contained in that vision of my youth. It is all in that moment when I opened my young eyes on it. I came upon it from a tussle with the sea—and I was young—and I saw it looking at me. And this is all that is left of it! Only a moment; a moment of strength, of romance, of glamour—of youth!* . . . A flick of sunshine upon a strange shore, the time to remember, the time for a sigh, and—goodbye!—Night—Goodbye . . . !"

He drank.

"Ah! The good old time—the good old time.* Youth and the sea.* Glamour and the sea! The good, strong sea, the salt, bitter sea, that could whisper to you and roar at you and knock your breath out of you."

He drank again.

"By all that's wonderful, it is the sea, I believe, the sea itself—or is it youth alone? Who can tell? But you here—you all had something out of life: money, love—whatever one gets on shore—and, tell me, wasn't that the best time, that time when we were young at sea; young and had nothing, on the sea that gives nothing, except hard knocks—and sometimes a chance to feel your strength—that only— what you all regret?"

And we all nodded at him: the man of finance, the man of accounts, the man of law, we all nodded at him over the polished table that like a still sheet of brown water reflected our faces, lined, wrinkled; our faces marked by toil, by deceptions, by success, by love; our weary eyes looking still, looking always, looking anxiously for something out of life, that while it is expected is already gone— has passed unseen, in a sigh, in a flash—together with the youth, with the strength, with the romance of illusions.*

# HEART OF DARKNESS

# HEART OF DARKNESS*

## I

THE *Nellie*, a cruising yawl, swung to her anchor without a flutter of the sails, and was at rest. The flood had made, the wind was nearly calm, and being bound down the river, the only thing for it was to come to and wait for the turn of the tide.

The sea-reach of the Thames stretched before us like the beginning of an interminable waterway. In the offing the sea and the sky were welded together without a joint, and in the luminous space the tanned sails of the barges drifting up with the tide seemed to stand still in red clusters of canvas sharply peaked, with gleams of varnished sprits. A haze rested on the low shores that ran out to sea in vanishing flatness. The air was dark above Gravesend, and farther back still seemed condensed into a mournful gloom, brooding motionless over the biggest, and the greatest, town on earth.

The Director of Companies was our captain and our host.* We four affectionately watched his back as he stood in the bows looking to seaward. On the whole river there was nothing that looked half so nautical. He resembled a pilot, which to a seaman is trustworthiness personified.* It was difficult to realise his work was not out there in the luminous estuary, but behind him, within the brooding gloom.

Between us there was, as I have already said somewhere, the bond of the sea.* Besides holding our hearts together through long periods of separation, it had the effect of making us tolerant of each other's yarns—and even convictions. The Lawyer—the best of old fellows—had, because of his many years and many virtues, the only cushion on deck, and was lying on the only rug. The Accountant had brought out already a box of dominoes, and was toying architecturally with the bones.* Marlow sat cross-legged right aft, leaning against the mizzen-mast. He had sunken cheeks, a yellow complexion, a straight back, an ascetic aspect, and, with his arms dropped, the palms of hands outwards, resembled an idol.* The Director, satisfied the anchor had good hold, made his way aft and sat down amongst us. We exchanged a few words lazily. Afterwards there was silence on board the yacht. For some reason or other we did not begin that game of dominoes. We felt meditative, and fit for nothing but placid staring. The day was ending in a serenity of still and exquisite brilliance. The water shone pacifically; the sky, without a speck, was a benign immensity of unstained light; the very mist on the Essex marshes was like a gauzy and radiant fabric, hung from the wooded rises inland, and draping the low shores in diaphanous folds. Only the gloom to the west, brooding over the upper reaches, became more sombre every minute, as if angered by the approach of the sun.

And at last, in its curved and imperceptible fall, the sun sank low, and from glowing white changed to a dull red without rays and without heat, as if about to go out suddenly, stricken to death by the touch of that gloom brooding over a crowd of men.

Forthwith a change came over the waters, and the serenity became less brilliant but more profound. The old river in its broad reach rested unruffled at the decline of day, after ages of good service done to the race that peopled its banks, spread out in the tranquil dignity of a waterway leading to the uttermost ends of the earth. We looked at the venerable stream not in the vivid flush of a short day that comes and departs for ever, but in the august light of abiding memories. And indeed nothing is easier for a man who has, as the phrase goes, "followed the sea" with reverence and affection, than to evoke the great spirit of the past upon the lower reaches of the Thames. The tidal current runs to and fro in its unceasing service, crowded with memories of men and ships it had borne to the rest of home or to the battles of the sea. It had known and served all the men of whom the nation is proud, from Sir Francis Drake to Sir John Franklin, knights all, titled and untitled—the great knights-errant of the sea. It had borne all the ships whose names are like jewels flashing in the night of time, from the *Golden Hind* returning with her round flanks full of treasure, to be visited by the Queen's Highness and thus pass out of the gigantic tale, to the *Erebus* and *Terror*, bound on other conquests—and that never returned.* It had known the ships and the men. They had sailed from Deptford, from Greenwich, from Erith—the adventurers and the settlers; kings' ships and the ships of men on 'Change; captains, admirals, the dark "interlopers" of the Eastern trade, and the commissioned "generals" of East India fleets.* Hunters for gold or pursuers of fame, they all had gone out on that stream, bearing the sword, and often the torch, messengers of the might within the land, bearers of a spark from the sacred fire. What greatness had not floated on the ebb of that river into the mystery of an unknown earth! . . . The dreams of men, the seed of commonwealths, the germs of empires.

The sun set; the dusk fell on the stream, and lights began to appear along the shore. The Chapman lighthouse, a three-legged thing erect on a mud-flat, shone strongly. Lights of ships moved in the fairway—a great stir of lights going up and going down. And farther west on the upper reaches the place of the monstrous town was still marked ominously on the sky, a brooding gloom in sunshine, a lurid glare under the stars.

"And this also," said Marlow suddenly, "has been one of the dark places of the earth."*

He was the only man of us who still "followed the sea." The worst that could be said of him was that he did not represent his class. He was a seaman, but he was a wanderer too, while most seamen lead, if one may so express it, a sedentary life. Their minds are of the stay-at-home order, and their home is always with them—the ship; and so is their country—the sea. One ship is very much like another, and the sea is always the same. In the immutability of their surroundings the foreign shores, the foreign faces, the changing immensity of life, glide past, veiled not by a sense of mystery but by a slightly disdain-ful ignorance; for there is nothing mysterious to a seaman unless it be the sea itself, which is the mistress of his existence and as inscrutable as Destiny. For the rest, after his hours of work, a casual stroll or a casual spree on shore suffices to unfold for him the secret of a whole continent, and generally he finds the secret not worth knowing. The yarns of seamen have a direct simplicity, the whole meaning of which lies within the shell of a cracked nut. But Marlow was not typical (if his propensity to spin yarns be excepted), and to him the meaning of an episode was not inside like a kernel but outside, enveloping the tale which brought it out only as a glow brings out a haze, in the likeness of one of these misty halos that sometimes are made visible by the spectral illumination of moonshine.

His remark did not seem at all surprising. It was just like Marlow. It was accepted in silence. No one took the trouble to grunt even; and presently he said, very slow,—

"I was thinking of very old times, when the Romans first came here, nineteen hundred years ago—the other day.* . . . Light came out

of this river since—you say 'knights'?* Yes; but it is like a running
blaze on a plain, like a flash of lightning in the clouds. We live in the
flicker—may it last as long as the old earth keeps rolling! But darkness was here yesterday. Imagine the feelings of a commander of a
fine—what d'ye call 'em?—trireme in the Mediterranean, ordered
suddenly to the north; run overland across the Gauls in a hurry; put
in charge of one of these craft the legionaries,—a wonderful lot of
handy men they must have been too—used to build, apparently by
the hundred, in a month or two, if we may believe what we read.*
Imagine him here—the very end of the world, a sea the colour of
lead, a sky the colour of smoke, a kind of ship about as rigid as a
concertina—and going up this river with stores, or orders, or what
you like. Sandbanks, marshes, forests, savages,—precious little to eat
fit for a civilised man, nothing but Thames water to drink. No Falernian wine here, no going ashore. Here and there a military camp lost
in a wilderness, like a needle in a bundle of hay—cold, fog, tempests,
disease, exile, and death,—death skulking in the air, in the water, in
the bush. They must have been dying like flies here. Oh yes—he did
it. Did it very well, too, no doubt, and without thinking much about
it either, except afterwards to brag of what he had gone through in
his time, perhaps. They were men enough to face the darkness. And
perhaps he was cheered by keeping his eye on a chance of promotion
to the fleet at Ravenna by-and-by, if he had good friends in Rome
and survived the awful climate. Or think of a decent young citizen in
a toga—perhaps too much dice, you know—coming out here in the
train of some prefect, or tax-gatherer, or trader even, to mend his
fortunes.* Land in a swamp, march through the woods, and in some
inland post feel the savagery, the utter savagery, had closed round
him,—all that mysterious life of the wilderness that stirs in the
forest, in the jungles, in the hearts of wild men. There's no initiation
either into such mysteries. He has to live in the midst of the
incomprehensible, which is also detestable. And it has a fascination,
too, that goes to work upon him. The fascination of the
abomination—you know. Imagine the growing regrets, the longing
to escape, the powerless disgust, the surrender, the hate."

He paused.

"Mind," he began again, lifting one arm from the elbow, the palm
of the hand outwards, so that, with his legs folded before him, he had
the pose of a Buddha preaching in European clothes and without a

lotus-flower*—"Mind, none of us would feel exactly like this. What saves us is efficiency—the devotion to efficiency.* But these chaps were not much account, really. They were no colonists; their administration was merely a squeeze, and nothing more, I suspect. They were conquerors, and for that you want only brute force— nothing to boast of, when you have it, since your strength is just an accident arising from the weakness of others. They grabbed what they could get for the sake of what was to be got.* It was just robbery with violence, aggravated murder on a great scale, and men going at it blind—as is very proper for those who tackle a darkness.* The conquest of the earth, which mostly means the taking it away from those who have a different complexion or slightly flatter noses than ourselves, is not a pretty thing when you look into it too much. What redeems it is the idea only. An idea at the back of it; not a sentimental pretence but an idea; and an unselfish belief in the idea—something you can set up, and bow down before, and offer a sacrifice to. . . ."

He broke off. Flames glided in the river, small green flames, red flames, white flames, pursuing, overtaking, joining, crossing each other—then separating slowly or hastily.* The traffic of the great city went on in the deepening night upon the sleepless river.* We looked on, waiting patiently—there was nothing else to do till the end of the flood; but it was only after a long silence, when he said, in a hesitating voice, "I suppose you fellows remember I did once turn fresh-water sailor for a bit," that we knew we were fated, before the ebb began to run, to hear about one of Marlow's inconclusive experiences.

"I don't want to bother you much with what happened to me personally," he began, showing in this remark the weakness of many tellers of tales who seem so often unaware of what their audience would best like to hear; "yet to understand the effect of it on me you ought to know how I got out there, what I saw, how I went up that river to the place where I first met the poor chap. It was the farthest point of navigation and the culminating point of my experience. It seemed somehow to throw a kind of light on everything about me— and into my thoughts. It was sombre enough too—and pitiful—not extraordinary in any way—not very clear either. No, not very clear. And yet it seemed to throw a kind of light.

"I had then, as you remember, just returned to London after a lot of Indian Ocean, Pacific, China Seas—a regular dose of the

East—six years or so, and I was loafing about, hindering you fellows in your work and invading your homes, just as though I had got a heavenly mission to civilise you. It was very fine for a time, but after a bit I did get tired of resting. Then I began to look for a ship—I should think the hardest work on earth. But the ships wouldn't even look at me. And I got tired of that game too.

"Now when I was a little chap I had a passion for maps. I would look for hours at South America, or Africa, or Australia, and lose myself in all the glories of exploration. At that time there were many blank spaces on the earth, and when I saw one that looked particularly inviting on a map (but they all look that) I would put my finger on it and say, When I grow up I will go there.* The North Pole was one of these places, I remember. Well, I haven't been there yet, and shall not try now. The glamour's off. Other places were scattered about the Equator, and in every sort of latitude all over the two hemispheres. I have been in some of them, and . . . well, we won't talk about that. But there was one yet—the biggest, the most blank, so to speak—that I had a hankering after.

"True, by this time it was not a blank space any more. It had got filled since my boyhood with rivers and lakes and names. It had ceased to be a blank space of delightful mystery—a white patch for a boy to dream gloriously over.* It had become a place of darkness. But there was in it one river especially, a mighty big river, that you could see on the map, resembling an immense snake uncoiled, with its head in the sea, its body at rest curving afar over a vast country, and its tail lost in the depths of the land. And as I looked at the map of it in a shop-window, it fascinated me as a snake would a bird—a silly little bird. Then I remembered there was a big concern, a Company for trade on that river.* Dash it all! I thought to myself, they can't trade without using some kind of craft on that lot of fresh water— steamboats! Why shouldn't I try to get charge of one. I went on along Fleet Street, but could not shake off the idea. The snake had charmed me.

"You understand it was a Continental concern, that Trading Society; but I have a lot of relations living on the Continent, because it's cheap and not so nasty as it looks, they say.

"I am sorry to own I began to worry them. This was already a fresh departure for me. I was not used to get things that way, you know. I always went my own road and on my own legs where I had a mind to go. I wouldn't have believed it of myself; but, then—you see—I felt somehow I must get there by hook or by crook. So I worried them. The men said 'My dear fellow,' and did nothing. Then—would you believe it?—I tried the women. I, Charlie Marlow, set the women to work—to get a job. Heavens! Well, you see, the notion drove me. I had an aunt, a dear enthusiastic soul.* She wrote: 'It will be delightful. I am ready to do anything, anything for you. It is a glorious idea. I know the wife of a very high personage in the Administration, and also a man who has lots of influence with,' &c., &c. She was determined to make no end of fuss to get me appointed skipper of a river steamboat, if such was my fancy.

"I got my appointment—of course; and I got it very quick. It appears the Company had received news that one of their captains had been killed in a scuffle with the natives. This was my chance, and it made me the more anxious to go. It was only months and months afterwards, when I made the attempt to recover what was left of the body, that I heard the original quarrel arose from a misunderstanding about some hens. Yes, two black hens. Fresleven—that was the fellow's name, a Dane—thought himself wronged somehow in the bargain, so he went ashore and started to hammer the chief of the village with a stick.* Oh, it didn't surprise me in the least to hear this, and at the same time to be told that Fresleven was the gentlest, quietest creature that ever walked on two legs. No doubt he was; but he had been a couple of years already out there engaged in the noble cause, you know, and he probably felt the need at last of asserting his self-respect in some way. Therefore he whacked the old nigger mercilessly, while a big crowd of his people watched him, thunderstruck, till some man,—I was told the chief's son,—in desperation at hearing the old chap yell, made a tentative jab with a spear at the white man—and of course it went quite easy between the shoulder-blades. Then the whole population cleared into the forest, expecting all kinds of calamities to happen, while, on the other hand, the steamer Fresleven commanded left also in a bad panic, in charge of the engineer, I believe. Afterwards nobody seemed to trouble much about Fresleven's remains, till I got out and stepped into his shoes. I couldn't let it rest, though; but when an opportunity offered at last to meet my predecessor, the grass growing through his ribs was tall enough to hide his bones. They were all there. The supernatural being had not been touched after he fell. And the village was deserted, the huts gaped black, rotting, all askew within the fallen enclosures. A calamity had come to it, sure enough. The people had vanished. Mad terror had scattered them, men, women, and children, through the bush, and they had never returned. What became of the hens I don't know either. I should think the cause of progress got them, anyhow. However, through this glorious affair I got my appointment, before I had fairly begun to hope for it.

"I flew around like mad to get ready, and before forty-eight hours I was crossing the Channel to show myself to my employers, and sign the contract. In a very few hours I arrived in a city that always makes me think of a whited sepulchre.* Prejudice no doubt. I had no difficulty in finding the Company's offices. It was the biggest thing in the town, and everybody I met was full of it. They were going to run an over-sea empire, and make no end of coin by trade.

"A narrow and deserted street in deep shadow, high houses, innumerable windows with venetian blinds, a dead silence, grass sprouting between the stones, imposing carriage archways right and left, immense double doors standing ponderously ajar. I slipped through one of these cracks, went up a swept and ungarnished staircase, as arid as a desert, and opened the first door I came to. Two women, one fat and the other slim, sat on straw-bottomed chairs, knitting black wool.* The slim one got up and walked straight at me—still knitting with down-cast eyes—and only just as I began to think of getting out of her way, as you would for a somnambulist, stood still, and looked up. Her dress was as plain as an umbrella-cover, and she turned round without a word and preceded me into a waiting-room. I gave my name, and looked about. Deal table in the middle, plain chairs all round the walls, on one end a large shining map, marked with all the colours of a rainbow. There was a vast amount of red—good to see at any time, because one knows that some real work is done in there, a deuce of a lot of blue, a little green, smears of orange, and, on the East Coast, a purple patch, to show where the jolly pioneers of progress drink the jolly lager-beer. However, I wasn't going into any of these. I was going into the yellow.* Dead in the centre. And the river was there—fascinating—deadly— like a snake. Ough! A door opened, a white-haired secretarial head, but wearing a compassionate expression, appeared, and a skinny forefinger beckoned me into the sanctuary. Its light was dim, and a heavy writing-desk squatted in the middle. From behind that structure came out an impression of pale plumpness in a frock-coat.* The great man himself. He was five feet six, I should judge, and had his grip on the handle-end of ever so many millions. He shook hands, I fancy, murmured vaguely, was satisfied with my French. *Bon voyage*.

"In about forty-five seconds I found myself again in the waiting-room with the compassionate secretary, who, full of desolation and sympathy, made me sign some document. I believe I undertook amongst other things not to disclose any trade secrets.* Well, I am not going to.

"I began to feel slightly uneasy. You know I am not used to such ceremonies, and there was something ominous in the atmosphere. It was just as though I had been let into some conspiracy—I don't know—something not quite right; and I was glad to get out. In the outer room the two women knitted black wool feverishly. People were arriving, and the younger one was walking back and forth introducing them. The old one sat on her chair. Her flat cloth slippers were propped up on a foot-warmer, and a cat reposed on her lap. She wore a starched white affair on her head, had a wart on one cheek, and silver-rimmed spectacles hung on the tip of her nose. She glanced at me above the glasses. The swift and indifferent placidity of that look troubled me. Two youths with foolish and cheery countenances were being piloted over, and she threw at them the same quick glance of unconcerned wisdom. She seemed to know all about them and about me too. An eerie feeling came over me. She seemed uncanny and fateful. Often far away there I thought of these two, guarding the door of Darkness,* knitting black wool as for a warm pall, one introducing, introducing continuously to the unknown, the other scrutinising the cheery and foolish faces with unconcerned old eyes. *Ave!* Old knitter of black wool. *Morituri te salutant*.* Not many of those she looked at ever saw her again—not half, by a long way.

"There was yet a visit to the doctor. 'A simple formality,' assured me the secretary,* with an air of taking an immense part in all my sorrows. Accordingly a young chap wearing his hat over the left eyebrow, some clerk I suppose,—there must have been clerks in the business, though the house was as still as a house in a city of the dead,—came from somewhere up-stairs, and led me forth. He was shabby and careless, with ink-stains on the sleeves of his jacket, and his cravat was large and billowy, under a chin shaped like the toe of an old boot. It was a little too early for the doctor, so I proposed a

drink, and thereupon he developed a vein of joviality. As we sat over
our vermuths he glorified the Company's business, and by-and-by I
expressed casually my surprise at him not going out there. He
became very cool and collected all at once. 'I am not such a fool as I
look, quoth Plato to his disciples,'* he said sententiously, emptied his
glass with great resolution, and we rose.

"The old doctor felt my pulse, evidently thinking of something
else the while. 'Good, good for there,' he mumbled, and then with a
certain eagerness asked me whether I would let him measure my
head.* Rather surprised, I said Yes, when he produced a thing like
calipers and got the dimensions back and front and every way, taking
notes carefully. He was an unshaven little man in a threadbare coat
like a gaberdine, with his feet in slippers, and I thought him a harmless fool. 'I always ask leave, in the interests of science, to measure
the crania of those going out there,' he said. 'And when they come
back too?' I asked. 'Oh, I never see them,' he remarked; 'and, moreover, the changes take place inside, you know.' He smiled, as if at
some quiet joke. 'So you are going out there. Famous. Interesting
too.' He gave me a searching glance, and made another note. 'Ever
any madness in your family?' he asked, in a matter-of-fact tone. I felt
very annoyed. 'Is that question in the interests of science too?' 'It
would be,' he said, without taking notice of my irritation, 'interesting for science to watch the mental changes of individuals, on the
spot, but . . .' 'Are you an alienist?' I interrupted. 'Every doctor
should be—a little,' answered that original, imperturbably. 'I have a
little theory which you Messieurs who go out there must help me to
prove. This is my share in the advantages my country shall reap from
the possession of such a magnificent dependency. The mere wealth I
leave to others. Pardon my questions, but you are the first Englishman coming under my observation . . .' I hastened to assure him I
was not in the least typical. 'If I were,' said I, 'I wouldn't be talking
like this with you.' 'What you say is rather profound, and probably
erroneous,' he said, with a laugh. 'Avoid irritation more than
exposure to the sun. Adieu. How do you English say, eh? Goodbye.
Ah! Goodbye. Adieu. In the tropics one must before everything keep
calm.' . . . He lifted a warning forefinger. . . . '*Du calme, du calme.
Adieu.*'*

"One thing more remained to do—say goodbye to my excellent
aunt. I found her triumphant. I had a cup of tea—the last decent cup

of tea for many days—and in a room that most soothingly looked just as you would expect a lady's drawing-room to look, we had a long quiet chat by the fireside. In the course of these confidences it became quite plain to me I had been represented to the wife of the high dignitary, and goodness knows to how many more people besides, as an exceptional and gifted creature—a piece of good fortune for the Company—a man you don't get hold of every day. Good heavens! and I was going to take charge of a twopenny-halfpenny river-steamboat with a penny whistle attached! It appeared, however, I was also one of the Workers, with a capital—you know.* Something like an emissary of light, something like a lower sort of apostle.* There had been a lot of such rot let loose in print and talk just about that time,* and the excellent woman, living right in the rush of all that humbug, got carried off her feet. She talked about 'weaning those ignorant millions from their horrid ways,' till, upon my word, she made me quite uncomfortable. I ventured to hint that the Company was run for profit.

"'You forget, dear Charlie, that the labourer is worthy of his hire,'* she said, brightly. It's queer how out of touch with truth women are. They live in a world of their own, and there had never been anything like it, and never can be. It is too beautiful altogether, and if they were to set it up it would go to pieces before the first sunset. Some confounded fact we men have been living contentedly with ever since the day of creation would start up and knock the whole thing over.*

"After this I got embraced, told to wear flannel, be sure to write often, and so on—and I left. In the street—I don't know why—a queer feeling came to me that I was an impostor. Odd thing that I, who used to clear out for any part of the world at twenty-four hours' notice, with less thought than most men give to the crossing of a street, had a moment—I won't say of hesitation, but of startled pause, before this commonplace affair. The best way I can explain it to you is by saying that, for a second or two, I felt as though, instead of going to the centre of a continent, I were about to set off for the centre of the earth.*

"I left in a French steamer, and she called in every blamed port they have out there, for, as far as I could see, the sole purpose of landing soldiers and custom-house officers. I watched the coast. Watching a coast as it slips by the ship is like thinking about an enigma. There it is before you—smiling, frowning, inviting, grand, mean, insipid, or savage, and always mute with an air of whispering, Come and find out. This one was almost featureless, as if still in the making, with an aspect of monotonous grimness. The edge of a colossal jungle, so dark-green as to be almost black, fringed with white surf, ran straight, like a ruled line, far, far away along a blue sea whose glitter was blurred by a creeping mist. The sun was fierce, the land seemed to glisten and drip with steam. Here and there greyish-whitish specks showed up, clustered inside the white surf, with a flag flying above them perhaps. Settlements some centuries old, and still no bigger than pin-heads on the untouched expanse of their back-ground. We pounded along, stopped, landed soldiers; went on, landed custom-house clerks to levy toll in what looked like a God-forsaken wilderness, with a tin shed and a flag-pole lost in it; landed more soldiers—to take care of the custom-house clerks, presumably. Some, I heard, got drowned in the surf; but whether they did or not, nobody seemed particularly to care. They were just flung out there, and on we went. Every day the coast looked the same, as though we had not moved; but we passed various places—trading places—with names like Gran' Bassam, Little Popo,* names that seemed to belong to some sordid farce acted in front of a sinister backcloth. The idle-ness of a passenger, my isolation amongst all these men with whom I had no point of contact, the oily and languid sea, the uniform sombreness of the coast, seemed to keep me away from the truth of things, within the toil of a mournful and senseless delusion. The  voice of the surf heard now and then was a positive pleasure, like the speech of a brother. It was something natural, that had its reason, that had a meaning. Now and then a boat from the shore gave one a momentary contact with reality. It was paddled by black fellows. You could see from afar the white of their eyeballs glistening. They shouted, sang; their bodies streamed with perspiration; they had faces like grotesque masks—these chaps; but they had bone, muscle, a wild vitality, an intense energy of movement, that was as natural and true as the surf along their coast. They wanted no excuse for being there. They were a great comfort to look at. For a time I would feel I belonged still to a world of straightforward facts; but the feeling would not last long. Something would turn up to scare it away. Once, I remember, we came upon a man-of-war anchored off the coast. There wasn't even a shed there, and she was shelling the bush. It appears the French had one of their wars going on there-abouts.* Her ensign dropped limp* like a rag; the muzzles of the long eight-inch guns stuck out all over the low hull; the greasy, slimy swell swung her up lazily and let her down, swaying her thin masts. In the empty immensity of earth, sky, and water, there she was, incomprehensible, firing into a continent. Pop, would go one of the eight-inch guns; a small flame would dart and vanish, a little white smoke would disappear, a tiny projectile would give a feeble screech—and nothing happened. Nothing could happen. There was a touch of insanity in the proceeding, a sense of lugubrious drollery in the sight; and it was not dissipated by somebody on board assuring me earnestly there was a camp of natives—he called them enemies!—hidden out of sight somewhere.

"We gave her her letters (I heard the men in that lonely ship were dying of fever at the rate of three a day) and went on. We called at some more places with farcical names, where the merry dance of death and trade goes on in a still and earthy atmosphere as of an overheated catacomb; all along the formless coast bordered by dangerous surf, as if Nature herself had tried to ward off intruders; in and out of rivers, streams of death in life, whose banks were rotting into mud, whose waters, thickened into slime, invaded the contorted mangroves, that seemed to writhe at us in the extremity of an impotent despair. Nowhere did we stop long enough to get a particularised impression, but the general sense of vague and oppressive wonder grew upon me. It was like a weary pilgrimage amongst hints for nightmares.

"It was upward of thirty days before I saw the mouth of the big river. We anchored off the seat of the government.* But my work would not begin till some two hundred miles farther on. So as soon as I could I made a start for a place thirty miles higher up.

"I had my passage on a little sea-going steamer. Her captain was a Swede, and knowing me for a seaman, invited me on the bridge. He was a young man, lean, fair, and morose, with lanky hair and a shuffling gait. As we left the miserable little wharf, he tossed his head contemptuously at the shore. 'Been living there?' he asked. I said, 'Yes.' 'Fine lot these government chaps—are they not?' he went on, speaking English with great precision and considerable bitterness. 'It is funny what some people will do for a few francs a month. I wonder what becomes of that kind when it goes up country?' I said to him I expected to see that soon. 'So-o-o!' he exclaimed. He shuffled athwart, keeping one eye ahead vigilantly. 'Don't be too sure,' he continued. 'The other day I took up a man who hanged himself on the road. He was a Swede, too.' 'Hanged himself! Why, in God's name?' I cried. He kept on looking out watchfully. 'Who knows? The sun too much for him, or the country perhaps.'

At last we opened a reach. A rocky cliff appeared, mounds of turned-up earth by the shore, houses on a hill, others, with iron roofs, amongst a waste of excavations, or hanging to the declivity. A continuous noise of the rapids above hovered over this scene of inhabited devastation. A lot of people, mostly black and naked, moved about like ants. A jetty projected into the river. A blinding sunlight drowned all this at times in a sudden recrudescence of glare. 'There's your Company's station,' said the Swede, pointing to three wooden barrack-like structures on the rocky slope.* 'I will send your things up. Four boxes did you say? So. Farewell.'

"I came upon a boiler wallowing in the grass, then found a path leading up the hill. It turned aside for the boulders, and also for an undersized railway-truck lying there on its back with its wheels in the air. One was off. The thing looked as dead as the carcass of some animal. I came upon more pieces of decaying machinery, a stack of rusty rails. To the left a clump of trees made a shady spot, where dark things seemed to stir feebly. I blinked, the path was steep. A horn tooted to the right, and I saw the black people run. A heavy and dull detonation shook the ground, a puff of smoke came out of the cliff, and that was all. No change appeared on the face of the rock. They were building a railway.* The cliff was not in the way of anything; but this objectless blasting was all the work going on.

"A slight clinking behind me made me turn my head. Six black men advanced in a file, toiling up the path. They walked erect and slow, balancing small baskets full of earth on their heads, and the clink kept time with their footsteps. Black rags were wound round their loins, and the short ends behind wagged to and fro like tails. I could see every rib, the joints of their limbs were like knots in a rope; each had an iron collar on his neck, and all were connected together with a chain whose bights swung between them, rhythmically clinking. Another report from the cliff made me think suddenly of that ship of war I had seen firing into a continent. It was the same kind of ominous voice; but these men could by no stretch of imagination be called enemies. They were called criminals, and the outraged law, like the bursting shells, had come to them, an insoluble mystery from over the sea. All their meagre breasts panted together, the violently dilated nostrils quivered, the eyes stared stonily up-hill. They passed me within six inches, without a glance, with that complete, deathlike indifference of unhappy savages.* Behind this raw matter one of the reclaimed, the product of the new forces at work, strolled despondently, carrying a rifle by its middle. He had a uniform jacket with one button off, and seeing a white man on the path, hoisted his weapon to his shoulder with alacrity. This was simple prudence, white men being so much alike at a distance that he could not tell who I might be. He was speedily reassured, and with a large, white, rascally grin, and a glance at his charge, seemed to take me into partnership in his exalted trust. After all, I also was a part of the great cause of these high and just proceedings.

"Instead of going up, I turned and descended to the left. My idea was to let that chain-gang get out of sight before I climbed the hill. You know I am not particularly tender; I've had to strike and to fend off. I've had to resist and to attack sometimes—that's only one way of resisting—without counting the exact cost, according to the demands of such sort of life as I had blundered into. I've seen the devil of violence, and the devil of greed, and the devil of hot desire; but, by all the stars! these were strong, lusty, red-eyed devils, that swayed and drove men—men, I tell you. But as I stood on this hillside, I foresaw that in the blinding sunshine of that land I would become acquainted with a flabby, pretending, weak-eyed devil of a rapacious and pitiless folly. How insidious he could be, too, I was only to find out several months later and a thousand miles farther. For a moment I stood appalled, as though by a warning. Finally I descended the hill, obliquely, towards the trees I had seen.

"I avoided a vast artificial hole somebody had been digging on the slope, the purpose of which I found it impossible to divine. It wasn't a quarry or a sandpit, anyhow. It was just a hole. It might have been connected with the philanthropic desire of giving the criminals something to do. I don't know. Then I nearly fell into a very narrow ravine, almost no more than a scar in the hillside. I discovered that a lot of imported drainage-pipes for the settlement had been tumbled in there. There wasn't one that was not broken. It was a wanton smash-up. At last I got under the trees. My purpose was to stroll into the shade for a moment; but no sooner within than it seemed to me I had stepped into the gloomy circle of some Inferno.* The rapids were near, and an uninterrupted, uniform, headlong, rushing noise filled the mournful stillness of the grove, where not a breath stirred, not a leaf moved, with a mysterious sound—as though the tearing pace of the launched earth had suddenly become audible.

"Black shapes crouched, lay, sat between the trees, leaning against the trunks, clinging to the earth, half coming out, half effaced within the dim light, in all the attitudes of pain, abandonment, and despair. Another mine on the cliff went off, followed by a slight shudder of the soil under my feet. The work was going on. The work! And this was the place where some of the helpers had withdrawn to die.*

"They were dying slowly—it was very clear. They were not enemies, they were not criminals, they were not earthly now,—nothing but black shadows of disease and starvation, lying confusedly in the greenish gloom. Brought from all the recesses of the coast in all the legality of time contracts,* lost in uncongenial surroundings, fed on unfamiliar food, they sickened, became inefficient, and were then allowed to crawl away and rest. These moribund shapes were free as air—and nearly as thin. I began to distinguish the gleam of eyes under the trees. Then, glancing down, I saw a face near my hand. The black bones reclined at full length with one shoulder against the tree, and slowly the eyelids rose and the sunken eyes looked up at me, enormous and vacant, a kind of blind, white flicker in the depths of the orbs, which died out slowly. The man seemed young—almost a boy—but you know with them it's hard to tell. I found nothing else to do but to offer him one of my good Swede's ship's biscuits I had in my pocket. The fingers closed slowly on it and held—there was no other movement and no other glance. He had tied a bit of white worsted round his neck—Why?* Where did he get it? Was it a badge—an ornament—a charm—a propitiatory act? Was there any idea at all connected with it? It looked startling round his black neck, this bit of white thread from beyond the seas.

"Near the same tree two more bundles of acute angles sat with their legs drawn up. One, with his chin propped on his knees, stared at nothing, in an intolerable and appalling manner: his brother phantom rested its forehead, as if overcome with a great weariness; and all about others were scattered in every pose of contorted collapse, as in some picture of a massacre or a pestilence. While I stood horror-struck, one of these creatures rose to his hands and knees, and went off on all-fours towards the river to drink. He lapped out of his hand, then sat up in the sunlight, crossing his shins in front of him, and after a time let his woolly head fall on his breastbone.

"I didn't want any more loitering in the shade, and I made haste towards the station. When near the buildings I met a white man, in such an unexpected elegance of get-up that in the first moment I took him for a sort of vision. I saw a high starched collar, white cuffs, a light alpaca jacket, snowy trousers, a clear necktie,* and varnished boots. No hat. Hair parted, brushed, oiled, under a green-lined parasol held in a big white hand. He was amazing, and had a penholder behind his ear.

"I shook hands with this miracle, and I learned he was the Company's chief accountant, and that all the book-keeping was done at this station. He had come out for a moment, he said, 'to get a breath of fresh air.' The expression sounded wonderfully odd, with its suggestion of sedentary desk-life. I wouldn't have mentioned the fellow to you at all, only it was from his lips that I first heard the name of the man who is so indissolubly connected with the memories of that time. Moreover, I respected the fellow. Yes; I respected his collars, his vast cuffs, his brushed hair. His appearance was certainly that of a hairdresser's dummy; but in the great demoralisation of the land he kept up his appearance. That's backbone. His starched collars and got-up shirt-fronts were achievements of character. He had been out nearly three years; and, later on, I could not help asking him how he managed to sport such linen. He had just the faintest blush, and said modestly, 'I've been teaching one of the native women about the station. It was difficult. She had a distaste for the work.' Thus this man had verily accomplished something. And he was devoted to his books, which were in apple-pie order.

"Everything else in the station was in a muddle,—heads, things, buildings. Strings of dusty niggers with splay feet arrived and departed; a stream of manufactured goods, rubbishy cottons, beads, and brass-wire set into the depths of darkness, and in return came a precious trickle of ivory.

"I had to wait in the station for ten days—an eternity. I lived in a hut in the yard, but to be out of the chaos I would sometimes get into the accountant's office. It was built of horizontal planks, and so badly put together that, as he bent over his high desk, he was barred from neck to heels with narrow strips of sunlight. There was no need to open the big shutter to see. It was hot there too; big flies buzzed fiendishly, and did not sting, but stabbed. I sat generally on the floor, while, of faultless appearance (and even slightly scented), perching on a high stool, he wrote, he wrote. Sometimes he stood up for exercise. When a truckle-bed with a sick man (some invalided agent from up-country) was put in there, he exhibited a gentle annoyance. 'The groans of this sick person,' he said, 'distract my attention. And without that it is extremely difficult to guard against clerical errors in this climate.'

"One day he remarked, without lifting his head, 'In the interior you will no doubt meet Mr Kurtz.'* On my asking who Mr Kurtz was, he said he was a first-class agent; and seeing my disappointment at this information, he added slowly, laying down his pen, 'He is a very remarkable person.' Further questions elicited from him that Mr Kurtz was at present in charge of a trading post, a very import-ant one, in the true ivory-country, at 'the very bottom of there. Sends in as much ivory as all the others put together . . .' He began to write again. The sick man was too ill to groan. The flies buzzed in a great peace.

"Suddenly there was a growing murmur of voices and a great tramping of feet. A caravan had come in. A violent babble of uncouth sounds burst out on the other side of the planks. All the carriers were speaking together, and in the midst of the uproar the lamentable voice of the chief agent was heard 'giving it up' tearfully for the twentieth time that day. . . . He rose slowly. 'What a frightful row,' he said. He crossed the room gently to look at the sick man, and returning, said to me, 'He does not hear.' 'What! Dead?' I asked, startled. 'No, not yet,' he answered, with great composure. Then, alluding with a toss of the head to the tumult in the station-yard, 'When one has got to make correct entries, one comes to hate those savages—hate them to the death.' He remained thoughtful for a moment. 'When you see Mr Kurtz,' he went on, 'tell him from me that everything here'—he glanced at the desk—'is very satisfactory. I don't like to write to him—with those messengers of ours you never know who may get hold of your letter—at that Central Station.' He stared at me for a moment with his mild, bulging eyes. 'Oh, he will go far, very far,' he began again. 'He will be a somebody in the Administration before long. They, above—the Council in Europe, you know—mean him to be.'

"He turned to his work. The noise outside had ceased, and presently in going out I stopped at the door. In the steady buzz of flies the homeward-bound agent was lying flushed and insensible; the other, bent over his books, was making correct entries of perfectly correct transactions; and fifty feet below the doorstep I could see the still tree-tops of the grove of death.

"Next day I left that station at last, with a caravan of sixty men, for a two-hundred-mile tramp.*

"No use telling you much about that. Paths, paths, everywhere; a stamped-in network of paths spreading over the empty land, through long grass, through burnt grass, through thickets, down and up chilly ravines, up and down stony hills ablaze with heat; and a solitude, a solitude, nobody, not a hut. The population had cleared out a long time ago.* Well, if a lot of mysterious niggers armed with all kinds of fearful weapons suddenly took to travelling on the road between Deal and Gravesend, catching the yokels right and left to carry heavy loads for them, I fancy every farm and cottage thereabouts would get empty very soon. Only here the dwellings were gone too. Still I passed through several abandoned villages. There's something pathetically childish in the ruins of grass walls. Day after day, with the stamp and shuffle of sixty pair of bare feet behind me, each pair under a 60-lb. load. Camp, cook, sleep, strike camp, march. Now and then a carrier dead in harness, at rest in the long grass near the path, with an empty water-gourd and his long staff lying by his side. A great silence around and above. Perhaps on some quiet night the tremor of far-off drums, sinking, swelling, a tremor vast, faint; a sound weird, appealing, suggestive, and wild—and perhaps with as profound a meaning as the sound of bells in a Christian country. Once a white man in an unbuttoned uniform, camping on the path with an armed escort of lank Zanzibaris,* very hospitable and festive—not to say drunk. Was looking after the upkeep of the road, he declared. Can't say I saw any road or any upkeep, unless the body of a middle-aged negro, with a bullet-hole in the forehead, upon which I absolutely stumbled three miles farther on, may be considered as a permanent improvement. I had a white companion too, not a bad chap, but rather too fleshy and with the exasperating habit of fainting on the hot hillsides, miles away from the least bit of shade and water. Annoying, you know, to hold your own coat like a parasol over a man's head while he is coming-to. I couldn't help asking him once what he meant by coming there at all. 'To make money, of course. What do you think?' he said, scornfully. Then he got fever, and had to be carried in a hammock slung under a pole. As he weighed sixteen stone I had no end of rows with the carriers.* They jibbed, ran away, sneaked off with their loads in the night—quite a mutiny. So, one evening, I made a speech in English with gestures, not one of which was lost to the sixty pairs of eyes before me, and the next morning I started the hammock off in front all right. An hour afterwards I came upon the whole concern wrecked in a bush—man, hammock, groans, blankets, horrors. The heavy pole had skinned his poor nose. He was very anxious for me to kill somebody, but there wasn't the shadow of a carrier near. I remembered the old doctor,— 'It would be interesting for science to watch the mental changes of individuals, on the spot.' I felt I was becoming scientifically interesting. However, all that is to no purpose. On the fifteenth day I came in sight of the big river again, and hobbled into the Central Station. It was on a back water surrounded by scrub and forest, with a pretty border of smelly mud on one side, and on the three others enclosed by a crazy fence of rushes. A neglected gap was all the gate it had, and the first glance at the place was enough to let you see the flabby devil was running that show. White men with long staves in their hands appeared languidly from amongst the buildings, strolling up to take a look at me, and then retired out of sight somewhere. One of them, a stout, excitable chap with black moustaches, informed me with great volubility and many digressions, as soon as I told him who I was, that my steamer was at the bottom of the river. I was thunderstruck. What, how, why? Oh, it was 'all right.' The 'manager himself' was there. All quite correct. 'Everybody had behaved* splendidly! splendidly!'—'You must,' he said in agitation, 'go and see the general manager at once. He is waiting!'

'I did not see the real significance of that wreck at once.* I fancy I see it now, but I am not sure—not at all. Certainly the affair was too stupid—when I think of it—to be altogether natural. Still. . . . But at the moment it presented itself simply as a confounded nuisance. The steamer was sunk. They had started two days before in a sudden hurry up the river with the manager on board, in charge of some volunteer skipper, and before they had been out three hours they tore the bottom out of her on stones, and she sank near the south bank. I asked myself what I was to do there, now my boat was lost. As a matter of fact, I had plenty to do in fishing my command out of the river. I had to set about it the very next day. That, and the repairs when I brought the pieces to the station, took some months.

"My first interview with the manager was curious. He did not ask me to sit down after my twenty-mile walk that morning. He was commonplace in complexion, in feature, in manners, and in voice. He was of middle size and of ordinary build. His eyes, of the usual blue, were perhaps remarkably cold, and he certainly could make his glance fall on one as trenchant and heavy as an axe. But even at these times the rest of his person seemed to disclaim the intention. Otherwise there was only an indefinable, faint expression of his lips, something stealthy—a smile—not a smile—I remember it, but I can't explain. It was unconscious, this smile was, though just after he had said something it got intensified for an instant. It came at the end of his speeches like a seal applied on the words to make the meaning of the commonest phrase appear absolutely inscrutable. He was a common trader, from his youth up employed in these parts— nothing more. He was obeyed, yet he inspired neither love nor fear, nor even respect.* He inspired uneasiness. That was it! Uneasiness. Not a definite mistrust—just uneasiness—nothing more. You have no idea how effective such a . . . a . . . faculty can be. He had no genius for organising, for initiative, or for order even. That was evident in such things as the deplorable state of the station. He had no learning, and no intelligence. His position had come to him— why? Perhaps because he was never ill . . . He had served three terms of three years out there . . . Because triumphant health in the general rout of constitutions is a kind of power in itself. When he went home on leave he rioted on a large scale—pompously. Jack ashore—with a difference—in externals only. This one could gather from his casual talk. He originated nothing, he could keep the routine going—that's all. But he was great. He was great by this little thing that it was impossible to tell what could control such a man. He never gave that secret away. Perhaps there was nothing within him. Such a suspicion made one pause—for out there there were no external checks. Once when various tropical diseases had laid low almost every 'agent' in the station, he was heard to say, 'Men who come out here should have no entrails.'* He sealed the utterance with that smile of his, as though it had been a door opening into a darkness he had in his keeping. You fancied you had seen things—but the seal was on. When annoyed at meal-times by the constant quarrels of the white men about precedence, he ordered an immense round table to be made, for which a special house had to be built. This was the station's mess-room. Where he sat was the first place—the rest were nowhere. One felt this to be his unalterable conviction. He was neither civil nor uncivil. He was quiet. He allowed his 'boy'—an overfed young negro from the coast—to treat the white men, under his very eyes, with provoking insolence.

"He began to speak as soon as he saw me. I had been very long on the road. He could not wait. Had to start without me. The up-river stations had to be relieved. There had been so many delays already that he did not know who was dead and who was alive, and how they got on—and so on, and so on. He paid no attention to my explanations, and, playing with a stick of sealing-wax, repeated several times that the situation was 'very grave, very grave.' There were rumours that a very important station was in jeopardy, and its chief, Mr Kurtz, was ill. Hoped it was not true. Mr Kurtz was . . . I felt weary and irritable. Hang Kurtz, I thought. I interrupted him by saying I had heard of Mr Kurtz on the coast. 'Ah! So they talk of him down there,' he murmured to himself. Then he began again, assuring me Mr Kurtz was the best agent he had, an exceptional man, of the greatest importance to the Company; therefore I could understand his anxiety. He was, he said, 'very, very uneasy.' Certainly he fidgeted on his chair a good deal, exclaimed, 'Ah, Mr Kurtz!', broke the stick of sealing-wax and seemed dumfounded by the accident. Next thing he wanted to know 'how long it would take to' . . . I interrupted him again. Being hungry, you know, and kept on my feet too, I was getting savage. 'How could I tell?' I said. 'I hadn't even seen the wreck yet—some months, no doubt.'* All this talk seemed to me so futile. 'Some months,' he said. 'Well, let us say three months before we can make a start. Yes. That ought to do the affair.' I flung out of his hut (he lived all alone in a clay hut with a sort of verandah) muttering to myself my opinion of him. He was a chattering idiot. Afterwards I took it back when it was borne in upon me startlingly with what extreme nicety he had estimated the time requisite for the 'affair.'

"I went to work the next day, turning, so to speak, my back on that station. In that way only it seemed to me I could keep my hold on the redeeming facts of life. Still, one must look about sometimes; and then I saw this station, these men strolling aimlessly about in the sunshine of the yard. I asked myself sometimes what it all meant. They wandered here and there with their absurd long staves in their hands, like a lot of faithless pilgrims bewitched inside a rotten fence. The word 'ivory' rang in the air, was whispered, was sighed. You would think they were praying to it. A taint of imbecile rapacity blew through it all, like a whiff from some corpse. By Jove! I've never seen anything so unreal in my life. And outside, the silent wilderness surrounding this cleared speck on the earth struck me as something great and invincible, like evil or truth, waiting patiently for the passing away of this fantastic invasion.

"Oh, these months! Well, never mind. Various things happened. One evening a grass shed full of calico, cotton prints, beads, and I don't know what else, burst into a blaze so suddenly that you would have thought the earth had opened to let an avenging fire consume all that trash. I was smoking my pipe quietly by my dismantled steamer, and saw them all cutting capers in the light, with their arms lifted high, when the stout man with moustaches came tearing down to the river, a tin pail in his hand, assured me that everybody was 'behaving splendidly, splendidly,' dipped about a quart of water and tore back again. I noticed there was a hole in the bottom of his pail.

"I strolled up. There was no hurry. You see the thing had gone off like a box of matches. It had been hopeless from the very first. The flame had leaped high, driven everybody back, lighted up everything—and collapsed. The shed was already a heap of embers glowing fiercely. A nigger was being beaten near by. They said he had caused the fire in some way; be that as it may, he was screeching most horribly. I saw him, later on, for several days, sitting in a bit of shade looking very sick and trying to recover himself: afterwards he arose and went out—and the wilderness without a sound took him into its bosom again. As I approached the glow from the dark I found myself at the back of two men, talking. I heard the name of Kurtz pronounced, then the words, 'take advantage of this unfortunate accident.'* One of the men was the manager. I wished him a good evening. 'Did you ever see anything like it—eh? it is incredible,' he said, and walked off. The other man remained. He was a first-class agent, young, gentlemanly, a bit reserved, with a forked little beard and a hooked nose. He was stand-offish with the other agents, and they on their side said he was the manager's spy upon them. As to me, I had hardly ever spoken to him before. We got into talk, and by-and-by we strolled away from the hissing ruins. Then he asked me to his room, which was in the main building of the station. He struck a match, and I perceived that this young aristocrat had not only a silver-mounted dressing-case but also a whole candle all to himself. Just at that time the manager was the only man supposed to have any right to candles. Native mats covered the clay walls; a collection of spears, assegais, shields, knives was hung up in trophies. The business intrusted to this fellow was the making of bricks—so I had been informed; but there wasn't a fragment of a brick anywhere in the station, and he had been there more than a year—waiting. It seems he could not make bricks without something, I don't know what—straw maybe.* Anyway, it could not be found there, and as it was not likely to be sent from Europe, it did not appear clear to me what he was waiting for. An act of special creation perhaps.* However, they were all waiting—all the sixteen or twenty pilgrims of them—for something; and upon my word it did not seem an uncongenial occupation, from the way they took it, though the only thing that ever came to them was disease—as far as I could see. They beguiled the time by backbiting and intriguing against each other in a foolish kind of way. There was an air of plotting about that station, but nothing came of it, of course. It was as unreal as everything else—as the philanthropic pretence of the whole concern, as their talk, as their government, as their show of work. The only real feeling was a desire to get appointed to a trading-post where ivory was to be had, so that they could earn percentages.* They intrigued and slandered and hated each other only on that account,—but as to effectually lifting a little finger—oh, no. By heavens! there is something after all in the world allowing one man to steal a horse while another must not look at a halter.* Steal a horse straight out. Very well. He has done it. Perhaps he can ride. But there is a way of looking at a halter that would provoke the most charitable of saints into a kick.

"I had no idea why he wanted to be sociable, but as we chatted in there it suddenly occurred to me the fellow was trying to get at something—in fact, pumping me. He alluded constantly to Europe, to the people I was supposed to know there—putting leading questions as to my acquaintances in the sepulchral city, and so on. His little eyes glittered like mica discs—with curiosity,—though he tried to keep up a bit of superciliousness. At first I was astonished, but very soon I became awfully curious to see what he would find out from me. I couldn't possibly imagine what I had in me to make it worth his while.* It was very pretty to see how he baffled himself, for in truth my body was full of chills, and my head had nothing in it but that wretched steamboat business. It was evident he took me for a perfectly shameless prevaricator. At last he got angry, and, to conceal a movement of furious annoyance, he yawned. I rose. Then I noticed a small sketch in oils, on a panel, representing a woman, draped and blindfolded, carrying a lighted torch.* The background was sombre—almost black. The movement of the woman was stately, and the effect of the torchlight on the face was sinister.

"It arrested me, and he stood by civilly, holding a half-pint champagne bottle (medical comforts) with the candle stuck in it. To my question he said Mr Kurtz had painted this—in this very station more than a year ago—while waiting for means to go to his trading-post. 'Tell me, pray,' said I, 'who is this Mr Kurtz?'

"'The chief of the Inner Station,' he answered in a short tone, looking away. 'Much obliged,' I said, laughing. 'And you are the brickmaker of the Central Station. Every one knows that.' He was silent for a while. 'He is a prodigy,' he said at last. 'He is an emissary of pity, and science, and progress, and devil knows what else.* We want,' he began to declaim suddenly, 'for the guidance of the cause intrusted to us by Europe, so to speak, higher intelligence, wide sympathies, a singleness of purpose.' 'Who says that?' I asked. 'Lots of them,' he replied. 'Some even write that; and so *he* comes here, a special being, as you ought to know.' 'Why ought I to know?' I interrupted, really surprised. He paid no attention. 'Yes. Today he is chief of the best station, next year he will be assistant-manager, two years more and . . . but I daresay you know what he will be in two years' time. You are of the new gang—the gang of virtue. The same people who sent him specially also recommended you. Oh, don't say no. I've my own eyes to trust.' Light dawned upon me. My dear aunt's influential acquaintances were producing an unexpected effect upon that young man. I nearly burst into a laugh. 'Do you read the Company's confidential correspondence?' I asked. He hadn't a word

to say. It was great fun. 'When Mr Kurtz,' I continued severely, 'is
General Manager, you won't have the opportunity.'

"He blew the candle out suddenly, and we went outside. The
moon had risen. Black figures strolled about listlessly, pouring water
on the glow, whence proceeded a sound of hissing; steam ascended in
the moonlight; the beaten nigger groaned somewhere. 'What a row
the brute makes!' said the indefatigable man with the moustaches,
appearing near us. 'Serve him right. Transgression—punishment—
bang! Pitiless, pitiless. That's the only way. This will prevent all
conflagrations for the future. I was just telling the manager . . .' He
noticed my companion, and became crestfallen all at once. 'Not in
bed yet,' he said, with a kind of servile heartiness; 'it's so natural.
Ha! Danger—agitation.' He vanished. I went on to the river-side,
and the other followed me. I heard a scathing murmur at my ear,
'Heap of muffs—go to.' The pilgrims could be seen in knots gesticu-
lating, discussing. Several had still their staves in their hands. I verily
believe they took these sticks to bed with them. Beyond the fence the
forest stood up spectrally in the moonlight, and through the dim stir,
through the faint sounds of that lamentable courtyard, the silence of
the land went home to one's very heart,—its mystery, its greatness,
the amazing reality of its concealed life. The hurt nigger moaned
feebly somewhere near by, and then fetched a deep sigh that made
me mend my pace away from there. I felt a hand introducing itself
under my arm. 'My dear sir,' said the fellow, 'I don't want to be
misunderstood, and especially by you, who will see Mr Kurtz long
before I can have that pleasure. I wouldn't like him to get a false idea
of my disposition. . . .'

"I let him run on, this papier-mâché Mephistopheles,* and it
seemed to me that if I tried I could poke my forefinger through him,
and would find nothing inside but a little loose dirt, maybe. He,
don't you see, had been planning to be assistant-manager by-and-by
under the present man, and I could see that the coming of that Kurtz
had upset them both not a little. He talked precipitately, and I did
not try to stop him. I had my shoulders against the wreck of my
steamer, hauled up on the slope like a carcass of some big river
animal. The smell of mud, of primeval mud, by Jove! was in my
nostrils, the high stillness of primeval forest was before my eyes;
there were shiny patches on the black creek. The moon had spread
over everything a thin layer of silver—over the rank grass, over the

mud, upon the wall of matted vegetation standing higher than the wall of a temple, over the great river I could see through a sombre gap glittering, glittering, as it flowed broadly by without a murmur. All this was great, expectant, mute, while the man jabbered about himself. I wondered whether the stillness on the face of the immensity looking at us two were meant as an appeal or as a menace. What were we who had strayed in here? Could we handle that dumb thing, or would it handle us? I felt how big, how confoundedly big, was that thing that couldn't talk, and perhaps was deaf as well. What was in there? I could see a little ivory coming out from there, and I had heard Mr Kurtz was in there. I had heard enough about it too—God knows! Yet somehow it didn't bring any image with it—no more than if I had been told an angel or a fiend was in there. I believed it in the same way one of you might believe there are inhabitants in the planet Mars. I knew once a Scotch sailmaker who was certain, dead sure, there were people in Mars. If you asked him for some idea how they looked and behaved, he would get shy and mutter something about 'walking on all-fours.' If you as much as smiled, he would— though a man of sixty—offer to fight you. I would not have gone so far as to fight for Kurtz, but I went for him near enough to a lie. You know I hate, detest, and can't bear a lie, not because I am straighter than the rest of us, but simply because it appals me. There is a taint of death, a flavour of mortality in lies,—which is exactly what I hate and detest in the world—what I want to forget. It makes me miserable and sick, like biting something rotten would do. Temperament, I suppose. Well, I went near enough to it by letting the young fool there believe anything he liked to imagine as to my influence in Europe. I became in an instant as much of a pretence as the rest of the bewitched pilgrims. This simply because I had a notion it somehow would be of help to that Kurtz whom at the time I did not see— you understand. He was just a word for me. I did not see the man in the name any more than you do. Do you see him? Do you see the story? Do you see anything? It seems to me I am trying to tell you a dream—making a vain attempt, because no relation of a dream can convey the dream-sensation, that commingling of absurdity, surprise, and bewilderment in a tremor of struggling revolt, that notion of being captured by the incredible which is of the very essence of dreams. . . ."

He was silent for a while.

". . . No, it is impossible; it is impossible to convey the life-sensation of any given epoch of one's existence,—that which makes its truth, its meaning—its subtle and penetrating essence. It is impossible. We live, as we dream—alone. . . ."*

He paused again as if reflecting, then added—

"Of course in this you fellows see more than I could then. You see me, whom you know. . . ."

It had become so pitch dark that we listeners could hardly see one another. For a long time already he, sitting apart, had been no more to us than a voice. There was not a word from anybody. The others might have been asleep, but I was awake. I listened, I listened on the watch for the sentence, for the word, that would give me the clue to the faint uneasiness inspired by this narrative that seemed to shape itself without human lips in the heavy night-air of the river.

". . . Yes—I let him run on," Marlow began again, "and think what he pleased about the powers that were behind me. I did! And there was nothing behind me! There was nothing but that wretched, old, mangled steamboat I was leaning against, while he talked fluently about 'the necessity for every man to get on.' 'And when one comes out here, you conceive, it is not to gaze at the moon.' Mr Kurtz was a 'universal genius,' but even a genius would find it easier to work with 'adequate tools—intelligent men.' He did not make bricks—why, there was a physical impossibility in the way—as I was well aware; and if he did secretarial work for the manager, it was because 'no sensible man rejects wantonly the confidence of his superiors.' Did I see it? I saw it. What more did I want? What I really wanted was rivets, by heaven! Rivets. To get on with the work—to stop the hole. Rivets I wanted. There were cases of them down at the coast—cases—piled up—burst—split! You kicked a loose rivet at every second step in that station yard on the hillside. Rivets had rolled into the grove of death. You could fill your pockets with rivets for the trouble of stooping down—and there wasn't one rivet to be found where it was wanted. We had plates that would do, but nothing to fasten them with. And every week the messenger, a lone negro, letter-bag on shoulder and staff in hand, left our station for the coast. And several times a week a coast caravan came in with trade goods,—ghastly glazed calico that made you shudder only to look at it, glass beads value about a penny a quart, confounded spotted cotton handkerchiefs. And no rivets.

Three carriers could have brought all that was wanted to set that steamboat afloat.

"He was becoming confidential now, but I fancy my unresponsive attitude must have exasperated him at last, for he judged it necessary to inform me he feared neither God nor devil, let alone any mere man. I said I could see that very well, but what I wanted was a certain quantity of rivets—and rivets were what really Mr Kurtz wanted, if he had only known it. Now letters went to the coast every week. . . . 'My dear sir,' he cried, 'I write from dictation.' I demanded rivets. There was a way—for an intelligent man. He changed his manner; became very cold, and suddenly began to talk about a hippopotamus;* wondered whether sleeping on board the steamer (I stuck to my salvage night and day) I wasn't disturbed. There was an old hippo that had the bad habit of getting out on the bank and roaming at night over the station grounds. The pilgrims used to turn out in a body and empty every rifle they could lay hands on at him. Some even had sat up o' nights for him. All this energy was wasted, though. 'That animal has a charmed life,' he said; 'but you can say this only of brutes in this country. No man—you apprehend me?—no man here bears a charmed life.' He stood there for a moment in the moonlight with his delicate hooked nose set a little askew, and his mica eyes glittering without a wink, then, with a curt Good night, he strode off. I could see he was disturbed and considerably puzzled, which made me feel more hopeful than I had been for days. It was a great comfort to turn from that chap to my influential friend, the battered, twisted, ruined, tin-pot steamboat. I clambered on board. She rang under my feet like an empty Huntley & Palmer biscuit-tin* kicked along a gutter; she was nothing so solid in make, and rather less pretty in shape, but I had expended enough hard work on her to make me love her. No influential friend would have served me better. She had given me a chance to come out a bit—to find out what I could do. No, I don't like work. I had rather laze about and think of all the fine things that can be done. I don't like work—no man does—but I like what is in the work,—the chance to find yourself. Your own reality—for yourself, not for others—what no other man can ever know. They can only see the mere show, and never can tell what it really means.

"I was not surprised to see somebody sitting aft, on the deck, with his legs dangling over the mud. You see I rather chummed with the few mechanics there were in that station, whom the other pilgrims naturally despised—on account of their imperfect manners, I suppose. This was the foreman—a boiler-maker by trade—a good worker. He was a lank, bony, yellow-faced man, with big intense eyes. His aspect was worried, and his head was as bald as the palm of my hand; but his hair in falling seemed to have stuck to his chin, and had prospered in the new locality, for his beard hung down to his waist. He was a widower with six young children (he had left them in charge of a sister of his to come out there), and the passion of his life was pigeon-flying. He was an enthusiast and a connoisseur. He would rave about pigeons. After work hours he used sometimes to come over from his hut for a talk about his children and his pigeons; at work, when he had to crawl in the mud under the bottom of the steamboat, he would tie up that beard of his in a kind of white serviette he brought for the purpose. It had loops to go over his ears. In the evening he could be seen squatted on the bank rinsing that wrapper in the creek with great care, then spreading it solemnly on a bush to dry.

"I slapped him on the back and shouted 'We shall have rivets!' He scrambled to his feet exclaiming. 'No! Rivets!' as though he couldn't believe his ears. Then in a low voice, 'You . . . eh?' I don't know why we behaved like lunatics. I put my finger to the side of my nose and nodded mysteriously. 'Good for you!' he cried, snapped his fingers above his head, lifting one foot. I tried a jig. We capered on the iron deck. A frightful clatter came out of that hulk, and the virgin forest on the other bank of the creek sent it back in a thundering roll upon the sleeping station. It must have made some of the pilgrims sit up in their hovels. A dark figure obscured the lighted doorway of the manager's hut, vanished, then, a second or so after, the doorway itself vanished too. We stopped, and the silence driven away by the stamping of our feet flowed back again from the recesses of the land. The great wall of vegetation, an exuberant and entangled mass of trunks, branches, leaves, boughs, festoons, motionless in the moonlight, was like a rioting invasion of soundless life, a rolling wave of plants, piled up, crested, ready to topple over the creek, to sweep every little man of us out of his little existence. And it moved not. A deadened burst of mighty splashes and snorts reached us from afar, as though an ichthyosaurus had been taking a bath of glitter in the great river. 'After all,' said the boiler-maker in a reasonable tone, 'why shouldn't we get the rivets?' Why not, indeed! I did not know of any reason why we shouldn't. 'They'll come in three weeks,' I said, confidently.

"But they didn't. Instead of rivets there came an invasion, an infliction, a visitation. It came in sections during the next three weeks, each section headed by a donkey carrying a white man in new clothes and tan shoes, bowing from that elevation right and left to the impressed pilgrims. A quarrelsome band of footsore sulky niggers trod on the heels of the donkey; a lot of tents, camp-stools, tin boxes, white cases, brown bales would be shot down in the courtyard, and the air of mystery would deepen a little over the muddle of the station. Five such instalments came, with their absurd air of disorderly flight with the loot of innumerable outfit shops and provision stores, that, one would think, they were lugging, after a raid, into the wilderness for equitable division. It was an inextricable mess of things decent in themselves but that human folly made look like the spoils of thieving.

"This devoted band called itself the Eldorado Exploring Expedition,* and I believe they were sworn to secrecy. Their talk, however, was the talk of sordid buccaneers: it was reckless without hardihood, greedy without audacity, and cruel without courage; there was not an atom of foresight or of serious intention in the whole batch of them, and they did not seem aware these things are wanted for the work of the world. To tear treasure out of the bowels of the land was their desire, with no more moral purpose at the back of it than there is in burglars breaking into a safe. Who paid the expenses of the noble enterprise I don't know; but the uncle of our manager was leader of that lot.

"In exterior he resembled a butcher in a poor neighbourhood, and his eyes had a look of sleepy cunning. He carried his fat paunch with ostentation on his short legs, and during the time his gang infested the station spoke to no one but his nephew. You could see these two roaming about all day long with their heads close together in an everlasting confab.

"I had given up worrying myself about the rivets. One's capacity for that kind of folly is more limited than you would suppose. I said Hang!—and let things slide. I had plenty of time for meditation, and now and then I would give some thought to Kurtz. I wasn't very interested in him. No. Still, I was curious to see whether this man, who had come out equipped with moral ideas of some sort, would climb to the top after all, and how he would set about his work when there."

## II

"ONE evening as I was lying flat on the deck of my steamboat, I heard voices approaching—and there were the nephew and the uncle strolling along the bank. I laid my head on my arm again, and had nearly lost myself in a doze, when somebody said in my ear, as it were: 'I am as harmless as a little child, but I don't like to be dictated to. Am I the manager—or am I not? I was ordered to send him there. It's incredible.' . . . I became aware that the two were standing on the shore alongside the forepart of the steamboat, just below my head. I did not move; it did not occur to me to move: I was sleepy. 'It *is* unpleasant,' grunted the uncle. 'He has asked the Administration to be sent there,' said the other, 'with the idea of showing what he could do; and I was instructed accordingly. Look at the influence that man must have. Is it not frightful?' They both agreed it was frightful, then made several bizarre remarks: 'Make rain and fine weather—one man—the Council—by the nose'—bits of absurd sentences that got the better of my drowsiness, so that I had pretty near the whole of my wits about me when the uncle said, 'The climate may do away with this difficulty for you. Is he alone there?' 'Yes,' answered the manager; 'he sent his assistant down the river with a note to me in these terms: "Clear this poor devil out of the country, and don't bother sending more of that sort. I had rather be alone than have the kind of men you can dispose of with me." It was more than a year ago. Can you imagine such impudence!' 'Anything since then?' asked the other, hoarsely. 'Ivory,' jerked the nephew; 'lots of it—prime sort—lots—most annoying, from him.' 'And with that?' questioned the heavy rumble. 'Invoice,' was the reply fired out, so to speak. Then silence. They had been talking about Kurtz.

"I was broad awake by this time, but, lying perfectly at ease, remained still, having no inducement to change my position. 'How did that ivory come all this way?' growled the elder man, who seemed very vexed. The other explained that it had come with a fleet of canoes in charge of an English half-caste clerk Kurtz had with him; that Kurtz had apparently intended to return himself, the station being by that time bare of goods and stores, but after coming three hundred miles, had suddenly decided to go back, which he started to do alone in a small dug-out with four paddlers, leaving the half-caste to continue down the river with the ivory. The two fellows there seemed astounded at anybody attempting such a thing. They were at a loss for an adequate motive. As to me, I seemed to see Kurtz for the first time. It was a distinct glimpse: the dug-out, four paddling savages, and the lone white man turning his back suddenly on the headquarters, on relief, on thoughts of home—perhaps; setting his face towards the depths of the wilderness, towards his empty and desolate station. I did not know the motive. Perhaps he was just simply a fine fellow who stuck to his work for its own sake. His name, you understand, had not been pronounced once. He was 'that man.' The half-caste, who, as far as I could see, had conducted a difficult trip with great prudence and pluck, was invariably alluded to as 'that scoundrel.' The 'scoundrel' had reported that the 'man' had been very ill—had recovered imperfectly. . . . The two below me moved away then a few paces, and strolled back and forth at some little distance. I heard: 'Military post—doctor—two hundred miles— quite alone now—unavoidable delays—nine months—no news— strange rumours.' They approached again, just as the manager was saying, 'No one, as far as I know, unless a species of wandering trader—a pestilential fellow, snapping ivory from the natives.' Who was it they were talking about now? I gathered in snatches that this was some man supposed to be in Kurtz's district, and of whom the manager did not approve. 'We will not be free from unfair competition till one of these fellows is hanged for an example,' he said. 'Certainly,' grunted the other; 'get him hanged! Why not?* Anything—anything can be done in this country. That's what I say; nobody here, you understand, *here*, can endanger your position. And why? You stand the climate—you outlast them all. The danger is in Europe; but there before I left I took care to——' They moved off and whispered, then their voices rose again. 'The extraordinary series of delays is not my fault. I did my possible.'* The fat man sighed, 'Very sad.' 'And the pestiferous absurdity of his talk,' continued the other; 'he bothered me enough when he was here. "Each station should be like a beacon on the road towards better things, a centre for trade of course, but also for humanising, improving, instructing." Conceive you—that ass! And he wants to be manager! No, it's——' Here he got choked by excessive indignation, and I lifted my head the least bit. I was surprised to see how near they were—right under me. I could have spat upon their hats. They were looking on the ground, absorbed in thought. The manager was switching his leg with a slender twig: his sagacious relative lifted his head. 'You have been well since you came out this time?' he asked. The other gave a start. 'Who? I? Oh! Like a charm—like a charm. But the rest—oh, my goodness! All sick. They die so quick, too, that I haven't the time to send them out of the country—it's incredible!' 'H'm. Just so,' grunted the uncle. 'Ah! my boy, trust to this—I say, trust to this.' I saw him extend his short flipper of an arm for a gesture that took in the forest, the creek, the mud, the river,—seemed to beckon with a dishonouring flourish before the sunlit face of the land a treacherous appeal to the lurking death, to the hidden evil, to the profound darkness of its heart. It was so startling that I leaped to my feet and looked back at the edge of the forest, as though I had expected an answer of some sort to that black display of confidence. You know the foolish notions that come to one sometimes. The high stillness confronted these two figures with its ominous patience, waiting for the passing away of a fantastic invasion.

"They swore aloud together—out of sheer fright, I believe—then pretending not to know anything of my existence, turned back to the station. The sun was low; and leaning forward side by side, they seemed to be tugging painfully uphill their two ridiculous shadows of unequal length, that trailed behind them slowly over the tall grass without bending a single blade.

"In a few days the Eldorado Expedition went into the patient wilderness, that closed upon it as the sea closes over a diver. Long afterwards the news came that all the donkeys were dead. I know nothing as to the fate of the less valuable animals. They, no doubt, like the rest of us, found what they deserved. I did not inquire. I was then rather excited at the prospect of meeting Kurtz very soon. When I say very soon I mean it comparatively. It was just two months from the day we left the creek when we came to the bank below Kurtz's station.

"Going up that river was like travelling back to the earliest beginnings of the world, when vegetation rioted on the earth and the big trees were kings. An empty stream, a great silence, an impenetrable forest. The air was warm, thick, heavy, sluggish. There was no joy in the brilliance of sunshine. The long stretches of the waterway ran on, deserted, into the gloom of overshadowed distances. On silvery sandbanks hippos and alligators sunned themselves side by side. The broadening waters flowed through a mob of wooded islands; you lost your way on that river as you would in a desert, and butted all day long against shoals, trying to find the channel, till you thought yourself bewitched and cut off for ever from everything you had known once—somewhere—far away—in another existence perhaps. There were moments when one's past came back to one, as it will sometimes when you have not a moment to spare to yourself; but it came in the shape of an unrestful and noisy dream, remembered with wonder amongst the overwhelming realities of this strange world of plants, and water, and silence. And this stillness of life did not in the least resemble a peace. It was the stillness of an implacable force brooding over an inscrutable intention. It looked at you with a vengeful aspect. I got used to it afterwards; I did not see it any more; I had no time. I had to keep guessing at the channel; I had to discern, mostly by inspiration, the signs of hidden banks; I watched for sunken stones; I was learning to clap my teeth smartly before my heart flew out, when I shaved by a fluke some infernal sly old snag that would have ripped the life out of the tin-pot steamboat and drowned all the pilgrims; I had to keep a look-out for the signs of dead wood we could cut up in the night for next day's steaming.* When you have to attend to things of that sort, to the mere incidents of the surface, the reality—the reality, I tell you—fades. The inner truth is hidden—luckily, luckily. But I felt it all the same; I felt often its mysterious stillness watching me at my monkey tricks, just as it watches you fellows performing on your respective tight-ropes for— what is it? half-a-crown a tumble——"

"Try to be civil, Marlow," growled a voice, and I knew there was at least one listener awake besides myself.

"I beg your pardon. I forgot the heartache which makes up the rest of the price. And indeed what does the price matter, if the trick be well done? You do your tricks very well. And I didn't do badly either, since I managed not to sink that steamboat on my first trip. It's a wonder to me yet. Imagine a blindfolded man set to drive a van over a bad road. I sweated and shivered over that business considerably, I can tell you. After all, for a seaman, to scrape the bottom of the thing that's supposed to float all the time under his care is the unpardonable sin. No one may know of it, but you never forget the thump—eh? A blow on the very heart. You remember it, you dream of it, you wake up at night and think of it—years after—and go hot and cold all over. I don't pretend to say that steamboat floated all the time. More than once she had to wade for a bit, with twenty cannibals splashing around and pushing.* We had enlisted some of these chaps on the way for a crew. Fine fellows—cannibals—in their place. They were men one could work with, and I am grateful to them. And, after all, they did not eat each other before my face: they had brought along a provision of hippo-meat which went rotten, and made the mystery of the wilderness stink in my nostrils. Phoo! I can sniff it now. I had the manager on board and three or four pilgrims with their staves—all complete.* Sometimes we came upon a station close by the bank, clinging to the skirts of the unknown, and the white men rushing out of a tumble-down hovel, with great gestures of joy and surprise and welcome, seemed very strange,—had the appearance of being held there captive by a spell. The word 'ivory' would ring in the air for a while—and on we went again into the silence, along empty reaches, round the still bends, between the high walls of our winding way, reverberating in hollow claps the ponderous beat of the stern-wheel. Trees, trees, millions of trees, massive, immense, running up high; and at their foot, hugging the bank against the stream, crept the little begrimed steamboat, like a sluggish beetle crawling on the floor of a lofty portico. It made you feel very small, very lost, and yet it was not altogether depressing that feeling. After all, if you were small, the grimy beetle crawled on— which was just what you wanted it to do. Where the pilgrims imagined it crawled to I don't know. To some place where they expected to get something, I bet! For me it crawled towards Kurtz— exclusively;* but when the steam-pipes started leaking we crawled very slow. The reaches opened before us and closed behind, as if the forest had stepped leisurely across the water to bar the way for our return. We penetrated deeper and deeper into the heart of darkness.  It was very quiet there. At night sometimes the roll of drums behind the curtain of trees would run up the river and remain sustained faintly, as if hovering in the air high over our heads, till the first break of day. Whether it meant war, peace, or prayer we could not tell. The dawns were heralded by the descent of a chill stillness; the wood-cutters slept, their fires burned low; the snapping of a twig would make you start. We were wanderers on a prehistoric earth, on an earth that wore the aspect of an unknown planet. We could have fancied ourselves the first of men taking possession of an accursed inheritance, to be subdued at the cost of profound anguish and of excessive toil. But suddenly, as we struggled round a bend, there would be a glimpse of rush walls, of peaked grass-roofs, a burst of yells, a whirl of black limbs, a mass of hands clapping, of feet stamping, of bodies swaying, of eyes rolling, under the droop of heavy and motionless foliage. The steamer toiled along slowly on the edge of a black and incomprehensible frenzy. The prehistoric man was cursing us, praying to us, welcoming us—who could tell? We were cut off from the comprehension of our surroundings; we glided past like phantoms, wondering and secretly appalled, as sane men would be before an enthusiastic outbreak in a madhouse. We could not understand, because we were too far and could not remember, because we were travelling in the night of first ages, of those ages that are gone, leaving hardly a sign—and no memories.

"The earth seemed unearthly. We are accustomed to look upon the shackled form of a conquered monster, but there—there you could look at a thing monstrous and free. It was unearthly, and the men were—— No, they were not inhuman. Well, you know, that was the worst of it—this suspicion of their not being inhuman. It would come slowly to one. They howled, and leaped, and spun, and made horrid faces; but what thrilled you was just the thought of their humanity—like yours—the thought of your remote kinship with this wild and passionate uproar. Ugly. Yes, it was ugly enough; but if you were man enough you would admit to yourself that there was in you just the faintest trace of a response to the terrible frankness of that noise, a dim suspicion of there being a meaning in it which you—you so remote from the night of first ages—could comprehend. And why not? The mind of man is capable of anything*— because everything is in it, all the past as well as all the future. What was there after all? Joy, fear, sorrow, devotion, valour, rage—who can tell?—but truth—truth stripped of its cloak of time. Let the fool gape and shudder—the man knows, and can look on without a wink. But he must at least be as much of a man as these on the shore. He must meet that truth with his own true stuff—with his own inborn strength. Principles? Principles won't do. Acquisitions, clothes, pretty rags—rags that would fly off at the first good shake. No; you want a deliberate belief. An appeal to me in this fiendish row—is there? Very well; I hear; I admit, but I have a voice too, and for good or evil mine is the speech that cannot be silenced. Of course, a fool, what with sheer fright and fine sentiments, is always safe. Who's that grunting? You wonder I didn't go ashore for a howl and a dance? Well, no—I didn't. Fine sentiments, you say? Fine sentiments, be hanged! I had no time. I had to mess about with white-lead and strips of woollen blanket helping to put bandages on those leaky steam-pipes—I tell you. I had to watch the steering, and circumvent those snags, and get the tin-pot along by hook or by crook. There was surface-truth enough in these things to save a wiser man. And between whiles I had to look after the savage who was fireman. He was an improved specimen; he could fire up a vertical boiler. He was there below me, and, upon my word, to look at him was as edifying as seeing a dog in a parody of breeches and a feather hat, walking on his hind-legs. A few months of training had done for that really fine chap. He squinted at the steam-gauge and at the water-gauge with an evident effort of intrepidity—and he had filed teeth too, the poor devil, and the wool of his pate shaved into queer patterns, and three ornamental scars on each of his cheeks. He ought to have been clapping his hands and stamping his feet on the bank, instead of which he was hard at work, a thrall to strange witchcraft, full of improving knowledge. He was useful because he had been instructed; and what he knew was this—that should the water in that transparent thing disappear, the evil spirit inside the boiler would get angry through the greatness of his thirst, and take a terrible vengeance. So he sweated and fired up and watched the glass fearfully (with an impromptu charm, made of rags, tied to his arm, and a piece of polished bone, as big as a watch, stuck flatways through his lower lip), while the wooded banks slipped past us slowly, the short noise was left behind, the interminable miles of silence—and we crept on, towards Kurtz. But the snags were thick, the water was treacherous and shallow, the boiler seemed indeed to have a sulky devil in it, and thus neither that fireman nor I had any time to peer into our creepy thoughts.

"Some fifty miles below the Inner Station we came upon a hut of reeds, an inclined and melancholy pole, with the unrecognisable tatters of what had been a flag of some sort flying from it, and a neatly stacked wood-pile. This was unexpected. We came to the bank, and on the stack of firewood found a flat piece of board with some faded pencil-writing on it. When deciphered it said: 'Wood for you. Hurry up. Approach cautiously.' There was a signature, but it was illegible—not Kurtz—a much longer word. Hurry up. Where? Up the river? 'Approach cautiously.' We had not done so. But the warning could not have been meant for the place where it could be only found after approach. Something was wrong above. But what—and how much? That was the question. We commented adversely upon the imbecility of that telegraphic style. The bush around said nothing, and would not let us look very far, either. A torn curtain of red twill hung in the doorway of the hut, and flapped sadly in our faces. The dwelling was dismantled; but we could see a white man had lived there not very long ago. There remained a rude table—a plank on two posts; a heap of rubbish reposed in a dark corner, and by the door I picked up a book. It had lost its covers, and the pages had been thumbed into a state of extremely dirty softness; but the back had been lovingly stitched afresh with white cotton thread, which looked clean yet. It was an extraordinary find. Its title was, *An Inquiry into Some Points of Seamanship*, by a man Towser, Towson—some such name—Master in his Majesty's Navy.* The matter looked dreary reading enough, with illustrative diagrams and repulsive tables of figures, and the copy was sixty years old. I handled this amazing antiquity with the greatest possible tenderness, lest it should dissolve in my hands. Within, Towson or Towser was inquiring earnestly into the breaking strain of ships' chains and tackle, and other such matters. Not a very enthralling book; but at the first glance you could see there a singleness of intention, an honest concern for the right way of going to work, which made these humble pages, thought out so many years ago, luminous with another than a professional light. The simple old sailor, with his talk of chains and purchases, made me forget the jungle and the pilgrims in a delicious sensation of having come upon something unmistakably real. Such a book being there was wonderful enough; but still more astounding were the notes pencilled in the margin, and plainly referring to the text. I couldn't believe my eyes! They were in cipher! Yes, it looked like cipher. Fancy a man lugging with him a book of that description into this nowhere and studying it—and making notes—in cipher at that! It was an extravagant mystery.

"I had been dimly aware for some time of a worrying noise, and when I lifted my eyes I saw the wood-pile was gone, and the manager, aided by all the pilgrims, was shouting at me from the river-side. I slipped the book into my pocket. I assure you to leave off reading was like tearing myself away from the shelter of an old and solid friendship.

"I started the lame engine ahead. 'It must be this miserable trader—this intruder,' exclaimed the manager, looking back malevolently at the place we had left. 'He must be English,' I said. 'It will not save him from getting into trouble if he is not careful,' muttered the manager darkly. I observed with assumed innocence that no man was safe from trouble in this world.

"The current was more rapid now, the steamer seemed at her last gasp, the stern-wheel flopped languidly, and I caught myself listening on tiptoe for the next beat of the float, for in sober truth I expected the wretched thing to give up every moment. It was like watching the last flickers of a life. But still we crawled. Sometimes I would pick out a tree a little way ahead to measure our progress towards Kurtz by, but I lost it invariably before we got abreast. To keep the eyes so long on one thing was too much for human patience. The manager displayed a beautiful resignation. I fretted and fumed and took to arguing with myself whether or no I would talk openly with Kurtz; but before I could come to any conclusion it occurred to me that my speech or my silence, indeed any action of mine, would be a mere futility. What did it matter what any one knew or ignored? What did it matter who was manager? One gets sometimes such a flash of insight. The essentials of this affair lay deep under the surface, beyond my reach, and beyond my power of meddling.

"Towards the evening of the second day we judged ourselves about eight miles from Kurtz's station. I wanted to push on; but the manager looked grave, and told me the navigation up there was so dangerous that it would be advisable, the sun being very low already, to wait where we were till next morning. Moreover, he pointed out that if the warning to approach cautiously were to be followed, we must approach in daylight—not at dusk, or in the dark. This was sensible enough. Eight miles meant nearly three hours' steaming for us, and I could also see suspicious ripples at the upper end of the reach. Nevertheless, I was annoyed beyond expression at the delay, and most unreasonably too, since one night more could not matter much after so many months. As we had plenty of wood, and caution was the word, I brought up in the middle of the stream. The reach was narrow, straight, with high sides like a railway cutting. The dusk

came gliding into it long before the sun had set. The current ran
smooth and swift, but a dumb immobility sat on the banks. The
living trees, lashed together by the creepers and every living bush of
the undergrowth, might have been changed into stone, even to the
slenderest twig, to the lightest leaf. It was not sleep—it seemed
unnatural, like a state of trance. Not the faintest sound of any kind
could be heard. You looked on amazed, and began to suspect yourself of being deaf—then the night came suddenly, and struck you
blind as well. About three in the morning some large fish leaped, and
the loud splash made me jump as though a gun had been fired. When
the sun rose there was a white fog, very warm and clammy, and more
blinding than the night. It did not shift or drive; it was just there,
standing all round you like something solid. At eight or nine, perhaps, it lifted as a shutter lifts. We had a glimpse of the towering
multitude of trees, of the immense matted jungle, with the blazing
little ball of the sun hanging over it—all perfectly still—and then the
white shutter came down again, smoothly, as if sliding in greased
grooves. I ordered the chain, which we had begun to heave in, to be
paid out again. Before it stopped running with a muffled rattle, a cry,
a very loud cry, as of infinite desolation, soared slowly in the opaque
air. It ceased. A complaining clamour, modulated in savage discords,
filled our ears. The sheer unexpectedness of it made my hair stir
under my cap. I don't know how it struck the others: to me it seemed
as though the mist itself had screamed, so suddenly, and apparently
from all sides at once, did this tumultuous and mournful uproar
arise. It culminated in a hurried outbreak of almost intolerably
excessive shrieking, which stopped short, leaving us stiffened in a
variety of silly attitudes, and obstinately listening to the nearly as
appalling and excessive silence. 'Good God! What is the
meaning——?' stammered at my elbow one of the pilgrims,—a little
fat man, with sandy hair and red whiskers, who wore side-spring
boots, and pink pyjamas tucked into his socks. Two others remained
open-mouthed a whole minute, then dashed into the little cabin, to
rush out incontinently and stand darting scared glances, with Winchesters at 'ready' in their hands. What we could see was just the
steamer we were on, her outlines blurred as though she had been on
the point of dissolving, and a misty strip of water, perhaps two feet
broad, around her—and that was all. The rest of the world was
nowhere, as far as our eyes and ears were concerned. Just nowhere.

Gone, disappeared; swept off without leaving a whisper or a shadow behind.

"I went forward, and ordered the chain to be hauled in short, so as to be ready to trip the anchor and move the steamboat at once if necessary. 'Will they attack?' whispered an awed voice. 'We will be all butchered in this fog,' murmured another. The faces twitched with the strain, the hands trembled slightly, the eyes forgot to wink. It was very curious to see the contrast of expressions of the white men and of the black fellows of our crew, who were as much strangers to that part of the river as we, though their homes were only eight hundred miles away. The whites, of course greatly discomposed, had besides a curious look of being painfully shocked by such an outrageous row. The others had an alert, naturally interested expression; but their faces were essentially quiet, even those of the one or two who grinned as they hauled at the chain. Several exchanged short, grunting phrases, which seemed to settle the matter to their satisfaction. Their headman, a young, broad-chested black, severely draped in dark-blue fringed cloths, with fierce nostrils and his hair all done up artfully in oily ringlets, stood near me. 'Aha!' I said, just for good fellowship's sake. 'Catch 'im,' he snapped, with a bloodshot widening of his eyes and a flash of sharp teeth—'catch 'im. Give 'im to us.' 'To you, eh?' I asked; 'what would you do with them?' 'Eat 'im!' he said, curtly, and, leaning his elbow on the rail, looked out into the fog in a dignified and profoundly pensive attitude. I would no doubt have been properly horrified, had it not occurred to me that he and his chaps must be very hungry: that they must have been growing increasingly hungry for at least this month past. They had been engaged for six months (I don't think a single one of them had any clear idea of time, as we at the end of countless ages have. They still belonged to the beginnings of time—had no inherited experience to teach them as it were), and of course, as long as there was a piece of paper written over in accordance with some farcical law or other made down the river, it didn't enter anybody's head to trouble how they would live. Certainly they had brought with them some rotten hippo-meat, which couldn't have lasted very long, anyway, even if the pilgrims hadn't, in the midst of a shocking hullabaloo, thrown a considerable quantity of it overboard. It looked like a high-handed proceeding; but it was really a case of legitimate self-defence. You can't breathe dead hippo waking, sleeping, and eating, and at the same time keep your precarious grip on existence. Besides that, they had given them every week three pieces of brass wire, each about nine inches long; and the theory was they were to buy their provisions with that currency in river-side villages.* You can see how *that* worked. There were either no villages, or the people were hostile, or the director, who like the rest of us fed out of tins, with an occasional old he-goat thrown in, didn't want to stop the steamer for some more or less recondite reason. So, unless they swallowed the wire itself, or made loops of it to snare the fishes with, I don't see what good their extravagant salary could be to them. I must say it was paid with a regularity worthy of a large and honourable trading company. For the rest, the only thing to eat—though it didn't look eatable in the least—I saw in their possession was a few lumps of some stuff like half-cooked dough,* of a dirty lavender colour, they kept wrapped in leaves, and now and then swallowed a piece of, but so small that it seemed done more for the looks of the thing than for any serious purpose of sustenance. Why in the name of all the gnawing devils of hunger they didn't go for us—they were thirty to five—and have a good tuck-in for once, amazes me now when I think of it. They were big powerful men, with not much capacity to weigh the consequences, with courage, with strength, even yet, though their skins were no longer glossy and their muscles no longer hard. And I saw that something restraining, one of those human secrets that baffle probability, had come into play there. I looked at them with a swift quickening of interest—not because it occurred to me I might be eaten by them before very long, though I own to you that just then I perceived—in a new light, as it were—how unwholesome the pilgrims looked, and I hoped, yes, I positively hoped, that my aspect was not so—what shall I say?—so—unappetising: a touch of fantastic vanity which fitted well with the dream-sensation that pervaded all my days at that time. Perhaps I had a little fever too. One can't live with one's finger everlastingly on one's pulse. I had often 'a little fever,' or a little touch of other things—the playful paw-strokes of the wilderness, the preliminary trifling before the more serious onslaught which came in due course. Yes; I looked at them as you would on any human being, with a curiosity of their impulses, motives, capacities, weaknesses, when brought to the test of an inexorable physical necessity. Restraint! What possible restraint? Was it superstition, disgust, patience, fear—or some kind of primitive honour? No fear can stand up to hunger, no patience can wear it out, disgust simply does not exist where hunger is; and as to superstition, beliefs, and what you may call principles, they are less than chaff in a breeze. Don't you know the devilry of lingering starvation, its exasperating torment, its black thoughts, its sombre and brooding ferocity? Well, I do. It takes a man all his inborn strength to fight hunger properly. It's really easier to face bereavement, dishonour, and the perdition of one's soul—than this kind of prolonged hunger. Sad, but true. And these chaps too had no earthly reason for any kind of scruple. Restraint! I would just as soon have expected restraint from a hyena prowling amongst the corpses of a battlefield. But there was the fact facing me—the fact dazzling, to be seen, like the foam on the depths of the sea, like a ripple on an unfathomable enigma, a mystery greater—when I thought of it— than the curious, inexplicable note of desperate grief in this savage clamour that had swept by us on the river-bank, behind the blind whiteness of the fog.

"Two pilgrims were quarrelling in hurried whispers as to which bank. 'Left.' 'No, no; how can you? Right, right, of course.' 'It is very serious,' said the manager's voice behind me; 'I would be desolated if anything should happen to Mr Kurtz before we came up.' I looked at him, and had not the slightest doubt he was sincere. He was just the kind of man who would wish to preserve appearances. That was his restraint. But when he muttered something about going on at once, I did not even take the trouble to answer him. I knew, and he knew, that it was impossible. Were we to let go our hold of the bottom, we would be absolutely in the air—in space. We wouldn't be able to tell where we were going to—whether up or down stream, or across—till we fetched against one bank or the other,—and then we wouldn't know at first which it was. Of course I made no move. I had no mind for a smash-up. You couldn't imagine a more deadly place for a shipwreck. Whether drowned at once or not, we were sure to perish speedily in one way or another. 'I authorise you to take all the risks,' he said, after a short silence. 'I refuse to take any,' I said shortly; which was just the answer he expected, though its tone might have surprised him. 'Well, I must defer to your judgment. You are captain,' he said, with marked civility. I turned my shoulder to him in sign of my appreciation, and looked into the fog. How long would it last? It was the most hopeless look-out. The approach to this Kurtz grubbing for ivory in the wretched bush was beset by as many dangers as though he had been an enchanted princess sleeping in a fabulous castle.* 'Will they attack, do you think?' asked the manager, in a confidential tone.

"I did not think they would attack, for several obvious reasons. The thick fog was one. If they left the bank in their canoes they would get lost in it, as we would be if we attempted to move. Still, I had also judged the jungle of both banks quite impenetrable—and yet eyes were in it, eyes that had seen us. The river-side bushes were certainly very thick; but the undergrowth behind was evidently penetrable. However, during the short lift I had seen no canoes anywhere in the reach—certainly not abreast of the steamer. But what made the idea of attack inconceivable to me was the nature of the noise—of the cries we had heard. They had not the fierce character boding of immediate hostile intention. Unexpected, wild, and violent as they had been, they had given me an irresistible impression of sorrow. The glimpse of the steamboat had for some reason filled those savages with unrestrained grief. The danger, if any, I expounded, was from our proximity to a great human passion let loose. Even extreme grief may ultimately vent itself in violence—but more generally takes the form of apathy. . . .

"You should have seen the pilgrims stare! They had no heart to grin, or even to revile me; but I believe they thought me gone mad—with fright, maybe. I delivered a regular lecture. My dear boys, it was no good bothering. Keep a look-out? Well, you may guess I watched the fog for the signs of lifting as a cat watches a mouse; but for anything else our eyes were of no more use to us than if we had been buried miles deep in a heap of cotton-wool. It felt like it too—choking, warm, stifling. Besides, all I said, though it sounded extravagant, was absolutely true to fact. What we afterwards alluded to as an attack was really an attempt at repulse. The action was very far from being aggressive—it was not even defensive, in the usual sense: it was undertaken under the stress of desperation, and in its essence was purely protective.

"It developed itself, I should say, two hours after the fog lifted, and its commencement was at a spot, roughly speaking, about a mile and a half below Kurtz's station. We had just floundered and flopped round a bend, when I saw an islet, a mere grassy hummock of bright green, in the middle of the stream. It was the only thing of the kind;

but as we opened the reach more, I perceived it was the head of a long sandbank, or rather of a chain of shallow patches stretching down the middle of the river. They were discoloured, just awash, and the whole lot was seen just under the water, exactly as a man's backbone is seen running down the middle of his back under the skin. Now, as far as I did see, I could go to the right or to the left of this. I didn't know either channel, of course. The banks looked pretty well alike, the depth appeared the same; but as I had been informed the station was on the west side, I naturally headed for the western passage.

"No sooner had we fairly entered it than I became aware it was much narrower than I had supposed. To the left of us there was the long uninterrupted shoal, and to the right a high, steep bank heavily overgrown with bushes. Above the bush the trees stood in serried ranks. The twigs overhung the current thickly, and from distance to distance a large limb of some tree projected rigidly over the stream. It was then well on in the afternoon, the face of the forest was gloomy, and a broad strip of shadow had already fallen on the water. In this shadow we steamed up—very slowly, as you may imagine. I sheered her well inshore—the water being deepest near the bank, as the sounding-pole informed me.

"One of my hungry and forbearing friends was sounding in the bows just below me. This steamboat was exactly like a decked scow. On the deck there were two little teak-wood houses, with doors and windows. The boiler was in the fore-end, and the machinery right astern. Over the whole there was a light roof, supported on stanchions. The funnel projected through that roof, and in front of the funnel a small cabin built of light planks served for a pilot-house. It contained a couch, two camp-stools, a loaded Martini-Henry leaning in one corner, a tiny table, and the steering-wheel. It had a wide door in front and a broad shutter at each side. All these were always thrown open, of course. I spent my days perched up there on the extreme fore-end of that roof, before the door. At night I slept, or tried to, on the couch. An athletic black belonging to some coast tribe, and educated by my poor predecessor, was the helmsman. He sported a pair of brass earrings, wore a blue cloth wrapper from the waist to the ankles, and thought all the world of himself. He was the most unstable kind of fool I had ever seen. He steered with no end of a swagger while you were by; but if he lost sight of you, he became instantly the prey of an abject funk, and would let that cripple of a steamboat get the upper hand of him in a minute.

"I was looking down at the sounding-pole, and feeling much annoyed to see at each try a little more of it stick out of that river, when I saw my poleman give up the business suddenly, and stretch himself flat on the deck, without even taking the trouble to haul his pole in. He kept hold on it though, and it trailed in the water. At the same time the fireman, whom I could also see below me, sat down abruptly before his furnace and ducked his head. I was amazed. Then I had to look at the river mighty quick, because there was a snag in the fairway. Sticks, little sticks, were flying about—thick: they were whizzing before my nose, dropping below me, striking behind me against my pilot-house. All this time the river, the shore, the woods, were very quiet—perfectly quiet. I could only hear the heavy splashing thump of the stern-wheel and the patter of these things. We cleared the snag clumsily. Arrows, by Jove! We were being shot at! I stepped in quickly to close the shutter on the land-side. That fool-helmsman, his hands on the spokes, was lifting his knees high, stamping his feet, champing his mouth, like a reined-in horse. Confound him! And we were staggering within ten feet of the bank. I had to lean right out to swing the heavy shutter, and I saw a face amongst the leaves on the level with my own, looking at me very fierce and steady; and then suddenly, as though a veil had been removed from my eyes, I made out, deep in the tangled gloom, naked breasts, arms, legs, glaring eyes,—the bush was swarming with human limbs in movement, glistening, of bronze colour. The twigs shook, swayed, and rustled, the arrows flew out of them, and then the shutter came to. 'Steer her straight,' I said to the helmsman. He held his head rigid, face forward; but his eyes rolled, he kept on lifting and setting down his feet gently, his mouth foamed a little. 'Keep quiet!' I said in a fury. I might just as well have ordered a tree not to sway in the wind. I darted out. Below me there was a great scuffle of feet on the iron deck; confused exclamations; a voice screamed, 'Can you turn back?' I caught sight of a V-shaped ripple on the water ahead. What? Another snag! A fusillade burst out under my feet. The pilgrims had opened with their Winchesters, and were simply squirting lead into that bush. A deuce of a lot of smoke came up and drove slowly forward. I swore at it. Now I couldn't see the ripple or the snag either. I stood in the doorway, peering, and the arrows came in swarms. They might have been poisoned, but they looked as though they wouldn't kill a cat. The bush began to howl. Our wood-cutters raised a warlike whoop; the report of a rifle just at my back deafened me. I glanced over my shoulder, and the pilot-house was yet full of noise and smoke when I made a dash at the wheel. The fool-nigger had dropped everything, to throw the shutter open and let off that Martini-Henry. He stood before the wide open-ing, glaring, and I yelled at him to come back, while I straightened the sudden twist out of that steamboat. There was no room to turn even if I had wanted to, the snag was somewhere very near ahead in that confounded smoke, there was no time to lose, so I just crowded her into the bank—right into the bank, where I knew the water was deep.

"We tore slowly along the overhanging bushes in a whirl of broken twigs and flying leaves. The fusillade below stopped short, as I had foreseen it would when the squirts got empty. I threw my head back to a glinting whizz that traversed the pilot-house, in at one shutter-hole and out at the other. Looking past that mad helmsman, who was shaking the empty rifle and yelling at the shore, I saw vague forms of men running bent double, leaping, gliding, distinct, incomplete, evanescent. Something big appeared in the air before the shutter, the rifle went overboard, and the man stepped back swiftly, looked at me over his shoulder in an extraordinary, profound, familiar manner, and fell upon my feet. The side of his head hit the wheel twice, and the end of what appeared a long cane clattered round and knocked over a little camp-stool. It looked as though after wrenching that thing from somebody ashore he had lost his balance in the effort. The thin smoke had blown away, we were clear of the snag, and looking ahead I could see that in another hundred yards or so I would be free to sheer off, away from the bank; but my feet felt so very warm and wet that I had to look down. The man had rolled on his back and stared straight up at me; both his hands clutched that cane. It was the shaft of a spear that, either thrown or lounged* through the opening, had caught him in the side just below the ribs; the blade had gone in out of sight, after making a frightful gash; my shoes were full; a pool of blood lay very still, gleaming dark-red under the wheel; his eyes shone with an amazing lustre. The fusil-lade burst out again. He looked at me anxiously, gripping the spear like something precious, with an air of being afraid I would try to take it away from him. I had to make an effort to free my eyes from his gaze and attend to the steering. With one hand I felt above my head for the line of the steam-whistle, and jerked out screech after screech hurriedly.* The tumult of angry and warlike yells was checked instantly, and then from the depths of the woods went out such a tremulous and prolonged wail of mournful fear and utter despair as may be imagined to follow the flight of the last hope from the earth. There was a great commotion in the bush; the shower of arrows stopped, a few dropping shots rang out sharply—then silence, in which the languid beat of the stern-wheel came plainly to my ears. I put the helm hard a-starboard at the moment when the pilgrim in pink pyjamas, very hot and agitated, appeared in the doorway. 'The manager sends me——' he began in an official tone, and stopped short. 'Good God!' he said, glaring at the wounded man.

"We two whites stood over him, and his lustrous and inquiring glance enveloped us both. I declare it looked as though he would presently put to us some question in an understandable language; but he died without uttering a sound, without moving a limb, without twitching a muscle. Only in the very last moment, as though in response to some sign we could not see, to some whisper we could not hear, he frowned heavily, and that frown gave to his black death-mask an inconceivably sombre, brooding, and menacing expression. The lustre of inquiring glance faded swiftly into vacant glassiness. 'Can you steer?' I asked the agent eagerly. He looked very dubious; but I made a grab at his arm, and he understood at once I meant him to steer whether or no. To tell you the truth, I was morbidly anxious to change my shoes and socks. 'He is dead,' murmured the fellow, immensely impressed. 'No doubt about it,' said I, tugging like mad at the shoe-laces. 'And, by the way, I suppose Mr Kurtz is dead as well by this time.'

"For the moment that was the dominant thought. There was a sense of extreme disappointment, as though I had found out I had been striving after something altogether without a substance. I couldn't have been more disgusted if I had travelled all this way for the sole purpose of talking with Mr Kurtz. Talking with. . . . I flung one shoe overboard, and became aware that that was exactly what I had been looking forward to—a talk with Kurtz. I made the strange discovery that I had never imagined him as doing, you know, but as discoursing. I didn't say to myself, 'Now I will never see him,' or 'Now I will never shake him by the hand,' but, 'Now I will never hear him.' The man presented himself as a voice. Not of course that I did not connect him with some sort of action. Hadn't I been told in all the tones of jealousy and admiration that he had collected, bartered, swindled, or stolen more ivory than all the other agents together. That was not the point. The point was in his being a gifted creature, and that of all his gifts the one that stood out preeminently, that carried with it a sense of real presence, was his ability to talk, his words—the gift of expression, the bewildering, the illuminating, the most exalted and the most contemptible, the pulsating stream of light, or the deceitful flow from the heart of an impenetrable darkness.

"The other shoe went flying unto the devil-god of that river. I thought, By Jove! it's all over. We are too late; he has vanished—the gift has vanished, by means of some spear, arrow, or club. I will never hear that chap speak after all,—and my sorrow had a startling extravagance of emotion, even such as I had noticed in the howling sorrow of these savages in the bush. I couldn't have felt more of lonely desolation somehow, had I been robbed of a belief or had missed my destiny in life.* . . . Why do you sigh in this beastly way, somebody? Absurd? Well, absurd. Good Lord! mustn't a man ever—— Here, give me some tobacco." . . .

There was a pause of profound stillness, then a match flared, and Marlow's lean face appeared, worn, hollow, with downward folds and dropped eyelids, with an aspect of concentrated attention; and as he took vigorous draws at his pipe, it seemed to retreat and advance out of the night in the regular flicker of the tiny flame. The match went out.

"Absurd!" he cried. "This is the worst of trying to tell. . . . Here you all are, each moored with two good addresses, like a hulk with two anchors, a butcher round one corner, a policeman round another, excellent appetites, and temperature normal—you hear— normal from year's end to year's end. And you say, Absurd! Absurd be—exploded! Absurd! My dear boys, what can you expect from a man who out of sheer nervousness had just flung overboard a pair of new shoes? Now I think of it, it is amazing I did not shed tears. I am, upon the whole, proud of my fortitude. I was cut to the quick at the idea of having lost the inestimable privilege of listening to the gifted

Kurtz. Of course I was wrong. The privilege was waiting for me. Oh
yes, I heard more than enough. And I was right, too. A voice. He was
very little more than a voice. And I heard—him—it—this voice—
other voices—all of them were so little more than voices—and the
memory of that time itself lingers around me, impalpable, like a
dying vibration of one immense jabber, silly, atrocious, sordid, savage, or simply mean, without any kind of sense. Voices, voices—even
the girl herself—now——"

He was silent for a long time.

"I laid the ghost of his gifts at last with a lie," he began suddenly.
"Girl! What? Did I mention a girl? Oh, she is out of it—completely.
They—the women I mean—are out of it—should be out of it. We
must help them to stay in that beautiful world of their own, lest ours
gets worse. Oh, she had to be out of it. You should have heard the
disinterred body of Mr Kurtz saying, 'My Intended.' You would
have perceived directly then how completely she was out of it. And
the lofty frontal bone of Mr Kurtz! They say the hair goes on growing sometimes,* but this—ah—specimen, was impressively bald. The
wilderness had patted him on the head, and, behold, it was like a
ball—an ivory ball; it had caressed him, and—lo!—he had withered;
it had taken him, loved him, embraced him, got into his veins, consumed his flesh, and sealed his soul to its own by the inconceivable
ceremonies of some devilish initiation. He was its spoiled and pam-
pered favourite. Ivory? I should think so. Heaps of it, stacks of it.
The old mud shanty was bursting with it. You would think there was
not a single tusk left either above or below the ground in the whole
country. 'Mostly fossil,' the manager had remarked disparagingly. It
was no more fossil than I am; but they call it fossil when it is dug up.
It appears these niggers do bury the tusks sometimes—but evidently
they couldn't bury this parcel deep enough to save the gifted Mr
Kurtz from his fate. We filled the steamboat with it, and had to pile a
lot on the deck. Thus he could see and enjoy as long as he could see,
because the appreciation of this favour had remained with him to the
last. You should have heard him say, 'My ivory.' Oh yes, I heard him.
'My Intended, my ivory, my station, my river, my——' everything
belonged to him. It made me hold my breath in expectation of hearing the wilderness burst into a prodigious peal of laughter that
would shake the fixed stars in their places. Everything belonged to
him—but that was a trifle. The thing was to know what he belonged

to, how many powers of darkness claimed him for their own. That was the reflection that made you creepy all over. It was impossible— it was not good for one either—trying to imagine. He had taken a high seat amongst the devils of the land—I mean literally. You can't understand. How could you?—with solid pavement under your feet, surrounded by kind neighbours ready to cheer you or to fall on you, stepping delicately between the butcher and the policeman, in the holy terror of scandal and gallows and lunatic asylums—how can you imagine what particular region of the first ages a man's untrammelled feet may take him into by the way of solitude—utter solitude without a policeman—by the way of silence—utter silence, where no warning voice of a kind neighbour can be heard whispering of public opinion? These little things make all the great difference. When they are gone you must fall back upon your own innate strength, upon your own capacity for faithfulness. Of course you may be too much of a fool to go wrong—too dull even to know you are being assaulted by the powers of darkness. I take it, no fool ever made a bargain for his soul with the devil: the fool is too much of a fool, or the devil too much of a devil—I don't know which. Or you may be such a thunderingly exalted creature as to be altogether deaf and blind to anything but heavenly sights and sounds. Then the earth for you is only a standing place—and whether to be like this is your loss or your gain I won't pretend to say. But most of us are neither one nor the other. The earth for us is a place to live in, where we must put up with sights, with sounds, with smells too, by Jove!— breathe dead hippo, so to speak, and not be contaminated. And there, don't you see? your strength comes in, the faith in your ability for the digging of unostentatious holes to bury the stuff in—your power of devotion, not to yourself, but to an obscure, back-breaking business. And that's difficult enough. Mind, I am not trying to excuse or even explain—I am trying to account to myself for—for— Mr Kurtz—for the shade of Mr Kurtz. This initiated wraith from the back of Nowhere honoured me with its amazing confidence before it vanished altogether. This was because it could speak English to me. The original Kurtz had been educated partly in England, and—as he was good enough to say himself—his sympathies were in the right place. His mother was half-English, his father was half-French.* All Europe contributed to the making of Kurtz; and by-and-by I learned that, most appropriately, the International Society for the Suppression of Savage Customs* had intrusted him with the making of a report, for its future guidance. And he had written it too. I've seen it. I've read it. It was eloquent, vibrating with eloquence, but too high-strung, I think. Seventeen pages of close writing he had found time for! But this must have been before his—let us say—nerves, went wrong, and caused him to preside at certain midnight dances ending with unspeakable rites, which—as far as I reluctantly gathered from what I heard at various times—were offered up to him—do you understand?—to Mr Kurtz himself.* But it was a beautiful piece of writing. The opening paragraph, however, in the light of later information, strikes me now as ominous. He began with the argument that we whites, from the point of development we had arrived at, 'must necessarily appear to them [savages] in the nature of supernatural beings—we approach them with the might as of a deity,' and so on, and so on. 'By the simple exercise of our will we can exert a power for good practically unbounded,' &c., &c. From that point he soared and took me with him. The peroration was magnificent, though difficult to remember, you know. It gave me the notion of an exotic Immensity ruled by an august Benevolence. It made me tingle with enthusiasm. This was the unbounded power of eloquence—of words—of burning noble words. There were no practical hints to interrupt the magic current of phrases, unless a kind of note at the foot of the last page, scrawled evidently much later, in an unsteady hand, may be regarded as the exposition of a method. It was very simple, and at the end of that moving appeal to every altruistic sentiment it blazed at you, luminous and terrifying, like a flash of lightning in a serene sky: 'Exterminate all the brutes!' The curious part was that he had apparently forgotten all about that valuable postscriptum, because, later on, when he in a sense came to himself, he repeatedly entreated me to take good care of 'my pamphlet' (he called it), as it was sure to have in the future a good influence upon his career. I had full information about all these things, and, besides, as it turned out, I was to have the care of his memory. I've done enough for it to give me the indisputable right to lay it, if I choose, for an everlasting rest in the dust-bin of progress, amongst all the sweepings and, figuratively speaking, all the dead cats of civilisation. But then, you see, I can't choose. He won't be forgotten. Whatever he was, he was not common. He had the power to charm or frighten rudimentary souls into an aggravated witch-dance in his honour; he could also fill the small souls of the pilgrims with bitter misgivings: he had one devoted friend at least, and he had conquered one soul in the world that was neither rudimentary nor tainted with self-seeking. No; I can't forget him, though I am not prepared to affirm the fellow was exactly worth the life we lost in getting to him. I missed my late helmsman awfully,—I missed him even while his body was still lying in the pilot-house. Perhaps you will think it passing strange this regret for a savage who was no more account than a grain of sand in a black Sahara. Well, don't you see, he had done something, he had steered; for months I had him at my back—a help—an instrument. It was a kind of partnership. He steered for me—I had to look after him, I worried about his deficiencies, and thus a subtle bond had been created, of which I only became aware when it was suddenly broken. And the intimate profundity of that look he gave me when he received his hurt remains to this day in my memory—like a claim of distant kinship affirmed in a supreme moment.

"Poor fool! If he had only left that shutter alone. He had no restraint, no restraint—just like Kurtz—a tree swayed by the wind. As soon as I had put on a dry pair of slippers, I dragged him out, after first jerking the spear out of his side, which operation I confess I performed with my eyes shut tight. His heels leaped together over the little door-step; his shoulders were pressed to my breast; I hugged him from behind desperately. Oh! he was heavy, heavy; heavier than any man on earth, I should imagine. Then without more ado I tipped him overboard. The current snatched him as though he had been a wisp of grass, and I saw the body roll over twice before I lost sight of it for ever. All the pilgrims and the manager were then congregated on the awning-deck about the pilot-house, chattering at each other like a flock of excited magpies, and there was a scandalised murmur at my heartless promptitude. What they wanted to keep that body hanging about for I can't guess. Embalm it, maybe. But I had also heard another, and a very ominous, murmur on the deck below. My friends the wood-cutters were likewise scandalised, and with a better show of reason—though I admit that the reason itself was quite inadmissible. Oh, quite! I had made up my mind that if my late helmsman was to be eaten, the fishes alone should have him. He had been a very second-rate helmsman while alive, but now he was dead he might have become a first-class temptation, and possibly cause some startling trouble. Besides, I was anxious to take the wheel, the man in pink pyjamas showing himself a hopeless duffer at the business.

"This I did directly the simple funeral was over. We were going half-speed, keeping right in the middle of the stream, and I listened to the talk about me. They had given up Kurtz, they had given up the station; Kurtz was dead, and the station had been burnt—and so on—and so on. The red-haired pilgrim was beside himself with the thought that at least this poor Kurtz had been properly revenged. 'Say! We must have made a glorious slaughter of them in the bush. Eh? What do you think? Say?' He positively danced, the bloodthirsty little gingery beggar. And he had nearly fainted when he saw the wounded man! I could not help saying, 'You made a glorious lot of smoke, anyhow.' I had seen, from the way the tops of the bushes rustled and flew, that almost all the shots had gone too high. You can't hit anything unless you take aim and fire from the shoulder; but these chaps fired from the hip with their eyes shut. The retreat, I maintained—and I was right—was caused by the screeching of the steam-whistle. Upon this they forgot Kurtz, and began to howl at me with indignant protests.

"The manager stood by the wheel murmuring confidentially about the necessity of getting well away down the river before dark at all events, when I saw in the distance a clearing on the river-side and the outlines of some sort of building. 'What's this?' I asked. He clapped his hands in wonder. 'The station!' he cried. I edged in at once, still going half-speed.

"Through my glasses I saw the slope of a hill interspersed with rare trees and perfectly free from undergrowth. A long decaying building on the summit was half buried in the high grass; the large holes in the peaked roof gaped black from afar; the jungle and the woods made a background. There was no enclosure or fence of any kind; but there had been one apparently, for near the house half-a-dozen slim posts remained in a row, roughly trimmed, and with their upper ends ornamented with round carved balls. The rails, or whatever there had been between, had disappeared. Of course the forest surrounded all that. The river-bank was clear, and on the water-side I saw a white man under a hat like a cart-wheel beckoning persistently with his whole arm. Examining the edge of the forest above and below, I was almost certain I could see movements—human

forms gliding here and there. I steamed past prudently, then stopped
the engines and let her drift down. The man on the shore began to
shout, urging us to land. 'We have been attacked,' screamed the
manager. 'I know—I know. It's all right,' yelled back the other, as
cheerful as you please. 'Come along. It's all right. I am glad.'

"His aspect reminded me of something I had seen—something
funny I had seen somewhere. As I manœuvred to get alongside, I was
asking myself, 'What does this fellow look like?' Suddenly I got it.
He looked like a harlequin.* His clothes had been made of some stuff
that was brown holland probably, but it was covered with patches all
over, with bright patches, blue, red, and yellow,—patches on the
back, patches on front, patches on elbows, on knees; coloured bind-
ing round his jacket, scarlet edging at the bottom of his trousers; and
the sunshine made him look extremely gay and wonderfully neat
withal, because you could see how beautifully all this patching had
been done. A beardless, boyish face, very fair, no features to speak of,
nose peeling, little blue eyes, smiles and frowns chasing each other
over that open countenance like sunshine and shadow on a wind-
swept plain. 'Look out, captain!' he cried; 'there's a snag lodged in
here last night.' What! Another snag? I confess I swore shamefully. I
had nearly holed my cripple, to finish off that charming trip. The
harlequin on the bank turned his little pug nose up to me. 'You
English?' he asked, all smiles. 'Are you?' I shouted from the wheel.
The smiles vanished, and he shook his head as if sorry for my disappointment. Then he brightened up. 'Never mind!' he cried
encouragingly. 'Are we in time?' I asked. 'He is up there,' he replied,
with a toss of the head up the hill, and becoming gloomy all of a
sudden. His face was like the autumn sky, overcast one moment and
bright the next.

"When the manager, escorted by the pilgrims, all of them armed
to the teeth, had gone to the house, this chap came on board. 'I say, I
don't like this. These natives are in the bush,' I said. He assured me
earnestly it was all right. 'They are simple people,' he added; 'well, I
am glad you came. It took me all my time to keep them off.' 'But you
said it was all right,' I cried. 'Oh, they meant no harm,' he said; and
as I stared he corrected himself, 'Not exactly.' Then vivaciously, 'My
faith, your pilot-house wants a clean up!' In the next breath he
advised me to keep enough steam on the boiler to blow the whistle in
case of any trouble. 'One good screech will do more for you than all

your rifles. They are simple people,' he repeated. He rattled away at such a rate he quite overwhelmed me. He seemed to be trying to make up for lots of silence, and actually hinted, laughing, that such was the case. 'Don't you talk with Mr Kurtz?' I said. 'You don't talk with that man—you listen to him,' he exclaimed with severe exaltation. 'But now——' He waved his arm, and in the twinkling of an eye was in the uttermost depths of despondency. In a moment he came up again with a jump, possessed himself of both my hands, shook them continuously, while he gabbled: 'Brother sailor . . . honour . . . pleasure . . . delight . . . introduce myself . . . Russian . . . son of an arch-priest . . . Government of Tambov* . . . What? Tobacco! English tobacco; the excellent English tobacco! Now, that's brotherly. Smoke? Where's a sailor that does not smoke?'

"The pipe soothed him, and gradually I made out he had run away from school, had gone to sea in a Russian ship; ran away again; served some time in English ships; was now reconciled with the arch-priest. He made a point of that. 'But when one is young one must see things, gather experience, ideas; enlarge the mind.' 'Here!' I interrupted. 'You can never tell! Here I have met Mr Kurtz,' he said, youthfully solemn and reproachful. I held my tongue after that. It appears he had persuaded a Dutch trading-house on the coast* to fit him out with stores and goods, and had started for the interior with a light heart, and no more idea of what would happen to him than a baby. He had been wandering about that river for nearly two years alone, cut off from everybody and everything. 'I am not so young as I look. I am twenty-five,' he said. 'At first old Van Shuyten* would tell me to go to the devil,' he narrated with keen enjoyment; 'but I stuck to him, and talked and talked, till at last he got afraid I would talk the hind-leg off his favourite dog, so he gave me some cheap things and a few guns, and told me he hoped he would never see my face again. Good old Dutchman, Van Shuyten. I've sent him one small lot of ivory a year ago, so that he can't call me a little thief when I get back. I hope he got it. And for the rest I don't care. I had some wood stacked for you. That was my old house. Did you see?'

"I gave him Towson's book. He made as though he would kiss me, but restrained himself. 'The only book I had left, and I thought I had lost it,' he said, looking at it ecstatically. 'So many accidents happen to a man going about alone, you know. Canoes get upset sometimes—and sometimes you've got to clear out so quick when the people get angry.' He thumbed the pages. 'You made notes in Russian?' I asked. He nodded. 'I thought they were written in cipher,' I said. He laughed, then became serious. 'I had lots of trouble to keep these people off,' he said. 'Did they want to kill you?' I asked. 'Oh no!' he cried, and checked himself. 'Why did they attack us?' I pursued. He hesitated, then said shamefacedly, 'They don't want him to go.' 'Don't they?' I said, curiously. He nodded a nod full of mystery and wisdom. 'I tell you,' he cried, 'this man has enlarged my mind.' He opened his arms wide, staring at me with his little blue eyes that were perfectly round."

## III

"I LOOKED at him, lost in astonishment. There he was before me, in motley, as though he had absconded from a troupe of mimes, enthusiastic, fabulous. His very existence was improbable, inexplicable, and altogether bewildering. He was an insoluble problem. It was inconceivable how he had existed, how he had succeeded in getting so far, how he had managed to remain—why he did not instantly disappear. 'I went a little farther,' he said, 'then still a little farther—till I had gone so far that I don't know how I'll ever get back. Never mind. Plenty time. I can manage. You take Kurtz away quick—quick—I tell you.' The glamour of youth enveloped his parti-coloured rags, his destitution, his loneliness, the essential desolation of his futile wanderings. For months—for years—his life hadn't been worth a day's purchase; and there he was gallantly, thoughtlessly alive, to all appearance indestructible solely by the virtue of his few years and of his unreflecting audacity. I was seduced into something like admiration—like envy. Glamour urged him on, glamour kept him unscathed. He surely wanted nothing from the wilderness but space to breathe in and to push on through. His need was to exist, and to move onwards at the greatest possible risk, and with a maximum of privation. If the absolutely pure, uncalculating, unpractical spirit of adventure had ever ruled a human being, it ruled this be-patched youth. I almost envied him the possession of this modest and clear flame. It seemed to have consumed all thought of self so completely, that, even while he was talking to you, you forgot that it was he—the man before your eyes—who had gone through these things. I did not envy him his devotion to Kurtz, though. He had not meditated over it. It came to him, and he accepted it with a sort of eager fatalism. I must say that to me it appeared about the most dangerous thing in every way he had come upon so far.

"They had come together unavoidably, like two ships becalmed near each other, and lay rubbing sides at last. I suppose Kurtz wanted an audience, because on a certain occasion, when encamped in the forest, they had talked all night, or more probably Kurtz had talked. 'We talked of everything,' he said, quite transported at the recollection. 'I forgot there was such a thing as sleep. The night did

not seem to last an hour. Everything! Everything! . . . Of love too.'
'Ah, he talked to you of love!' I said, much amused. 'It isn't what you
think,' he cried, almost passionately. 'It was in general. He made me
see things—things.'

"He threw his arms up. We were on deck at the time, and the
headman of my wood-cutters, lounging near by, turned upon him his
heavy and glittering eyes. I looked around, and I don't know why, but
I assure you that never, never before, did this land, this river, this
jungle, the very arch of this blazing sky, appear to me so hopeless and
so dark, so impenetrable to human thought, so pitiless to human
weakness. 'And, ever since, you have been with him, of course?' I
said.

"On the contrary. It appears their intercourse had been very much
broken by various causes. He had, as he informed me proudly, managed to nurse Kurtz through two illnesses (he alluded to it as you
would to some risky feat), but as a rule Kurtz wandered alone, far in
the depths of the forest. 'Very often coming to this station, I had to
wait days and days before he would turn up,' he said. 'Ah, it was
worth waiting for!—sometimes.' 'What was he doing? exploring or
what?' I asked. 'Oh yes, of course'; he had discovered lots of villages,
a lake too—he did not know exactly in what direction; it was dangerous to inquire too much—but mostly his expeditions had been for
ivory. 'But he had no goods to trade with by that time,' I objected.
'There's a good lot of cartridges left even yet,' he answered, looking
away. 'To speak plainly, he raided the country,' I said. He nodded.
'Not alone, surely!' He muttered something about the villages round
that lake. 'Kurtz got the tribe to follow him, did he?' I suggested. He
fidgeted a little. 'They adored him,' he said. The tone of these words
was so extraordinary that I looked at him searchingly. It was curious
to see his mingled eagerness and reluctance to speak of Kurtz. The
man filled his life, occupied his thoughts, swayed his emotions.
'What can you expect?' he burst out; 'he came to them with thunder
and lightning, you know—and they had never seen anything like it—
and very terrible. He could be very terrible. You can't judge Mr
Kurtz as you would an ordinary man. No, no, no! Now—just to give
you an idea—I don't mind telling you, he wanted to shoot me too
one day—but I don't judge him.' 'Shoot you!' I cried. 'What for?'
'Well, I had a small lot of ivory the chief of that village near my
house gave me. You see I used to shoot game for them. Well, he

wanted it, and wouldn't hear reason. He declared he would shoot me unless I gave him the ivory and then cleared out of the country, because he could do so, and had a fancy for it, and there was nothing on earth to prevent him killing whom he jolly well pleased. And it was true too. I gave him the ivory. What did I care! But I didn't clear out. No, no. I couldn't leave him. I had to be careful, of course, till we got friendly again for a time. He had his second illness then. Afterwards I had to keep out of the way; but I didn't mind. He was living for the most part in those villages on the lake. When he came down to the river, sometimes he would take to me, and sometimes it was better for me to be careful. This man suffered too much. He hated all this, and somehow he couldn't get away. When I had a chance I begged him to try and leave while there was time; I offered to go back with him. And he would say yes, and then he would remain; go off on another ivory hunt; disappear for weeks; forget himself amongst these people—forget himself—you know.' 'Why! he's mad,' I said. He protested indignantly. Mr Kurtz couldn't be mad. If I had heard him talk, only two days ago, I wouldn't dare hint at such a thing. . . . I had taken up my binoculars while we talked, and was looking at the shore, sweeping the limit of the forest at each side and at the back of the house. The consciousness of there being people in that bush, so silent, so quiet—as silent and quiet as the ruined house on the hill—made me uneasy. There was no sign on the face of nature of this amazing tale that was not so much told as suggested to me in desolate exclamations, completed by shrugs, in interrupted phrases, in hints ending in deep sighs. The woods were unmoved, like a mask—heavy, like the closed door of a prison—they looked with their air of hidden knowledge, of patient expectation, of unapproachable silence. The Russian was explaining to me that it was only lately that Mr Kurtz had come down to the river, bringing along with him all the fighting men of that lake tribe. He had been absent for several months—getting himself adored, I suppose—and had come down unexpectedly, with the intention to all appearance of making a raid either across the river or down stream. Evidently the appetite for more ivory had got the better of the—what shall I say?— less material aspirations. However he had got much worse suddenly. 'I heard he was lying helpless, and so I came up—took my chance,' said the Russian. 'Oh, he is bad, very bad.' I directed my glass to the house. There were no signs of life, but there was the ruined roof, the long mud wall peeping above the grass, with three little square window-holes, no two of the same size; all this brought within reach of my hand, as it were. And then I made a brusque movement, and one of the remaining posts of that vanished fence leaped up in the field of my glass. You remember I told you I had been struck at the distance by certain attempts at ornamentation, rather remarkable in the ruinous aspect of the place. Now I had suddenly a nearer view, and its first result was to make me throw my head back as if before a blow. Then I went carefully from post to post with my glass, and I saw my mistake. These round knobs were not ornamental but symbolic;* they were expressive and puzzling, striking and disturbing— food for thought and also for the vultures if there had been any looking down from the sky; but at all events for such ants as were industrious enough to ascend the pole. They would have been even more impressive, those heads on the stakes,* if their faces had not been turned to the house. Only one, the first I had made out, was facing my way. I was not so shocked as you may think. The start back I had given was really nothing but a movement of surprise. I had expected to see a knob of wood there, you know. I returned deliberately to the first I had seen—and there it was, black, dried, sunken, with closed eyelids,—a head that seemed to sleep at the top of that pole, and, with the shrunken dry lips showing a narrow white line of the teeth, was smiling too, smiling continuously at some endless and jocose dream of that eternal slumber.

"I am not disclosing any trade secrets. In fact the manager said afterwards that Mr Kurtz's methods had ruined the district. I have no opinion on that point, but I want you clearly to understand that there was nothing exactly profitable in these heads being there. They only showed that Mr Kurtz lacked restraint in the gratification of his various lusts, that there was something wanting in him—some small matter which, when the pressing need arose, could not be found under his magnificent eloquence. Whether he knew of this deficiency himself I can't say. I think the knowledge came to him at last—only at the very last. But the wilderness had found him out early, and had taken on him a terrible vengeance for the fantastic invasion.* I think it had whispered to him things about himself which he did not know, things of which he had no conception till he took counsel with this great solitude—and the whisper had proved irresistibly fascinating. It echoed loudly within him because he was hollow at the core.* . . . I put down the glass, and the head that had appeared near enough to be spoken to seemed at once to have leaped away from me into inaccessible distance.

"The admirer of Mr Kurtz was a bit crestfallen. In a hurried, indistinct voice he began to assure me he had not dared to take these—say, symbols—down. He was not afraid of the natives; they would not stir till Mr Kurtz gave the word. His ascendancy was extraordinary. The camps of these people surrounded the place, and the chiefs came every day to see him. They would crawl. . . . 'I don't want to know anything of the ceremonies used when approaching Mr Kurtz,' I shouted. Curious, this feeling that came over me that such details would be more intolerable than those heads drying on the stakes under Mr Kurtz's windows. After all, that was only a savage sight, while I seemed at one bound to have been transported into some lightless region of subtle horrors, where pure, uncomplicated savagery was a positive relief, being something that had a right to exist—obviously—in the sunshine. The young man looked at me with surprise. I suppose it did not occur to him Mr Kurtz was no idol of mine. He forgot I hadn't heard any of these splendid monologues on, what was it? on love, justice, conduct of life—or what not. If it had come to crawling before Mr Kurtz, he crawled as much as the veriest savage of them all. I had no idea of the conditions, he said: these heads were the heads of rebels. I shocked him excessively by laughing. Rebels! What would be the next definition I was to hear? There had been enemies, criminals, workers—and these were rebels. Those rebellious heads looked very subdued to me on their sticks. 'You don't know how such a life tries a man like Kurtz,' cried Kurtz's last disciple. 'Well, and you?' I said. 'I! I! I am a simple man. I have no great thoughts. I want nothing from anybody. How can you compare me to . . . ?' His feelings were too much for speech, and suddenly he broke down. 'I don't understand,' he groaned. 'I've been doing my best to keep him alive, and that's enough. I had no hand in all this. I have no abilities. There hasn't been a drop of medicine or a mouthful of invalid food for months here. He was shamefully abandoned. A man like this, with such ideas. Shamefully! Shamefully! I—I—haven't slept for the last ten nights. . . .'

"His voice lost itself in the calm of the evening. The long shadows of the forest had slipped down hill while we talked, had gone far beyond the ruined hovel, beyond the symbolic row of stakes. All this was in the gloom, while we down there were yet in the sunshine, and the stretch of the river abreast of the clearing glittered in a still and dazzling splendour, with a murky and overshadowed bend above and below. Not a living soul was seen on the shore. The bushes did not rustle.

"Suddenly round the corner of the house a group of men appeared, as though they had come up from the ground. They waded waist-deep in the grass, in a compact body, bearing an improvised stretcher in their midst. Instantly, in the emptiness of the landscape, a cry arose whose shrillness pierced the still air like a sharp arrow flying straight to the very heart of the land; and, as if by enchantment, streams of human beings—of naked human beings—with spears in their hands, with bows, with shields, with wild glances and savage movements, were poured into the clearing by the dark-faced and pensive forest. The bushes shook, the grass swayed for a time, and then everything stood still in attentive immobility.

" 'Now, if he does not say the right thing to them we are all done for,' said the Russian at my elbow. The knot of men with the stretcher had stopped too, half-way to the steamer, as if petrified. I saw the man on the stretcher sit up, lank and with an uplifted arm, above the shoulders of the bearers. 'Let us hope that the man who can talk so well of love in general will find some particular reason to spare us this time,' I said. I resented bitterly the absurd danger of our situation, as if to be at the mercy of that atrocious phantom had been a dishonouring necessity. I could not hear a sound, but through my glasses I saw the thin arm extended commandingly, the lower jaw moving, the eyes of that apparition shining darkly far in its bony head that nodded with grotesque jerks. Kurtz—Kurtz—that means 'short' in German—don't it? Well, the name was as true as every-thing else in his life—and death. He looked at least seven feet long. His covering had fallen off, and his body emerged from it pitiful and appalling as from a winding-sheet. I could see the cage of his ribs all astir, the bones of his arm waving. It was as though an animated image of death carved out of old ivory had been shaking its hand with menaces at a motionless crowd of men made of dark and glitter-ing bronze. I saw him open his mouth wide—it gave him a weirdly voracious aspect, as though he had wanted to swallow all the air, all the earth, all the men before him. A deep voice reached me faintly.

He must have been shouting. He fell back suddenly. The stretcher shook as the bearers staggered forward again, and almost at the same time I noticed that the crowd of savages was vanishing without any perceptible movement of retreat, as if the forest that had ejected these beings so suddenly had drawn them in again as the breath is drawn in a long aspiration.

"Some of the pilgrims behind the stretcher carried his arms—two shot-guns, a heavy rifle, and a light revolver-carbine—the thunder-bolts of that pitiful Jupiter. The manager bent over him murmuring as he walked beside his head. They laid him down in one of the little cabins—just a room for a bed-place and a camp-stool or two, you know. We had brought his belated correspondence, and a lot of torn envelopes and open letters littered his bed. His hand roamed feebly amongst these papers. I was struck by the fire of his eyes and the composed languor of his expression. It was not so much the exhaustion of disease. He did not seem in pain. This shadow looked satiated and calm, as though for the moment it had had its fill of all the emotions.

"He rustled one of the letters, and looking straight in my face said, 'I am glad.' Somebody had been writing to him about me. These special recommendations were turning up again. The volume of tone he emitted without effort, almost without the trouble of moving his lips, amazed me. A voice! a voice! It was grave, profound, vibrating, while the man did not seem capable of a whisper. However, he had enough strength in him—factitious no doubt—to very nearly make an end of us, as you shall hear directly.

"The manager appeared silently in the doorway; I stepped out at once and he drew the curtain after me. The Russian, eyed curiously by the pilgrims, was staring at the shore. I followed the direction of his glance.

"Dark human shapes could be made out in the distance, flitting indistinctly against the gloomy border of the forest, and near the river two bronze figures, leaning on tall spears, stood in the sunlight under fantastic head-dresses of spotted skins, warlike and still in statuesque repose. And from right to left along the lighted shore moved a wild and gorgeous apparition of a woman.

"She walked with measured steps, draped in striped and fringed cloths, treading the earth proudly, with a slight jingle and flash of barbarous ornaments. She carried her head high; her hair was done in the shape of a helmet; she had brass leggings to the knee, brass wire gauntlets to the elbow, a crimson spot on her tawny cheek, innumerable necklaces of glass beads on her neck; bizarre things, charms, gifts of witch-men, that hung about her, glittered and trembled at every step. She must have had the value of several elephant tusks upon her. She was savage and superb, wild-eyed and magnificent; there was something ominous and stately in her deliberate progress. And in the hush that had fallen suddenly upon the whole sorrowful land, the immense wilderness, the colossal body of the fecund and mysterious life seemed to look at her, pensive, as though it had been looking at the image of its own tenebrous and passionate soul.

"She came abreast of the steamer, stood still, and faced us. Her long shadow fell to the water's edge. Her face had a tragic and fierce aspect of wild sorrow and of dumb pain mingled with the fear of some struggling, half-shaped resolve. She stood looking at us without a stir, and like the wilderness itself, with an air of brooding over an inscrutable purpose. A whole minute passed, and then she made a step forward. There was a low jingle, a glint of yellow metal, a sway of fringed draperies, and she stopped as if her heart had failed her.* The young fellow by my side growled. The pilgrims murmured at my back. She looked at us all as if her life had depended upon the unswerving steadiness of her glance. Suddenly she opened her bared arms and threw them up rigid above her head, as though in an uncontrollable desire to touch the sky, and at the same time the swift shadows darted out on the earth, swept around on the river, gathering the steamer into a shadowy embrace. A formidable silence hung over the scene.*

"She turned away slowly, walked on, following the bank, and passed into the bushes to the left. Once only her eyes gleamed back at us in the dusk of the thickets before she disappeared.

"'If she had offered to come aboard I really think I would have tried to shoot her,' said the man of patches, nervously. 'I had been risking my life every day for the last fortnight to keep her out of the house. She got in one day and kicked up a row about those miserable rags I picked up in the storeroom to mend my clothes with. I wasn't decent. At least it must have been that, for she talked like a fury to Kurtz for an hour, pointing at me now and then. I don't understand the dialect of this tribe. Luckily for me, I fancy Kurtz felt too ill that day to care, or there would have been mischief. I don't understand. . . . No—it's too much for me. Ah, well, it's all over now.'

"At this moment I heard Kurtz's deep voice behind the curtain, 'Save me!—save the ivory, you mean. Don't tell me. Save *me!* Why, I've had to save you. You are interrupting my plans now. Sick! Sick! Not so sick as you would like to believe. Never mind. I'll carry my ideas out yet—I will return. I'll show you what can be done. You with your little peddling notions—you are interfering with me. I will return. I . . .'

"The manager came out. He did me the honour to take me under the arm and lead me aside. 'He is very low, very low,' he said. He considered it necessary to sigh, but neglected to be consistently sorrowful. 'We have done all we could for him—haven't we? But there is no disguising the fact, Mr Kurtz has done more harm than good to the Company. He did not see the time was not ripe for vigorous action. Cautiously, cautiously—that's my principle. We must be cautious yet. The district is closed to us for a time. Deplorable! Upon the whole, the trade will suffer. I don't deny there is a remarkable quantity of ivory—mostly fossil. We must save it, at all events—but look how precarious the position is—and why? Because the method is unsound.' 'Do you,' said I, looking at the shore, 'call it "unsound method"?' 'Without doubt,' he exclaimed, hotly. 'Don't you?' . . . 'No method at all,' I murmured after a while. 'Exactly,' he exulted. 'I anticipated this. Shows a complete want of judgment. It is my duty to point it out in the proper quarter.' 'Oh,' said I, 'that fellow—what's his name?—the brickmaker, will make a readable report for you.' He appeared confounded for a moment. It seemed to me I had never breathed an atmosphere so vile, and I turned mentally to Kurtz for relief—positively for relief. 'Nevertheless I think Mr Kurtz is a remarkable man,' I said with emphasis. He started, dropped on me a cold heavy glance, said very quietly, 'He *was*,' and turned his back on me. My hour of favour was over; I found myself lumped along with Kurtz as a partisan of methods for which the time was not ripe: I was unsound! Ah! but it was something to have at least a choice of nightmares.

"I had turned to the wilderness really, not to Mr Kurtz, who, I was ready to admit, was as good as buried. And for a moment it seemed to me as if I also were buried in a vast grave full of unspeakable secrets. I felt an intolerable weight oppressing my breast, the smell of the damp earth, the unseen presence of victorious corruption, the darkness of an impenetrable night. . . . The Russian tapped me on the shoulder. I heard him mumbling and stammering something about 'brother seaman—couldn't conceal—knowledge of matters that would affect Mr Kurtz's reputation.' I waited. For him evidently Mr Kurtz was not in his grave; I suspect that for him Mr Kurtz was one of the immortals. 'Well!' said I at last, 'speak out. As it happens, I am Mr Kurtz's friend—in a way.'

"He stated with a good deal of formality that had we not been 'of the same profession,' he would have kept the matter to himself without regard to consequences. He suspected there was an active ill-will towards him on the part of these white men that—— 'You are right,' I said, remembering a certain conversation I had overheard. 'The manager thinks you ought to be hanged.' He showed a concern at this intelligence which amused me at first. 'I had better get out of the way quietly,' he said, earnestly. 'I can do no more for Kurtz now, and they would soon find some excuse. What's to stop them? There's a military post three hundred miles from here.' 'Well, upon my word,' said I, 'perhaps you had better go if you have any friends amongst the savages near by.' 'Plenty,' he said. 'They are simple people—and I want nothing, you know.' He stood biting his lip, then: 'I don't want any harm to happen to these whites here, but of course I was thinking of Mr Kurtz's reputation—but you are a brother seaman and——' 'All right,' said I, after a time. 'Mr Kurtz's reputation is safe with me.' I did not know how truly I spoke.

"He informed me, lowering his voice, that it was Kurtz who had ordered the attack to be made on the steamer. 'He hated sometimes the idea of being taken away—and then again. . . . But I don't understand these matters. I am a simple man. He thought it would scare you away—that you would give it up, thinking him dead. I could not stop him. Oh, I had an awful time of it this last month.' 'Very well,' I said. 'He is all right now.' 'Ye-e-es,' he muttered, not very convinced apparently. 'Thanks,' said I; 'I shall keep my eyes open.' 'But quiet—eh?' he urged, anxiously. 'It would be awful for his reputation if anybody here——' I promised a complete discretion with great gravity. 'I have a canoe and three black fellows waiting not very far. I am off. Could you give me a few Martini-Henry cartridges?' I could, and did, with proper secrecy. He helped himself, with a wink at me, to a handful of my tobacco. 'Between sailors—you know—good English tobacco.' At the door of the pilot-house he turned round—'I say, haven't you a pair of shoes you could spare?' He raised one leg. 'Look.' The soles were tied with knotted strings sandal-wise under his bare feet. I rooted out an old pair, at which he looked with admiration before tucking it under his left arm. One of his pockets (bright red) was bulging with cartridges, from the other (dark blue) peeped *Towson's Inquiry*, &c., &c. He seemed to think himself excellently well equipped for a renewed encounter with the wilderness. 'Ah! I'll never, never meet such a man again. You ought to have heard him recite poetry—his own too it was, he told me. Poetry!' He rolled his eyes at the recollection of these delights. 'Oh, he enlarged my mind!' 'Goodbye,' said I. He shook hands and vanished in the night. Sometimes I ask myself whether I had ever really seen him—whether it was possible to meet such a phenomenon! . . .

"When I woke up shortly after midnight his warning came to my mind with its hint of danger that seemed, in the starred darkness, real enough to make me get up for the purpose of having a look round. On the hill a big fire burned, illuminating fitfully a crooked corner of the station-house. One of the agents with a picket of a few of our blacks, armed for the purpose, was keeping guard over the ivory; but deep within the forest, red gleams that wavered, that seemed to sink and rise from the ground amongst confused columnar shapes of intense blackness, showed the exact position of the camp where Mr Kurtz's adorers were keeping their uneasy vigil. The monotonous beating of a big drum filled the air with muffled shocks and a lingering vibration. A steady droning sound of many men chanting each to himself some weird incantation came out from the black, flat wall of the woods as the humming of bees comes out of a hive, and had a strange narcotic effect upon my half-awake senses. I believe I dozed off leaning over the rail, till an abrupt burst of yells, an overwhelming outbreak of a pent-up and mysterious frenzy, woke me up in a bewildered wonder. It was cut short all at once, and the low droning went on with an effect of audible and soothing silence. I glanced casually into the little cabin. A light was burning within, but Mr Kurtz was not there.

"I think I would have raised an outcry if I had believed my eyes. But I didn't believe them at first—the thing seemed so impossible. The fact is I was completely unnerved by a sheer blank fright, pure abstract terror, unconnected with any distinct shape of physical danger. What made this emotion so overpowering was—how shall I define it?—the moral shock I received, as if something altogether monstrous, intolerable to thought and odious to the soul, had been thrust upon me unexpectedly. This lasted of course the merest fraction of a second, and then the usual sense of commonplace, deadly danger, the possibility of a sudden onslaught and massacre, or something of the kind, which I saw impending, was positively welcome and composing. It pacified me, in fact, so much, that I did not raise an alarm.

"There was an agent buttoned up inside an ulster and sleeping on a chair on deck within three feet of me. The yells had not awakened him; he snored very slightly; I left him to his slumbers and leaped ashore. I did not betray Mr Kurtz—it was ordered I should never betray him—it was written I should be loyal to the nightmare of my choice. I was anxious to deal with this shadow by myself alone,—and to this day I don't know why I was so jealous of sharing with any one the peculiar blackness of that experience.

"As soon as I got on the bank I saw a trail—a broad trail through the grass. I remember the exultation with which I said to myself, 'He can't walk—he is crawling on all-fours—I've got him.' The grass was wet with dew. I strode rapidly with clenched fists. I fancy I had some vague notion of falling upon him and giving him a drubbing. I don't know. I had some imbecile thoughts. The knitting old woman with the cat obtruded herself upon my memory as a most improper person to be sitting at the other end of such an affair. I saw a row of pilgrims squirting lead in the air out of Winchesters held to the hip. I thought I would never get back to the steamer, and imagined myself living alone and unarmed in the woods to an advanced age. Such silly things—you know. And I remember I confounded the beat of the drum with the beating of my heart, and was pleased at its calm regularity.

"I kept to the track though—then stopped to listen. The night was very clear: a dark blue space, sparkling with dew and starlight, in which black things stood very still. I thought I could see a kind of motion ahead of me. I was strangely cocksure of everything that night. I actually left the track and ran in a wide semicircle (I verily believe chuckling to myself) so as to get in front of that stir, of that motion I had seen—if indeed I had seen anything. I was circumventing Kurtz as though it had been a boyish game.

"I came upon him, and, if he had not heard me coming, I would have fallen over him too, but he got up in time. He rose, unsteady, long, pale, indistinct, like a vapour exhaled by the earth, and swayed slightly, misty and silent before me; while at my back the fires loomed between the trees, and the murmur of many voices issued from the forest. I had cut him off cleverly; but when actually confronting him I seemed to come to my senses, I saw the danger in its right proportion. It was by no means over yet. Suppose he began to shout? Though he could hardly stand, there was still plenty of vigour in his voice. 'Go away—hide yourself,' he said, in that profound tone. It was very awful. I glanced back. We were within thirty yards from the nearest fire. A black figure stood up, strode on long black legs, waving long black arms, across the glow. It had horns—antelope horns, I think—on its head. Some sorcerer, some witch-man, no doubt: it looked fiend-like enough. 'Do you know what you are doing?' I whispered. 'Perfectly,' he answered, raising his voice for that single word: it sounded to me far off and yet loud, like a hail through a speaking-trumpet. If he makes a row we are lost, I thought to myself. This clearly was not a case for fisticuffs, even apart from the very natural aversion I had to beat that Shadow—this wandering and tormented thing. 'You will be lost,' I said—'utterly lost.' One gets sometimes such a flash of inspiration, you know. I did say the right thing, though indeed he could not have been more irretrievably lost than he was at this very moment, when the foundations of our intimacy were being laid—to endure—to endure—even to the end—even beyond.

"'I had immense plans,' he muttered irresolutely. 'Yes,' said I; 'but if you try to shout I'll smash your head with——' there was not a stick or a stone near. 'I will throttle you for good,' I corrected myself. 'I was on the threshold of great things,' he pleaded, in a voice of longing, with a wistfulness of tone that made my blood run cold. 'And now for this stupid scoundrel——' 'Your success in Europe is assured in any case,' I affirmed, steadily. I did not want to have the throttling of him, you understand—and indeed it would have been very little use for any practical purpose. I tried to break the spell—the heavy, mute spell of the wilderness—that seemed to draw him to its pitiless breast by the awakening of forgotten and brutal instincts, by the memory of gratified and monstrous passions. This alone, I was convinced, had driven him out to the edge of the forest, to the

bush, towards the gleam of fires, the throb of drums, the drone of
weird incantations; this alone had beguiled his unlawful soul beyond
the bounds of permitted aspirations. And, don't you see, the terror
of the position was not in being knocked on the head—though I had
a very lively sense of that danger too—but in this, that I had to deal
with a being to whom I could not appeal in the name of anything
high or low. I had, even like the niggers, to invoke him—himself—
his own exalted and incredible degradation. There was nothing
either above or below him, and I knew it. He had kicked himself
loose of the earth. Confound the man! he had kicked the very earth
to pieces. He was alone, and I before him did not know whether I
stood on the ground or floated in the air. I've been telling you what
we said—repeating the phrases we pronounced,—but what's the
good? They were common everyday words,—the familiar, vague
sounds exchanged on every waking day of life. But what of that?
They had behind them, to my mind, the terrific suggestiveness of
words heard in dreams, of phrases spoken in nightmares. Soul! If
anybody had ever struggled with a soul, I am the man. And I wasn't
arguing with a lunatic either. Believe me or not, his intelligence was
perfectly clear—concentrated, it is true, upon himself with horrible
intensity, yet clear; and therein was my only chance—barring, of
course, the killing him there and then, which wasn't so good, on
account of unavoidable noise. But his soul was mad. Being alone in
the wilderness, it had looked within itself, and, by heavens! I tell you,
it had gone mad. I had—for my sins, I suppose—to go through the
ordeal of looking into it myself. No eloquence could have been so
withering to one's belief in mankind as his final burst of sincerity. He
struggled with himself, too. I saw it,—I heard it. I saw the inconceivable mystery of a soul that knew no restraint, no faith, and no fear,
yet struggling blindly with itself. I kept my head pretty well; but
when I had him at last stretched on the couch, I wiped my forehead,
while my legs shook under me as though I had carried half a ton on
my back down that hill. And yet I had only supported him, his bony
arm clasped round my neck—and he was not much heavier than a
child.

"When next day we left at noon, the crowd, of whose presence
behind the curtain of trees I had been acutely conscious all the time,
flowed out of the woods again, filled the clearing, covered the slope
with a mass of naked, breathing, quivering, bronze bodies. I steamed

up a bit, then swung down-stream, and two thousand eyes followed the evolutions of the splashing, thumping, fierce river-demon beating the water with its terrible tail and breathing black smoke into the air. In front of the first rank, along the river, three men, plastered with bright red earth from head to foot, strutted to and fro restlessly. When we came abreast again, they faced the river, stamped their feet, nodded their horned heads, swayed their scarlet bodies; they shook towards the fierce river-demon a bunch of black feathers, a mangy skin with a pendent tail—something that looked like a dried gourd; they shouted periodically together strings of amazing words that resembled no sounds of human language; and the deep murmurs of the crowd, interrupted suddenly, were like the responses of some satanic litany.

"We had carried Kurtz into the pilot-house: there was more air there. Lying on the couch, he stared through the open shutter. There was an eddy in the mass of human bodies, and the woman with helmeted head and tawny cheeks rushed out to the very brink of the stream. She put out her hands, shouted something, and all that wild mob took up the shout in a roaring chorus of articulated, rapid, breathless utterance.

"'Do you understand this?' I asked.

"He kept on looking out past me with fiery, longing eyes, with a mingled expression of wistfulness and hate. He made no answer, but I saw a smile, a smile of indefinable meaning, appear on his colourless lips that a moment after twitched convulsively. 'Do I not?' he said slowly,* gasping, as if the words had been torn out of him by a supernatural power.

"I pulled the string of the whistle, and I did this because I saw the pilgrims on deck getting out their rifles with an air of anticipating a jolly lark. At the sudden screech there was a movement of abject terror through that wedged mass of bodies. 'Don't! don't! you frighten them away,' cried some one on deck disconsolately. I pulled the string time after time. They broke and ran, they leaped, they crouched, they swerved, they dodged the flying terror of the sound. The three red chaps had fallen flat, face down on the shore, as though they had been shot dead. Only the barbarous and superb woman did not so much as flinch, and stretched tragically her bare arms after us over the sombre and glittering river.

"And then that imbecile crowd down on the deck started their little fun, and I could see nothing more for smoke.

"The brown current ran swiftly out of the heart of darkness, bearing us down towards the sea with twice the speed of our upward progress; and Kurtz's life was running swiftly too, ebbing, ebbing out of his heart into the sea of inexorable time. The manager was very placid, he had no vital anxieties now, he took us both in with a comprehensive and satisfied glance: the 'affair' had come off as well as could be wished. I saw the time approaching when I would be left alone of the party of 'unsound method.' The pilgrims looked upon me with disfavour. I was, so to speak, numbered with the dead. It is strange how I accepted this unforeseen partnership, this choice of nightmares forced upon me in the tenebrous land invaded by these mean and greedy phantoms.

"Kurtz discoursed. A voice! a voice! It rang deep to the very last. It survived his strength to hide in the magnificent folds of eloquence the barren darkness of his heart. Oh, he struggled! he struggled! The wastes of his weary brain were haunted by shadowy images now— images of wealth and fame revolving obsequiously round his unex- tinguishable gift of noble and lofty expression. My Intended, my station, my career, my ideas—these were the subjects for the occa- sional utterances of elevated sentiments. The shade of the original Kurtz frequented the bedside of the hollow sham, whose fate it was to be buried presently in the mould of primeval earth. But both the diabolic love and the unearthly hate of the mysteries it had penetrated fought for the possession of that soul satiated with primi- tive emotions, avid of lying fame, of sham distinction, of all the appearances of success and power.

"Sometimes he was contemptibly childish. He desired to have kings meet him at railway-stations on his return from some ghastly Nowhere, where he intended to accomplish great things. 'You show them you have in you something that is really profitable, and then there will be no limits to the recognition of your ability,' he would say. 'Of course you must take care of the motives—right motives— always.' The long reaches that were like one and the same reach, monotonous bends that were exactly alike, slipped past the steamer with their multitude of secular trees looking patiently after this grimy fragment of another world, the forerunner of change, of conquest, of trade, of massacres, of blessings. I looked ahead—piloting. 'Close the shutter,' said Kurtz suddenly one day; 'I can't bear to look at this.' I did so. There was a silence. 'Oh, but I will wring your heart yet!' he cried at the invisible wilderness.

"We broke down—as I had expected—and had to lie up for repairs at the head of an island. This delay was the first thing that shook Kurtz's confidence. One morning he gave me a packet of papers and a photograph,—the lot tied together with a shoe-string. 'Keep this for me,' he said. 'This noxious fool' (meaning the manager) 'is capable of prying into my boxes when I am not looking.' In the afternoon I saw him. He was lying on his back with closed eyes, and I withdrew quietly, but I heard him mutter, 'Live rightly, die, die . . .'\* I listened. There was nothing more. Was he rehearsing some speech in his sleep, or was it a fragment of a phrase from some newspaper article? He had been writing for the papers and meant to do so again, 'for the furthering of my ideas. It's a duty.'

"His was an impenetrable darkness. I looked at him as you peer down at a man who is lying at the bottom of a precipice where the sun never shines. But I had not much time to give him, because I was helping the engine-driver to take to pieces the leaky cylinders, to straighten a bent connecting-rod, and in other such matters. I lived in an infernal mess of rust, filings, nuts, bolts, spanners, hammers, ratchet-drills—things I abominate, because I don't get on with them. I tended the little forge we fortunately had aboard; I toiled wearily in a wretched scrap-heap—unless I had the shakes too bad to stand.

"One evening coming in with a candle I was startled to hear him say a little tremulously, 'I am lying here in the dark waiting for death.' The light was within a foot of his eyes. I forced myself to murmur, 'Oh, nonsense!' and stood over him as if transfixed.

"Anything approaching the change that came over his features I have never seen before, and hope never to see again. Oh, I wasn't touched. I was fascinated. It was as though a veil had been rent. I saw on that ivory face the expression of sombre pride, of ruthless power, of craven terror—of an intense and hopeless despair.\* Did he live his life again in every detail of desire, temptation, and surrender during that supreme moment of complete knowledge? He cried in a whisper at some image, at some vision,—he cried out twice, a cry that was no more than a breath—

"'The horror! The horror!'*

"I blew the candle out and left the cabin. The pilgrims were dining in the mess-room, and I took my place opposite the manager, who lifted his eyes to give me a questioning glance, which I successfully ignored. He leaned back, serene, with that peculiar smile of his sealing the unexpressed depths of his meanness. A continuous shower of small flies streamed upon the lamp, upon the cloth, upon our hands and faces. Suddenly the manager's boy put his insolent black head in the doorway, and said in a tone of scathing contempt—

"'Mistah Kurtz—he dead.'

"All the pilgrims rushed out to see. I remained, and went on with my dinner. I believe I was considered brutally callous. However, I did not eat much. There was a lamp in there—light, don't you know—and outside it was so beastly, beastly dark. I went no more near the remarkable man who had pronounced a judgment upon the adventures of his soul on this earth. The voice was gone. What else had been there? But I am of course aware that next day the pilgrims buried something in a muddy hole.

"And then they very nearly buried me.*

"However, as you see, I did not go to join Kurtz there and then. I did not. I remained to dream the nightmare out to the end, and to show my loyalty to Kurtz once more. Destiny. My destiny! Droll thing life is—that mysterious arrangement of merciless logic for a futile purpose. The most you can hope from it is some knowledge of yourself—that comes too late—a crop of unextinguishable regrets. I have wrestled with death. It is the most unexciting contest you can imagine. It takes place in an impalpable greyness, with nothing underfoot, with nothing around, without spectators, without clamour, without glory, without the great desire of victory, without the great fear of defeat, in a sickly atmosphere of tepid scepticism, without much belief in your own right, and still less in that of your adversary. If such is the form of ultimate wisdom, then life is a greater riddle than some of us think it to be. I was within a hair's-breadth of the last opportunity for pronouncement, and I found with humiliation that probably I would have nothing to say. This is the reason why I affirm that Kurtz was a remarkable man. He had something to say. He said it. Since I had peeped over the edge myself, I understand better the meaning of his stare, that could not see the flame of the candle, but was wide enough to embrace the whole universe, piercing enough to penetrate all the hearts that beat in the darkness. He had summed up—he had judged. 'The horror!' He was a remarkable man. After all, this was the expression of some sort of belief; it had candour, it had conviction, it had a vibrating note of revolt in its whisper, it had the appalling face of a glimpsed truth—the strange commingling of desire and hate. And it is not my own extremity I remember best—a vision of greyness without form filled with physical pain, and a careless contempt for the evanescence of all things—even of this pain itself. No! It is his extremity that I seem to have lived through. True, he had made that last stride, he had stepped over the edge, while I had been permitted to draw back my hesitating foot. And perhaps in this is the whole difference; perhaps all the wisdom, and all truth, and all sincerity, are just compressed into that inappreciable moment of time in which we step over the threshold of the invisible. Perhaps! I like to think my summing-up would not have been a word of careless contempt. Better his cry—much better. It was an affirmation, a moral victory paid for by innumerable defeats, by abominable terrors, by abominable satisfactions. But it was a victory! That is why I have remained loyal to Kurtz to the last, and even beyond, when a long time after I heard once more, not his own voice, but the echo of his magnificent eloquence thrown to me from a soul as translucently pure as a cliff of crystal.

"No, they did not bury me, though there is a period of time which I remember mistily, with a shuddering wonder, like a passage through some inconceivable world that had no hope in it and no desire. I found myself back in the sepulchral city resenting the sight of people hurrying through the streets to filch a little money from each other, to devour their infamous cookery, to gulp their unwhole-some beer, to dream their insignificant and silly dreams. They tres-passed upon my thoughts. They were intruders whose knowledge of life was to me an irritating pretence, because I felt so sure they could not possibly know the things I knew. Their bearing, which was simply the bearing of commonplace individuals going about their business in the assurance of perfect safety, was offensive to me like the outrageous flauntings of folly in the face of a danger it is unable to comprehend. I had no particular desire to enlighten them, but I had some difficulty in restraining myself from laughing in their faces, so full of stupid importance.* I daresay I was not very well at that time. I tottered about the streets—there were various affairs to settle—grinning bitterly at perfectly respectable persons. I admit my behaviour was inexcusable, but then my temperature was seldom normal in these days. My dear aunt's endeavours to 'nurse up my strength' seemed altogether beside the mark. It was not my strength that wanted nursing, it was my imagination that wanted soothing. I kept the bundle of papers given me by Kurtz, not knowing exactly what to do with it. His mother had died lately, watched over, as I was told, by his Intended. A clean-shaved man, with an official manner and wearing gold-rimmed spectacles, called on me one day and made inquiries, at first circuitous, afterwards suavely pressing, about what he was pleased to denominate certain 'documents.' I was not surprised, because I had had two rows with the manager on the subject out there. I had refused to give up the smallest scrap out of that package, and I took the same attitude with the spectacled man. He became darkly menacing at last, and with much heat argued that the Company had the right to every bit of information about its 'territories.' And, said he, 'Mr Kurtz's knowledge of unexplored regions must have been necessarily extensive and peculiar—owing to his great abilities and to the deplorable circumstances in which he had been placed: therefore——' I assured him Mr Kurtz's knowledge, however extensive, did not bear upon the problems of commerce or administration. He invoked then the name of science. 'It would be an incalculable loss if,' &c., &c. I offered him the report on the 'Suppression of Savage Customs,' with the postscriptum torn off. He took it up eagerly, but ended by sniffing at it with an air of contempt. 'This is not what we had a right to expect,' he remarked. 'Expect nothing else,' I said. 'There are only private letters.' He withdrew upon some threat of legal proceedings, and I saw him no more; but another fellow, calling himself Kurtz's cousin, appeared two days later, and was anxious to hear all the details about his dear relative's last moments. Incidentally he gave me to understand that Kurtz had been essentially a great musician. 'There was the making of an immense success,' said the man, who was an organist, I believe, with lank grey hair flowing over a greasy coat-collar. I had no reason to doubt his statement; and to this day I am unable to say what was Kurtz's profession, whether he ever had any—which was the greatest of his talents. I had taken him for a painter who wrote for the papers, or else for a journalist who could paint—but even the cousin (who took snuff during the interview) could not tell me what he had been—exactly. He was a universal genius—on that point I agreed with the old chap, who thereupon blew his nose noisily into a large cotton handkerchief and withdrew in senile agitation, bearing off some family letters and memoranda without importance. Ultimately a journalist anxious to know something of the fate of his 'dear colleague' turned up. This visitor informed me Kurtz's proper sphere ought to have been politics 'on the popular side.' He had furry straight eyebrows, bristly hair cropped short, an eye-glass on a broad ribbon, and, becoming expansive, confessed his opinion that Kurtz really couldn't write a bit—'but heavens! how that man could talk! He electrified large meetings. He had faith—don't you see?—he had the faith. He could get himself to believe anything—anything. He would have been a splendid leader of an extreme party.'* 'What party?' I asked. 'Any party,' answered the other. 'He was an—an—extremist.' Did I not think so? I assented. Did I know, he asked, with a sudden flash of curiosity, 'what it was that had induced him to go out there?' 'Yes,' said I, and forthwith handed him the famous Report for publication, if he thought fit. He glanced through it hurriedly, mumbling all the time, judged 'it would do,' and took himself off with this plunder.

"Thus I was left at last with a slim packet of letters and the girl's portrait. She struck me as beautiful—I mean she had a beautiful expression. I know that the sunlight can be made to lie too, yet one felt that no manipulation of light and pose could have conveyed the delicate shade of truthfulness upon those features.* She seemed ready to listen without mental reservation, without suspicion, without a thought for herself. I concluded I would go and give her back her portrait and those letters myself. Curiosity? Yes; and also some other feeling perhaps.* All that had been Kurtz's had passed out of my hands: his soul, his body, his station, his plans, his ivory, his career. There remained only his memory and his Intended—and I wanted to give that up too to the past, in a way,—to surrender personally all that remained of him with me to that oblivion which is the last word of our common fate. I don't defend myself. I had no clear perception of what it was I really wanted. Perhaps it was an impulse of unconscious loyalty, or the fulfilment of one of these ironic necessities that lurk in the facts of human existence. I don't know. I can't tell. But I went.

"I thought his memory was like the other memories of the dead that accumulate in every man's life,—a vague impress on the brain of shadows that had fallen on it in their swift and final passage; but before the high and ponderous door, between the tall houses of a street as still and decorous as a well-kept alley in a cemetery, I had a vision of him on the stretcher, opening his mouth voraciously, as if to devour all the earth with all its mankind. He lived then before me; he lived as much as he had ever lived—a shadow insatiable of splendid appearances, of frightful realities; a shadow darker than the shadow of the night, and draped nobly in the folds of a gorgeous eloquence. The vision seemed to enter the house with me—the stretcher, the phantom-bearers, the wild crowd of obedient worshippers, the gloom of the forests, the glitter of the reach between the murky bends, the beat of the drum, regular and muffled like the beating of a heart—the heart of a conquering darkness. It was a moment of triumph for the wilderness, an invading and vengeful rush which, it seemed to me, I would have to keep back alone for the salvation of another soul. And the memory of what I had heard him say afar there, with the horned shapes stirring at my back, in the glow of fires, within the patient woods, those broken phrases came back to me, were heard again in their ominous and terrifying simplicity.* I remembered his abject pleading, his abject threats, the colossal scale of his vile desires, the meanness, the torment, the tempestuous anguish of his soul. And later on I seemed to see his collected languid manner, when he said one day, 'This lot of ivory now is really mine. The Company did not pay for it. I collected it myself at a very great personal risk. I am afraid they will try to claim it as theirs though. H'm. It is a difficult case. What do you think I ought to do—resist? Eh? I want no more than justice.' ... He wanted no more than justice—no more than justice. I rang the bell before a mahogany door on the first floor, and while I waited he seemed to stare at me out of the glassy panel—stare with that wide and immense stare embracing, condemning, loathing all the universe. I seemed to hear the whispered cry, 'The horror! The horror!'*

"The dusk was falling. I had to wait in a lofty drawing-room with three long windows from floor to ceiling that were like three luminous and bedraped columns. The bent gilt legs and backs of the furniture shone in indistinct curves. The tall marble fireplace had a cold and monumental whiteness. A grand piano stood massively in a corner, with dark gleams on the flat surfaces like a sombre and polished sarcophagus. A high door opened—closed. I rose.

"She came forward, all in black, with a pale head, floating towards me in the dusk. She was in mourning. It was more than a year since his death, more than a year since the news came; she seemed as though she would remember and mourn for ever. She took both my hands in hers and murmured, 'I had heard you were coming.' I noticed she was not very young—I mean not girlish. She had a mature capacity for fidelity, for belief, for suffering. The room seemed to have grown darker, as if all the sad light of the cloudy evening had taken refuge on her forehead. This fair hair, this pale visage, this pure brow, seemed surrounded by an ashy halo from which the dark eyes looked out at me. Their glance was guileless, profound, confident, and trustful. She carried her sorrowful head as though she were proud of that sorrow, as though she would say, I—I alone know how to mourn for him as he deserves. But while we were still shaking hands, such a look of awful desolation came upon her face that I perceived she was one of those creatures that are not the playthings of Time. For her he had died only yesterday. And, by Jove! the impression was so powerful that for me too he seemed to have died only yesterday—nay, this very minute. I saw her and him in the same instant of time—his death and her sorrow—I saw her sorrow in the very moment of his death. Do you understand? I saw them together—I heard them together. She had said, with a deep catch of the breath, 'I have survived'; while my strained ears seemed to hear distinctly, mingled with her tone of despairing regret, the summing-up whisper of his eternal condemnation. I asked myself what I was doing there, with a sensation of panic in my heart as though I had blundered into a place of cruel and absurd mysteries not fit for a human being to behold.* She motioned me to a chair. We sat down. I laid the packet gently on the little table, and she put her hand over it. . . . 'You knew him well,' she murmured, after a moment of mourning silence.

"'Intimacy grows quick out there,' I said. 'I knew him as well as it is possible for one man to know another.'

"'And you admired him,' she said. 'It was impossible to know him and not to admire him. Was it?'

"'He was a remarkable man,' I said, unsteadily. Then before the appealing fixity of her gaze, that seemed to watch for more words on my lips, I went on, 'It was impossible not to——'

"'Love him,' she finished eagerly, silencing me into an appalled dumbness. 'How true! How true! But when you think that no one knew him so well as I! I had all his noble confidence. I knew him best.'

"'You knew him best,' I repeated. And perhaps she did. But with every word spoken the room was growing darker, and only her forehead, smooth and white, remained illumined by the unextinguishable light of belief and love.

"'You were his friend,' she went on. 'His friend,' she repeated, a little louder. 'You must have been, if he had given you this, and sent you to me. I feel I can speak to you—and oh! I must speak. I want you—you who have heard his last words—to know I have been worthy of him. . . . It is not pride. . . . Yes! I am proud to know I understood him better than any one on earth—he told me so himself. And since his mother died I have had no one—no one— to—to——'

"I listened. The darkness deepened. I was not even sure whether he had given me the right bundle. I rather suspect he wanted me to take care of another batch of his papers which, after his death, I saw the manager examining under the lamp.* And the girl talked, easing her pain in the certitude of my sympathy; she talked as thirsty men drink. I had heard that her engagement with Kurtz had been disapproved by her people. He wasn't rich enough or something. And indeed I don't know whether he had not been a pauper all his life. He had given me some reason to infer that it was his impatience of comparative poverty that drove him out there.

"'. . . Who was not his friend who had heard him speak once?' she was saying. 'He drew men towards him by what was best in them.' She looked at me with intensity. 'It is the gift of the great,' she went on, and the sound of her low voice seemed to have the accompaniment of all the other sounds, full of mystery, desolation, and sorrow, I had ever heard—the ripple of the river, the soughing of the trees swayed by the wind, the murmurs of wild crowds, the faint ring of incomprehensible words cried from afar, the whisper of a voice speaking from beyond the threshold of an eternal darkness. 'But you have heard him! You know!' she cried.

"'Yes, I know,' I said with something like despair in my heart, but bowing my head before the faith that was in her, before that great and saving illusion that shone with an unearthly glow in the darkness, in the triumphant darkness from which I could not have defended her—from which I could not even defend myself.

"'What a loss to me—to us!'—she corrected herself with beautiful generosity; then added in a murmur, 'To the world.' By the last gleams of twilight I could see the glitter of her eyes, full of tears—of tears that would not fall.

"'I have been very happy—very fortunate—very proud,' she went on. 'Too fortunate. Too happy for a little while. And now I am unhappy for—for life.'

"She stood up; her fair hair seemed to catch all the remaining light in a glimmer of gold. I rose too.

"'And of all this,' she went on, mournfully, 'of all his promise, and of all his greatness, of his generous mind, of his noble heart, nothing remains—nothing but a memory. You and I——'

"'We shall always remember him,' I said, hastily.

"'No!' she cried. 'It is impossible that all this should be lost—that such a life should be sacrificed to leave nothing—but sorrow. You know what vast plans he had. I knew of them too—I could not perhaps understand,—but others knew of them. Something must remain. His words, at least, have not died.'

"'His words will remain,' I said.

"'And his example,' she whispered to herself. 'Men looked up to him,—his goodness shone in every act. His example——'

"'True,' I said; 'his example too. Yes, his example. I forgot that.'

"'But I do not. I cannot—I cannot believe—not yet. I cannot believe that I shall never see him again, that nobody will see him again, never, never, never.'

"She put out her arms as if after a retreating figure, stretching them black and with clasped pale hands* across the fading and narrow sheen of the window. Never see him! I saw him clearly enough then. I shall see this eloquent phantom as long as I live, and I shall see her too, a tragic and familiar Shade, resembling in this gesture another one, tragic also, and bedecked with powerless charms, stretching bare brown arms over the glitter of the infernal stream, the stream of darkness.* She said suddenly very low, 'He died as he lived.'

"'His end,' said I, with dull anger stirring in me, 'was in every way worthy of his life.'

"'And I was not with him,' she murmured. My anger subsided before a feeling of infinite pity.

"'Everything that could be done——' I mumbled.

"'Ah, but I believed in him more than any one on earth—more than his own mother, more than—himself. He needed me! Me! I would have treasured every sigh, every word, every sign, every glance.'

"I felt like a chill grip on my chest. 'Don't,' I said, in a muffled voice.

"'Forgive me. I—I—have mourned so long in silence—in silence. . . . You were with him—to the last? I think of his loneliness. Nobody near to understand him as I would have understood. Perhaps no one to hear . . .'

"'To the very end,' I said, shakily. 'I heard his very last words. . . .' I stopped in a fright.

"'Repeat them,' she said in a heart-broken tone. 'I want—I want—something—something—to—to live with.'

"I was on the point of crying at her, 'Don't you hear them?' The dusk was repeating them in a persistent whisper all around us, in a whisper that seemed to swell menacingly like the first whisper of a rising wind. 'The horror! the horror!'

"'His last word—to live with,' she murmured. 'Don't you understand I loved him—I loved him—I loved him!'

"I pulled myself together and spoke slowly.

"'The last word he pronounced was—your name.'

"I heard a light sigh, and then my heart stood still, stopped dead short by an exulting and terrible cry, by the cry of inconceivable triumph and of unspeakable pain. 'I knew it—I was sure!' . . . She knew. She was sure. I heard her weeping; she had hidden her face in her hands. It seemed to me that the house would collapse before I could escape, that the heavens would fall upon my head. But nothing happened. The heavens do not fall for such a trifle. Would they have fallen, I wonder, if I had rendered Kurtz that justice which was his due? Hadn't he said he wanted only justice?* But I couldn't. I could not tell her. It would have been too dark—too dark altogether. . . ."

Marlow ceased, and sat apart, indistinct and silent, in the pose of a meditating Buddha. Nobody moved for a time. "We have lost the first of the ebb," said the Director, suddenly. I raised my head. The offing was barred by a black bank of clouds, and the tranquil waterway leading to the uttermost ends of the earth flowed sombre under an overcast sky—seemed to lead into the heart of an immense darkness.

# EXTRACT FROM THE
# AUTHOR'S NOTE (1917)

## TO *YOUTH | A NARRATIVE | AND TWO OTHER STORIES*

THE three stories in this volume lay no claim to unity of artistic purpose. The only bond between them is that of the time in which they were written. They belong to the period immediately following the publication of the *Nigger of the Narcissus*, and preceding the first conception of *Nostromo*, two books which, it seems to me, stand apart and by themselves in the body of my work. It is also the period during which I contributed to "Maga"; a period dominated by *Lord Jim* and associated in my grateful memory with the late Mr. William Blackwood's encouraging and helpful kindness.

*Youth* was not my first contribution to "Maga." It was the second. But that story marks the first appearance in the world of the man Marlow, with whom my relations have grown very intimate in the course of years. The origins of that gentleman (nobody as far as I know had ever hinted that he was anything but that)—his origins have been the subject of some literary speculation of, I am glad to say, a friendly nature.

One would think that I am the proper person to throw a light on the matter; but in truth I find that it isn't so easy. It is pleasant to remember that nobody had charged him with fraudulent purposes or looked down on him as a charlatan; but apart from that he was supposed to be all sorts of things: a clever screen, a mere device, a "personator," a familiar spirit, a whispering "dæmon." I myself have been suspected of a meditated plan for his capture.

That is not so. I made no plans. The man Marlow and I came together in the casual manner of those health-resort acquaintances which sometimes ripen into friendships. This one has ripened. For all his assertiveness in matters of opinion he is not an intrusive person. He haunts my hours of solitude, when, in silence, we lay our heads together in great comfort and harmony; but as we part at the end of a tale I am never sure that it may not be for the last time. Yet I don't think that either of us would care much to survive the other. In his case, at any rate, his occupation would be gone and he would suffer from that extinction, because I suspect him of some vanity. I don't mean vanity in the Solomonian sense. Of all my people he's the one that has never been a vexation to my spirit. A most discreet, understanding man. . . .

Even before appearing in book-form *Youth* was very well received. It lies on me to confess at last, and this is as good a place for it as another, that I have been all my life--all my two lives--the spoiled adopted child of Great Britain and even of the Empire; for it was Australia that gave me my first command. I break out into this declaration not because of a lurking tendency to megalomania, but, on the contrary, as a man who has no very notable illusions about himself. I follow the instincts of vain-glory and humility natural to all mankind. For it can hardly be denied that it is not their own deserts that men are most proud of, but rather of their pro-digious luck, of their marvellous fortune: of that in their lives for which thanks and sacrifices must be made on the altars of the inscrutable gods.

*Heart of Darkness* also received a certain amount of notice from the first; and of its origins this much may be said: it is well known that curious men go prying into all sorts of places (where they have no business) and come out of them with all kinds of spoil. This story, and one other ['An Outpost of Progress'] [. . .], are all the spoil I brought out from the centre of Africa, where, really, I had no sort of business. More ambitious in its scope and longer in the telling, *Heart of Darkness* is quite as authentic in fundamentals as *Youth*. It is, obviously, written in another mood. I won't characterize the mood precisely, but anybody can see that it is anything but the mood of wistful regret, of reminiscent tenderness.

One more remark may be added. *Youth* is a feat of memory. It is a record of experience; but that experience, in its facts, in its inwardness and in its outward colouring, begins and ends in myself. *Heart of Darkness* is experience too; but it is experience pushed a little (and only very little) beyond the facts of the case for the perfectly legitimate, I believe, purpose of bringing it home to the minds and bosoms of the readers. There it was no longer a matter of sincere colouring. It was like another art altogether. That sombre theme had to be given a sinister resonance, a tonality of its own, a continued vibration that, I hoped, would hang in the air and dwell on the ear after the last note had been struck [. . .]

1917.                                                                                    J. C.

# EXPLANATORY NOTES

Nautical and foreign terms, and various place-names, are listed in the Glossary. In these notes, the following abbreviations are used:

AB      Andrzej Busza, 'Conrad's Polish Literary Background and Some Illustrations of the Influence of Polish Literature on his Work', *Antemurale*, 10 (Rome: Institutum Historicum Polonicum, 1966).

*BP*     Gustave Flaubert, *Bouvard et Pécuchet* (Paris: Lemerre, 1881).

*CD*     Zdzisław Najder (ed.), *Congo Diary and Other Uncollected Pieces* (New York: Doubleday, 1978).

*CEW*     Norman Sherry, *Conrad's Eastern World* (London: Cambridge University Press, 1966).

*CWW*     Norman Sherry, *Conrad's Western World* (London: Cambridge University Press, 1971).

*FF*     Yves Hervouet, *The French Face of Joseph Conrad* (Cambridge: Cambridge University Press, 1990).

HH     Hunt Hawkins, 'Conrad's Critique of Imperialism in *Heart of Darkness*', *Publications of the Modern Language Association of America*, 94 (1989), 286–99.

HS     Henry Morton Stanley, *The Congo and the Founding of Its Free State: A Story of Work and Exploration* (2 volumes; New York: Harper, 1885).

*LE*     Joseph Conrad, *Last Essays* (London: Dent, 1926).

*Letters*     Frederick R. Karl and Laurence Davies (ed.), *The Collected Letters of Joseph Conrad* (Cambridge: Cambridge University Press; vol. i, 1983; vol. ii, 1986; vol. iii, 1988).

*LP*     Guy Burrows, *The Land of the Pigmies* (London: Pearson, 1898).

*MOS*     Joseph Conrad, *The Mirror of the Sea* (London: Methuen, 1906).

*NE*     Rodney Mundy, *Narrative of Events in Borneo and Celebes* (2 volumes; London: Murray, 1848).

RH     Robert Hampson (ed.), Joseph Conrad: *Heart of Darkness* (London: Penguin, 1995).

RK     Robert Kimbrough (ed.), Joseph Conrad: *Heart of Darkness* (3rd edn.; New York: Norton, 1988).

*SR*     Joseph Conrad, *Some Reminiscences* (London: Eveleigh Nash, 1912).

Quotations from Shakespeare are taken from the 'Globe' edition: *The Works of William Shakespeare*, ed. W. G. Clark and W. A. Wright (London: Macmillan, 1864), which would have been available to Conrad.

### An Outpost of Progress

3 *Kayerts . . . Carlier . . . legs*: when Conrad made his journey through the Congo in 1890, the commercial agent Alphonse Kayaerts travelled with

him in the *Roi des Belges* from Stanley Pool to Stanley Falls. The captain of the steamer *Lualaba*, which in the same year plied between Antwerp and the Congo, was named Carlier (*CWW* 21, 43). When describing 'An Outpost of Progress', Conrad told his publisher: 'It is a story of the Congo [. . .] The most common incidents are related—the life in a lonely station on the Kassai. I have divested myself of everything but pity—and some scorn—while putting down the insignificant events that bring on the catastrophe' (*Letters*, i. 294).

*The third . . . Price*: Sierra Leone, on the west coast of Africa, was popu-lated partly by liberated slaves and their descendants. In 1808 its coastal settlement became a British colony, and in 1896 the colony and its hinter-land were proclaimed a British protectorate. (In the magazine text, Henry Price's name is 'James Price'.)

*for all furniture*: a Gallicism. Subsequent Gallicisms include 'He regretted the streets' (for 'He missed the streets') and 'this dog of a country'.

*torn wearing apparel*: later editions have 'town wearing apparel', but 'torn' fits the context better.

4  *He made a speech . . . station*: H. M. Stanley, in *The Congo* (HS ii. 244–5), gives an example of the disappointments he encountered. At one trading-post, he made an encouraging speech to the agent in charge, but to no avail:

I am absent ten months from the scene, but I find on my return that the condition of the place is far worse than when I departed. The warm promises made by him created in me an ideal paradise; but instead of my bright, and, alas! too florid an ideal, I see the wild grass has overrun our native village, so that it is scarcely visible [. . .]; famine beleaguers the garrison [. . .]; the stores are empty [. . .] The natives leave him and his station so severely alone that he is in actual risk of starvation.

*an army guaranteed from harm by several European Powers*: Article VII of the Treaty of London (1839) declared that Belgium was 'an independent and perpetually neutral state' under the collective guarantee of Great Britain, France, Prussia, Russia, and Austria. In a letter of 1903 (*Letters*, iii. 94), Conrad remarked:

Kayerts is not a French name. Carlier perhaps, but as soon as I name him, I hasten to say that he is a former cavalry n.c.o. of an army *protected from all danger by several European powers*. I took the trouble to make a soldier out of that animal deliberately. They are gallant Belgians—God bless them: and they were recognized as such here and in Brussels when the tale appeared [. . .]

*to begin*: the serial version reads: 'to begin. The two most useless men I ever saw.' A few lines later, the phrase 'The two men watched' at the start of a paragraph reads, in the serial, 'The two useless men watched'.

5 *of its police and of its opinion*: in 'Signs of the Times' (1829), as later published in *Critical and Miscellaneous Essays*, vol. ii (London: Chapman & Hall, 1899), Thomas Carlyle declared (p. 78):

For the 'superior morality,' of which we have heard so much, we too would desire to be thankful: at the same time, it were but blindness to deny that this 'superior morality' is properly rather an 'inferior criminality,' produced not by greater love of Virtue, but by greater perfection of Police; and of that far subtler and stronger Police, called Public Opinion.

8 *On the sands . . . side*: in 'Heart of Darkness' (pp. 136–7), there is very similar alliterative phrasing: 'On silvery sandbanks hippos and alligators sunned themselves side by side.' 'Alligators' is Conrad's error for 'crocodiles'.

*Richelieu . . . people*: Richelieu and d'Artagnan appear in *Les Trois Mousquetaires* (*The Three Musketeers*), by Alexandre Dumas the Elder; Hawk-eye (Natty Bumppo) appears in *The Last of the Mohicans* and the other Leather-Stocking narratives of James Fenimore Cooper; and Father Goriot is prominent in *La Comédie humaine* (*The Human Comedy*), a sequence of novels by Honoré de Balzac. The rather naïve responses of Kayerts and Carlier to their reading-matter partly resemble the more elaborate responses of the eponymous heroes of Flaubert's *Bouvard et Pécuchet*, whose choice of novels (in chapter 5) also includes work by Dumas and Balzac. 'Melie', the name of Kayerts's daughter, appears in Flaubert's text as 'Mélie', the name of a maidservant.

9 *It spoke much . . . dark places of the earth*: in widely reported speeches, King Leopold II of Belgium (the proprietor, from 1885 to 1908, of the 'Congo Free State') had proclaimed the nobly civilizing mission of Belgian traders in the Congo. He said, for instance:

I am pleased to think that our agents, nearly all of whom are volunteers drawn from the ranks of the Belgian army, have always present in their minds a strong sense of the career of honour in which they are engaged, and are animated with a pure feeling of patriotism; not sparing their own blood, they will the more spare the blood of the natives, who will see in them the all-powerful protectors of their lives and their property, benevolent teachers of whom they have so great a need. Our only programme [. . .] is the work of moral and material regeneration, and we must do this among a population whose degeneration in its inherited conditions it is difficult to measure. The many horrors and atrocities which disgrace humanity give way little by little before our intervention [. . .] [O]ur progress [. . .] will soon introduce into the vast region of the Congo all the blessings of Christian civilization (*LP* 286–7, 288).

In 1903, Conrad remarked to Roger Casement (*Letters*, iii. 96):

It is an extraordinary thing that the conscience of Europe which seventy years ago has put down the slave trade on humanitarian grounds tolerates the Congo State to day. It is as if the moral clock had been put back many hours [. . .] and the Belgians are worse than the seven plagues of Egypt [. . .]

10 *Father Gobila*: Henry Morton Stanley's account (HS i. 507, 510) of Lieutenant Janssen's station in the Upper Congo stated:

His residence is like a genteel farmhouse in appearance, with a cool and shady porch, where he holds his palavers and chats twice a day with Papa Gobila [. . .] This old gentleman, stout of form, hearty and genial in manner, came up breathlessly and held out his fat hands, and welcomed Bula Matari ['Breaker of Rocks', the sobriquet of Stanley] after his long absence [. . .] Gobila, genial, aldermanic Gobila—Papa Gobila [. . .]

Conrad's Gobila is thin rather than stout, but he shares with his real-life namesake both the paternal attitude and the staff 'tall as himself' (which is shown in Stanley's picture of Gobila: HS i. 508).

19 *exterminating all the niggers . . . habitable*: this anticipation of Kurtz's 'Exterminate all the brutes!' is one of many connections between 'An Outpost of Progress' and 'Heart of Darkness'. (Other connections include the manager's cynicism, the steamboat's delay, the incompetence of the traders, and the demoralizing effect on Europeans of isolation within a wilderness.)

20 *". . . Bring out that sugar, Kayerts!"*: one source of this sequence is the fierce and almost suicidal quarrel between Bouvard and Pécuchet over two spoonfuls of tea (*BP* 299–300).

23 *with his right eye blown out—*: the serial reads 'with half his face blown away—'.

## Karain: A Memory

30 *Karain*: Conrad may have derived this name from Captain Rodney Mundy's *Narrative of Events in Borneo and Celebes*, which mentions that a 'rajah Karain' was a ruler in the Wajo region of south-west Celebes (*NE* i. 110–11). 'Kara-eng' is Makasarese for 'lord, descendant of rulers'.

32 *All that . . . immobility of a painted scene*: the phrasing echoes that of Flaubert's *Madame Bovary*: 'Ainsi vu d'en haut, le paysage tout entier avait l'air immobile comme une peinture' (*FF* 50).

35 *which he would politely conceal . . . threshold*: Frederick McNair's *Perak and the Malays* (London: Tinsley, 1878), 245, says: 'Considered an almost indispensable article of his dress, the Malay always wears his kris on the left side, where it is held up by the twisting of the sarong, with which during an interview it is considered respectful to conceal the weapon.'

37 *His mother . . . Gulf of Boni*: the Gulf of Boni (also spelt Bone) is a large gulf extending deeply into southern Celebes (Sulawesi). B. H. M.

Vlekke, in *Nusantara* (The Hague: Van Hoeve, 1959), 299, states that in the 1850s,

[t]here was fighting on Celebes where a proud queen of the Buginese had ordered her skippers to display the Dutch flag upside down on their ships. Batavia retaliated with armed force, and the campaign gave the Dutch the opportunity to renew their old alliance with the Aru Palacca of Bone.

The 'revolt' by Base Kajuara (the Queen of Boni) and her people was crushed by Dutch forces in 1859–60. *The Times* (29 March 1860, p. 11) reported: 'The people have submitted, the Queen has taken to flight, and her successor will hold office as a vassal of Holland.'

37  *a Korinchi man of no family*: according to Hans van Marle, it would have been as unlikely for a Bugis queen to marry a Korinchi trader (a Muslim Malay from West Sumatra) as for Queen Victoria to have married John Brown.

47  *the great trouble that broke the alliance of the four states of Wajo*: in south-western Celebes during the 1840s and 1850s, the states of Wajo, Boni (or Bone), Soping (Sopeng), and Si Dendring (Sidenring) fell to dissension over the choice of successor to the Rajah of Si Dendring. The outcome of the strife was that the Dutch extended their influence in the region. The Dutch expeditions of 1859–60 defeated the Queen, Base Kajuara, and brought to the throne the pretender, Aru Palaka (also spelt Aru Palacca and Aroe Palakka). In 1860 Boni and Soping entered a treaty recognizing Dutch sovereignty; this was confirmed in 1880. Wajo did the same in 1888.

*Pata Matara*: 'Pata' means 'Lord' (title of a high nobleman). 'Matara' was the name of a Bugis nobleman who guided Captain Mundy during his visit to Celebes in 1840; Conrad may have derived the name from Mundy's book (*NE* i. 31, 34, 79).

49  *a great mountain burning in the midst of water*: possibly Gunung Api ('Fire Mountain'), a volcanic island located at 8° 12′ south, 119° east, near the meeting-point of the Selat Sape and the Flores Sea. (Not the Moluccan Gunung Api.)

*a foreign sword*: Captain Mundy, whose writings were consulted by Conrad, argued that in Java, Celebes, and the other states of the Malay Archipelago, European domination had proved disastrous for the indigenes. See, for example, *NE* i. 70:

The first voyagers from the west found the natives rich and powerful, with strong established governments, and a thriving trade with all parts of the world. The rapacious European has reduced them to their present condition. Their governments have been broken up; the old states decomposed by treachery, by bribery, and intrigue; their possessions wrested from them under flimsy pretences; their trade restricted, their virtues repressed, and their energies paralysed or rendered desperate.

51 *Bajow people, who have no country*: Captain Mundy (*NE* i. 45), says: 'The Orang Bajow [Bajow people] resemble the Bugis and Malays. They have no country, live in boats, carry on a trade in tortoise-shell, bêche de mer, &c. [. . .] They say they have [. . .] a tradition that they originally came from the kingdom of Luwu.'

52 *Atjeh, where there was war*: the Atjehnese (or Achinese) War of 1873–1904 was a colonial campaign in which the Dutch repeatedly strove, with eventual success, to conquer the Muslim state of Atjeh in northern Sumatra. In March 1873, the Dutch declared war; and in 1874, after heavy losses (increased by cholera), they gained dominance; but sporadic warfare continued for thirty years.

53 *scraped the flint with his thumb-nail*: Andrzej Busza points out (AB 211) that this detail derives from Adam Mickiewicz's ballad 'Czaty' ('The Ambush'), which provided the basis of Conrad's tale. In 'Czaty', the governor, who seeks to kill his unfaithful young wife, tells his henchman: '[P]our in some priming and scrape the flint with your nail.'

58 *We served the Sultan of Sulu. We fought the Spaniards*: the sultans of the Sulu Archipelago in the south-western Philippines long opposed Spanish domination.

59 *'Give me your protection . . . charm . . . a weapon!'*: Mundy claimed that the Bugis people of southern Celebes were not only deeply superstitious but also great admirers of the English: 'They look to them for protection . . .' (*NE* i. 115, 82).

60 *We felt . . . illusions*: in classical mythology, Minos, Aeacus, and Rhadamanthus are the appointed judges of the souls of the dead on their entry to the underworld.

61 *'It's on account of its being a likeness—an engraved image'*: one tradition of the Muslim religion is aniconism, which forbids the representation of human beings and other living creatures; so Hollis fears that if Karain is a strict Muslim, he may deem idolatrous a talismanic image of the Queen. (Some Muslims maintain the aniconic tradition; others tolerate pictorial representations in restricted areas; and others openly display portraits of the holy family, the prophets, and religious leaders.)

62 *Jubilee sixpence . . . gilt . . . rim*: in 1887, to commemorate the Golden Jubilee (the fiftieth anniversary of Queen Victoria's accession to the throne), a new coinage was issued. It included a silver sixpenny piece bearing the Queen's head on one side and the royal coat of arms on the other. Unfortunately, this coin, which was of relatively low value, had a close resemblance in size and design to the gold half-sovereign, which was of relatively high value; so forgers gilded it in order to pass it fraudulently as the half-sovereign. In an appropriate irony, Hollis's 'gilt' sixpence appears more valuable than it really is: the coin is doubly deceptive. (The 'hole punched near the rim' enabled it to be worn as an ornament.)

*Suleiman the Wise, who commanded the genii*: the Koran (Sura XXXIV) states that Suleiman the Wise (Solomon) was served by spirits (djinn or genii) who 'made for him whatever he pleased'.

63 *thing like those Italian peasants wear, you know*: Italian peasants used to wear Madonna amulets, which could be made of gold, silver or tin, on neck-chains.

65 *Bland's window*: the shop of Thomas Bland and Sons, the gunsmiths, stood at 430, West Strand; the Strand being a busy street of central London, with theatres, hotels, and prosperous shops.

66 *A watery gleam . . . voices*: Hervouet (*FF* 51–2) suggests that this passage echoes phrases of a sentence in Flaubert's 'La Légende de Saint Julien l'Hospitalier', notably 'une confusion de toits pressés', 'des rues noires', and 'd'où montait jusqu'à lui un bourdonnement continuel'.

67 *a line of yellow boards . . . hats*: the boards are advertising-placards on a frame or yoke, extending above the shoulders of each of the bearers (the 'sandwich men'). Sometimes (as here) a procession of boards spelt out the name of a firm or product. (In other cases, a pair of boards hung from the shoulders of the bearer, one at the front and one at the back: hence the names 'sandwich boards' and 'sandwich men'.)

## Youth: A Narrative

71 *The director had been a 'Conway' boy*: the *Conway*, moored in the River Mersey at Liverpool, was a prestigious training-ship for naval cadets. The group of men described here reappears in 'Heart of Darkness' and was based on a group of Conrad's friends: G. F. W. Hope (a company director and former *Conway* boy), W. B. Keen (an accountant), and T. L. Mears (a lawyer). Charles Marlow, whose voyages resemble Conrad's, was an invention.

*It was my first voyage to the East, . . . skipper's first command*: the ensuing tale is based on Conrad's first voyage to the East, as second mate of the *Palestine* in 1881–3. The *Palestine* was a wooden barque of 427 tons, built at Sunderland in 1857 and owned by John Wilson (the 'Wilmer, Wilcox' of the tale); her captain was Elijah (not John) Beard, who in 1881 was 57 years old; and the first mate was H. Mahon. The *Palestine*'s disastrous odyssey was summarized in the report of the Marine Court of Enquiry which was held in Singapore on 2 April 1883:

On the 29th November 1881 she sailed from Newcastle-upon-Tyne with a cargo of 557 tons of West Hartley coal, bound to Bang Kok, and a crew of 13 hands all told. Arriving in the chops of the English Channel, the vessel encountered a succession of heavy gales, losing sails and springing a leak on the 24th of December 1881, the crew refusing to proceed, the vessel put into Falmouth. The coal was there discharged and stored under cover, with the exception of about 90 tons, and the vessel thoroughly repaired in dock. On the 17th September 1882 the 'Palestine' sailed from Falmouth with a complement of 13 hands all told, and proceeded on her voyage to Bang Kok. The passage was tedious owing to persistent high winds, but nothing unusual occurred until noon of the 11th March, when a strong smell resembling paraffin oil was perceived; at this time the vessel's position was lat. 2 36 S and long. 105 45 E. Banca Strait. Next day smoke was discovered issuing from the coals on the port side of main hatch. Water was thrown over them until the smoke abated, the boats were lowered, water placed in them. On the 13th some coals were thrown overboard, about 4 tons, and more water poured down the hold. On the 14th, the hatches being on but not battened down, the decks blew up fore and aft as far as the poop. The boats were then provisioned and the vessel headed for the Sumatra shore. About 3 p.m. the S. S. 'Somerset' came alongside in answer to signals and about 6 p.m. she took the vessel in tow. Shortly afterwards the fire rapidly increased and the master of the 'Palestine' requested the master of the 'Somerset' to tow the barque on shore. This being refused, the tow-rope was slipped and about 11 p.m. the vessel was a mass of fire, and all hands got into the boats, 3 in number. The mate and 4 seamen in one boat, the 2nd mate with three hands in another and the master in the long boat with 3 men. The boats remained by the vessel until 8.30 a.m. on the 15th. The boats arrived at Mintok at 10 p.m. on the 15th [. . .] The officers and crew came on to Singapore in the British steamer 'Sissie'. . . .

The Court considers that the cause of the fire was spontaneous combustion, the passage having been unusually protracted.

The Court is further of opinion that the vessel was not prematurely abandoned and that no blame is attached to the master, officers or crew (*CEW* 297–8).

72 *I had come out . . . I was just twenty*: in 1880, Conrad had worked as third mate of the *Loch Etive*, a 'crack clipper' that voyaged from London to Sydney. He was 23 when he joined the *Palestine* in September 1881.

*'Do or Die' underneath*: 'Let's [. . .] either doe, or dye' (John Fletcher, *The Island Princess*, 1621, II. ii. 67).

74 *Abraham*: in the serial version of 'Youth', between 'Abraham.' and 'Mrs Beard' appears the following sentence: 'It rained every day, and in the cabin we lived *en famille*.'

*'Sartor Resartus' and Burnaby's 'Ride to Khiva'*: Thomas Carlyle's *Sartor Resartus* (1834) is an elaborately satiric philosophical work. Although Marlow is unenthusiastic about it, Carlyle's text does include (in chapter 5) a passage which, by stressing the contrast between youthful ardour and subsequent disillusionment, anticipates one of the main themes of Conrad's tale:

Happy season of virtuous youth, when shame is still an impassable celestial barrier; and the sacred air-cities of Hope have not shrunk into the mean clay-hamlets of Reality; and man, by his nature, is yet infinite and free!

Captain Frederick G. Burnaby's *A Ride to Khiva: Travels and Adventures in Central Asia* (London: Cassell, 1877) would have appealed to Conrad in various ways. First, it is a warning against Russian expansionism, and particularly against the threat that Russia may offer to British interests in India. Secondly, the narrative depicts the backwardness of Russia and the oppressiveness of her rulers. Thirdly, the quixotic courage of Burnaby's venture would have appealed to the author of 'Youth'. Burnaby claimed that it was precisely because the Russian authorities had forbidden foreigners to travel in central Asia that he conceived his plan of traversing Russia from St Petersburg to Khiva, a journey of about 2,000 miles in icy and perilous conditions.

74  *I watched . . . remained*: a 'head-light' is a white light on or in front of a foremast, and the starboard side of a vessel has a green light, while the port side has a red light.

75  *A sailor . . . wife—I say*: in Conrad's *Nostromo*, Captain Mitchell says: 'I was never married myself. A sailor should exercise self-denial.'

79  *blessed name. Mesopotamia*: the celebrated actor, David Garrick, is reputed to have remarked, 'That blessed word Mesopotamia', when declaring that George Whitefield (a renowned Methodist preacher) 'could make men laugh or cry' by his pronunciation of this name of an Iraqi region.

81  *concluded to clear out*: a Gallicism; the meaning is 'decided to clear out'.

*the superstition about them*: proverbially, rats instinctively desert a ship that is doomed to sink.

> A rotten carcass of a boat, not rigg'd,
> Nor tackle, sail, nor mast; the very rats
> Instinctively had quit it.
> (Shakespeare, *The Tempest*, i. ii. 146–8)

82  *on fire*: Robert W. Stevens's *On the Stowage of Ships and Their Cargoes* (6th edn., London: Longmans, Green, Reader, & Dyer, 1873), 120, says:

Coal is liable to danger of two kinds, totally different, although often confounded together; one is from spontaneous combustion, and the other the liability of ignition and explosion of the gas evolved from the coal, and remaining in the ship [. . .] Any coal containing a large quantity of iron pyrites is apt to heat when saturated with water, and after some time to burst into flame; the only prevention is said to be to keep the coal dry [. . .]

Stevens advocates (on p. 121) use of a system of ventilation to prevent the accumulation of flammable gas in a vessel.

*You see . . . anything else*: Stevens (pp. 121–2) states that coal which is free from iron pyrites is relatively safe, whereas 'brassey coal and steam coal' are relatively dangerous. 'Smithy coal' is small and soft bituminous coal of the kind used in a blacksmith's forge.

*by want of air*: Stevens's advice (p. 135) is this:

Fire cannot continue without a constant supply of air, therefore use the utmost diligence in stopping every hole and crevice through which air can obtain access to the combustible; and prevent as much as possible the passing off of the smoke produced, because it contains carbonic acid, which is even a more active extinguisher of fire than water itself.

83 *And she crawled on ... splendour of sea and sky*: in this fine passage of Conradian poetic prose, the rhetorical devices include alliteration, assonance, asyndeton (phrases associated without conjunctions), parison (structural parallelism), and ploce (systematic repetition of words).

85 *all round me like*: a Gallicism; 'all round me something like' would be better English.

*the explosion*: Stevens (p. 121) says:

Every kind of steam and other coal, especially when rapidly transferred from the mine to the ship, gives out carburetted hydrogen gas or fire damp, which is explosive when mixed with atmospheric air, on the application of a flame [. . .] If the hatches are fastened down directly the cargo is received, which is frequently done to keep out the rain or cold, or to prepare for sea, the gas finds its way from the coal to the spaces under the deck, and penetrates through the bulk-heads into the lazarette, cabin, and forecastle, and when a match is lit, or a lighted candle exposed [. . .], an explosion may take place and damage the decks, and jeopardize the lives of the crew.

*The coal-dust suspended ... on the cargo*: in the serial, this passage reads:

You see, she had blown up her decks, and the coal-dust suspended in the air of the hold glowed dull-red for an instant. In the twinkling of an eye, in an infinitesimal fraction of a second since the first tilt of the bench, I struck full length on the coals.

87 *and be done with our ridiculous troubles*: the serial reads: 'and thus end the poignant comedy of that voyage'.

*I wonder what will happen. O youth!*: the serial reads: 'I wonder what will happen. I exulted as if after a triumph. O youth! And are we not all descendants of Don Quixote, all the wise, all the simple—all of us in the quixotism of our youth?'

89 *I don't say positively ... same way*: the serial reads: 'I don't say positively that the crew of a vulgar French or German merchantman wouldn't have done it, but I doubt it. And it wouldn't have been done in the same way.'

90 *The old man ... gear*: the serial reads: 'The old man informed us it was part of our duty to save as much as we could out of the ship.'

91 *the sparks flew upwards, as man is born to trouble*: 'Yet man is born unto trouble, as the sparks fly upward' (Job 5: 7).

93  *The silly . . . youth*: the use of the definite article here is another Gallicism.

95  *handful of dust*: Meditation IV of John Donne's *Devotions upon Emergent Occasions* (1624) says: '[W]hats become of mans great extent & proportion, when himselfe shrinkes himselfe, and consumes himselfe to a handfull of dust?'

98–9  *Only a moment . . . youth!*: the serial reads: 'My God! Only a moment, an instant, a beat of the eyelid, and all is gone. All! The strength, the ignorance, the romance, the hopes, the glamour—youth!'

99  *the good old time*: Lord Byron's 'The Age of Bronze' (I. 1–2) says:

> The 'good old times'—all times when old are good—
> Are gone; the present might be if they would [. . .]

*Youth and the sea*: the serial reads: 'Youth and the sea. You have known it. What was it? What was there in it? Eh? Not the life itself. Hey? What?'

*already gone . . . illusions*: the serial reads: 'already gone, gone past, gone unseen, gone in a flash—gone together with the youth, with the strength, with the romance of illusions.'

### Heart of Darkness

103  *HEART OF DARKNESS*: the title is richly ambiguous, even more so than its original form in the serial (which began with the definite article). The phrase 'heart of darkness' could mean the centre of a dark (obscure, mysterious, sinister, or evil) place. It suggests the interior of Africa, which was then widely termed 'The Dark Continent' (and the tale refers to 'the profound darkness of its heart'); but London is described as the centre of 'a brooding gloom'. The phrase could also mean 'A person with a dark (obscure, mysterious, sinister, or evil) heart', so that it anticipates the depiction of Kurtz, as when 'the darkness of his heart' is mentioned by Marlow. In the tale, the word 'darkness' also connotes: the death of the individual or of the human race; 'dark ages' between periods of civilization; the abominable; the primordial; the inscrutable; the unknown; the mapped. Light is associated with civilization and truth but also with the brightness and destructiveness of fire. Whiteness is associated with hypocrisy, ivory, bones, death, fog, and the unmapped. In Virgil's *Aeneid*, Bk. VI, the ivory gates of the Underworld are the gates by which 'false dreams' are sent to the world above. Kurtz's career may occasionally evoke that of Lucifer (whose name means 'Light-bringer'), the brightest of the angels, who fell through pride and reigned in Hell.

*The Director of Companies . . . host*: the 'Director' was G. F. W. Hope (a director of the South African Mercantile Company and the Thames Sand Dredging Company), who owned the yawl *Nellie*, moored at Greenhithe. He made occasional sailing expeditions in her with his friends T. L. Mears (a lawyer), W. B. Keen (an accountant), and Conrad. When at anchor, they would exchange yarns. Mears had served in the *Duke of Sutherland*, as had Hope and Conrad at different times. (See Hope's 'Friend of Conrad' in *The Conradian*, 25: 2 (Autumn 2000), 1–56.)

*He resembled a pilot, . . . trustworthiness personified*: Hampson (RH 126) notes that the typescript contains a fuller description: 'The sunburnt neck, the broad shoulders, the set of the blue clothes, the balance and solid aspect of the whole figure suggested the idealized type of a pilot [. . .] '

*as I have already said somewhere, the bond of the sea*: the 'somewhere' is paragraph two of 'Youth', which mentions this bond.

*bones*: 'bones' was a familiar term for dominoes, which were then often made of ivory (so that, in contrast to most dominoes today, they were white and bore black spots). The term introduces the tale's thematic association of ivory with death. G. F. W. Hope used to play dominoes with his friends aboard the *Nellie*.

*He . . . resembled an idol*: Conrad's purposes in comparing Marlow to 'an idol' here (and subsequently to 'a Buddha preaching' and 'a meditating Buddha') are partly ironic, for this 'Buddha' is 'in European clothes and without a lotus-flower' and offers no road to Nirvana: Marlow is a sceptic. Like the eastern idol to a western tourist, Marlow may seem the possessor of more knowledge than he can express. Nevertheless, like the Buddha Gautama, Marlow teaches by means of paradoxes; he warns of the perils of the appetites; and he indicates the impermanence and possible illusoriness of the phenomenal world.

104 *It had known . . . Drake . . . Franklin . . . never returned*: Sir Francis Drake (*c*.1542–1596) was knighted by Queen Elizabeth I at Deptford aboard *The Golden Hind*, the ship in which he had circumnavigated the globe and harried the Spaniards, returning with pillaged wealth. Sir John Franklin (1786–1847) commanded an expedition to find a north-west passage linking the North Atlantic to the North Pacific. Both its ships, the *Erebus* and the *Terror*, became ice-bound in the Arctic, and all the men died. Subsequently, Dr John Rae alleged that the last survivors had resorted to cannibalism in the unsuccessful attempt to save their lives. Conrad, when praising Franklin (*LE* 15–16) refers to the termination of that expedition as 'the end of the darkest drama perhaps played behind the curtain of Arctic mystery'.

*"interlopers" . . . "generals" . . . fleets*: 'interlopers' were traders who breached a legal monopoly. Brian Gardner's *The East India Company* (London: Hart-Davis, 1971), 50, says:

Another bane of the [East India] Company was the activity of the merchant interlopers [. . .] [I]n 1685 the Company mounted 48 prosecutions for interloping. In 1701, the notorious Captain Kidd was executed for piracy in the Indian Ocean [. . .]

The 'commissioned "generals" of East India fleets' were the commanders of the company's fleets: James Lancaster, for instance, was termed 'our Generall' (Gardner, 26). The East India Company, originally chartered by Queen Elizabeth I in 1600, gradually took control of most of the Indian subcontinent until, in 1857–8, its authority there was transferred to the British government.

105 *one of the dark places of the earth*: Psalms 74:20. William Booth, in his *In Darkest England and the Way Out* (London: Salvation Army, 1890), 11, said: 'As there is a darkest Africa is there not also a darkest England?' Booth's volume was partly a response to a work published earlier in 1890: *In Darkest Africa*, by H. M. Stanley, the renowned explorer. (Previously, Rudyard Kipling's tale 'The Man Who would be King' had referred to the Indian 'Native States' as 'the dark places of the earth'.)

*when the Romans first came here . . . the other day*: *The Times* (4 October 1892, p. 5) reported a speech by H. M. Stanley which quoted as follows the oratory of William Pitt in 1792:

'It has been alleged that Africa labours under a natural incapacity for civilization [. . .] Allow of this principle as applied to Africa, and I should be glad to know why it might not also have been applied to ancient and uncivilized Britain. Why might not some Roman Senator have predicted with equal boldness—"There is a people destined never to be free, a people depressed by the hand of nature below the level of the human species, and created to form a supply of slaves for the rest of the world"? Sir, we were once as obscure among the nations of the earth, as debased in our morals, as savage in our manners, as degraded in our understandings as these unhappy Africans are at present. But, in the lapse of a long series of years, by a progression slow and, for a time, almost imperceptible, we have become rich in a variety of acquirements, favoured above measure with the gifts of Providence [. . .] God forbid that we should any longer subject Africa to the same dreadful scourge and preclude the light of knowledge which has reached every other quarter of the globe from having access into her coasts.'

Conrad's friend Cunninghame Graham, in his *Notes on the District of Menteith* (London: Black, 1891), 81, wrote:

History informs us that the Romans once ruled the greater part of Scotland [. . .] What an abode of horror it must have been to the unfortunate centurion, say from Naples, stranded in a marsh far from the world, in a climate of the roughest, and blocked on every side by painted savages!

Hampson (RH 128) notes the irony that the Roman legions would have included soldiers from North Africa.

106 *you say 'knights'?*: this interjection retrospectively modifies the status of the anonymous narrator's reflections on the Thames and her 'knights all, titled and untitled'. Evidently the statements from 'The tidal current' to

'germs of empires' should be regarded mainly as tacitly reported speech, representing words originally uttered aloud, and thus justifying the shift to the past perfect tense during that descriptive passage. (Conrad sometimes, however, uses the past perfect where the present perfect is correct.)

*if we may believe what we read*: in, for example, Julius Caesar's *De Bello Gallico*, v. 1–2, which claims that 628 ships were built in one winter by Romans preparing to invade Britain.

*mend his fortunes*: in this proleptic paragraph, the account of the 'trireme commander' partly anticipates the description of Marlow's experiences, while the account of this 'decent young citizen' partly anticipates what will be said of Kurtz. Section XXX of Conrad's *The Mirror of the Sea* (1906) again imagines a Roman galley-commander's first voyage up the Thames: see *MOS* 158–60.

106–7 *without a lotus-flower*: Buddhist scriptures confer many symbolic meanings on the lotus-flower: these include 'enlightening doctrine', 'spiritual grace', 'paradisal beauty', 'purity', and 'the support and ground of manifestation'. In paintings and sculptures of the Buddha, a cross-legged posture indicates meditation or preaching, and a raised forearm with palm outwards signifies reassurance.

107 *efficiency*: efficiency was a quality highly recommended in the 1890s by Social Darwinists, Liberal imperialists, and Fabian imperialists. In 1899, Conrad remarked to William Blackwood about 'The Heart of Darkness': 'The criminality of inefficiency and pure selfishness when tackling the civilizing work in Africa is a justifiable idea.' In 1901, however, Conrad said that *The Inheritors* (which he co-authored with F. M. Hueffer) attacked the fashionable 'worship' of 'unscrupulous efficiency' (see *Letters*, ii. 139–40, 348).

*to be got*: Hampson (RH 129) notes that a cancelled passage in the manuscript continues: 'but at any rate they had no pretty fictions about it. They had no international associations from motives of philanthropy with some third rate king for head [. . .]' This passage, indicting King Leopold II of Belgium, was superseded by an expanded version which also appears in the typescript.

*blind . . . darkness*: cf. Deuteronomy 28: 29: 'the blind gropeth in darkness'.

*Flames glided . . . hastily*: the 'flames' are the lights of vessels and their reflections in the water. Sailing vessels carried a green light on the starboard side and a red one on the port side; a steamer carried, in addition, a white light on or in front of the foremast.

*sleepless river*: there follows in the manuscript a lengthy description of 'a big steamer [. . .] bound to the uttermost ends of the earth', followed by a comparison of the earth to 'a pea spinning in the heart of an immense darkness'. The typescript contains an equivalent passage.

108 *I will go there*: Marlow's recollections resemble Conrad's, as given in *SR* 41:

> It was in 1868, when nine years old or thereabouts, that while looking at a map of Africa of the time and putting my finger on the blank space then representing the unsolved mystery of that continent, I said to myself with absolute assurance and an amazing audacity which are no longer in my character now: 'When I grow up I shall go *there*.'

There is a similar passage in 'Geography and Some Explorers' (*LE* 24).

*dream gloriously over*: in 'Geography and Some Explorers (*LE* 20), Conrad recalls that in his childhood atlas, printed in 1852, '[t]he heart of its Africa was white and big'. The explorations of David Livingstone, Sir Richard Burton, and Captain J. H. Speke then helped to fill such space with details of the interior of the continent.

*a Company for trade on that river*: the river is evidently the Congo, and the company corresponds to the Société Anonyme Belge pour le Commerce du Haut-Congo (the Belgian Limited Company for Trade on the Upper Congo), which had its headquarters in Brussels.

109 *I had an aunt ... enthusiastic soul*: she is based partly on Marguerite Poradowska, whom Conrad addressed as 'Aunt' (though she was really the wife of his maternal grandmother's first cousin) and who lived in Brussels. In November 1889 Conrad was interviewed in that city by Captain Albert Thys, director of the Société Anonyme Belge, and was apparently promised the command of the *Florida*, a paddle-steamer in the Congo. In February 1890, around the time of her husband's death, Conrad visited Madame Poradowska; he was again interviewed, but doubted the outcome; yet, in April, the appointment was confirmed. Apparently she had exerted her influence on Conrad's behalf. (Her friends included A. J. Wauters, secretary-general of the Compagnies Belges du Congo.)

*Fresleven ... stick*: Otto Lütken, in 'Joseph Conrad in the Congo' (*London Mercury*, 22 May 1930, p. 43), states:

> [Johannes] Freiesleben, a Danish captain, and Conrad's predecessor in command of the *Florida*, was killed by the natives at Tchumbe[r]i in some dispute over firewood or fresh provisions; but his bones were recovered on the 24th March, 1890[,] by the two steamers [. . .] The steamers had soldiers on board and some Belgian officers [. . .]; and there was a good deal of shooting and burning of native huts [. . .] Duhst, who *was* there, tells of the grass growing through the bones of the skeleton which lay where it had fallen.

110 *whited sepulchre*: according to St Mark's Gospel (23: 27–8), Jesus said:

> Woe unto you, scribes and Pharisees, hypocrites! for ye are like unto whited sepulchres, which indeed appear beautiful outward, but are within full of dead *men's* bones, and all uncleanness.

Even so ye also outwardly appear righteous unto men, but within ye are full of hypocrisy and iniquity.

Marlow associates Brussels with hypocrisy because of the 'philanthropic pretence' masking the desire to 'make no end of coin by trade'. In the typescript of 'Heart of Darkness' the description of the city is expanded: its big houses, for example, 'suggest the reserve of discreet turpitude'.

*Two women . . . knitting black wool*: this description may distantly recall Charles Dickens's *A Tale of Two Cities*, in which Madame Defarge knits 'with the steadfastness of Fate'. She says she is knitting shrouds; her companion in the task is called 'Vengeance'; and the knitwork incorporates the names of the exploiters who are to incur retribution. Given that one of the knitters is 'uncanny and fateful' and that both are associated with death, another connotation (though tenuous and partly parodic) is with the classical Fates, Clotho, Lachesis, and Atropos: Clotho and Lachesis spin the thread of each person's life, and Atropos lethally shears it. Ivan Turgenev's *A House of Gentlefolk* mentions 'three old women' who, 'like the Fates, swiftly and silently plied their knitting-needles'. Incidentally, in a letter of 1897, Conrad described the universe as a remorseless knitting machine: 'It knits us in and it knits us out' (*Letters*, i. 425).

*red . . . yellow*: British late nineteenth-century maps of the world usually coloured British territories red, French territories blue, Italian green, Portuguese orange, German purple, and Belgian yellow: this was a standard code. (Tanganyika, on the east coast of Africa, became a German protectorate in 1891.)

111  *pale plumpness in a frock-coat*: probably a recollection of Captain Albert Thys (1849–1915), the director who had interviewed Conrad. (In photographs taken between 1887 and 1892, Thys is markedly plump.) In 1885 Thys was praised by H. M. Stanley (HS i, p. xiii) for supplying Stanley's expeditions in the Congo.

*trade secrets*: compare: 'I am destined to the command of a steamboat [. . .] but I know nothing for certain as everything is supposed to be kept secret' (Conrad to Karol Zagórski, 22 May 1890: *Letters*, i. 52).

*guarding the door of Darkness*: the Sybil in Virgil's *Aeneid* guards 'the door of gloomy Dis', the entrance of the underworld into which Aeneas is to descend.

*Ave! . . . Morituri te salutant*: the original Latin form was 'Ave Caesar [*or* Ave imperator], morituri te salutant': 'Hail, Caesar [*or* Hail, Emperor], those about to die salute you': the gladiators' salutation on entering the arena of combat.

*assured me the secretary*: one of Conrad's lapses into French word-order.

112  *quoth Plato to his disciples*: a facetious tag, not a genuine attribution.

*measure my head*: the doctor is a craniologist and craniometrist: he measures crania in order to compare and classify the characteristics of different individuals and races. In the late nineteenth century, this was a flourishing though controversial area of research; and in 1881 Conrad had been asked to collect skulls during his travels and send them to a museum in Kraków. Alfred Russel Wallace's *The Malay Archipelago* (1869), one of Conrad's favourite books, contains an appendix in which Wallace, while noting that the value of craniology has been questioned by T. H. Huxley, specifies the results of his own researches, which appear to reveal a correlation between cranial volume and 'capacity for civilization'.

*Du calme, du calme. Adieu*: '[Keep] calm, calm. Goodbye.'

113 *Workers, with a capital—you know*: as in Thomas Carlyle's *Past and Present* [1843] (London: Chapman & Hall, 1858), 302:

But it is to you, ye Workers, [. . .] that the whole world calls for new work and nobleness. Subdue mutiny, discord, widespread despair, by manfulness, justice, mercy and wisdom. Chaos is dark, deep as Hell; let light be, and there is instead a green flowery World [. . .] It is work for a God. Sooty Hell of mutiny and savagery and despair can, by man's energy, be made a kind of Heaven.

In 1898, H. M. Stanley quoted this passage to justify King Leopold's activities in the Congo, adding: 'Who can doubt that God chose the King for His instrument to redeem this vast slave park' (RK 79).

*sort of apostle*: Hampson notes that in 1882 the French press had described the explorer Pierre de Brazza as an 'apostle of liberty' who had dealt 'a death blow to slavery in West Africa' (RH 132).

*rot let loose . . . time*: in 1889, for example, Leopold II opened the international 'Brussels Conference for the Abolition of the Slave-Trade', which was widely publicized; and Albert Thys published his proposals for the Lower Congo Railway, concluding:

We must also appeal to philanthropists and men of goodwill who are horrified by the barbarities of the slave-trade; [. . .] to religious and believing men who suffer to see the unfortunate blacks held in the ignorance of fetish-worship. All these friends of humanity will find that the Congo railway is the means *par excellence* of allowing civilisation to penetrate rapidly and surely into the unknown depths of Africa.

(Quotation from Ruth Slade's *King Leopold's Congo* (Oxford: Oxford University Press, 1962), 75.)

*the labourer is worthy of his hire*: Luke 10: 7. This maxim was cited by H. M. Stanley in *The Congo and the Founding of Its Free State* (HS vol. i, p. xiv).

*It's queer . . . whole thing over*: in *Chance* (London: Methuen, 1914), 131, Marlow says the opposite:

'The women's rougher, simpler, more upright judgment, embraces the whole truth, which their tact, their mistrust of masculine idealism, ever prevents them speaking in its entirety [. . .] We could not stand women speaking the truth [. . .] It would cause infinite misery and bring about most awful disturbances in this rather mediocre, but still idealistic fool's paradise in which each of us lives his own little life.'

*centre of the earth*: Jules Verne's *Voyage au centre de la terre* had appeared in 1864; but Marlow's phrasing also evokes Dante, who (in *Inferno*, Canto II) paused fearfully before setting out for Hell, 'this centre here below'.

114 *Gran' Bassam, Little Popo*: in 1890, when Conrad voyaged from Bordeaux to the mouth of the Congo in the steamer *Ville de Maceio*, the vessel called at Grand Bassam (or Bassa) on the Ivory Coast and at Grand Popo in Dahomey (Benin). Little Popo (or Anecho) is in Togo, formerly Togoland.

115 *wars going on thereabouts*: Conrad later explained (*Letters*, iii. 94): 'If I say that the ship which bombarded the coast was French, it is quite simply because *it was* a French ship. I recall its name—the *Seignelay*. It was during the war (!) with Dahomey.' Between February and October 1890, the French attempted to conquer the African kingdom of Dahomey by bombardment and invasion. The campaign resumed between 1892 and 1894, until in 1894 King Behanzin surrendered and Dahomey became a French protectorate.

*dropped limp*: this is the version in the Blackwood and Dent texts. The manuscript and the Heinemann 1921 edition give 'drooped limp'.

*seat of the government*: Conrad stayed one night at Boma, the 'seat of government' of the Congo Free State. In the manuscript of 'Heart of Darkness', Marlow speaks scornfully of the place, particularly its 'greasy and dingy' hotel. Sherry (*CWW* 27) says that in 1890 Boma, with its steam-tramway, hotel and post office, was actually 'a well-established, well-organised seat of government'.

116 *Company's station . . . slope*: the location corresponds to Matadi.

*building a railway*: construction of the 270-mile railway line from Matadi to Kinshasa was beset by difficulties, and it took eight years (until completion in 1898) instead of the expected four.

117 *unhappy savages*: 'On 8 August 1890, a royal decree [by Leopold II] permitted the railway company to establish a militia to impress workers from the surrounding area' (HH 290). Forced labour, under various pre-texts, became widespread in the Congo. In 1890 George Grenfell reported that he had seen 'nine slaves chained neck to neck in the State Station at Upoto' (RK 101).

118 *gloomy circle of some Inferno*: Marlow's journey has intermittent (though distant) analogies with Dante's journey through the nine circles of hell: he sees suffering beings, learns of various kinds of corruption, and, on meeting Kurtz, encounters a flagrant malefactor who is described as a 'tormented soul'.

118  *helpers had withdrawn to die*: Louis Goffin's *Le Chemin de fer du Congo* (Brussels: Weissenbruch, 1907), 43–4, emphasizes the high mortality rate among the black workers during the construction of the railway through the Congo. In one month alone, 15 November to 15 December 1891, 150 men (nearly 8 per cent of the black workforce of 1,951) perished. Goffin remarks that they often withdrew into the bush to die. Numerous Europeans either died or (like Conrad) were sent home suffering from tropical diseases.

*time contracts*: G. W. Williams, who traversed the Congo in 1890, reported that labourers were often recruited from distant coastal regions and were expected to work for one year (RK 95, 106).

*white worsted . . . Why?*: probably as an amulet supposed to ward off diseases of the throat. See *Astonishment and Power* (exhibition catalogue; Washington: Smithsonian Institution Press, 1993), 84.

119  *clear necktie*: as Hampson (RH 133) points out, 'clear silk necktie' in the manuscript became 'clear necktie' in the 1902 edition and, after Conrad's proof-correction, 'clean necktie' in the Heinemann text. (There may be a Gallicism: the French adjective 'clair' can mean 'light in colour' as well as 'clear'.)

120  *Kurtz*: in the manuscript, Conrad initially used the name 'Klein' before changing it to 'Kurtz'. When Conrad, in the *Roi des Belges*, reached Stanley Falls in September 1890, the vessel took on board an agent of the company, Georges Antoine Klein. The agent was suffering from dysentery, and died while the paddle-steamer was making her way downstream. 'Klein' is German for 'small'; 'kurz' is German for 'short'. Marlow later explains the doubly ironic significance of Kurtz's name.

121  *two-hundred-mile tramp*: this part of Marlow's journey corresponds geographically to Conrad's overland trek from Matadi to Kinshasa between June and August 1890. Sherry (*CWW* 38–9) notes that whereas Marlow describes a depopulated region, 'Conrad's journey took him to many market places, to various stations, and he passed *en route* other caravans'. Nevertheless, G. W. Williams reported in 1890 that numerous inhabitants had moved away or been killed 'by war or small pox epidemic' (RK 93), and E. D. Morel lists areas depopulated after raids and outrages by the State soldiers (*Red Rubber* (London: Unwin, 1906), 44–6).

*the population had cleared out a long time ago*: H. M. Stanley reported of the Matadi–Boma region (HS i. 96):

Boma (Mboma) has a history, a cruel blood-curdling history, fraught with horror, and woe, and suffering. Inhumanity of man to man has been exemplified here for over two centuries by the pitiless persecution of black men, by sordid whites [. . .] Now do you wonder, as you look about over the large area of wilderness and sterility, that so much of those rich plains, now covered with mournfully rustling grass, lies untilled?

*Zanzibaris*: the soldiers in the Congo were 'very largely imported from Zanzibar' (G. W. Williams: RK 106).

122 *rows with the carriers*: on Conrad's trek, his European companion, Prosper Harou, became very ill with fever and had to be carried in a hammock by the African porters. He was heavy, and quarrels ensued. (See 'Congo Diary', RH 159.) Harou's older brother had accompanied Stanley on his 1879–82 expedition (RH 134).

*had behaved*: as this is direct speech, 'has behaved' would be correct.

*the real significance of that wreck at once*: when Conrad reached Kinshasa at the beginning of August 1890, he found that the *Florida* (the paddle-steamer he expected to command) had been wrecked. In the tale, Conrad has converted this fact into part of a covert plot. The 'real significance' of the fictional wreck is the probability that the central station's manager devised the 'mishap'. The manager hopes to destroy Kurtz, his main rival for promotion, by delaying the relief of the inner station until Kurtz has become mortally ill. After the steamer has been wrecked, the manager then impedes the repairs for three months by intercepting Marlow's requests for rivets. By the time the vessel reaches its goal, Kurtz (who has thus been isolated for well over a year) is dying. In reality, the *Florida* was wrecked, salvaged, and brought back to Kinshasa by 23 July; and Conrad was not delayed, nor was he involved in salvage work (see *CWW* 40–1). Norman Sherry points out that Conrad had taken an exceptionally long time to trek from Matadi to Kinshasa (35 days instead of the usual 17–20) and might well have been reproached for tardiness. If so, the tale imaginatively transfers culpability from Conrad to the manager (*CWW* 44–7).

123 *nor even respect*: while staying at Kinshasa, Conrad wrote to Marguerite Poradowska (*Letters*, i. 62):

From the manager in Africa who has taken the trouble to tell one and all that I offend him supremely, down to the lowest mechanic, they all have the gift of irritating my nerves—so that I am not as agreeable to them perhaps as I should be. The manager is a common ivory dealer with base instincts who considers himself a merchant though he is only a kind of African shop-keeper. His name is Delcommune. He detests the English, and out here I am naturally regarded as such.

The 'common ivory dealer' was Camille Delcommune (1859–92), manager of the Société Belge du Haut-Congo.

124 *no entrails*: Arthur Hodister, a trader in the Congo, was depicted by his critics as 'a man with no heart and no entrails' (*CWW* 114–15).

*'How could I tell?... I hadn't... doubt.'*: although these quotation-marks signify direct speech, Conrad uses the tenses of indirect (reported) speech. In page proofs for the Heinemann edition, Conrad changed 'could' to 'can' and 'hadn't' to 'haven't'.

125 *take advantage of this unfortunate accident*: the implication is that the destruction of the shed which contained trading goods could be used as

another pretext for delaying Kurtz's relief. The manager, however, does not need to exploit this possibility.

126 *bricks without . . . straw maybe*: Exodus 5: 7 quotes Pharaoh's command: 'Ye shall no more give the people straw to make brick, as heretofore: let them go and gather straw for themselves.' Sherry (*CWW* 43–4) remarks that the actual brick-maker at Kinshasa made plenty of bricks.

*act of special creation perhaps*: Marlow mockingly alludes to those people who, in the nineteenth-century controversy about evolutionary theories, maintained that species were not a product of natural evolution but were individually created by God.

*percentages*: agents were paid a commission on ivory which rose in inverse proportion to the sums they paid for it. 'The less the native got [. . .], the larger the Official's commission!' (Morel, *Red Rubber*, 32.)

*steal a horse while another must not look at a halter*: as 'halter' means (here) 'rope or strap for leading a horse', Marlow is offering a witty variant of the old proverb, 'One man may steal a horse, while another may not look over a hedge' (meaning that some people commit crimes with impunity, though others are punished for trivial or imaginary misdemeanours).

127 *worth his while*: in the manuscript and the serial, these words are followed by the sentence: 'His allusions were Chinese to me.'

*a woman, draped and blindfolded, carrying a lighted torch*: Astraea, goddess of Justice, is often depicted as blindfolded (meaning that ideal justice is impartial), and Liberty is famously depicted as brandishing a lighted torch; but Kurtz has created a new and highly ironic symbol. From his viewpoint, the painting presumably expresses the idea that the advance of civilization into the darkness of Africa lacks vision (hence the blindfold). His idealistic writings were designed to provide that vision. Marlow has sarcastically referred to Roman colonists as 'men going at it blind—as is very proper for those who tackle a darkness'. The primary narrator had described British adventurers positively as bearers of 'the torch', 'bearers of a spark from the sacred fire'. Conrad, however, provides various indications that the torch is an ambiguous symbol, for it may be incendiary (starting a conflagration) rather than illuminative: hence, perhaps, the 'sinister' effect of the torchlight on the bearer's face. What makes the picture so fully symbolic is that, while it solicits decipherment, it retains a residue of the indeterminable.

*devil knows what else*: Norman Sherry (*CWW* 95–118) suggests that Kurtz is based partly on Arthur Hodister, the ivory-collector and explorer who was ambitious, courageous, idealistic, eloquent, and corruptible. (In view of the tale's Faustian theme, Marlow's colloquialism—'devil knows'—has thematic resonance.)

128 *papier-mâché Mephistopheles*: papier-mâché is paper (or paper-pulp) treated to make such items as trays, boxes, light furniture, and imitation plaster moulding. It is cheap, deceptive, and lacks strength: hence, 'if I

tried I could poke my forefinger through him'. Mephistopheles, who is prominent in Marlowe's and Goethe's versions of the Faust legend, is the diabolic agent of Lucifer.

130 *We live, as we dream—alone*: Conrad sometimes quoted Calderón's maxim, 'La vida es sueño' ('Life is a dream'); and Decoud, in *Nostromo*, remarks: 'All this is life, must be life, since it is so much like a dream.' Among writers whose works were studied by Conrad, Schopenhauer quoted Calderón's phrase and emphasized 'the frailty, vanity and dream-like quality of all things', Maupassant repeatedly voiced the fear of utter solitude, and Walter Pater (in *Marius the Epicurean*, 1885) let Marius reflect: 'The ideas we are somehow impelled to form of an outer world, and of other minds akin to our own, are, it may be, but a day-dream.' Marlow's words 'We live [. . .] alone' constitute an oxymoron, for the solipsism of 'alone' is contradicted by the collectivity of 'We'.

131 *hippopotamus*: the connection between the hippopotamus and the rivets is soon implied. Whereas the hippopotamus 'has a charmed life', 'no man here bears a charmed life'. Kurtz is vulnerable, and the manager is increasing his vulnerability by protracting the steamer's repair. The brick-maker's remark, 'I write from dictation', implies that the manager has prevented the transmission of Marlow's request for rivets; and, since the brick-maker 'had been planning to be assistant-manager by-and-by under the present man', his loyalty is to the manager rather than to Kurtz. Marlow fails to perceive the brick-maker's logic, and therefore wrongly assumes that he has persuaded the man to transmit the request: hence his subsequent assurance to the boiler-maker—'We shall have rivets!'

*Huntley & Palmer biscuit-tin*: Marlow omits the 's' from the name 'Palmers'. Huntley & Palmers, famous biscuit-makers based at Reading in England, exported their products worldwide (and to the table of King Leopold II).

133 *Eldorado Exploring Expedition*: Sherry (*CWW* 85) says that Alexandre Delcommune's Katanga expedition arrived at Kinshasa in three groups on 20 and 23 September and 5 October 1890, leaving on 17 October. (Alexandre was the elder brother of Camille Delcommune.) 'El Dorado' (meaning 'the golden place' or 'the gilded man') was the name given by the Spanish *conquistadores* to the fabulous land, rich in gold, which they sought in vain. In 'Geography and Some Explorers' (*LE* 5), Conrad writes:

I suppose it is not very charitable of me, but I must say that to this day I feel a malicious pleasure at the many disappointments of those pertin-acious searchers for El Dorado who climbed mountains, pushed through forests, swam rivers, floundered in bogs, without giving a single thought to the science of geography.

135 *hanged! Why not?*: in 1895, a Belgian officer in the Congo arrested and hanged on the spot a British lay-missionary, Charles Stokes, who had

sold arms to Arabs. The British government protested, but the officer was acquitted. (Neil Ascherson, *The King Incorporated* (London: Allen & Unwin, 1963), 243.) Conrad may have read about this incident.

135  *I did my possible*: a Gallicism; a literal translation of 'J'ai fait mon possible' ('I've done all I could'— or 'I did my best', as Conrad rendered it in later editions). Another example, a few lines later, is 'Conceive you' (recalling 'concevez-vous' or 'conçois-tu'); the meaning is 'Can you imagine?' Other instances are 'Famous' (for 'Splendid', p. 112), 'you conceive' (p. 130), 'My faith' (p. 158), and 'I felt like a chill grip on my chest' (p. 186).

137  *next day's steaming*: when Conrad voyaged up the Congo from Kinshasa to Stanley Falls in the *Roi des Belges*, the captain was Ludvig Koch, and Conrad made navigational notes in preparation for the time when (he expected) he himself would be captain of one of the company's vessels. The *Roi des Belges*, a paddle-steamer fuelled by timber, closely resembled the vessel described in the tale; and Conrad's notes make evident the dangers presented by snags, stones, and sandbanks in the river. See 'Up-river Book' in *CD*.

138  *twenty cannibals . . . pushing*: S. L. Hinde, who travelled on the Congo at this period, reported (*LP* 142):

When I was returning from Stanley Falls on my homeward journey six of the [Bangala] crew were in irons on board ship, whom the captain delivered up to justice at Bangala for having eaten two of their number during the voyage up to the falls.

Norman Sherry (*CWW* 59–60) comments:

The crews of steamers were from the upper Congo, mostly from Bangala [. . .] Like Marlow's cannibal crew, the Bangalas were joyfully cannibalistic. The brother of Bapulula (popular pilot on the mission steamer *Peace* on the river at this time), when asked if he ate human flesh, answered, 'Ah! I wish I could eat everybody on earth'. Dr Bentley, the missionary, recalls talking to an old man at Bangala, three years before Conrad went up the river, who was reported to have killed and eaten seven of his wives.

G. W. Williams, a black observer, noted in 1890 that some of the soldiers in the Congo were 'bloodthirsty cannibalistic Bangalas' who ate the bodies of slain children (RK 110).

*I had the manager . . . complete*: in the *Roi des Belges*, Conrad's European companions were Captain Koch, Camille Delcommune, three agents, and a mechanic.

*exclusively*: Hampson (RH 136) notes that in the manuscript a cancelled passage here includes the words: 'Towards the man possessed of moral ideals holding a torch in the heart of darkness.'

139  *The mind . . . anything*: Maupassant's 'La Chevelure' concludes: 'L'esprit de l'homme est capable de tout' (*FF* 63).

141  *Towser, Towson—some such name—Master in his Majesty's Navy*: the serial
and the 1902 text have 'Tower' as the first name, but 'Towser' (which
appears subsequently in this paragraph) is the spelling at this point in the
manuscript. J. A. Arnold, in *Conradiana*, 7 (1976), 121–6, suggests that
Marlow or Conrad linked the name of J. T. Towson to a book by Nicholas
Tinmouth. Towson published navigational tables but not a handbook,
whereas Tinmouth published in 1845 *An Inquiry Relative to Various
Important Points of Seamanship, Considered as a Branch of Practical Science*. Its preface manifests both the humility and the 'concern for the
right way of going to work' that Marlow notes; and the subsequent
chapters, based on 'half-a-century' of maritime experience, do indeed
'inquir[e] earnestly into the breaking strain of ships' chains and tackle'.
The book also includes eighteen of the 'illustrative diagrams' and three
of the 'repulsive tables of figures' mentioned by Marlow. Tinmouth,
however, was not a 'Master in his Majesty's Navy' but a Master-
Attendant at Her Majesty's dockyard at Woolwich.

145  *brass wire . . . villages*: J. Rose Troup, in *With Stanley's Rear Column*
(London: Chapman & Hall, 1890), 103–4, states:

The mitako, or brass rod, is the currency among the natives at Leopoldville and most of the regions of the Upper Congo. It is in general
imported to the Congo by the State in large rolls or coils of 60 lbs. in
weight. After its arrival at Leopoldville it is cut up into the regulation
lengths (about 2 feet) [. . .]; the value of each of these pieces at Leopoldville is reckoned at 1½*d*.

*stuff like half-cooked dough*: kwanga, i.e. cassava (also known as manioc or
tapioca), steeped and boiled to form a stiff dough; sometimes combined
with ground millet and preservatives. It can indeed be 'of a dirty lavender
colour' but is long-lasting and sustaining.

147  *beset . . . castle*: in Charles Perrault's version of the fairy tale 'The Sleeping Beauty', the sleeping princess's castle is surrounded by an apparently
impenetrable thicket of trees and briars, and is said to be haunted by
ghosts or sorcerers or a cannibalistic ogre.

150  *lounged*: alternative spelling (now archaic) of 'lunged'.

151  *steam-whistle . . . hurriedly*: as Hampson notes (RH 137), W. Holman
Bentley's *Pioneering on the Congo* (London: Religious Tract Society,
1900), ii. 139, says that, during Bentley's voyage by steamboat on a
tributary of the Congo, four local men (armed with guns) in a canoe tried
to levy toll:

They demanded blackmail, and lay across our bows. The two whistles of
the *Peace* [*sic*: the name of the steamer] shrieked their loudest [. . .]
There was an instant collapse in the canoe; guns were dropped and
paddles were seized and plied to their utmost.

152  *had I been . . . or had missed my destiny in life*: grammatically, Marlow
should have said 'missed' (or 'had I missed') instead of 'had missed'.

153 *the hair goes on growing sometimes*: i.e. on corpses, Marlow having previously referred to 'the disinterred body of Mr Kurtz'. Subsequently Kurtz will be termed 'an initiated wraith', 'a shade', and a 'phantom'.

154 *His mother was half-English, his father was half-French*: Conrad remarked: 'I took great care to give Kurtz a cosmopolitan origin' (*Letters*, iii. 94).

155 *International Society for the Suppression of Savage Customs*: Conrad was perhaps recalling the International Association for the Exploration and Civilizing of Africa ('l'Association Internationale pour l'Exploration et la Civilisation en Afrique'), of which King Leopold II was the president. Arthur Hodister was associated with the Belgian Anti-Slavery Society ('la Société Antiesclavagiste de Belgique').

*nerves, went wrong . . . unspeakable rites . . . himself*: H. M. Stanley alleged that the 'unfledged' European in Africa would 'very readily explode his unspeakable passions' (HS i. 517). Norman Sherry notes that Arthur Hodister assisted at the fifteenth wedding of a chieftain, Tyabo, and witnessed human sacrifices decreed by Tyabo during funerary rites. In 1892 *The Times* reported that, during further explorations in the Congo, Hodister was captured and killed, his head stuck on a pole, and his body eaten (*CWW* 100–1, 110–11).

158 *harlequin*: a type found in French folk-literature, the Italian *commedia dell'arte*, and English pantomime: a lively, acrobatic character, dressed in bright particoloured costume.

159 *Government of Tambov*: 'Government of' here means '(from the) administrative region called'. Tambov is one of the largest provinces of western Russia, and its chief city and administrative centre (also called Tambov) has a seventeenth-century cathedral and was an archiepiscopal see of the Russian Orthodox Church.

*Dutch trading-house on the coast*: the most powerful trading company on the Congolese coast was the Nieuwe Afrikaansche Handels-Vennootschap (see *CWW* 69, and Bentley's *Pioneering on the Congo*, i. 68–9).

*Van Shuyten*: 'impossible as a Dutch name; Van Schuyten will do', comments Hans van Marle. Sherry (*CWW* 117) suggests that Conrad adapted the name of Schouten, a Belgian associated with Hodister.

164 *symbolic*: in the serial, the wording between 'symbolic;' and 'expressive' is: 'they were symbolic of some cruel and forbidden knowledge. They were'.

*heads on the stakes*: in 1892, it was reported that fifty-two human heads on stakes surrounded a station at Yanga (in the Congo) where two white men stayed (*CWW* 117–18). E. J. Glave noted in 1895 that at Stanley Falls 'twenty-one heads [. . .] have been used by Captain Rom as a decoration round a flower-bed in front of his house' ('Cruelty in the Congo Free State', *Century Illustrated Monthly Magazine*, 54 (1897), 706).

*fantastic invasion*: in the serial, the wording between 'fantastic' and 'I think' is: 'invasion. It had tempted him with all the sinister suggestions of its loneliness.'

165 *hollow at the core*: the ancient proverb, 'The empty vessel makes the greatest sound' (Shakespeare, *Henry V*, IV. iv. 73–4), partly explains Kurtz's combination of 'hollowness' and exceptional eloquence.

168 *she stopped . . . failed her*: in the serial, the wording between 'she' and 'The young fellow' is:

stopped. Had her heart failed her, or had her eyes, veiled with that mournfulness that lies over all the wild things of the earth, seen the hopelessness of longing that will find out sometimes even a savage soul in the lonely darkness of its being? Who can tell. Perhaps she did not know herself.

*A formidable silence hung over the scene*: this short sentence replaces the longer version in the serial: 'Her sudden gesture seemed to demand a cry, but the unbroken silence that hung over the scene was more formidable than any sound could be.'

175 *'Do I not?' he said slowly*: in the serial, the wording is: ' "I will return," he said, slowly'.

177 *'Live rightly, die, die . . .'*: in the manuscript, the phrase 'die nobly' completes the maxim.

*face the expression . . . despair*: in the serial, the wording between 'face' and 'Did he live' is: 'the expression of savage pride, of mental power, of avarice, of blood-thirstiness, of cunning, of excessive terror, of an intense and hopeless despair.'

178 *'The horror! The horror!'*: Marlow interprets these words in different ways, thus setting the precedent for many subsequent commentators. He suggests the following meanings. (1) Kurtz condemns as horrible his corrupt actions, so that this 'judgment upon the adventures of his soul on this earth' is 'an affirmation, a moral victory'. (2) Kurtz deems hateful but also desirable the temptations to which he has succumbed: the whisper has 'the strange commingling of desire and hate'. (3) Kurtz deems horrible the inner nature of everybody: 'no eloquence could have been so withering as his final burst of sincerity' when his stare 'penetrate[d] all the hearts that beat in the darkness'. (4) Kurtz deems horrible the whole universe: 'that wide and immense stare embracing, condemning, loathing all the universe . . . "The horror!" '

The words 'The horror! The horror!' thus serve as a thematic nexus, a climactic but highly ambiguous utterance which sums up, without resolving, several of the paradoxical themes of the tale. As is customary with symbols, the various meanings suggested do not exhaust the phrase's potential: it retains some opacity. Co-ordinated enigmas are a structural principle of 'Heart of Darkness'.

(Incidentally, Conrad may have recalled here Psalms 55: 4–5: 'My heart is sore pained within me: and the terrors of death are fallen upon

me. Fearfulness and trembling are come upon me, and horror hath overwhelmed me.')

*they very nearly buried me*: Conrad, suffering from fever and dysentery,
was allowed to return early from the Congo to Europe.

179 *I found myself back in the sepulchral city resenting the sight of people . . . so
full of stupid importance*: there are analogies with Gulliver's distaste for a
humankind 'smitten with *pride*' (in the closing pages of Swift's *Gulliver's
Travels*) and with Prendick's revulsion as he walks through the crowded
streets (near the close of Wells's *The Island of Doctor Moreau*).

181 *leader of an extreme party*: Conrad knew the work of Max Nordau, and in
Nordau's *Degeneration* (London: Heinemann, 1895), the description of
the 'highly-gifted degenerate' (pp. 22–4) may have provided hints for the
characterization of Kurtz:

'The degenerate,' says Legrain, 'may be a genius. A badly balanced mind
is susceptible of the highest conceptions, while, on the other hand, one
meets in the same mind with traits of meanness and pettiness all the more
striking from the fact that they co-exist with the most brilliant qualities.'
[. . .] 'As regards their intellect, they can,' says Roubinovitch, 'attain to a
high degree of development, but from a moral point of view their existence is completely deranged . . . A degenerate will employ his brilliant
faculties quite as well in the service of some grand object as in the
satisfaction of the basest propensities.' [. . .] I do not share Lombroso's
opinion that highly gifted degenerates are an active force in the progress
of mankind. They corrupt and delude; they do, alas! frequently exercise a
deep influence, but this is always a baneful one [. . .] They, likewise, are
leading men along the paths they themselves have found to new goals, but
these goals are abysses or waste places. They are guides to swamps like
will-o'-the-wisps, or to ruin like the ratcatcher of Hammelin.

*yet . . . features*: in the serial, the wording after 'yet' and before 'She
seemed' is:

that face on paper seemed to be a reflection of truth itself. One felt that
no manipulation of light and pose could have conveyed the delicate shade
of truthfulness upon those features. She looked out truthfully.

*some other feeling perhaps*: Conrad told David Meldrum that the tale
offered '[a] mere shadow of love interest just in the last pages' (*Letters*,
ii. 145–6). This motif reaches its ironic conclusion in the closing pages of
*Chance*, when Marlow, an ageing bachelor, successfully acts as
matchmaker for a younger seafarer and a widow.

182 *terrifying simplicity*: in the serial, the wording after 'terrifying' and before
'I remembered' is:

simplicity: 'I have lived—supremely!' 'What do you want here? I have
been dead—and damned.' 'Let me go—I want more of it.' More of what?
More blood, more heads on stakes, more adoration, rapine, and murder.

*he seemed to stare at me . . . The horror!*: the memory of Kurtz's face perhaps suffuses the reflection of Marlow's in the 'glassy panel'; and the description may be influenced by the incident in Dickens's *A Christmas Carol* when Scrooge, about to open the door of his house, sees the staring face of the dead Marley, and associates it with a vision of horror:

[T]hough the eyes were wide open, they were perfectly motionless. That, and its livid colour, made it horrible; but its horror seemed to be in spite of the face and beyond its control, rather than a part of its own expression.

183 *to behold*: in the serial, after 'to' and before 'She', the wording is: 'behold. I wanted to get out.'

184 *under the lamp*: in the serial, after 'lamp.' and before 'And the girl', the wording is: 'But in the box I had brought to his bedside there were several packages pretty well alike, all tied with shoe-strings, and probably he had made a mistake.'

185 *stretching them black and with clasped pale hands*: her arms appear black because she is wearing a long-sleeved mourning dress. The sense would be clearer if the punctuation were thus: 'stretching them, black and with clasped pale hands,'.

*Shade . . . arms . . . darkness*: Virgil's *Aeneid* (vi. 314) says that the Shades in the underworld 'stretched their arms out in longing' to Charon as they stood on the shore of Styx, the river of darkness.

186 *It seemed . . . that the heavens would fall . . . justice*: Marlow is recalling the Latin maxim, 'Fiat iustitia ruat caelum [*or* coelum]': 'Let justice be done, though the heavens fall'. Conrad quoted this as 'fiat justicia ruat coelum' when writing to Marguerite Poradowska in March 1890, six weeks before setting out for the Congo (*Letters*, i. 43). The recurrence of the tag is one of several features suggesting that the description of Marlow's meeting with the Intended is based, in part, on Conrad's relationship with 'Aunt' Marguerite in 1890. Marguerite lived in Brussels, as does Kurtz's fiancée. Marguerite was 42; the fiancée is 'not very young'. When Conrad visited Marguerite in April 1890, she, like the Intended, was bereaved and in mourning, because her husband, Aleksander Poradowski, had died recently. (Aleksander had apparently strayed morally 'into an abyss' during his mortal illness.) Marlow admires and is attracted to the Intended; Conrad admired and was attracted to Marguerite. Indeed, Conrad's uncle, Tadeusz Bobrowski, wrote to warn him against an infatuation which could not lead to marriage.

# GLOSSARY

**abaft, aft** behind, towards the stern of a vessel

*ad patres* (Latin) to the fathers; 'send (them) *ad patres*': kill them

**after-hatch** rearmost hatch in main deck

**Ahoy!** traditional nautical cry to hail a ship or attract attention

**alienist** psychiatrist

**alpaca** cloth made of wool from the South American mammal, the alpaca

**amok, amuck** (Malay) (in) a state of murderous frenzy

**Anjer** coastal town in north-west Java

**appeal** (noun, p. 12) call (Gallicism, from *appel*)

**assegai** light spear

**a-starboard** to the right

**athwart** (p. 116) sideways

**Atjeh** Muslim state (also termed Achin, Aceh, etc) in northern Sumatra

**attap** (Malay) palm fronds (particularly from the nipa palm) used for thatching

**Bajow people** maritime Malays (often nomadic traders known as 'sea gypsies') inhabiting the coastal regions of Borneo, Celebes, and the southern Philippines

**Batavia** (subsequently Jakarta) capital of Indonesia; located in north-west Java; founded in 1619, and ruled by the Dutch until 1945

**beggar** (p. 157, slang) (mildly derogatory term for) person, fellow

**bend sails** secure sails to spars

**berth** (i) sleeping-place; (ii) mooring-place

**billet** (colloquial) job, position

**blab** divulge a secret

**blamed** (p. 113) (euphemism for) blasted

**bluff of her bow** upper part of a vessel's front end

**boat-hook** pole ending in a hook, for pulling or pushing off a boat

**Boni, Gulf of** long gulf, later called Teluk Bone, in southern Celebes (Sulawesi)

**bow, bows** forward part of vessel, where it curves to the stem

**bowman** oarsman at the bow of a boat

**brought up** (p. 142) halted and anchored; 'brought up with the deep-sea lead-line' (p. 96): halted by employing as an anchor the lead-weighted line normally used for assessing the depth of water in fathoms ('Deep-sea' was pronounced '*dip*-see')

**buckler** small round shield

**Bugis** inhabitants (or their descendants) of the south-western part of Celebes

**bulkhead** upright partition between compartments

**bulwarks** ship's sides above deck-level

**bunt** baggy part of a sail

**caballeros** (Spanish) cavaliers or gentlemen; (p. 66) Spanish authorities in the region

**cabinet photograph** photograph measuring approximately 6½ by 4½ inches (16.5 by 11.4 cm)

**calabash** gourd-shell used as a container

**Calashes** (Malay) Malay seamen

**calipers** (usually 'callipers') compasses with legs suitable for measuring inner or outer diameters

**campong** (Malay) village or cluster of buildings, enclosed and sometimes fortified with palisades

**Canal** Suez Canal

**cat-heads** beams supporting anchor-tackle

**caulk her topsides** make watertight with oakum the upper parts of the vessel's sides (between the waterline and the ship's rail)

**Celebes** island in the Dutch East Indies; later known as Sulawesi in Indonesia

**chain-hook** iron rod ending in a hook, used for hauling chain-cables

**chain-plates** iron plates to which shrouds (ropes supporting a mast) are secured

**'Change** place such as the Royal Exchange or the Stock Exchange in London, where merchants, financiers, and their employees transact business. 'Men on 'Change': merchants, businessmen

**Chapman lighthouse** screw-pile lighthouse, erected in 1849 on a mud-flat off Canvey Island in the Thames

**chased hilt** ornamented handle

**Chips** customary nickname of a ship's carpenter

**cipher** code

**come to** (p. 103) anchor

**companion** (i) ladder or stairway; (ii) entrance to a stairway

**confab** (colloquial) confabulation, conversation

**coppered** sheathed in copper

*cortège* (French) procession of attendants

**counter** curving part of a vessel's hull towards the stern

**crack** (adjective) first-rate, excellent

**crew of runners** crew engaged for a single short voyage

**cuddy** (i) in a large vessel (such as the schooner in 'Karain'), a saloon serving as a common room for meals, etc; (ii) in a smaller vessel, a cabin; (iii) in an even smaller vessel, a shelter or locker

**davits** small cranes by which a ship's boat is raised or lowered

**Deal** town on the east coast of Kent

**Delli** (Deli) region of north-east Sumatra

**Deptford** eastern suburb of London, on the south side of the Thames; once noted for its dockyard established by Henry VIII

**Dogger Bank** submerged sandbank in the North Sea between northern England and Denmark

**Eastern Archipelago** the Malay Archipelago, whose many islands include Borneo, Sumatra, Java, and Celebes (Sulawesi)

**Eldorado** the Golden Land sought in vain by the Spanish Conquistadores in America (from the Spanish *el dorado*, the gilded man or golden place)

**Erith** port and township on the south side of the Thames, 3 miles north-west of Dartford

**evolutions** (p. 175) manœuvres

**fairway** navigable part of a river

**Falernian wine** fine wine from the district of Falernus Ager, lying inland from Neapolis (now Napoli or Naples)

**famous** (p. 112) splendid (Gallicism, from *fameux*)

**fife-rail** pin-rail (to hold belaying-pins) in a semi-circle round the mast near its base

**Fleet Street** busy street of central London, famed as a centre for newspaper publishing

**float** (p. 142) blade of a paddle-wheel

**foot-warmer** perforated box containing a pan for hot coals

**force-pump** piston-operated pump which ejects liquid forcibly, under pressure (as opposed to a lift-pump, which emits—rather than ejects—the liquid)

**Forelands** two headlands (North Foreland and South Foreland) in south-eastern England, on the coast of Kent

**forepeak scuttle** hatch of compartment in the forward part of a vessel, close to the bow

**foresail** lowest of the sails on the foremast (mast nearest bow)

**gasket** canvas band to tie a furled sail to a yard

**Gauls** Cisalpine Gaul and Transalpine Gaul. The former was bordered by the Alps and the Apennines, the latter by the Alps, the Mediterranean, the Pyrenees, the Atlantic, and the Rhine

**Geordie** person who hails from (or lives in) Tyneside, in north-east England

**get-up** (slang) attire

**Goram men** Muslim traders from the island of Goram in eastern Indonesia

**Gran' Bassam** Grand Bassam, a coastal town of Ivory Coast

**Gravesend** town and port on the south side of the Thames, opposite Tilbury Docks, approximately 20 miles from central London

**Greenwich** an eastern borough of London, on the south bank of the Thames; former port, and location of a palace

**Greenwich Time** clock-time co-ordinated by the Royal Observatory located on the zero meridian at Greenwich

**gripes** bands and fastenings retaining a boat in its cradle

**grog-blossoms** purplish blotches attributed to the frequent drinking of grog (rum)

**Gulf of Boni** long gulf (later called Teluk Bone) in southern Celebes

**gunwale** (pronounced '*gunn*el') upper edge of a boat's side

**'Harbour furl—aloft there!'** 'You hands up there, furl the sails neatly as if for docking!'

**hard a-starboard** as far as possible to the right

**head-light** white navigation-light carried on the mast-head

**head-pump** small manual lift-pump fixed at vessel's bow, to draw sea water aboard; normally used for washing the 'heads' (lavatories) and decks

**helm** wheel

**helmsman** man who steers a vessel

**holland** coarse linen cloth

**hooker** old-fashioned or clumsy vessel

**ichthyosaurus** gigantic prehistoric marine reptile

**incontinently** (i) immediately; (ii) impetuously

**intelligence** news, report, information

**interlopers** (p. 104) venturers trespassing on the trade monopoly of the East India Company

**Java Head** the western tip of Java, where the Sunda Strait meets the Indian Ocean

**jury-rig** makeshift rigging

**kedge-anchor** small anchor for steadying and manœuvring a ship

**knot** unit of speed: one nautical mile (1.85 km) per hour

**Korinchi man** Muslim Malay from western Sumatra

**kriss** (Malay) Malayan or Indonesian dagger with scalloped or wavy edges

**Land's End** granite headland at the south-western tip of Cornwall

**lazarette** (from Italian *lazzaretto*) storeroom between decks near the stern of a ship

**lee bow** downwind side of the front part of a vessel

**leeward** downwind

**Little Popo** Anecho, a coastal town in Togo

**Lizards** Cornwall's southernmost promontory and its offshore rocks

**Loanda** a port on the Atlantic coast of Angola (then in Portuguese West Africa)

**long-boat** largest boat of a ship

**long-shore loafers** waterfront idlers

**lounged** (p. 150; now-archaic spelling) lunged

**main-chains** metal fixtures to which the shrouds from the mainmast are secured

**main-deck** uppermost of the decks which span the length and breadth of a ship

**mainmast** chief mast of a sailing-vessel with two or more masts: (i) on a yawl or ketch, the foremast; (ii) on most other vessels, the second mast from the bow

**mainsail** largest and lowest sail on the mainmast

**mainyard** lowest yard (horizontal spar) on the mainmast

**Martini-Henry** breech-action rifle, its breech designed by F. Martini, its barrel-rifling by A. Henry

**Mephistopheles** a devil who, as Lucifer's agent, is prominent in the Faust legend

**Mesopotamia** region of south-west Asia between the lower and middle reaches of the rivers Tigris and Euphrates

**mess** (p. 80) meal

**Mindanao** the second largest island of the Philippines

**mizzen-mast** rear mast on a two- or three-masted vessel; third mast from front on a four-masted vessel

**mizzen-shrouds** ropes extending from the vessel's sides to the head of the mizzen-mast

**mizzly** (rain) rain falling in a light misty drizzle of droplets

**mooned, mooned about** was listlessly idle

**motley** particoloured garb, as worn by harlequins

**muff** bungler, incompetent person

**mulatto** person having one black and one white parent

**Nemesis** (i) retribution; (ii) the Greek goddess of retribution

**Nero** Roman emperor from AD 54 to 68, notorious for despotism and cruelty

**non-commissioned officer** subordinate officer (e.g. sergeant) who is appointed from the ranks and does not hold a commission

**oakum** tarred rope-fibres used for caulking seams

**Odyssey** (p. 56) long and arduous journey comparable to that of the legendary Odysseus (Ulysses)

**offing** part of the sea that is visible from the shore

**omnibus** large four-wheeled horse-drawn passenger-vehicle

**Ough!** exclamation of distaste or disgust, loosely corresponding to the more recent exclamation 'Yuck!'

**P. & O.** Peninsular and Oriental Steamship Company

**painter** rope in the bow of a boat, for securing or towing it

**palaver** discussion or negotiation

**palm wine** the fermented sap of the palm tree

**papier-mâché** paper or paper-pulp treated with adhesive and moulded

**Perak** state on the north-west coast of the Malay Peninsula

**plantain** plant yielding banana-type fruit

**poop** high deck and enclosed area beneath it, at the stern of a vessel

**port** (side) left side of a vessel, relative to a forward-facing position aboard

**prau** Malay boat, usually undecked

**purchases** leverages; mechanical advantages in raising or lowering

**put back** (a vessel) reverse the vessel's course

**rattans** climbing palms whose stems are used for wickerwork and canes

**Ravenna** town of north-east Italy near the Adriatic coast. Augustus (Roman emperor from 29 BC to AD 14) made its port, Classis, into a naval station

**reach** length of river between bends

**'ready': at 'ready'** pointed outwards, ready for firing

**recaulked** rendered watertight again by pressing oakum into the seams

**recrudescence** new outbreak

**regret the streets** (Gallicism) miss (sadly recall) the streets

**revolver-carbine** light rifle with a rotating magazine

**rumour** (pp. 39, 66; Gallicism) murmur; humming noise

**runner** seaman engaged for a single short voyage

**salamander** (p. 92) amphibious creature reputed to live in fire

**sardine box** sardine tin

**sarong** (Malay) garment resembling a long skirt

**schooner** two-masted sailing-ship with fore-and-aft rigging

**scow** flat-bottomed boat

**scratch** (p. 32) hastily gathered

**scuttling** (p. 88) deliberately flooding a ship's holds

**secular** age-old, long-lived, ancient

**Selangore** (Selangor) state of Peninsular Malaya, on the Strait of Malacca

**serang** (from Persian and Urdu *sarhang*) native boatswain

**shade** (pp. 154, 176, 185) ghost

**Shadwell basin** channel at Wapping which connects the London Docks to the River Thames

**shakes** (slang) uncontrollable trembling caused by fever

**sheered** (p. 148) steered on a deviating course

**ship's biscuit** hard biscuit (also called 'ship's bread') for seamen

**shot down** (p. 133) thrown down, dumped

**shrouds** ropes supporting a mast

**side-spring boots** boots with elasticized side-strips

**Sierra Leone** then a British colony on the west coast of Africa, populated partly by freed slaves and their descendants

**smithy coal** small and soft bituminous coal used in a blacksmith's forge

**snag** hazard to navigation, particularly a submerged or semi-submerged part of a tree

**Solomon** King of Israel in the tenth century BC; credited with great wisdom

**soughing** sighing

**sounding-rod** metal rod used to measure the depth of water in the bilges

**spontaneous combustion** ignition resulting from the oxidation process

**sprit** spar set diagonally upwards from the mast, to extend and elevate a fore-and-aft sail

**square-rigged** fitted with rectangular sails slung athwartship

**square the foreyard** set, at a right-angle to the fore-and-aft line of the vessel, the spar on the foremast from which the lowest sail is suspended

**squirts** (p. 150; slang) repeating rifles

**stanchion** upright supporting-post

**starboard** right-hand side of a vessel, relative to a forward-facing position aboard

**stem-head** top end of the stem (the curving post at the front of a boat)

**step** (a mast) fix a mast in place

**sternports** openings at the stern of a vessel

**stream-anchor** medium-sized anchor used for warping or to moor a ship in a sheltered position

**stream-cable** cable or hawser of the stream-anchor

**strophe** division of a song

**stun'-sail** studding-sail, a light auxiliary sail set outboard on a spar on either side of a square sail

**Sulu** the Sulu Archipelago in the south-western Philippines

**taffrail** aftermost rail of a vessel, following the curve of the stern

**tale: lost the tale** lost count

**tallow dip** candle made by dipping a wick in fat or grease

**Tambov** city and region of central Russia, about 300 miles south-east of Moscow

**thwarts** planks which extend transversely across a boat and may be used as seats

**tier** (i) row of ships anchored or moored; (ii) anchorage or mooring-place where ships lie in rows or columns

**told off as** appointed to the post of

**told off to** allocated to

**top-gallant mast** mast extending above topmast

**trim the yards** adjust the spars

**trireme** galley with three banks of oars on each side

**truck** flat circular wooden cap at the top of a mast

**truckle-bed** low bed on wheels, capable of being stored beneath another bed

**twill** woven fabric showing diagonal lines

**twopenny-halfpenny** (pronounced '*tup*nee-*hape*nee') cheap and of inferior quality

**Tyne** river in northern England which flows into the North Sea

**valiance** valour

**Wajo** region and town (later called Kaluwaja) in south-western Celebes (Sulawesi) on the Gulf of Boni (Teluk Bone)

**warp** (a ship) move a ship by hauling on a 'warp' (towing-rope)

**watch** (i) period of duty; (ii) group of men allotted to a period of duty. 'Watch and watch' (pp. 76–7): in turn, the two halves of the crew taking duty alternately every four hours

**waterman** man who plies a boat for hire

**weather-cloth** protective tarpaulin

**white-lead** type of putty made from lead carbonate and linseed oil

**whizz** (noun, p. 150) sound of an object moving rapidly through the air

**Winchester** American repeating rifles named after O. F. Winchester, their manufacturer

**windlass** rotating cylinder used for raising or lowering the anchor

**wink** (p. 144) blink

**yard** (on vessel) spar to bear or extend a sail

**Yarmouth roads** anchorage outside the port of Great Yarmouth in Norfolk

**yawl** two-masted sailing vessel, rigged fore-and-aft, with a large mainmast and a small mizzen-mast (rear mast)